Dark Light

Edited by Carl Hose

© 2012 MARLvision Publishing

Printed in the United States of America

Published by MARLvision Publishing

Sarasota, FL

ISBN: 978-0-615-65706-6

Dark Light

Horror anthology to benefit Ronald McDonald House Charities

4

Carl would like to thank:

My wife and kids, each of whom I love with all my heart—without you, all of this would have less meaning.

Marcee and Carl would like to thank:

All Children's Hospital and its staff in St. Petersburg, FL.—you took care of our daughter and we will never forget.

The Ronald McDonald House Charities, particularly in St. Petersburg, FL.—you made our stay pleasant and kept us near our daughter when she needed us most.

Each of the authors who participated in the *Dark Light* project—your generosity is beyond compare and your words will help families for years to come.

We would also like to thank:

My mother-in-law Pat Stuart for diligently reading through this manuscript and editing with a careful eye (and for taking care of our boys while Marcee and I were away)

Innovative Online Book Tours for organizing a spectacular blog tour to help out. Consider using them for your next book tour: http://innovativeonlinebooktours.com/

Carl Porter, who gave *Dark Light* sight and sound with a killer trailer. Check out his work at http://carlericporter.com/wp/

Contents

Introduction

My daughter Ireland Joy Hose was due to come into the world on March 3rd, 2012. Since my wife Marcee was going to have a C-section, her doctor scheduled her to deliver Ireland February 13th. It's typical to schedule C-sections about two weeks before the actual due date, but in my wife's case, the C-section was scheduled a little earlier because she had complete placenta previa, meaning her placenta was blocking the birth canal. This is normally not a problem unless the previa turns into accreta, which means the placenta attaches to body organs and actually begins to grow into them (pretty alien-like). This can result in severe hemorrhaging and may require a partial or even a complete hysterectomy.

All of this is beside the point. Ireland decided she wanted to show up on January 27th at 10:35 P.M. She was six weeks premature, 18 inches long, and weighed just 4 lbs. 13 oz.

Marcee had gone to the gynecologist that day. He told her she was having contractions. We went to the hospital, where they tried to stop her contractions. It didn't happen. Marcee started bleeding, and while I write about blood all the time, seeing it pour from my wife's body was pretty damn scary.

I was in the operating room when Ireland was delivered. She came out fine, although she would have her own struggles ahead of her in the coming weeks. Shortly after the nurses began cleaning Ireland up, one of the doctors said to another doctor that Marcee had accreta and would need a hysterectomy. I was caught between the joy of my daughter's birth and my wife's fragile situation.

The doctors began pumping my wife full of anesthesia and she was fading fast. All she wanted was to hear our baby girl cry, to know Ireland was all right. "Cry, baby girl," she said, and when Ireland began to wail, Marcee drifted off.

I was ushered from the OR with Ireland in my arms. What followed was a two-and-a-half-hour wait while the doctors performed surgery on Marcee. There was a lot of blood loss, but in the end she came through the surgery alive and eager to see Ireland. Barely able to sit up, she insisted I wheel her to the nursery, where she held Ireland for the first time, a full four hours after Ireland was born.

Because Ireland was premature, she was going to be spending time in the NICU. She was moved to a different hospital—one that was further away from where we lived—the next night. Marcee and I agreed I should go with Ireland. There was really no discussion necessary. This, however, left Marcee alone to deal with the trauma of her experience without me or her newborn daughter to comfort her.

One of the memories that haunts me still is seeing an ambulance with the words *Neonatal Transport Unit* on the side and thinking, *that's a baby ambulance and it's here for my baby.*

I arrived at the hospital where my daughter was taken late that night. The blur begins here, so I don't have the exact time. The NICU staff suggested I get a room at the Ronald McDonald House. I insisted I didn't need one, that I would be staying at my daughter's side day and night. They worked hard to convince me a room at the Ronald McDonald House made more sense—that it would be more comfortable than a chair in the NICU. If it had just been me, they probably wouldn't have changed my mind, but since I knew Marcee was planning to join me as soon as she could strong arm the doctor's into discharging her (which she did in record time), I relented and allowed one of the nurses to contact the Ronald McDonald House nearby to reserve us a spot.

It turns out no reservation was needed that night. Hospital security drove me to the Ronald McDonald House where we would be staying. It so happened I was the only guest at the time. The house was a quaint looking affair that reminded me of a bed and breakfast in the country—from the outside. Inside was a maze of stairways and narrow hallways that housed about thirty rooms. The security guard said I wouldn't be able to get a key until morning, so once he left, I wouldn't be able to get in and out. The doors lock automatically.

After the security guard left, I wandered around the house. It was beautiful. Hardwood floors, stocked library, fully-stocked kitchen (help yourself to anything you want), fireplace, and a playground outside for kids. It was amazing.

And a little creepy.

The house sat in a beautiful residential area with red brick streets and lots of gorgeous trees, but at night, alone as I was, still a little in shock over the premature birth of my daughter and the bloody mess that was Marcee's surgery, my mind began working overtime. I imagined all sorts of creaking floors and shadows moving through the house—hell, maybe it wasn't my imagination. In any case, sleep did not come easy that night. I'd seen far too many horror movies, written far too many horror stories myself, not to know what usually becomes of lone visitors in quaint country homes in the middle of the night. I called Marcee to let her know I was settled in and that I thought I had the company of ghosts, or maybe something much worse.

With no key, I used my overnight bag to prop the door open so I could step outside and have a cigarette.

It was a foggy night—isn't it always?

One cigarette became two, two became three. I stood outside in the fog, looking through the chilly darkness, grateful to have a new daughter, but afraid for how fragile she seemed to be; happy Marcee came through the surgery alive, but sad she was alone at another hospital; missing our boys, who would end up seeing us very little over the next three weeks (although they were well taken care of, thanks to Marcee's mom and dad).

It was 3:00 A.M when I finally went back inside and stretched out on the bed, fully clothed, lying on top of the covers.

Marcee arrived the next day. She shouldn't have been walking at all, but she wouldn't be denied her daughter. We spent the next three weeks living at the Ronald McDonald House (they moved us from the bed-and-breakfast model to one that resembled a fairly expensive hotel). Our days were filled with walking from the Ronald McDonald House to the hospital and back again. We would feed and change our daughter, hold her, and watch as she began to overcome the challenges of prematurity. She did those things like the little champ she is. I believe having us with her day and night helped contribute to her impressive adjustment to being thrust into the world so early. She is just over two months old at the time of this writing and healthy as can be. Marcee is doing great too.

The Ronald McDonald House played a big part in making this happen. They provided food, shelter, homemade gifts from volunteers, and even cards for Valentine's Day. We didn't need to do anything except be there for Ireland. If not for the Ronald McDonald House, Marcee and I would have had to travel every day to see Ireland, or we would have had to sleep in the NICU to be with her. We would have gladly done either, but the Ronald McDonald House made it so we didn't need to.

The Ronald McDonald House does this for thousands of families every hour of every day of every year.

I came up with the idea for this anthology one night while Marcee and I were in our room at RMH. We wanted to give back to the organization not only for what it was doing for us, but what it has done for families since the first Ronald McDonald House opened its doors in 1974. The organization operates strictly on donations, and the best way I could think to give back was to use my talent with words.

I knew I couldn't do it alone, however, so I called upon some of the best names in horror fiction to help out. The response was overwhelming. With very few exceptions, every author I contacted was willing to participate. I also received stories from writers who saw the call for submissions on Dark Markets. It wasn't long before I had more stories than I could possibly use—enough to fill two volumes of *Dark Light*.

I can remember where I was and at what time of the day it was when I received word from each of these fine writers that he or she would be happy to contribute. It isn't that difficult, though. I was either at the hospital or at the Ronald McDonald House. The days and nights ran together, but each one of these authors responding that he or she would be willing to participate in *Dark Light* was an uplifting moment.

I am grateful to the 42 authors included here, as well as to those who wanted to participate but couldn't be included. I would also like to thank ahead of time all of you who will be helping promote the book after its release (there are several commitments already). Without each of you, this project could not have been realized. Your generosity warms my heart.

John Sadness

Jeffrey Thomas

Sobs wrenched Jane Thistle as holy men carried the tiny raft to the water's edge. She walked in the procession, though she was still weak from the long labor that had delivered the blighted infant. Her husband John Thistle helped support her. Others, deemed more important in the ritual, walked ahead of them, even though John and Jane were the parents. There was the mayor of the village, John Stout, and the village surgeon, John Copper, their black top hats severe like parading towers. The four religious men in their robes and sandaled feet, bearing along the flower-decorated raft, took the lead.

The nameless lake spread out before them, vast and black, misted gray where it blended with a distant horizon, lapping the shore with an insidious calm. Violent storms never blew in off this lake and the oily waves never much varied their steady, somnambulant rhythm. Fish were not caught from this lake and boats were never sailed upon it. Even travelers from the villages on its far side would rather spend months skirting around it than weeks sailing across it. Too many had been lost in the attempt. Too many had died eating the fish. It was said that these waters were tainted with the fluids from the machinery of those ancient people who had once populated this land, but had died out many ages ago, extinguishing themselves so thoroughly that they took most of their artifacts along with them.

But there was an island at the center of the lake, Jane Thistle had been assured by the surgeon who examined her newborn, and by the mayor who had given the Word in accordance with the laws of their religion. No one alive had ever set foot upon this island, but it had been sighted before travel on the lake had finally been entirely outlawed. Though never visible from the shore, it was a large island, thick with black fir trees choked in swirling mist. It was the island to which the waters would either literally—or symbolically—carry her child.

And now the robed men set the raft down in the thin water that slurped around their ankles (they would take long purifying baths to cleanse themselves later). All throughout the walk from the village, the infant had been quiet, had not fussed. Was he sleeping or blinking up innocently at the churning gray skies and the faces of the strangers who bore him toward his fate?

His name was John Sadness. The parents of the blighted were discouraged from naming these infants when they were, upon occasion, born. But Jane Thistle had named him secretly. Even her husband did not know his name.

Now, as if the infant knew he was to be sent to an obvious death, John Sadness began to cry. So did his mother, who in a burst of anguish sought to rush to his side. Her husband held her back. He was afraid that if he didn't, one of the constables behind him would do so instead.

Mayor John Stout addressed the distraught woman in a deep, oratorical voice that belched steam into the chill air. "Madam, I have given the Word, in accordance with the laws of our Lord and Master, and upon the advice of Surgeon John Copper. You need no surgeon's eyes to see that your child is blighted and must be sent from us to the place where his brothers dwell."

"No other blighted children dwell on that island!" Jane Thistle cried, a vein standing out on her flushed forehead like a brand of disgrace. "You know as well as I that they all perish from the cold, or in the water . . . or if they do wash up on the island, that they are too young and weak to care for themselves!"

"We do not murder these children. They are the Lord's children, howsoever malformed. We simply turn them over to the Lord's hands. But the Word tells us that they must not live amongst us, to spread their polluted seed. Would you have every child born of our village to be as this child?"

In her pain and helplessness, Jane's legs turned watery, insubstantial beneath her, so that she leaned more heavily into her husband's arms, however much she resented them at this moment. Her sobs increased as her child bawled more lustily. He wanted milk. He wanted his mother.

"He isn't that badly off!" she rasped, only half believing her own lie. She had had to drip milk into his twisted mouth with a dropper. She had screamed when first she saw his face—not only because she knew he would be sent away, but out of simple terror itself. "Couldn't we castrate him so that he won't breed? He has two arms, two legs . . . he could support himself when he's older . . . be of help to the village . . ."

"There are no exceptions. He would be sent away if he had but a cleft palate, a milky eye. It is the only way that the rest of us can be sure of our purity. We cast no blame on you, Jane Thistle. You did not ask for this curse, nor deserve it, I am sure. But the Word is the Word. We can delay the Lord's decree no longer . . ."

"Please . . . please," Jane pleaded, now nearly limp in her husband's embrace, no longer struggling, "let me kiss his brow one last time . . ."

The holy men either did not hear her beaten whimper or did not heed it as they pushed the miniature raft out into the lake of liquid obsidian. There it was rocked obscenely, if gently, like a cradle. Jane Thistle could see nothing of her son John Sadness upon that floating coffin but for the flowers and his two small arms—deformed as they were—reaching up for the neck of his mother, or in an appeal to their God.

* * *

Jane Thistle wore only long black mourning gowns for the ten years that followed the exile and death of her child. Her husband did not try to discourage her. The black attire, snug around her slim waist, the skirts voluminous, complemented the severe beauty of her dark hair and eyes and contrasted her colorless skin. Her husband was grateful that she would still bare that skin to him in its entirety, after the fruit their love had seeded.

18

There had been no further fruit, and that was no doubt why she permitted their love-making. The surgeon told her the child had probably damaged her womb in his birth. John Thistle felt his wife was relieved for this—that there would be no other children. But at the same time, he felt that her mourning garments were not only for their blighted son, but for her other children who would never be born at all.

Jane Thistle, twenty at the time of her son's exile, was now thirty. In that time, other women had watched their infants sail out to the unseen island. Some had sobbed, as Jane had. Some had watched in icy relief. In those ten years—as in all the years before—not one raft had washed back ashore. No flotsam of wood, no tiny fish-like bones. Only flowers . . . nothing more.

Then one day a cry went up. The whole village was gradually aroused. Some children casting rocks out into the ebony lake had seen something shadowy in the distant fog, and soon the constables were called to the water's edge. Other townspeople joined them. John Thistle told his wife about it as he hurried to their barn, slipping into his jacket as he went. Inside the barn, he took up a pitchfork.

"I'm going with you," Jane Thistle told him.

"They say it's a ship, Jane," John told her gravely. "At first the boys thought it was a whale—some great beast. But it's a ship . . . heading toward our shore . . ."

Jane pulled her fringed black shawl around her shoulders, the chill autumn breeze stirring her black curls about her face. "I'm coming with you."

At the edge of the lake, a brisk wind snapped at Jane's skirts. A gray Mayor John Stout held a plump hand to his top hat's brim to keep it from being dislodged. The constables had muskets in their fists.

The ship had already run aground by the time Jane and John Thistle arrived. Its prow was lodged in plowed-up mud. The vessel loomed; not even before craft had been outlawed from these waters had such a large vessel sailed them. The villagers murmured about how it resembled, in general outline and in size, an ocean-going vessel.

But resemblances ended there.

The hulking ship seemed to have a skin of glistening scales (no doubt why the boys had taken it for a living thing). These scales, up close, proved to be a mosaic of glossy white tiles, perhaps ceramic. There were no sails, nor even masts. Several small structures up top were also tiled and without windows or portholes. Here and there were pipes of a brassy color, up top and growing out of the sides of the ship, and thick black hoses like veins running in and out of white flesh. Atop the huge craft were, here and there, clusters of brassy and silvery machinery, like boilers and furnaces, with shiny chimneys that belched no smoke, but seemed only to vent a thin steam. The machinery made no sound.

"This can't be from the villages across the lake, and there are no rivers that connect with it," John Thistle breathed in awe. "It has to have come from the island."

"How could this have been built without us having heard any sounds of it?" surgeon John Copper wondered aloud. He had taken to dyeing his graying hair red. "Even across the distances, wouldn't we have heard something?"

"Perhaps it was built at the bottom of the lake and risen up," said Jane Mason, wife of one of the constables.

"Built by whom?" John Thistle asked.

"Look at it. Look at the machinery. This is the work of the Ancient People," said Jane Mason.

"The Ancient People were demons in the flesh," John Stout said, "and the Master cursed them and cleansed them from our lands. They are extinct, and rightly so."

"We don't know what exists on that island. It could be the Ancients still survive upon it, if only in small number. But look at that ship, John Stout! Who else could have created it?"

"Hallo!" John Stout bellowed, advancing further across the damp gritty sand, but not actually nearing the slithering membrane of the surf. "Hallo, in there! Show yourselves!"

In answer, the assemblage heard a grating of metal from above, then a whispery, scrabbling sound . . .

20

John Stout backed up several steps, and in a rather less confident tone, repeated, "Hallo?"

Below, they caught a fleeting glimpse of dark, silhouetted hands moving in quick darts and flurries, as fistfuls of flowers and broken petals were cast from atop the ship. The mayor stumbled backward now, frantically, as if the touch of the snow of petals might be poisonous.

With the petals still fluttering in the air like moths, a head rose up furtively to gaze down at the villagers. It was silhouetted and thus difficult to make out—difficult, even, to fathom—but seemed to resemble the fleshless skull of a horse. And then, timidly, the body followed. Ribs curled free of the chest like those of a skeleton and the vertebrae protruded in a line of jagged dorsal fins. The forelimbs were great pinchers, like those of a crab, and with these the thing was lowering a rope ladder over the side . . .

"Dear God!" one of the constables cried, and shouldered his musket and fired.

Thunder. The very air was burned. The skeletal apparition went back down out of sight abruptly at the impact. The villagers had all heard its inhuman shriek of pain and surprise.

"Demons!" cried John Kettle, the blacksmith. "It's the Ancient People!"

"No," said Jane Thistle in a voice so low only her husband beside her heard it. She clapped a hand over her heart, and in a tone of awed, anguished joy said, "It's our children!"

"It's our children!" said Jane Mason at the same moment, in a louder voice, and in a tone of absolute horror.

Now, from above, came other voices. Rumblings and chattering . . . hissing whispers, and panther-like growls . . .

"Jane," said John Thistle, "we must get back to the house."

"No!" she replied, moving forward.

He took her arm. "We must! Hurry!"

The first of them dropped off the back of the ship, where they were less vulnerable to the constables' muskets. The villagers could hear them splash as they landed.

And then they charged out of the ship's shadows, kicking up the poisonous black water as they came. In their speed, in their fury, and in their vast and varied hideousness, the deformed children made it difficult for the constables to take aim at them. A ragged line of shots cracked the air, and then the creatures were upon them . . .

"Run!" yelled John Thistle, violently pulling his wife along now, but still holding onto his pitchfork. "Run! Run!"

And despite her terrible joy, Jane did run when she saw one of the creatures embrace Mayor John Stout in four obese arms dangling folds of creased flesh. A translucent head—little more than a gelatinous bag—closed over the mayor's head like a caul.

As Jane turned and fled, holding hands with her husband, she saw the surgeon John Copper run past her. He was moving very fast for a man of his years, and then she realized he wasn't so much running as being propelled along by the momentum of a creature which had hold of him. The thing galloped on its hands and feet, but its body was normal enough; like all the creatures, it wore no clothing. From its eye sockets, however, writhed twin nests of milky tendrils like those of an anemone, and its bony hooked jaws pierced Copper's neck like the mandibles of an ant warrior.

Thistle let go of his wife and whirled about, gripping the pitchfork in both fists now. He lunged at the creature and the trident caught it through its neck. Jetting blood, it collapsed atop the surgeon, but the man was already jumping with his final electrified spasms. Thistle again took his wife's hand; again they ran. Jane's black skirts flapped the air like storm-lashed sails; the ground seemed to hammer with a maddened heartbeat under their thumping footfalls.

Something that squealed like a pig being slaughtered could be heard racing up behind them as they sprinted into their yard; whatever it was thudded against their door just as John got it closed and bolted. They rushed from window to window, locking them and drawing the curtains. Finally, John panted, "Upstairs, Jane . . . move!"

Jane's hair was in her face and her eyes gleamed madly from within its tangle. "They survived, John. Some of them . . . the strongest. And helped the weaker to survive. All these years they were building that ship. Building it from what they found on the island; machinery that the Ancients left behind. Building it all this while, so they could return to us . . ."

"For revenge, Jane!"

She wagged her head. Tears streamed down her flushed cheeks.

John again urged her upstairs, and this time she obeyed him. They entered their bedroom; John shut and barred its door. He turned to close the curtains to one window and saw the creature which had been waiting for them.

It had been struck by one of the constables' musket balls; dark blood was winding down its pallid flesh. It was stooped but still towered over them, emaciated yet also suggesting great strength. Its eyes, each as large as a normal man's head, were two great cloudy sacks hanging from a head that had not grown since its infancy. Its hair was still wispy as corn silk.

Though the eyes had grown so much larger, its cadaverous body so much taller, Jane Thistle recognized her son, John Sadness, instantly.

"My boy!" she sobbed, spreading her arms. "My boy!"

It took a lurching step toward her, fingers three times longer than they should be, curled into a skeleton's talons . . .

"No!" John Thistle cried, darting toward the small fireplace to seize up a poker . . .

The creature fell upon his wife and she struggled with it. But as Thistle raised the poker above his head, he realized that the thing had crumpled and Jane was fighting to hold it up. John dropped the poker and helped take hold of the scarecrow-like body . . . walked it to the bed with her, where they laid it down.

The creature gurgled up at them. Its pendulous orbs were nothing like eyes; in fact, the creature may have been blind. Maybe it was scent that had led it here. Or mere memory. It reached up feebly, unerringly to Jane's face, and stroked her cheek.

John took hold of its other hand and sat on the edge of his bed. In this bed, they had made this creature. Their son.

John watched as his wife bent over John Sadness. Her tears fell upon its tiny face and great eyes as she kissed it one last time, on the brow.

Then, with a small contented shudder, the creature died.

* * *

A dozen townspeople had perished in the battle. None of these victims had been children, however, for which the townspeople were grateful.

All of the monstrosities that had disembarked from the ship were finally slaughtered. It took several days to track down the last of them in the woods. Whether there were more aboard the ship, or back on the island, no one could tell . . . but the strange vessel was gone by the time anyone returned to the beach.

Sometimes Jane would stand at the spot where it had arrived, holding her husband's hand. There they would both look out across the black lake, staring at where the island must lie, as if hoping the mist would part and sunlight would beam down upon it. But it remained cloaked in its winding sheet of fog. And while most of the villagers no doubt gazed out at those waters in dread, Jane and John Thistle did so with tears in their eyes, and sad smiles on their lips.

–For Colin

Jeffrey Thomas is the author of such novels as Deadstock, Blue War, *and* Letters from Hades, *and collections such as* Punktown, Nocturnal Emissions, *and* Unholy Dimensions. *Thomas says of his inspiration for the story* John Sadness: *My son Colin is autistic, and so I can empathize with any parent whose child has faced tough challenges.* John Sadness *was one of several stories I wrote as a means of assimilating the news when Colin was first diagnosed as being autistic. It's a story about the unconditional love of parents for their children. Visit Jeffrey's blog at: http://punktalk.punktowner.com*

Crasher

Debbie Kuhn

They wanted Martin to finish the game. He refused to look at them, but he knew they were watching as he lifted the gun to his temple. His hand shook and he could smell his own fear in the sweat that trickled down his chest and back.

A gentle breeze wafted in through the window in front of him, carrying the scent of spring blossoms, while throaty female laughter drifted up from the sidewalk below his apartment. People were gathering at the cathedral across the street.

He thought about saying a desperate prayer, even though he didn't believe in God, but then the three of them moved into his peripheral vision. He felt the boy's hatred and anger wash over him in an ice-cold wave.

Martin pulled the trigger and heard a quiet *click*. No bullet.

He slumped in his chair, limp-limbed with both relief and disappointment. His foot knocked over what was left of the Maker's Mark.

He still had to finish the game.

Martin took a great gulp of sweet air and turned his head slowly to the left. As usual, the little girl's face wore a confused, frightened expression. Her mouth and neck were bleeding again, which had caused a few strands of her long black hair to become plastered against her pale cheek. When he made eye contact, she took a step forward and stretched out her hand to offer him a reminder. Her severed tongue wriggled around on her bloody palm.

The gaunt-faced woman stood behind her children, weeping incessantly and barely making a sound.

"You're dead," Martin whispered. "You're not really there."

According to his former shrink, the apparitions were simply manifestations of the anger, guilt, and grief he'd been feeling since returning home from Vietnam. Martin didn't argue against the theory because he didn't believe in ghosts.

But he was fucked either way. As long as he continued to breathe they would continue to exist, haunting his every waking moment and invading his whisky-soaked dreams.

"Keep taking your medicine, Mr. Sinclair. The pills I've prescribed should help you sleep and make those hallucinations go away."

Wrong. After eight weeks of treatment, which had included a brief hospital stay, Martin had pretended to be cured and had flushed the little white pills down the toilet. A few days after that he had marched into the bedroom and retrieved his dad's old service revolver from the bottom of the cedar chest.

There were no prescriptions, nor illegal drugs, that could give him any pleasure or peace—he had tried them all. There was only one way to end his torment.

Like father, like son.

Even with a generous dose of liquid courage in his veins, Martin had only been able to pull the trigger once the first couple of times he had played the game. He had fought like a savage to stay alive during his tour of duty. It was hard to give up on life now, a year later, when he was only twenty-two.

But they would never go away, never leave him alone. And he was just so *tired*.

Martin shuddered and tore his gaze away from the little girl. Time to finish it. He should have died with his friend Smitty, anyway. The scars on his face and body were nothing compared to the ones that crippled his soul.

He raised the revolver to his temple again. It felt even heavier.

Martin closed his eyes. *Click.*

Click.

He started to pull the trigger a fourth time but stopped. He could hear a woman singing. A soprano. The sound seemed to be coming from right across the street—inside Sacred Heart.

Ave Maria, gratia plena, Maria, gratia plena, Maria, gratia plena, Ave, ave dominus, Dominus tecum, Benedicta tu in mulieribus, Et benedictus, Et benedictus fructus ventris, Ventris tuae, Jesus. Ave Maria.

Martin lowered the gun, letting it rest in his lap. Tears sprang to his eyes and his whole body tingled with pleasure.

Ave Maria, mater Dei, Ora pro nobis peccatoribus, Ora pro nobis, Ora, ora pro nobis peccatoribus, Nunc et in hora mortis, Et in hora mortis nostrae, Ave Maria.

Martin felt warm, comforted. The apparitions—those figments of his tortured imagination—moved closer to his chair. The boy looked furious, but Martin couldn't be touched by it. He watched in amazement as the phantoms began to waver and then fade.

They disappeared completely with the last note of the song.

"Jesus." Martin jumped to his feet and the revolver clattered onto the hardwood floor.

He had to see the woman. He had to know who she was.

Martin paused just long enough to slip on a ratty pair of tennis shoes and then he raced out of his second floor apartment and down the hall, taking the stairs instead of the elevator.

The traffic on Waverly Place wasn't heavy for a Saturday evening in Greenwich Village. Martin was so excited he might have ended up as road kill otherwise.

The massive arched doors to the church were standing open—an invitation. The interior felt cool and dark after his exposure to the bright warm sun and Martin stood still for a moment to let his eyes adjust. The apparitions still had not returned. It had been ages since he'd been able to leave his apartment on his own and act like a normal person.

The woman was singing again. It was a song he didn't recognize this time, but he thought she sounded like an angel of mercy. He walked into the nave of the Gothic-style cathedral, and couldn't help feeling as though he were leaving the whole wicked world and his tragic past behind him.

White paper bells and streamers decorated the ends of the pews, which were crammed with people dressed in expensive suits and frilly dresses. Martin stayed next to the stone wall on the north side of the church, passing underneath the stained glass windows. He moved closer to the high altar where the middle-aged woman stood singing. She was tall and slender and her hair fell in dark ringlets around her face. Diffused, rose-colored sunlight poured in and bathed her in an ethereal glow—an effect magnified by the floor-length spangled dress she wore.

Martin knew the woman loved him. She loved everyone when she sang, and her singing was a gift that allowed her to bestow peace and the purest form of pleasure upon her audience.

When the song was finished, Martin realized that tears were streaming down his face.

The woman gracefully descended the steps of the high altar and chose a pew on the south side of the nave. The organist resumed her playing and Martin realized it was time for the wedding ceremony to commence. A bridesmaid appeared in the center aisle, followed by a half dozen others.

Martin moved to the back of the cathedral and sat on the edge of the last pew next to a heavy-set lady dressed in pink chiffon, who immediately covered her nose with a handkerchief. Her eyes filled with disdain at the sight of his stringy blond hair, stained white T-shirt, and torn bell-bottoms. She tried to put more distance between them, but Martin wouldn't let her.

"The woman who was singing—what's her name?" he whispered.

The lady stared at him like he was an idiot. She lowered her lace handkerchief just long enough to answer his question.

"Elaine Vittorio. She used to be an opera singer."

***

Martin had hailed a cab after the wedding ceremony and had followed the guests to the reception hall. He was hoping Elaine would sing again, but he didn't see her there. Soon after his arrival, a member of the wedding party insisted that he leave.

A week passed and Martin still felt euphoric. He had never believed in miracles before, but he was beginning to think Elaine's singing had somehow cured his insanity by chasing away the guilt-induced hallucinations.

Her voice had pushed the fragments of his mind back together in a bond tight enough to lock out the horrific memories of the war and keep his personal demons bound and gagged. Martin enjoyed life again. Hell, he didn't even need the crutches of cigarettes and alcohol.

Martin's mother noticed the change in him right away when she dropped by for her weekly visit that Saturday morning.

At ten A.M. sharp, Natalie Sinclair swept unannounced into the two-bedroom apartment she still owned, presumably to make sure the groceries she ordered for her son had been delivered, that the maid had shown up on Friday, and that Martin was still alive.

Yes, yes, and yes.

Martin was sitting at the breakfast table when his mother walked into the kitchen. He was eating a stack of pancakes fit for a lumberjack.

"Well, I'm glad to see your appetite has finally returned." She leaned over and planted a quick kiss on his right cheek. The left side of his face was scarred.

"And if I'm not mistaken, you've even had a shower today."

Martin nodded, his mouth full of syrupy flapjacks.

"Those sessions with Dr. Sylva are finally paying off. When's your next appointment?"

He didn't want to admit the truth, even though he had never told her about the hallucinations.

"Tuesday, I think."

"Good." His mother's expression softened a bit.

Martin had once been her "pretty blue-eyed prince." He knew she wanted him to see a plastic surgeon about his face.

Maybe he would. The last few days he'd been thinking a lot about his ex-girlfriend, Sharon Bohmer. He kept wondering what her reaction would be if he contacted her again.

Martin had enlisted in the army on Valentine's Day the year before. He'd been a senior at Columbia University with a college deferment. His grades were up and his I.Q. was down, or maybe he'd just been too drunk and pissed off to know better. His mother wanted to mold and shape him into a spineless replica of his father—make him president of one of the family's banks, perhaps set him up to fail. His softhearted girlfriend just wanted him to join a commune, protest at an occasional war rally, and pretend to be a vegetarian.

In retrospect, Martin wished he'd quit college and run off to California with Sharon to raise goats and chickens.

"Martin, are you listening to me?"

"Huh?" He looked up and saw his mother standing in the living room.

"When did *you* start liking opera?" She waved a hand at the pile of Elaine Vittorio albums on the coffee table.

"A week ago, actually." Martin had just bought the records the day before, hoping they would help keep the lunacy at bay.

"Hmm." His mother focused her attention on the gilded oval mirror that hung above the sofa. She pushed a lock of her frosted blonde hair back into place. "Elaine was a member of my club before she retired from the Met."

Martin was curious. "Why did she quit her career so early? She can't be more than forty."

"Her husband was in a car accident about a year ago. It left him in far worse shape than you've ever been."

***

Martin went to the library a week later and found some old newspaper articles about Elaine. They confirmed what his mother had told him. Al Vittorio was now a quadriplegic. Elaine had given up the career she loved to help care for him. Martin also learned the singer had joined Bob Hope's Christmas show in '68 and had traveled to Vietnam to entertain the troops. Now she only sang at the weddings and funerals of people she loved or admired, be they relatives, close friends, or celebrities.

It had now been exactly two weeks since Martin had seen Elaine perform in person. He had been able to sleep soundly at night and he had boundless amounts of energy during the day.

After visiting the library, Martin had gone to a Saturday matinee to see *The Godfather*. He had thought about asking his ex, Sharon, to come along, but he still didn't have the balls to call her. That night he lounged around eating junk food and watching sitcoms until the eleven o'clock news came on, at which time he flipped President Nixon the bird and went to bed.

***

Charlie Company's night assault at Phouc Vinh wound down as the sun came up. It had rained earlier and now the damp ground spawned a heavy mist as the heat and humidity worsened. Soon it would feel like a hundred degrees, even in the shade.

The straps of Martin's heavy pack bit into his shoulders and the weight strained his back. Exhaustion made his vision blur at times, but he tried to stay alert as he and Smitty approached a rubber plantation. Like the rest of their unit, they were headed to a nearby fire station to regroup and wait for instructions.

Lawrence "Smitty" Smith cursed under his breath at the insects swarming around his bronzed face. He dodged an old bomb crater and risked a glance back at Martin.

"One more month and you'll be kissing my sweet ass goodbye, Sinclair."

As usual, Martin grinned at Smitty's exaggerated southern drawl. "From what I've heard, Georgia ain't much better than 'Nam anyway."

His friend let out a snort. "Fuckin' Yankee."

Martin would have preferred to be in Georgia or any other place on earth. His nerves were shot after the night they'd had. But every hour was as horrible and boring as the next. You dealt with the stress whatever way you could. Half the grunts he knew were already heroin addicts.

At the moment, Martin just wanted to take a leak and have a cigarette. He'd started smoking again his first day in uniform.

"Smit, toss me your lighter, man." Martin had lost his in the jungle the night before.

His friend's Zippo was well worn and had "I Walk the Line" engraved on one side. Smitty had spent some time on the Demilitarized Zone, patrolling the border.

Martin caught the lighter and paused for a moment to fire up a damp cigarette. When he finally got it lit he shoved the Zippo into his breast pocket.

Smitty was now moving on toward a wide path bordered by a deep ditch. The rain had turned the red dirt into clay.

A faint sound reached Martin's ears, like a child crying. Smitty heard it too and stopped walking.

A boy around twelve years old dragged himself out of the ditch. He seemed injured, and before he could crawl any closer towards them a terrified woman rose up behind him and grabbed both his legs, trying to pull him back down into the trench.

The boy yelled something in Vietnamese, but Martin couldn't understand what he was saying.

Smitty began walking towards them. "Are you hurt, kid?"

The boy struggled with the woman and when he managed to break free of her grasp, he stood up and reached into the pockets of his filthy trousers.

Martin knew what was going to happen next and froze in his tracks, unable to fire his rifle or even shout a warning at his friend.

The grenade exploded in the air a few feet in front of Smitty. Martin was thrown back onto the ground as shrapnel and body parts rained down around him.

He tasted rancid blood, and as soon as he was able to pull more of the thick steamy air into his lungs, he screamed.

Martin struggled back to his feet, ignoring the pain coursing through him. He saw the boy running down the path away from the woman, who was crying. Another child, a little girl who appeared to be in shock, emerged from the ditch and grabbed on to her mother's skirts.

Martin took after the boy, and even though he was sobbing so hard he could barely see, he immediately raised his rifle and fired. The impact of the bullets lifted the kid off his feet and thrust him violently forward into the ground.

"Smitty! Goddammit, Smit!"

Martin didn't feel like Martin anymore.

He turned around and saw the woman charging at him with a knife. He swung his rifle up and knocked the weapon out of her hand. Then he brought the butt down against the side of her head—one, two, three times.

Shrill screams rent the air and hurt his ears. He flung his rifle back over his shoulder and picked up the knife.

The little girl was standing in the middle of the path, shrieking. Martin just wanted her to stop.

***

"Jesus Christ!" Martin sat straight up in bed, sweat pouring off his face, his heart thumping furiously in his chest.

The nightmare had felt so real, like he was actually reliving the incident with Smitty all over again. He swung his legs over the side of the bed and just sat there trembling for a minute.

A beer and a cigarette. That would help.

Martin stumbled down the short hallway to the kitchen and turned on a light. He kept Smitty's Zippo in a drawer by the refrigerator. He retrieved it and the pack of Marlboros that lay on the counter and took a seat at the table.

He puffed away furiously on a cigarette for several minutes and then snubbed it out.

When he was ready for the beer, Martin got up from the table with a yawn and opened the refrigerator door.

"Fuckin' Yankee."

Smitty's decaying head sat on a wire rack between the beer and the leftover pizza.

Martin thought for a brief moment that he might faint. He slammed the refrigerator door shut and then vomited all over his bare feet.

***

Things were much worse than before. And listening to Elaine's albums didn't help. Three weeks passed. Then he heard on the news that the mayor's daughter had died of leukemia.

He attended the funeral at St. Patrick's cathedral and listened to Elaine sing "Amazing Grace" and "Be Still My Soul."

The pleasure was so intense he could barely sit still. The peace lasted two weeks.

And then they were back.

Martin's body began to hurt all over just like it did when the grenade had gone off. He couldn't eat or sleep. He told his mother he had a bad case of the flu in hopes she would stay away.

Martin sat on the couch day and night, smoking and drinking and keeping an eye on his hallucinations. Their harassment reached new levels of torture. The little girl liked to float upside down above his head, letting the blood from her ravaged mouth and neck drip down onto his face. The boy dragged Smitty's arms and legs around the apartment, leaving red clay footprints and trails of blood all over the hardwood floor. Their mother's weeping had grown louder, like the death shrills of souls trapped in Hell.

Of course, his shrink would only tell him that he was punishing himself and that he really wanted to die.

But Martin realized he really wanted to live, whether he deserved to or not.

***

He needed to kill Elaine's husband. Al Vittorio was the reason she wasn't singing professionally anymore. Murder the cripple and all three of them would be put out of their mutual misery.

Being insane had its advantages. All of one's actions were easily justified.

Before Martin could plan the murder of Elaine's husband, he learned she would be singing at her niece's wedding the last Saturday in June—three days away.

On that afternoon, painful spasms wracked Martin's body, making it difficult for him to get into his suit. Still, he needed to blend into the Sacred Heart crowd as best he could.

Martin examined the program that was handed to him upon entering the cathedral and saw that Elaine and another female singer were to perform "Flower Duet" from Lakmé, an opera by Delibe.

Something seemed different about Elaine—she looked distracted and nervous and even a bit ill. But when the time came for her to sing, she didn't fail him.

***

Martin couldn't possibly plan a murder while feeling high on peace, love, and tranquility. He would have to wait until the effects of Elaine's singing wore off again. Having the nightmare about Smitty's death was the main warning sign that he was about to go into withdrawal.

The next time it happened was on a Saturday morning. Martin had fallen asleep on the couch the night before and was shaken awake from the dream by his mother.

"Martin, have you stopped taking your pills?"

Pain medication was what he needed. His head was about to explode and he felt nauseous.

His mother sighed and turned away. When he looked up he saw her staring at the photograph of his father that he kept on his bookshelf. The picture had been taken on their cabin cruiser one summer just off Martha's Vineyard. Robert Sinclair had posed proudly at the wheel, smiling broadly. A year later, on the 4th of July, he had used his World War II service revolver to splatter his brains all over the boat's newly decorated interior.

Martin had been sixteen at the time and he knew it was his mother's fault.

Natalie Sinclair looked back at her son, her face devoid of all emotion.

"Why did you have to end up like him, Martin? I had such high hopes for your future and now you've become just as weak and useless." She turned away from him again and began walking towards the apartment door. "Swallowing a bullet was the best decision your father ever made."

A few seconds later, his mother let out a startled yelp as he jerked her back around to face him. Even he was a little surprised when his hands closed around her throat.

***

The pain motivated Martin to fight for survival. Too bad about his mother, but she needed an attitude adjustment.

He had placed her body in the wingback chair with her legs splayed apart and her head tilted to one side—her cold eyes staring straight ahead. She really wasn't looking her best anymore, what with the bruises on her neck turning three different shades of purple. Her shoulder length hair was mussed and her makeup was smeared.

A casualty of war.

Martin paced back and forth in front of the body for a while, trying to think. The apparitions followed him.

He decided he should make it look like a mugging. In the wee hours of the morning, he would take her out to an alley somewhere closer to her townhouse and arrange the scene just so. He could report her missing the next afternoon.

Right in the middle of a spasm, Martin suddenly had a thought that made him smile despite his intense discomfort.

He could ask Elaine to sing at his mother's funeral. Everyone in New York knew the socialite and heiress. It was all so perfect.

Martin had several hours to wait before he could get rid of the body. He managed the best he could. He couldn't sit still anymore to watch television so he switched on the radio in the kitchen and turned up the volume to block out the cries of the children's mother.

He needed to find a way to contact Elaine or her assistant, and then realized with wry amusement that he should have asked Natalie about it before he killed her. Of course, he would have to hold off on calling anyone until the body was discovered.

It was later that evening, right after the DJ had played "Run Through the Jungle" by Credence Clearwater Revival, that he heard the news bulletin from hell.

"Former opera star Elaine Vittorio was admitted to the hospital early this morning of an apparent overdose. Sources close to the singer say she has been suffering from depression and hallucinations off and on over the last few months. She remains in serious condition."

Martin didn't want to accept it. He leaned back against the table and stared at the apparitions that surrounded him. Instead of his usual angry expression, the boy stared up at him with a smug little smile.

Martin felt a chill shimmy up his spine. "Son of a bitch."

His mother's disembodied laughter suddenly filled the room, mocking him as only she could do.

"Go to hell!"

There was only one way for Martin to confirm his fears—he would have to go see Elaine after visiting hours were over at the hospital.

***

St. Francis-St. George was six blocks away from Martin's apartment building. After swallowing two powerful painkillers, he headed out with the phantom trio and arrived at a quarter to midnight. When he sneaked into Elaine's fifth floor hospital room, he found her asleep. The dim glow from the nightlight overhead revealed the dark smudges beneath her eyes.

"Angel of mercy," he whispered.

Elaine stirred. When she woke and saw Martin standing there smiling, she merely gave him a puzzled stare. But then she noticed the three blood-soaked figures that hovered at the foot of her bed and he saw the horrified recognition on her face. Her eyes widened in terror.

Now Martin knew the truth. The spirits were real. He wasn't being haunted because he was insane. He was insane because he was being haunted.

Elaine looked as though she were going to start screaming so Martin spoke to her softly. "Shhh. You don't have to worry about them anymore."

"Who are they?" she asked, her voice shaking. "What do they want from me?"

"They want you to suffer for giving me peace and happiness. Your gift is so powerful that it drives them away—they can't torment me anymore. So they torment you."

"But . . . I don't understand."

"It'll be okay, Elaine. I know how to make them leave you alone. Just don't ever stop singing—not ever. Promise me?"

Elaine nodded, tears sliding down her face.

Martin thought about asking her to sing at his funeral, but then figured it would be a bit much to expect, considering the hell he'd put her through—and the fact he was a murderer.

He left the hospital as a light, cool rain began to fall, cleansing the air of its foul city odor. Steam rose off the warm pavement and mixed spookily with the glow of the streetlights. Traffic swished by at an easy pace.

His pain pills were beginning to wear off, but he wasn't worried.

When he reached Washington Square Park, the mother and her two children disappeared—but Martin knew they had simply gone home to wait for him.

Tonight he would finish the game.

Debbie Kuhn is a freelance writer and editor who currently lives in Kentucky. She writes across genres, but has no problem admitting that horror is her favorite. You can find out more info by visiting her website: www.debbiekuhn.com.

Harbinger

Carl Hose

Green Meadows was the last stop for its residents. It was a nice enough place, but it was *the last stop* nonetheless. There was no way to put a positive spin on it. Green Meadows was the place people came to die.

Harold Sanderson knew that. He'd long ago come to accept the fact. He was eighty-four and on his very last mile. His only friends these days were the other old farts who tottered around Green Meadows just waiting to die right along with him.

Harold didn't count the nurses and other staff at Green Meadows among his friends. How could he? Most of them were as cold and uncaring as an iceberg, here to collect a paycheck just as sure as Harold and the others were here to die.

Harold lay in bed, grateful he had it better than most of the others here. With the aid of a pair of very thick glasses, he was still able to read his Holy Bible, and on a good day he could walk up and down the hallway on his own two legs, wobbly as they were.

He stared at the thin line of moonlight creeping in through the closed blinds. Part of him wanted to get up and open the window to let the full light of the moon in, but another part of him wanted to remain in the dark, contemplating his very short future.

He wondered what he would do if he could turn back time. Would he have done anything different? Had he made the right choices in his life?

He caught movement over by the door and turned his head slowly to see what it was. Jasper, the orange and white mixed-breed cat that roamed the hallways of Green Meadows stood looking at Harold from the doorway, his piercing green eyes posing a threat.

Harold was full aware of what that threat was.

"Go away," he said to the cat. "Go somewhere else. I'm not near ready yet."

To Harold's great relief, Jasper turned and walked away. That was a good sign. It was a known fact at Green Meadows that Jasper knew who was next in line to die, and if that dang cat took post at your door, it was a fair bet he'd be there until they carted you out on a stretcher.

Harold turned back to the window. The strip of moonlight seemed to be getting wider. He stared at it and tried to collect his scattered thoughts. Where was he? Oh yeah, different. Would he do any different with his life if he could turn back time? A fellow thought about such things when he was at the end of his days, and Harold was no exception to the rule.

In retrospect, no, there was nothing he would have done any different. He'd raised a good family, though none of them came to see him except on the occasional holiday, and he'd stayed happily married to a good woman for fifty years, all the way up until the good Lord took her away from him. He'd worked hard to provide for his family, and they were all healthy and happy because of it. Not much more a man can do than that, and it was certainly something to be proud of, so there was nothing Harold would like to change about the life he'd lived.

No, sir, not a damn thing.

More movement from the door, only this time Harold looked and saw Edna in her wheelchair. Ninety-year-old Edna Bishop, not able to walk anymore, barely able to see . . .

"You still up, you old coot?" she asked.

. . . and still feisty as all get out.

She wheeled herself into his room.

"Saw that damn cat down here," she said.

"Didn't stay," Harold said without much enthusiasm.

"Well, just the same, don't like to see that cat at anybody's door," Edna said. "I don't know why they don't just take it out and shoot it."

"It's not the cat's fault people die," Harold said.

"That cat ain't right, Harry," she insisted. "That cat craves death."

"It's only a cat," he reminded her.

She huh-rumphed him but let the subject drop.

"Thanksgiving's coming up," she said. "Any of your family gonna make it this year?"

"Don't think so," Harold answered.

"Mine neither," she said. "Better chance one of yours would show up than mine, though. Guess that means we'll be eating the turkey and cranberry together this year, that is, if you don't mind."

"You know I don't mind," he said. "It's always a pleasure to spend time with you."

"Damn right it is," she said. She leaned up in her wheelchair to nudge him in the arm. "Why don't you get up out of that bed and use those two good legs ya got to push me around this joint."

He sighed and swung his legs over the edge of his bed, standing and going around behind Edna's wheelchair.

"Don't you pop none of them wheelies," she said.

"I don't think I'll be doing that," he replied, and then with a bit of effort he managed to point her toward the door.

* * *

Breakfast at the chow hall was the usual bland eggs poured from a container, and runny oatmeal. Harold drank a glass of orange juice. He noticed Edna was nowhere to be found. He asked around and no one knew anything about where she might be. One of the nurses overheard him and said that Edna had taken ill during the night, that she would be staying in her room for the day.

Harold ambled back to his room after breakfast. He passed Edna's room and saw her door was closed, with Jasper sitting right outside.

Harold continued down the hallway, looking over his shoulder now and then, checking to see if Jasper followed. The cat remained where he was, eyes straight ahead, taking his position as death sentinel quite seriously.

Harold thought he should shoo the cat away, but what good would it do? Time had shown that Jasper had a way of knowing when a resident of Green Meadows was going to die. Edna believed Jasper to be the actual bringer of death—the Grim Reaper himself—but Harold thought otherwise. He believed Jasper was, quite simply, in tune with the residents of Green Meadows in the way animals can be in tune with people sometimes.

Either way, Jasper's presence outside Edna's door was certainly a sign that her time was short. Harold felt a gentle tug at his heart. She wasn't the first he'd seen go, and God willing, maybe he'd outlive a few more. Awful as that sounded, Harold couldn't help it. He wasn't ready to die yet.

He went back to his room and sat on the edge of the bed. He thought about that damn cat. Maybe he *should* kill it. Would that change anything? He'd never believed that nonsense about the cat bringing death, but the facts were plain—somebody always died when Jasper came sniffing around.

Most of the day passed with Harold staying in his room, waiting for the news he was sure was forthcoming. He passed Jasper on his way to lunch. Edna's door was still shut. When he tried to approach it, Jasper hissed and showed teeth that Harold thought were longer and sharper than they should have been.

And the cat's eyes were yellow. Harold remembered them being green, not yellow. He was almost certain of that.

He returned to his room after lunch, smuggling some of the tuna that had been on the menu. He would need it to lure Jasper away from Edna's door, that is, assuming the cat would even fall for such a trick.

Harold spent the rest of the afternoon watching talk shows and game shows. He stayed away from the soaps. A lot of the ladies here liked those soaps. Most set their watches by them, but Harold couldn't stomach nary a single episode. Too much tragedy and too much drama. Ordinary folks could never handle so much.

Liquid shadows shifted across the walls of Harold's room as afternoon slipped into early evening. The cat remained outside Edna's door the whole time. Harold checked on the feline more than once, and Jasper would only glare at him, almost as if he *knew* something was afoot. At times the intensity of the animal's scrutiny made Harold shiver.

Harold waited until the night-duty nurse came on before he made his move. She was a fat, lazy hag of a woman who sat at the nurse's station with her nose in a cheap bodice-ripper paperback all night.

Harold unwrapped the tuna and stepped out into the silent hallway. He saw the night-duty nurse with her back to him, reading her paperback. Maybe she was even dozing, he couldn't be sure.

Harold hesitated when Jasper fixed him with those yellow eyes, wondering if maybe this wasn't the dumbest thing he'd ever done.

Nonsense. Jasper was just a cat. He was making too much of it.

He moved down the hallway, approaching Jasper slowly. When he was within a few feet of the cat, Harold squatted and held out the tuna.

His knees popped and nearly gave out.

He waved the tuna at Jasper.

The cat turned away from him, not the least bit interested.

"Come here, you stupid cat," Harold whispered.

Jasper shot him a dirty look and turned away again.

Harold inched closer, still squatting, and felt the pain in his bad knee joints. He kept his hand extended, tempting Jasper with the tuna, which by now had begun to take on a rather pungent odor.

Jasper glanced at the tuna, turned away, then looked back again.

"Gotcha now," Harold said in a low tone, taking a look down at the nurse's station to make sure Broom Hilda was still occupied.

Jasper moved toward Harold. He sniffed the tuna and took a little piece into his mouth, chewing greedily, his eyes still fixed on Harold as he did.

"That's a good cat," Harold said in his most comforting tone.

He stood up, wincing as a sharp pain raced along his spine, nearly bringing him back to his knees the hard way. He took a deep breath and gave the pain a moment to subside before he backed down the hallway, coaxing Jasper to follow.

Jasper looked at Edna's room, looked back at Harold, then gave one final look at Edna's room before opting to follow Harold.

Harold tossed bits of tuna onto the floor as he worked his way to his room. Jasper paused to scoop up each morsel with his tongue. Harold tossed one more piece of tuna onto the floor before he backed into his room. He squatted again, ignoring the pain in his knees as he held the last of the tuna out for Jasper. The cat crept forward, slinking into the room, and went straight for the tuna.

Harold watched the cat eat. When he knew the animal was engrossed in the meal, he lunged forward, slamming the door to his room shut. His knees hit the floor and he almost blacked out from the pain. The tuna fell across the floor and Jasper went at it, lapping up the rank-smelling fish without so much as a glance at Harold.

Harold leaned against the door, gasping for breath as he watched the cat eat. Now he had the blasted thing trapped. Jasper wouldn't be going anywhere near Edna's room. Not tonight at least, and just maybe, if there was anything at all to this nonsense, then Edna was going to be just fine.

* * *

Harold woke up curled on the floor in his room. He had such aches as he'd never known. He could hardly move at first, and when he finally did, it was only with an effort that nearly made him want to die.

He sat up and looked around his room. Jasper was nowhere in sight. The window was closed, the door was closed—there was no way that dang cat could have gotten out.

44

No way at all.

When he was able, Harold made a closer inspection of the room, and yep, the cat was nowhere to be found.

Harold passed Edna's room on his way to breakfast. The door was open. Edna was not in her room, but Jasper was once again standing vigil outside the door.

Good or bad sign, Harold couldn't be sure.

He found Edna in the chow hall, all smiles and full of vinegar. A great relief flooded over him.

"Come here, you old coot," she called to him, waving him to her table.

Harold sat with her. He had some of the awful oatmeal and a piece of dry toast, and even a couple strips of bacon the doctor told him was no good for his arteries, and all of it tasted good to him, mainly because Edna seemed in such high spirits and great health.

"Family's comin' to see me on Thanksgiving," Edna said.

"They are?" Harold asked, surprised to hear it.

As far as Harold could remember, no one in Edna's family had ever bothered to visit her. She'd always said she felt like a bit of discarded trash, and while she seemed to accept it most days, Harold could see it hurt her.

Her happiness now was proof of it in Harold's eyes. The thought of a visit from her family had Edna in better spirits than Harold had ever seen.

"I can't wait for you to meet them, Harry," Edna said. "My daughter and my granddaughter and all her young uns are going to be here, and my son, who I ain't seen in a devil's age."

"Can't wait to meet them, Edna," Harold said.

He couldn't help but wonder if Edna was going to be around for Thanksgiving. It was still a couple weeks away, and Jasper didn't seem to want to let her be.

Harold silently chastised himself for such foolish thoughts. That cat was no more the bringer of death than he himself was.

That's what he told himself, at least.

* * *

Harold was wide awake, staring at the ceiling, contemplating all that his life had been and all that was left in store for him.

Again, there was nothing he would change. He wasn't ready to die, but there was not much left ahead of him.

Nothing he couldn't do without, anyway.

The decision wasn't all that hard in the end.

All Harold needed was to convince Jasper to see things his way.

And there was no better time than the present.

Harold swung his feet over the edge of the bed and stood. His knees felt like rusted hinges. He stood still for a moment, waiting to see if he might fall, and then he moved to the door and stepped into the silent hallway.

He found Jasper outside Edna's door. The cat watched him approach.

It was just Harold, Jasper, and the lazy night-duty nurse at the end of the hall, and Harold wasn't worried about her. As usual, her nose was stuck in one of those cheap paperback novels. Harold faced Jasper and looked the cat in the eyes. "I think maybe we need to talk," he said.

Jasper yawned and his pink tongue wiped quickly across his mouth. The cat looked bored, that was Harold's thought.

"I guess maybe I believe what they say about you," Harold went on. "And I guess maybe you're here because it's Edna's time to go."

His knees were starting to hurt bad. He wasn't sure how much longer he could stand on them, and Lord knows he didn't want to try and squat.

"I don't know how much say you have in the matter of who goes and when they go, but if you have any say at all, I'd like you to consider taking me instead of her. She don't show it much, but it hurts her that her family don't come around. She doesn't feel like she's loved . . . and they're coming now, Jasper. Her family is coming to see her on Thanksgiving . . . and I'd sure like it if she could be around for that."

Harold took a slow, painful breath before finishing.

46

"You can take me instead. How would that be?"

The cat turned its head to look into Edna's room, then he looked back up at Harold. There was no sign anything had changed. No sign that Jasper understood anything at all that was being said, and Harold wondered exactly what kind of sign he'd expected.

"That's all I have to say on the matter, Jasper," Harold said. "That's all I have to say about it. You know where to find me."

Harold turned around and headed for his room. He glanced back one last time and saw Jasper was no longer sitting outside Edna's room.

Harold reached his own room and stopped just inside the door.

"It's good of you to come," he said.

Jasper was sitting on Harold's bed, licking his chops. Harold smiled. It was the first time he could remember feeling fond about the animal.

His knees suddenly felt better. He walked over to the bed and climbed in, lifting Jasper as he did, and then he lay back and set the cat on his chest.

"Let's go to sleep," he said.

Jasper licked Harold's nose.

Harold closed his eyes for the last time.

Carl Hose is the author of the anthologies Deadtown and Other Tales of Horror Set in the Old West, Fematales, Fematales Supernatural, Dead Horizon, *the zombie novella* Dead Rising, *the crime fiction novella* Blood Legacy, *and the erotic anthology* Pornocopia, *all published by MARLvision Publishing. Carl's work has appeared in the zombie anthology* Cold Storage, *which he co-edited. His work has also appeared in* DeathGrip: It Came from the Cinema, DeathGrip: Exit Laughing, Loving the Undead, *the erotic paranormal anthology* Beyond Desire, *the* Book of Tentacles, Through the Eyes of the Undead, Silver Moon, Bloody Bullets, *and* Lighthouse Digest *magazine. His poetry appears in the zombie poetry anthology* Vicious Verses and Reanimated Rhymes *and his nonfiction appears in* Writer's

Journal *and the horror film essay anthology* Butcher Knives and Body Counts. *His work can also be found in various magazines and on numerous websites. You can visit him online at www.carlhose.net or check him out on Facebook.*

A Sight for Sore Eyes

Deborah LeBlanc

It wasn't supposed to be this way.

Ever.

Instead of making rounds and dispensing meds as usual, Ariel found herself trudging through thigh-deep water with an eighty-eight-year-old man draped over her back. Stomach cancer had whittled Charlie Nichols down to a mere seventy-six pounds, but that was still more than half of Ariel's body weight. She struggled to keep moving, carefully placing one foot in front of the other, her knees threatening to buckle with each step. To make matters worse, she kept hearing odd noises, sounds that made her dizzy. Probably her blood pressure spiking. It certainly had reason to. A sudden rise in blood pressure usually caused ringing or buzzing in the ear, though. What she heard was a weird *clop . . . thump, clop,* and an occasional *chuuu,* like something hydraulic had been set into motion. Strange. But everything felt strange lately.

It seemed like only hours ago when these halls smelled of antiseptic and freshly waxed floors. Now they held the stench of contaminated water, an amalgam of sewage, oil, and rotted meat. Ariel cringed at the thought of the disease and parasites swirling through the murky water—around her legs.

The water was rising fast. Too fast. Dark ripples sent debris floating about haphazardly. Bedpans, hospital gowns, med trays, and swollen, soggy lumps she couldn't identify. She chewed her bottom lip to keep from crying. There was no time for tears or self-pity. She had to keep moving. They had to reach the second floor, and the stairwell that led to it was still a couple hundred feet away. Those stairs were their only salvation.

Salvation. The word seemed fantastical; something associated with knights on white horses, not a thirty-three-

49

year-old divorced nurse with quarter-inch hair stubble on her legs.

Even harder to believe was here and now—grasping that *this* was reality. Hurricane Katrina was supposed to have barreled toward the coast, then veered off in another direction at the last minute, just like the other hurricanes that had threatened New Orleans in the past had done. It was a pattern New Orleanians had counted on for decades. Some of the locals credited God for the many years of protection, others claimed specific saints were responsible. A few folks swore it was due to the diversion spells cast by the voodoo priests and priestesses who lived in the city. Regardless of who deserved the credit, He or they had obviously fallen asleep on the job because Katrina had rammed into New Orleans with a vengeance and it didn't look like she intended to let up any time soon.

The last time Ariel had dared to peek through the cracks in one of the boarded up windows, she'd seen little change. Torrential rains and triple-digit winds continued to rip through buildings, topple trees, and shatter glass, which filled the air with deadly flying shrapnel. The street that ran in front of St. Bernard's Hospital was now a river with a current strong enough to carry cars, mailboxes—dead bodies. People had prepared for some wind and rain, but not for this monster. And certainly not for the break in the levee that sent Lake Borgne rushing into the Ninth Ward.

Earlier, when it became painfully obvious the storm wasn't going to veer off course, many hospital employees simply walked off the job and hurried home to their families. As soon as news about the breach in the levee reached St. Bernard's, all but seven hospital employees fled. The entire medical staff now consisted of two doctors, one scrawny intern named Paul Struben, and five nurses, one of them being Ariel. She was the only one who'd chosen to stay with the geriatric patients on the first floor. Everyone else had rushed up to the second and third floors to help the younger, stronger patients, claiming they stood a better chance of survival. Although the reasoning sounded logical, Ariel couldn't bring herself to leave the elderly behind. It wasn't their fault they were old and unable to move quickly, if at all. Someone had to stay and help them. Paul had promised to come back and lend a hand, but that had been two hours ago. Not that she'd really expected him to return. The opportunistic jerk probably had his nose stuck up some doctor's ass, sniffing out kudos, and had forgotten all about her. Paul worked as hard at brown-nosing as any athlete training for the Olympics. A knight on a white horse he was not.

Charlie groaned against Ariel's right shoulder, and his hot, raspy breath reminded her he was only one of nine patients still in the ward. How was she supposed to get all of them to safety? She couldn't take the elevator. The power had gone out long ago, rendering it useless. Fortunately, the backup generator had kept the emergency lights going, but they'd recently started to flicker and dim. It didn't take an electrical engineer to figure out that wasn't a good sign.

Chuuu . . . clop, thump . . . clop . . .

Gripping Charlie's forearms, Ariel forced herself to keep moving. One more step—three more, meandering around floating utility carts, plastic trays, a toppled wheelchair. She kept her head down, her eyes on the water swirling about her legs. She struggled to block out the impossibility of it all—the roar of the wind that pummeled the building—the weird sounds in her head—the loud, desperate cries from the other patients. The fact that she had no family, no one to go home to. No one to worry about her.

By the time Ariel reached the heavy metal door that led to the stairwell, she wanted to collapse from exhaustion. The water had risen to hip level and had developed a current.

Chuuu . . . thump, thump . . .

She grabbed the doorknob, turned it, and pushed against the door. It didn't budge, but that didn't surprise her. Opening it usually required a hefty shove. She'd have to put a shoulder into it—but how on earth was she supposed to do that with an old man clinging to her back? *Thump, clop . . .* Even on a good day Charlie wasn't able to stand upright without help. If she allowed him to slide off her back, he'd surely drop into a heap and drown.

As Ariel racked her brain for a solution, a loud clatter, like so many pots tumbling from a high shelf, startled her. She glanced back toward the sound and spotted black smoke billowing out of a room directly behind them.

God, no—no, please . . .

A rush of adrenaline sent Ariel pushing and pounding frantically against the door. They *had* to reach the stairwell.

Charlie began to thrash against her, as though offering what little strength he had to the cause.

"Charlie, don't. You'll make us fall!"

He mumbled something incoherent and wiggled against her.

"Just hang on. Don't move!"

Chuuu . . . clop . . . clop, clop . . .

Charlie grunted and twisted his body slightly to the right, like he meant to break away from her and take the lead.

"Wait, stop! Stop moving or we'll—" Ariel felt her body tip forward, and in that moment bright light flashed in her periphery, and on its heels, a deafening explosion. Something big and solid slammed into them from behind, smashing Charlie against her. The force of the impact stole her breath, threw them into the water.

Then under it—

Deeper—

Deeper still.

Chuuu . . .

Someone needed to tell whoever was making those ridiculous gurgling sounds to shut up. This was supposed to be a peaceful, quiet place. A weightless zone. As weightless as her body felt this very moment. She wanted her mind to know that same buoyancy, but how could it with all the damn burbling . . . gurgling? Irritated, she started to say something—

Ariel's eyes flew open. Disoriented, it took a second for her to realize she was underwater and only half that time to know she needed air. She started to flail, but her arms and legs refused to work as a cohesive unit. She fought harder, frantic to break the water's surface, desperate to breathe.

But there was no surface. Only what felt like a heavy, wide wall hanging a foot or so over her head.

She squinted through the murk, eyes burning as she searched for a ledge, a corner of anything that might give her the leverage she needed to pull herself up to freedom. All she saw, though, was a beige, littered sea and Charlie Nichols' face as it bobbed into view. The old man's eyes held the blank gaze of a corpse, and his mouth hung open as if waiting to be fed. Without thinking, Ariel cried out and reached for him. Noxious water filled her mouth instantly, made her gag, seared her nostrils. Her lungs felt ready to explode.

Chuuu . . .

Breathe! Breathe! It was the only word on her mind, her sole prayer. But He or they must have fallen asleep on the job again because no air came.

Clop . . . thump . . . clop, clop.

The little energy she'd had earlier drained away, leaving her with only enough strength to swallow.

Swallow and blink.

Above her, the world had gone silent. She no longer heard the wail of the wind or the pitiful cries for help. Even the gurgling had stopped. All she heard was that annoying *clop . . . clop . . .* and voices?

Ariel's eyes felt scorched and she knew she should close them against the filthy water, but she wanted to—had to—see. Where were the voices coming from?

The water surrounding her suddenly turned into a shimmering silver veil, and through its sheen she saw . . . people. A black man wearing a short brimmed cap; a gray-haired woman standing beside a short, bald man . . .

"All dis was what we called de upper side of de Ninth," the black man said, holding his arms out wide.

"But there's nothing out here," the woman said.

"You right. Katrina, she took everything. Dere used to be little shops and restaurants out dis way. Good size neighborhood too. Back dere, over to de west side." He aimed his chin to indicate the direction.

"How many people were lost in this area?" the bald man asked, his voice low and sad.

"Well, from what everybody say, 'bout nine hundred, give or take. Some people dat used to live out here dey never did find."

The woman gasped and held a hand to her chest. Then she turned, walking in a slow, tight circle, scanning the vast emptiness around them. Her brown pumps gave voice to her faltering steps—*clop, clop . . . clop*—and the disbelief on her face spoke of her struggle to imagine that so many had died here.

"Nine hundred," the bald man repeated. "Unbelievable. It looks like nothing was ever here. It must have taken them, what . . . a year, year and a half to clear the debris?"

"No. More close to three, four years."

The bald man let out a low whistle. "Why so long?"

The black man shrugged. "All I know is de gov'ment's gonna do what dey wanna do, and dey gonna do it when dey wanna do it. Reg'lar folk like me don't got much say 'bout nothin.'"

"Oh, Ralphie, this is so sad," the woman said, taking hold of the bald man's arm.

"It sure is." Ralphie patted her hand. "Hard to believe so many people lived and worked here."

"I know," the woman agreed. Her voice sounded shaky, like she was about to cry. "All those poor, poor people. Dead . . . drowned."

"Oh, not all of dem died 'cause of de water," the black man said. "De wind did her part, too, and some people even got blowed up."

The woman gasped again. "You mean in an explosion?"

"Yes, ma'am. Dat's what happened to ol' St. Bernard's Hospital. Don't know 'xactly why, but it sure 'nough blowed up. And from what everybody say, de people dat was stuck inside it 'cause of de storm never came back out." He pointed to the woman's feet. "In fact, dat hospital used to be right dere where you standin,' on dat big concrete slab."

54

"O-oh, dear!" The woman looked down, seemingly panicked. She lifted one foot, then the other. *Clop . . . clop.* "We shouldn't be standing on it. It . . . it's sacrilegious. Let's go, Ralphie. I-I want to go back to the hotel. This is too . . . sad. And it's wrong. I didn't know it was going to be like this. All those poor souls. They need to be left in peace, not have people trampling over where they died."

"But we're not done with the tour," Ralphie said.

"I don't care," the woman cried. She turned to the black man and shook a finger at him. "You should be ashamed of yourself, exploiting the dead like that." Then she tugged on Ralphie's arm, forcing him to follow as she hurried across the slab. Her brown pumps hit the concrete with a rhythmic *clop, clop,* and Ralphie's sneakers with a steady *thump, thump . . .*

"Wait . . . what I did?" the black man asked, frowning.

"You making all that money off the misery of others," the woman said loudly, not bothering to look back at him. "It's a sin and a shame. That's what it is, a sin and a shame." Having reached the end of the slab, she stormed up three metal steps that stood a short distance away, Ralphie at her heels.

The black man shook his head and followed the woman and Ralphie up the three metal steps, climbing them slowly like it pained his knees. "I don't know nothin' 'bout no money. No, ma'am. I just drive dis here bus. Dat's my job. Drivin' de bus and tellin' people who wanna know what happened. Dat's all."

With that, he cleared the top step. Then two narrow glass doors closed behind him with a soft . . . *chuuu.*

It wasn't supposed to be this way.

Ever.

Best-selling author Deborah LeBlanc is a business owner, a licensed death scene investigator, and an active paranormal investigator. She served four years as president of the Horror Writers Association, eight years as president of The Writers Guild of Acadiana, and is currently President of the Mystery Writers of America's Southwest Chapter. Deborah is also the founder of the Literacy Challenge, an annual, national literacy campaign and Literacy, Inc., a non-profit organization with a mission to fight illiteracy in America's teens. Visit www.deborahleblanc.com and www.literacyinc.com

Confidence Man

David Tocher

The world we perceive with our five senses is in fact real. Yet *less real* than the one housed within it. Just think of tent caterpillars, who weave their silk tents in the branches of trees. That fibrous cocoon is our material world, a thin membrane with parasites swarming beneath the surface. The spiritual realm, then, is not a separate, parallel reality to our own; instead, it is the *source.* Instinctively, we know this and sense the movement of that world in those moments when we awaken from nightmares, or when we try to shake off the feeling of eyes watching us in the dark. It doesn't take much to open a hole in that silky tent. A smoldering ember will do, making way for the slithering mass of worms to come tumbling out like black vomit. That ember came to me in the form of a young Asian woman named Susan Lau. On the day she walked into my business, *The Intuitive Eye,* she scorched a hole open in the fabric of my world and showed me the monsters within.

* * *

My parents, both devout Catholics, named me Anthony. Hopefully, it wasn't after Anthony of Padua, the patron saint of lost things, because I grew up to be the *cause* of people's losses, not the redeemer.

Name any scam, yours truly has pulled it. I've phoned people's hotel rooms late at night, claiming to be from the front desk; after confirming their credit card numbers, the guests would wake up the next day to discover their cards maxed-out. I've also posed as a contractor, offering to paint people's homes for a low price; they'd wait for a crew that never arrived and I'd pocket the cash. Even job-seekers were my victims. Once they would apply for a position on my bogus website, I'd hold a telephone interview, gathering their social insurance numbers and bank account information for identity theft.

My shady career began in 1991. When I was twelve, living in Clydebank, British Columbia, a small town in the South West Kootenays, I'd stumbled upon my con-artist skills. It happened in the air cadets, when they'd asked for volunteers to sell chocolate bars. My parents had refused to buy the CD Walkman I'd asked for, so I concocted a plan: since I was the only cadet in my neighborhood, why not go door to door, charging an extra buck to pocket? That idea came to me as I sat on the porch one night, staring up at the sky. Ever since childhood, I could always think of a solution to my problems by looking at the black, star-spotted expanse above and just contemplating.

I sold three-hundred chocolate bars and got the electronic toy I wanted, simply because gazing at the darkness above somehow unlocked a door within my mind. Some people say they thank their lucky stars. Not me. I was thankful to the darkness *between* the stars.

Getting the Walkman wasn't the highlight for me, though. I'll never forget the exhilaration that rushed through me each time someone fell for my line. I had charmed them, out-thought them, and *overpowered* them. The realization was like a drug . . . and I've been chasing the high ever since.

As a teenager, I could walk into a grocery store with twenty dollars and walk out with thirty. The trick was simple. I asked for change on my twenty, confused the clerk on his math, and walked away with thirty in change without him being the wiser. At first, I didn't know it was a technique called *The Change Raising Con*. It was when I saw an investigative journalist on TV discussing how con-artists work that I noticed I was already putting many of these techniques to use. And that, people, is how to tell if you're gifted: you'll intuitively know how to do something.

Before anyone explains major and minor chords, certain folks will sit at a piano and just *know* what note to flatten if they want a darker sound. For others, they'll just *know* how to sketch a house as seen from above—long before anyone explains three point perspective. For me, I just *knew* how to scam people. And damn, was I good at it.

When I turned thirty, I was selling outdated stereo equipment online and advertising it as new. The customer got stuck with a cheap piece of crap, and I'd rake in a couple grand before making myself scarce. The police *almost* tracked me down, despite my precautions. That's when I knew it was time to think up some adjustments. And you know how I did it? Star-gazing. I came to these conclusions. Firstly, I needed an accomplice; secondly, I needed to stop running risky scams and go *legit*. Become an *honest* thief.

That's when I got into the psychic business. To appear credible, I got a diploma from The College of Metaphysical Science before opening an establishment on Pender Street in Vancouver, British Columbia. It was called *The Intuitive Eye*. A neon hand with an eye in the palm, the symbol of clairvoyance, buzzed in the window. Besides the dim lighting, I kept my office conservative-looking, furnished with bookshelves and oil paintings. There were no beads, crystals, or spread of tarot cards on display. I wanted the place to affect taste and professionalism, nothing too gypsy-ish.

How did I succeed? I'd tell my clients I needed at least forty-eight hours before the session to "connect with the energy" of their deceased loved one. During that time, my accomplice, an ex-cop, would dig up personal information about my clients. That way, I'd be able to bring up stuff "I couldn't possibly know" as validations. Can you hear a *cha-ching?*

Did I feel guilty for what I did? Of course not. People came to me with *a need*. A need for comfort and assurance. A word from beyond the grave. A dead mother to deliver belated forgiveness, perhaps. I delivered that message for a fee and they slept better. Both parties win, right? They wanted to believe the lie anyway, so that's what I sold them . . . *the very lie they wanted.* Now do you see what I mean by *honest* thief?

That's how I justified myself, at least until yesterday, when a real ghost appeared in my office.

* * *

"You," a female voice said, "are a fraud."

Startled, my head jolted up from the computer monitor. I was confirming a few appointments online before closing up for the night. A woman, dressed in a red skirt that hugged every curve, stood in front of my desk. She had raven-black hair, styled short and choppy. The perfume she wore was entrancing, arousing. Her presence dominated the room. She smiled without opening her mouth. Dark, hawk-like eyes fixed on mine. Her hands were trembling, clasped at her stomach.

How had she gotten in here? I should've heard the bell above the door jingle and the sound of her high heels clack across the floor.

I held her gaze, careful not to appear weak or deceitful. After all, I was a *confidence* man. "Excuse me, how did you get in here? Who are—"

She stabbed an accusatory finger at me. "Anthony Carter, you know damn well who I am."

My eyes widened when I recognized her face. She was Susan Lau, the deceased wife of Ben Lau, a client who'd had a reading with me a week earlier. She'd been mugged a year ago, stabbed in the face when she tried to get away. My accomplice had shown me several pictures of her (during my session with Ben, I'd said, "I see a woman . . . Asian . . . she's got short hair, she's wearing a necklace . . ." as I drew from my memory of the photos). My heart leapt into my throat. This had to be some kind of trick.

"Listen, lady," I said, standing up from my desk, "I have no idea who you are, but if you haven't booked an appointment, I'll have to ask you to kindly leave. My schedule is very busy."

She crossed her arms and shook her head. "Make me."

I walked around my desk and put my hand on her shoulder. My palm never touched what appeared to be her skin; instead, it sliced through empty air. Her form broke apart, then swirled together again, reminding me of mist in the breeze. I screamed, staggered backward, and stumbled to the floor. My back struck a bookshelf. Hardbacks and soft-covers rained on me.

I looked up again. Now an aura of white light radiated around her. There was a knife buried in Susan's nose, a twisted mess of meat and cartilage. Blood spouted from the gash, washing over her face. One of her eyes was cocked sideways in the socket. The side of her face was blue and puffy from bruising.

Seeing it made me flinch, almost feeling the pain of what had happened to her.

This is a dream. I'm gonna wake up in a minute. Just stay cool.

"Nope, this is not a dream. Staying cool ain't gonna do you any good." Her smile was hideous, the muscles forcing the knife handle, which jutted from her face like a growth, to bob up and down in its burrow of gristle.

Remember when I told you about reality being a flimsy membrane, one concealing another world beneath it? After Susan spoke my thoughts back, I witnessed the membrane of reality tear open all around me, the hole widening and widening to reveal the life beyond it. Spirit people shimmered out of the walls the way water sweats from a glass on a hot day. Men and women, young and old, each illuminated by white auras.

The crowd gathered around her. My gaze took in their faces, each one matching a photograph I'd studied.

"Our families trusted you," a man's voice spoke, "but you never told them what we were trying to say. You lied."

My heart jackhammered in my chest.

This can't be happening. It's impossible. *I refuse to belie—*

A teenage girl didn't so much step toward me as she did *float* toward me, her feet hovering an inch above the carpet. "Believe it. Now come with us. We have something to show you."

She extended her hand. I was reluctant to take it, sitting there on the floor with metaphysics books scattered around me.

"Now!" Susan's voice was a thundering echo, liquid silver being poured forth. The stereo on my desk suddenly turned on. The neon sign in my window fizzled and sparked, rattling against the glass. Lights began to flicker so quickly that when I stood up, my movements appeared choppy and stroboscopic.

I took the girl's hand. She smiled sweetly. At that moment, the world blurred as all of us rushed upward. I flinched, expecting to hit the ceiling, but we passed through it with the ease of an airplane rising through the clouds. Then we were standing on the rooftop of the building I'd leased an office in.

The breeze's chill raised gooseflesh on my arms. Vancouver was spread out before us, its rows of peaked high rises set unevenly against the backdrop of the horizon, a jagged blue outline of the distant mountains. Above, the dome of the nighttime sky sparkled with stars. And between those stars, the precious darkness. The rush of city traffic sounded below.

Susan and I stood in the center of the crowd, which had formed a loose circle around us. Chilly and frightened, I hopped from foot to foot, the soles of my shoes crunching over the gravel rooftop.

"Your antics, Anthony, have caused us a lot of trouble," Susan said. "Serious ones. You may *think* you aren't hurting anyone, but by pretending to be psychic, you've threatened to cause the destruction of the entire world, perhaps even the universe itself."

My mind still refused to accept what my eyes saw. "What are you talking about? How was I supposed to know? You can't hold me responsible for anything. I mean . . . how could anyone know ghosts are real?"

My argument was getting nowhere with them. They were just a sea of faces, each wearing an expression of cold, calculated rage.

A teenage girl, her skull caved in, stepped forward. The crowd of spirit people parted so she could pass. Her hair twinkled with windshield pebbles. One side of her body was skinned open, exposing torn muscle and splintered bones.

"Every culture in the world—from China to Ireland to Egypt—venerates the dead in some way," spoke the teenage girl, her voice low and grating. "The trappings change, but the idea remains constant: the living do things to help us who've died get by in the afterlife."

Susan Lau set a hand on the girl's shoulder. "In China, where my family comes from, they venerate the dead by erecting a spirit tablet in their homes and burning gifts to their relatives. Food, spirit money, clothing. These items are believed to translate into the spirit world and help those who've passed."

I nodded slowly. "Yes, I studied this at the metaphysics college. The Egyptians mummify their dead so their *ka*—the soul—can return to accept offerings from living—"

An older man with an Irish lilt stepped forward and cut me off. "The Celts at Samhain leave food on their porches as offerings to their departed loved ones."

"Ok," I said, scanning their faces warily, "Where are you going with this? Whatever I've done, just tell me."

Susan Lau crossed her arms over her chest. "These things are only symbolic; what the living are really doing is sending *energy* to us. The living are born with this knowledge programmed *into* them. They just *know* to honor those who've passed on. Why do you think this is?"

I understood the idea of being hardcoded with knowledge. Since childhood, I'd just *known* instinctively how to con people. Nevertheless, I shook my head, unable to answer the question.

The crowd of spirit people, their faces hard, closed in on me. Hands seized my shoulders, hair, legs, arms, and waist. My insides stirred with panic. I screamed, begging them not to hurt me, that whatever I'd done wrong, I'd change it, please, please.

"Shut your mouth," Susan snapped, cupping her hands to the sides of my head. "We're not going to hurt you. We're doing this to protect you. So you don't fall."

Don't fall? What the hell did she mean by that?

"Now look up," Susan commanded. "To your favorite place. The darkness between the stars."

I turned my eyes to the heavens. A sudden shift in perspective overcame me. The rooftop and Vancouver's cityscape suddenly became a ceiling. I was suspended upside down, above the deep and black abyss of the sky. My stomach rolled. My head swirled with vertigo.

"What do you see, Anthony?" Susan asked me.

"The-the-sky. B-b-below me . . ."

"No. Look *closer,*" she whispered forcefully.

Have you ever seen a stereogram—one of those pictures you stare at until a hidden three dimensional image comes into view? That's what it was like as I scanned the heavenly abyss. Its perimeter was the horizon's curve, studded with mountains, yet now, it appeared to be a jaw-line of crooked fangs. Beyond those fangs, the dark sky was the gaping mouth of a giant beast, now vomiting up innumerable monstrosities—tentacles, claws, goat-eyed spiders, fanged worms—all writhing and slithering as they tried to press through an invisible barrier, one that separated their world from ours. The sound of the rushing traffic was actually the auditory veil that hid their voices— screams, hisses, disembodied whispers, all madly chanting unintelligible things.

Two things filled me with a sense of maddening horror. The first thing was the substance of these *living, sentient* creatures was somehow intertwined with the atomic structure of the material world. The second thing, the *worst thing,* was when some of these monstrosities *noticed* me. I could *feel* their minds smiling with malevolent familiarity.

They recognized me.

Knew me.

I closed my eyes and screamed, high-pitched and squealing in terror, thrashing my head from side to side, begging the spirit people to take away the vision.

"You *must* look, Anthony, for we see these things every day," the old Irishman said. His words were sent by thought, echoing in my mind.

I felt invisible fingers pry my eyelids open.

"What are they?" I screamed.

"The *Thayne-too,*" Susan whispered in my ear. "There is a barrier between your world and theirs. We, the dead, *are* that barrier. When your kind, the living, do things to honor us, you are providing us energy, strengthening us so we may continue to *fight* against them and protect the universe. This is the real reason why we make contact with our living loved ones, letting them sense our presence in their lives. To encourage them to strengthen us with their energy.

"When you lie to our families about what we're saying, you are *blocking* that flow of energy. You are causing a breach in the barrier between your world . . . and the world of the *Thayne-too.*"

I closed my eyes again. "Ok, please, just make it stop!"

Silence.

I opened my eyes and the world was back to normal. The roof was below me, the sky above me. The traffic noise was just traffic noise; the horizon was only mountains; the sky was just a window to outer space. My mind, however, was still reeling with shock from the vision.

"But I'm nobody," I told them. "Just one guy. Con men like me are all over the place. How could I be so important? How could I cause the destruction of the universe?"

One of them stepped forward through the crowd. His face was pink and deformed like twisted wax. A burn victim. "All it takes is one smoldering cigarette butt and you can burn down an entire house, or a forest, even. Most con men like you would've been busted a long time ago. You've had a pretty good run. Why do you think that is? You have them,"—he pointed toward the sky—"the *Thayne-too* directing your thoughts, protecting you, guiding the course of your life."

"But why me? Why would they choose me?"

"Deep calls unto deep," Susan answered. "The darkness within them called to the darkness in you."

Now I knew why I'd always felt a compulsion to look toward the sky at night.

The teenage girl said, "The *Thayne-too* have left their mark on everything you've ever done in your life."

"What . . . are they? What do they want?"

"They're parasites," the girl replied. "They are no different than the Mountain Pine Beetle that destroy an entire forest just by laying eggs in the bark of trees."

I had read about those beetles before. They are a threat to British Columbia's ecosystem. "So we're talking . . . *cosmic* parasites? Eaters of worlds and universes?"

The crowd of spirits nodded.

Susan's white aura tinted an incandescent blue. "Have you been following the news? How in 2012 there've been strange noises in the sky, heard worldwide? This is a result of the barrier *you've* weakened, of the *Thayne-too* almost breaking through."

"Now that I know all this, what . . . do I do?" I asked.

"Your name is Anthony for a reason," Susan said, reaching behind her neck to undo her necklace. "He was the patron saint of *lost things*. It's now your duty to make sure the transference of energy from our loved ones to us doesn't get lost. While you're alive, from now on, help us to fight."

I nodded, shuddering at the thought of my past, of every wrong I'd done to people, my life wasted. This was a chance to redeem myself. "I understand."

"But before you go back, you give this to my husband," Mrs. Lau said, and opened her palm. In it was the necklace she'd removed. "He gave this to me years ago. I lost it. When you return this to him, tell him something for me."

She leaned forward, whispering her message in my ear.

The world around me began to darken. . . .

* * *

I awoke, finding myself collapsed on the floor among debris of books and papers. Reason tried to argue that it had all been a dream. After I'd passed out, my guilt-ridden subconscious had coughed up some fanciful delusions.

That . . . was all.

But how then could I explain the necklace in my hand? Or the bits of gravel and tar from the rooftop around my feet?

I looked up Ben Lau's number and phoned to ask if we could meet for a coffee somewhere later that night, that it was important and related to Susan. He agreed.

When I left *The Intuitive Eye,* I read the neon sign in the window, the one spelling my company's name. Some of the letters had burned out from all the frizzing and sparking earlier. It was most likely caused by the electromagnetic energy of all those spirit people who'd appeared in the room.

Now only the first seven letters glowed: THE INTU.

Theintu.

Or, its phonetic spelling: *Thayne-too.*

Remembering the words of the teenage ghost-girl, my heart chilled: *The* Theintu *have left their mark on everything you've ever done in your life.*

I sprinted down Pender Street, toward JB's Resto-Bar, clutching Susan's necklace in my fist. What I saw was very subtle, yet still identifiable. Everything glowed as if each object were its own light source. Alder trees lined the sidewalk. Halos of green light enrobed their leaves; the red bricks of a building glowed like coals; the silver necks of the street lights glowed with the bone color of moonlight.

My inner vision was now able to pierce through the veil—that is to say, *the flesh* of the universe—and perceive its spirit within.

This was the beginning of a new life, one where I no longer caused losses, but restored them.

For the living *and* the dead.

This man I'd speak with tonight, I no longer saw him—as I had seen others before him—as an opportunity, as someone to take advantage of. Instead, he was a person of great value, just as everyone else who passed me on the street. A person so valuable, in fact, that a myriad of souls would be willing to spend their eternity fighting to protect him.

I continued down Pender with the weight of Susan's necklace in my hand and the weight of her message burning in my heart.

Born and raised in British Columbia, David Tocher now lives in Eastern Canada, where he's currently at work on a novel. He appreciates literature which explores the paranormal and the dark side of human nature. He also loves heavy metal music. You can find his stories in the anthologies Evolve Two: Vampire Stories of the Future Undead, *edited by Nancy Kilpatrick and* Dreamspell Nightmares, *edited by Lisa Smith.*

Hunters

William Todd Rose

The sound of truck engines echoed through the valley like the roar of an angry god lurking within the pine-covered hills, as if it smelled our anger and fear mixed among the clouds of exhaust and knew we were coming for its bastard child; as if it could see the headlights cutting through the tendrils of fog creeping over the ground and hear the whoops and yells of men whose bellies were warmed with eighty-proof courage.

Bonfires blazed around the edge of the clearing we'd gathered in, the popping and crackling of dry twigs all but lost beneath the din of our war party. The light from these fires caused shadows to dance across the faces of the women who huddled around them, hugging themselves and standing a little closer to the flames than the cool autumn air demanded. Their eyes darted from their men to the children who played at the flickering edges of the glow and back to the men again.

I caught the eye of my wife and raised my hand to her with a smile I didn't feel. I wanted to appear brave, confident, and unshakable. I wanted her to think that this was no different than going coon hunting with the guys, that in a few hours we would all return, laughing and reeking of testosterone and stale cigarette smoke, congratulating each other on another successful foray into the wild.

She managed a weak smile before pulling her shawl around her shoulders and diverting her gaze into the glowing embers of the fire.

For a moment, the entire world faded like a scene in an old movie, where the spotlight slowly focuses on a single individual and everything else dissolves into a dark blur. I watched her push a strand of hair from her eyes, saw her cock her head as Sarah Jo Rucker leaned in to say something. She laughed in the same way she does when we're mingling with the congregation after a Sunday sermon, quick and sweet, just enough to be polite, but not loud or long enough to seem strained.

She hadn't wanted me to go, had begged me to stay home that night. Let the other men handle it, Carl. They don't need you out there. There's enough of 'em. They can take care of things just fine. You stay home. You stay with me."

Her bottom lip had quivered as she spoke and her eyes glistened as she blinked back tears. Her voice had been tinged with the slightest hint of panic and I wanted so desperately to pull her to me, to tell her that I would call Ernie Hendrickson and tell him I was sick, that our plumbing had burst again, any excuse to spare her from the worry. I stepped toward her, unsure of what I would say until the words spilled across my lips.

"I'll be fine, baby. Don't you worry about me, hear?"

Now Anna stood there, trying to make the best of the situation as always. Trying to be brave. But more likely than not, silently praying for my safe return.

"Carl, you gettin' in on this here thing or what?"

Bobby Rucker's voice cut through my thoughts like a fine-tooth hacksaw and I turned to face the other men. They were loading up into the trucks now. Those riding in the backs slid shells into their shotguns with faint clicks and others tucked pistols into their waistbands. Only the drivers and a few point men remained, clustered around the hood of Buck Mason's old Ford. A map was splayed out over the hood and Ernie Hendrickson bent over it, tracing lines with his index finger and speaking to the cluster of men who angled flashlights over his shoulder and nodded in silent agreement.

I climbed into the back of Bobby's truck and accepted a bottle of Wild Turkey that was making its rounds.

"Shit, this is gonna be like bear huntin' at a zoo."

"Reckon we'll get 'em tonight. Can feel it in the air."

I looked out at the silhouettes of the hills and imagined all the eyes hidden by the night. All the creatures looking down, perfectly blending with the shadows, noses twitching as they picked up our scent on the breeze, low growls rumbling in the back of throats lined with teeth twice as sharp as the hunting knife strapped to my belt. We were embarking into their domain, on the hunt for one of their own. And I could feel the presence of that creature out there somewhere, slinking through the trees and thickets, a dark mirage, a phantom existing somewhere in the dim borderlands between nightmare and reality, as silent and ruthless as sudden death.

And we were coming for it.

God help us all.

* * *

No one was ever really sure where it had come from. There were a lot of rumors and speculation, especially on two-for-one night at the Pit Stop down on Route 47. Some people said the chemical plants had taken to dumping their waste into the creeks and streams, that drinking from the tainted water had spurred some sort of abnormal growth spurt. Others claimed it had always been in these here parts but we'd never seen it until poaching had cleared out the deer population and forced it to seek other prey. Hell, Sadie Maris even said she'd seen it run out of a cave down by the Devil's Tea Table. Said it was dragging a broken chain behind it and she could hear something in the cavern bellowing in a language she didn't understand. Said it reminded her of the way Paul used to yell when the dogs would pull their leads out of the ground and chase off after a squirrel or rabbit.

"Satan's pet turned loose on th' world, that's what I reckon it is. I seen it. I *know*."

Of course, Sadie also sees Paul out in the fields, hoeing up potatoes or picking berries on the edge of the property with his little silver pail. And he's been dead going on five years now.

People like Sadie make the rest of the state think we just a bunch of superstitious bumpkins. Or drunkards. Or even both.

Hell, I'm the editor of the county paper and have a four-year degree in journalism. Rick Starkey is a doctor and Susan Mason, the only woman who headed out with us on that night, a game warden with over fifteen years of experience under her belt. We have a lot to lose by making something like this up. More than

71

we could ever gain from it. But we're not the ones who end up on the evening news when they need to fill a couple minutes with local color. We're not the ones interviewed in the larger papers. No, it's people like Sadie that they go for every time.

Which is probably one of the reasons we decided to take matters into our own hands. It had become obvious that no one was going to believe us, that no one would be coming to help. Never mind the cow carcasses, ripped apart and spread across the fields like some slaughterhouse had dropped their leftovers from a passing plane. Never mind all the missing dogs, the hen houses that looked like every bird inside had simultaneously exploded, or the fact that no one had seen a deer in almost half a year.

In fact, it was the deer that disappeared first, truth be told. It wasn't until after they were gone that the cows started being massacred. Once the cattle had been safely put away in barns for the night, dogs began to turn up missing and the raids on the chickens began. How much longer until someone's child happened to be playing near the woods just around dusk? How much longer until the only trace of that child was bloody swatches of fabric stuck in the briars and brambles of the forest?

It was a risk none of us were willing to take.

* * *

Bobby's truck crept along at a pace that made the minutes seem to stretch into eternity. This was partly strategic, as we did not want the sound of a revving engine to alert the prey to our presence. But there was also a bit of necessity involved. Our patrol had been assigned to Widow's Mountain, which was one of the roughest areas being covered that night. Ten years earlier the roads had been no more than deer paths that snaked through the ridges and streams. During a brief logging boom they had been widened to accommodate the semis that hauled felled trees out of the wilderness and back to civilization. They were never meant to be permanent roads and had therefore never been paved. Over time, rain had eroded deep ruts into the pass and those of us riding in the bed had to hang onto the sides as we bounced over terrain that, even with a four wheel drive, bordered on impassable.

Once we had left the safety of the clearing, silence had settled over our little group and we only spoke when necessary. Even then it was in whispers so soft that they almost couldn't be heard beneath the creaking of the suspension as another pothole jarred our bodies.

It was out there somewhere. Even as we prowled the countryside, it too was on the move. Days had passed since anyone had reported any dead or missing livestock. Unless it had found food elsewhere, it would be hungry. Perhaps desperate.

I tightened my grip on the shotgun with hands that felt too warm and slick for such a cool evening. Around us were the slight noises of a forest at night: the cracking of a twig, fluttering of wings as an unseen bird took flight, soft rustling in the underbrush. Anyone who lives in the country knows these sounds intimately. But on that night, even the smallest stirring seemed sinister and unfamiliar.

I glanced at the other men in the truck with me, trying to detect any signs of fear. There were three of us and we had taken up strategic locations, one looking out on either side of the vehicle and me looking back over the tailgate. With Bobby driving up front, this meant all sides were covered. We had formed a three hundred and sixty degree perimeter around our mobile base and the others could scamper to the required side in a matter of seconds if anything was spotted.

My quick look, though, revealed nothing. We had just rounded a curve in the road and entered the stretch children like to call The Tunnel. The sides of the hills towered over us to the left and right, rocks jutting out that had been formed when creatures as large as we were hunting were the norm. It was like we had suddenly entered a trench and the walls of dirt and stone blocked out what little light we had to begin with. Even though separated by mere feet, Paulie and Ray were nothing more than shadows.

"Ray . . ."

My voice was just a whisper, but after the silence of the last twenty minutes, I felt as if I were broadcasting through a megaphone.

"Ray, I gotta take a piss."

Ray's silhouette nodded and wrapped on the rear window of the cab four times, the signal to stop the truck.

I laid my gun in the bed and bounded over the side. My legs had gotten so used to crouching in the truck that the hard packed earth sent needles of pain through the soles of my feet.

I stood for a moment, listening to the silence and feeling my heart pound in my temples.

"Hurry up, Carl. Ain't got all night."

I fished a cigarette from the crumpled pack in my jacket and had to try three times before I managed to light it. I wondered if the others noticed the way the little flame quivered in the darkness, if they could see how I had to use both hands to steady the lighter as I held the fire to the tip of the smoke.

"Damn it, Carl . . ."

I walked about ten feet away from the truck, back the way we had come. In all honesty, I didn't really have to take a leak. I had needed to stretch my legs, to move around for a minute in hopes of releasing some of the tension that made every muscle in my body feel as though it had been pulled taut. With both sides of the road protected by the canyon-like walls of hillside, it had seemed like the perfect opportunity.

Away from my companions, however, I began to rethink the entire idea. The night seemed to press in on me and taking a drag from the cigarette took an act of willpower. It almost felt as if I had stumbled into the coils of some great snake that was slowly tightening its grasp. The smoke from my cigarette suddenly smelled too harsh, the ember like a beacon that betrayed my position in the darkness.

I shifted my weight from one foot to the other and realized that the only sound I could hear was the low rumble of the truck's engine behind me. There was no wind rustling the pine boughs overhead, no chirping or whirring from the millions of insects hiding within the forest.

A shiver tingled my spine as I listened for sounds that were not there.

Something was very, very wrong.

The forest is never that silent. There is always some little insect singing its praises to the trees, some small animal scrounging for a nut or root.

All of my instincts said to turn, to run back to the safety of the truck. The hairs along my arms tingled and I could feel sweat cooling against my forehead in the night air.

"Just turn and walk back calmly, Carl. No need to make an ass of yourself. Just get yourself back to that truck."

The silence was pierced with a shriek that sounded like a woman's scream amplified a hundred times, so loud and shrill that my eardrums felt as if they were vibrating with tremors of pain.

I spun in time to see a dark shape the size of a small car sailing through the air. It must have launched itself from the top of the hillside, maybe stalking us for hours, waiting on the perfect ambush.

There was a flash of muzzle fire and a thundering roar as Paulie unloaded his thirty-ought-six. I could see Ray banging the side of his gun as if something were stuck inside it. All of this in a fraction of a second.

In the time it took to blink, the creature had landed in the truck's bed. Paulie's body spun around and toppled over the side of the truck. Even through the darkness, I could see that his body was missing its head. At the same instant, I was also aware of the giant paw swinging out and of Ray's screams quickly being drowned by the creature's own.

"God damn son of a bitch mother fucker . . ."

It was Bobby's voice yelling. The creature sprang from the truck bed as more gunshots echoed off the hills. I knew it was pointless, that Bobby was just as dead as Ray and Paulie. And I knew that I would be next.

Without a second thought, I turned and ran.

I wish I could say I had the presence of mind to run with purpose, but that would be a lie. In fact, the entire time I was running, only a single thought kept repeating through my mind.

It killed them, oh Christ, it killed them all, oh God, it fucking killed them.

Trees went by in a blur and my chest felt as though it were on fire with every gasp of air. Was that the sound of paws bounding through the underbrush behind me? Was the warmth on the back of my neck the heat of its breath?

Part of me wanted to steal a look over my shoulder, to see how much ground it was gaining on me, but I was afraid of what I would see. Afraid those two curved fangs would be bearing down on the back of my head.

It wasn't supposed to have played out like this. We were supposed to have bagged the damn thing, not the other way around.

I thought of Anna, back in the clearing, watching as trucks slowly rolled back in from the patrols, hoping to see Bobby's Chevy with each set of headlights that appeared around the bend, biting on her bottom lip as she tends to do when she is worried.

Oh God, baby, I am so sorry, I'm so sorry . . .

Maybe the thoughts of my wife distracted me. Maybe on some level I had simply given up and subconsciously looked for a way out. Or perhaps it was something that just happened, but at that moment, I stumbled over a log I should have clearly seen. My body pitched forward and pain flared through my skull as my head smashed against a rock. For a moment the forest swam in and out of focus as I tried to push myself up into a standing position again, then darkness overtook me and I collapsed to the cold, hard ground.

* * *

I have no idea how long I was out. Perhaps hours, perhaps only a few minutes. When I came to, I was not alone. I could hear the giant creature as it paced around my body, its feet snapping twigs and a sound like the purring of the world's largest house cat coming in short bursts. I was lying on my stomach with my head to the side. I opened one eye just enough so I could see the world through a thin slit.

It paced into view, and for the first time I fully grasped the enormity of the beast we had hunted. Its paws were as large as hubcaps, its legs like the trunks of small trees. As it walked by, I could see muscles ripple beneath the tawny fur that covered its body.

Please God, please . . .

After what seemed like minutes, but could not have been more than seconds, the bulk of the behemoth had passed my field of vision and its tail brushed across my face, tickling my nose with coarse hairs.

Every ounce of my being fought to keep my body perfectly still, to keep from trembling or releasing the moan that was trapped somewhere in the back of my throat.

A paw batted at my shoulder blades, but the claws were retracted, as if it were trying to flip me over. Or testing me.

Without warning, a huge face appeared before my own, so large I could only see the leathery black nose and whiskers above its white mouth. It sniffed several times and then nudged me with its nose, its breath warm and smelling of rotted meat.

I could feel tears welling up behind my eyes, but knew if I were to give any sign I was aware of my surroundings, I would be ripped apart before I could even so much as draw the first breath for a scream.

The giant cat jerked its head up and its body seemed to stiffen. I heard it sniff the air and thought of the predators on nature shows, how they would remain alert, protecting their kill from any marauding scavengers that might be close by.

The night was silent and I could feel my heart pounding in my chest. Surely the beast could hear it. It had to know this was just a ruse, that I was not dead at all. Or was the ground muffling what seemed to me to be the loudest noise I had ever heard?

My mind raced, trying to remember all I had ever heard about mountain lions. Would they eat something they had not brought down themselves? If I laid still enough, would it eventually go away? Would it make a difference that this was a giant, a monster that never should have grown this large to begin with?

I became aware of a pressure digging into my stomach, something hard and painful. My hunting knife. For a moment hope flared within me, but as quickly as it had blossomed, it died again. There was no way I could reach it without betraying that I was not, indeed, dead. The moment I moved the slightest muscle, the cat would be upon me. I probably wouldn't even have time to roll over before its claws were tearing into my back.

The creature had apparently decided to dismiss whatever it had detected in the night and was sniffing me again. Maybe I should just end the charade and at least make an attempt to reach my knife. Would it not be better to die fighting than to be mauled without so much as showing the least bit of resistance?

Anna, baby, I am so sorry.

At that moment, the night exploded with a volley of gunfire. It seemed to come from all sides, as if I had somehow found myself transported from the forest floor into the middle of a battlefield.

The giant cat yowled in pain and I rolled to the left, away from the sound of its screams, while simultaneously jerking my knife from its sheath. Still the gunfire rang out in the night and I was peripherally aware of a ring of people closing in, fire licking from the ends of muzzles as clouds of spent gunpowder filled the forest.

After several minutes, the echo of the last shot faded and hands were roughly pulling me to my feet.

"He's alive!"

"It's Carl Smithers, he's alive!"

"You okay, buddy? Shit, we thought that thing had already killed ya."

I wanted to answer, but my body betrayed me. I stammered the beginnings of words and felt warm tears slide down my cheeks. I began to shake and my knees buckled. Only the quick hands of my saviors kept me from falling back to the ground again.

"Come on, old boy, it's okay now. Everything's gonna be all right."

They guided me to a small group of people who had clustered around the fallen monster. Its eyes had lost whatever sparkle of life they had once contained and it lay motionless in a pool of dark blood that had spewed from the bullet holes that riddled its body.

"My, god, would you look at the size of that thing."

One would have thought that there would be whoops of victory, slaps on the back in celebration of the beast that had been taken down. But for the most part we stared in relative silence and watched Susan Mason crouch beside the fallen creature.

Her eyes darted over the carcass and I noticed her stiffen, as if she had found something she had not expected. When she spoke, her voice was as cold and flat as the rock that balanced on the top of the Devil's Tea Table.

"Boys, we got ourselves a little problem, here."

She lifted the creature's tail in both hands. Susan was large for a woman, but the sheer size of the tail made her hands, probably for the first time in her life, look dainty in comparison.

"See these here rings around the tail?"

She nodded at the dark bands that broke up the rest of the dust colored fur.

"Mountain lions, they got a black tipped tail. No rings. Not like this."

Silence gripped us. I don't know about the others, but I held my breath, unsure of what she was driving at.

"What we got here," she said slowly, "is a juvenile. This thing is not much more than a baby."

At that moment, as if somehow aware that her child had been cut down in the dawn of life, a sound like a mix between a woman's scream and the roar of a jet engine rang out from somewhere in the night.

God help us all. . . .

Named by the Google+ Insider's Guide as one of their top 32 authors to follow, William Todd Rose writes dark fiction from his home in West Virginia. With short stories appearing in numerous magazines and anthologies, his longer works include Shadow of the Woodpile, Cry Havoc, *the short story collection* Sex in the Time of Zombies, The Dead & Dying, *and* The Seven Habits of Highly Infective People. *For more information, including a link to download the free novella* Apocalyptic Organ Grinder, *please visit the author online at www.williamtoddrose.com*

The Vampire Shortstop

Scott Nicholson

Jerry Shepherd showed up at first practice alone.

I mean, *showed*, as if he'd just popped into thin air at the edge of the woods that bordered Sawyer Field. Most kids, they come to first practice book-ended by their parents, who glower like Mafia heavies willing to break your kneecaps if their kid rides the pine for so much as an inning. So in a way, it was a relief to see Jerry materialize like that, with no threat implied.

But in another way, he made me nervous. Every year us Little League coaches get handed two or three players who either recently moved to the area or were given their release (yeah, we're that serious here) by their former teams. And if there's one thing that's just about universal, it's the fact that these Johnny-come-latelies couldn't hit their way out of a paper bag. So I figured, here's this spooky kid standing there at the fence, just chewing on his glove, real scared-like, so at least there's one brat who's not going to be squealing for playing time.

I figured him for a vampire right off. He had that pale complexion, the color of a brand new baseball before the outfield grass scuffs up the horsehide. But, hey, these are enlightened times, everybody's cool with everybody, especially since "Transylvania" Wayne Kazloski broke the major league undead barrier back in '29. And that old myth about vampires melting in the sun is just that, an old myth.

The league powers figured I wouldn't raise a fuss if they dumped an undesirable on me. I had eleven kids on the roster, only five of them holdovers from the year before, so I was starting from scratch anyway. I didn't mind a new face, even if I was pretty much guaranteed the vampire kid had two left feet. Coming off a three-and-thirteen season, the Maynard Solar Red Sox didn't have any great expectations to live up to.

All the other players had clustered around me as if I were giving out tickets to see a rock band, but Jerry just hung out around first base like a slow-thawing cryogenic.

"I'm Coach Ruttlemyer," I said, loudly enough to reach Jerry's pointy ears. "Some of you guys know each other and some of you don't. But on my team, it's not who you know that counts, it's how hard you play."

At this point in the first preseason speech, you always catch some kid with a finger in his or her nose. That year, it was a sweet-faced, red-headed girl. She had, at that moment, banished herself to right field.

"Now, everybody's going to play in every game," I said. "We're here to have fun, not just to win."

The kids looked at me like they didn't buy that line of bull. I barely believed it myself. But I always said it extra-loud so the parents could hear. It gave me something to fall back on at the end of a lousy season.

"We're going to be practicing hard because we only have two weeks before the first game," I said, pulling the bill of my cap down low over my eyes so they could see what a serious guy I was. "Now let's see who's who."

I went down the roster alphabetically, calling out each player's name. When the kid answered "Here," I glanced first at the kid, then up into the bleachers to see which parents were grinning and straining their necks. That's a good way to tell right off who's going to want their kid to pitch: the beefy, red-faced dad wearing sunglasses and too-tight polyester shorts, and the mom who's busy organizing which parent is bringing what snack for which game.

When I called out Jerry's name, he croaked out a weak syllable and grimaced, showing the tips of his fangs. I waved him over to join the rest of the team. He tucked his glove in his armpit and jogged to the end of the line. I watched him out of the corner of my eye, waiting for him to trip over the baseline chalk. But he didn't stumble once, and that's when I got my first glimmer of hope that maybe he'd be able to swipe a couple of bases for me. He was gaunt, which means that if he's clumsy you call him "gangly," but if he's well-coordinated you call him "sleek." So maybe we're not as enlightened as we claim to be, but hey, we're making progress.

I liked to start first practice by having the kids get on the infield dirt and snag some grounders. You can tell just about everything you need to know about a player that way. And I don't mean just gloving the ball and pegging it over to first. I mean footwork, hand-eye, hustle, aggressiveness, vision, all those little extras that separate the cellar-dwellers from the also-rans from the team that takes home the Sawyer Cup at the end of the season. And it's not just the way they act when it's their turn; you get a lot of clues by how they back each other up, whether they sit down between turns, whether they punch each other on the arm or hunt for four-leaf clovers.

By the first run through, ten ground balls had skittered through to the deep grass in centerfield. But one, *one,* made up for all those errors. Jerry Shepherd's grounder. He skimmed the ball off the dirt and whizzed it over to first as if the ball were a yo-yo and he held the string. My assistant coach and darling wife Dana grinned at me when the ball thwacked into her mitt. I winked at her, hoping the play wasn't a fluke.

But it was no fluke. Six turns through, and six perfect scoops and tosses by Jerry Shepherd. Some of the other kids were fifty-fifty risks, and one, you'd have guessed the poor little kid had the glove on the wrong hand. You know the kind, parents probably raised him on computer chess and wheat bran. Oops, there I go again, acting all unenlightened.

Another bright spot was Elise Stewart, my best returning player. She only made the one error on her first turn, and I could chalk that up to a long winter's layoff. She was not only sure-handed, she was also the kind of girl you'd want your son to date in high school. She had a happy heart and you just knew she'd be good at algebra.

All in all, I was pleased with the personnel. In fifteen years of coaching Little League, this was probably the best crop of raw talent I'd ever had. Now, I wasn't quite having delusions of being hauled out of the dugout on these guys' shoulders (me crushing their bones and hoisting the Sawyer Cup over my head), but with a little work, we had a chance at a winning season.

I made a boy named Biff put on the catcher's gear and get behind the plate. In baseball films, the chunky kid always plays catcher, but if you've ever watched even one inning of a real Little League game, you know the catcher needs to be quick. He spends all his time against the backstop, stumbling over his mask and jerking his head around looking for the baseball. Besides, Biff had a great name for a catcher, and what more could you ask for?

I threw batting practice, and again each kid had a turn while the others fanned out across the diamond. I didn't worry as much about hitting as I did fielding because I knew hitting was mostly a matter of practice and concentration. It was a skill that could be taught. So I kind of expected the team to be a little slow with the bat, and they didn't disappoint me.

Except when Jerry dug into the batter's box. He stared at me with his pupils glinting red under the brim of his batting helmet, just daring me to bring the heat. I chuckled to myself. I liked this kid's cockiness at the plate. But I used to be a decent scholarship prospect, and I still had a little of the old vanity myself. So instead of lobbing a cream puff, I kicked up my leg and brought the Ruttlemyer Express.

His line drive would have parted my hair, except for two things: I was wearing a cap and my hairline barely reached above my ears. But I felt the heat off his scorcher all the same, and it whistled like a bullet from a gun. I picked up the rosin bag and tossed it in the air a few times. Some of the parents had stopped talking among themselves to watch the confrontation.

Jerry dug in and Biff gave me a target painting the black on the inside corner. I snapped off a two-seamer curveball, hoping the poor batter didn't break his spine when he lunged at the dipping pitch. But Jerry kept his hips square, then twisted his wrists and roped the ball to right field for what would have been a stand-up double. I'd never seen a Little Leaguer who could go with a pitch like that. I tossed him a knuckleball; most grown-ups couldn't have hit it with a tennis racket, but Jerry drilled it over the fence in left-center.

Okay. *Okay.*

He did miss one pitch and hit a couple of fouls during his turn. I guess even vampires are only human.

After practice, I passed out uniforms and schedules and talked to the parents. I was hoping to tell Jerry what a good job he'd done and how I'd be counting on him to be a team leader, but he snatched up his goods and left before I had the chance. He got to the edge of the woods, then turned into a bat (the flying kind, not the kind you hit with) and flitted into the trees, his red jersey dangling from one of his little claws. His glove weighed him down a little and he was blind, of course, so he bumped into a couple of tree limbs before he got out of sight.

And so went the two weeks. Jerry was a natural shortstop; even the other kids saw that. Usually everybody wanted to pitch and play shortstop (both positions at the same time, you know), but nobody grumbled when I said Jerry would be our starting shortstop. Elise was starting pitcher, and Wheat Bran and the redhead were "designated pinch hitters." I told everybody to get a good night's sleep because we would be taking on the Piedmont Electric Half-Watts, which was always one of the better teams.

I could hardly sleep that night, I was so excited. Dana rolled over at about one A.M. and stole her pillow back.

"What's wrong?" she grunted.

"The game," I said. I was running through lineups in my mind, planning strategies for situations that might arise in the sixth inning.

"Go to sleep. Deadline's tomorrow."

"Yeah, yeah, yeah." I was editor of the Sawyer Creek E-Weekly, and Thursday noon was press time. I still had some unfinished articles. "That's just my job, but baseball is my lifeblood."

Thinking of lifeblood made me think of Jerry. The poor kid must have lost his parents. Back a few centuries ago, there had been a lot of purging and staking and garlic-baiting. Yeah, like I said, we're making progress, but sometimes I wonder if you can ever really change the human animal. I hoped nothing would come up about his being a vampire.

I knew how cruel Little League could be. Not the kids. They could play and play and play, making up rules as they went along, working things out. No, it was the parents who sometimes made things ugly, who threw tantrums and called names and threatened coaches. I'd heard parents boo their own kids.

In one respect, I was glad Jerry was an orphan. At least I didn't have to worry about his parents changing into wolves, leaping over the chain-link fence, and ripping my throat out over a bad managerial decision. Not that vampires perpetrated that sort of violence. Still, all myths contain a kernel of truth, and even a myth can make you shiver.

I finally went to sleep, woke up, and got the paper online. I drove out to the ballfield and there were four dozen vehicles in the parking lot. There's not much entertainment in Sawyer Creek. Like I said, Little League's a big deal in these parts, plus it was a beautiful April day, with the clouds all puffy and soft in the blue sky. Dana was already there, passing out baseballs so the kids could warm up. I looked around and noticed Jerry hadn't arrived.

"He'll be here," Dana said, reading my nervousness.

We took infield and I was filling out the lineup card when Elise pointed to centerfield. "Hey, looky there, Coach," she said.

Over the fence loped a big black dog with red socks and white pin-striped pants. Propped between the two stiff ears was a cockeyed cap. The upraised tail whipped back and forth in the breeze, a worn glove hooked over its tip. The dog transformed into Jerry when it got to second base.

A murmur rippled through the crowd. I felt sorry for Jerry then. The world may be enlightened, but the light's a little slower in reaching Sawyer Creek than it is most places. There are always a few bigots around. Red, yellow, black, and white,— we had all gotten along and interbred and become one race. But when you get down to the equality of the living and the living dead, some people just don't take to that notion of unity as easily.

And there was something else that set the crowd on edge, and even bothered *me* for a second. Hanging by a strap around his neck was one of those sports bottles all the kids have these days. Most of the kids put in juice or Super-Ade or something advertised by their favorite big leaguers. But Jerry's drink was thick and blood-red. Perfectly blood-red.

"Sorry I'm late," he said, sitting down on the end of the bench. I winced as he squirted some of the contents of the sports bottle into his throat.

"Play ball," the umpire yelled, and Elise went up to the plate and led off with a clean single to right. The next kid bunted her over, then Jerry got up. The first pitch bounced halfway to home plate and Elise stole third. Dana, who was coaching third base, gave her the "hold" sign. I wanted to give Jerry a chance to drive her in.

The next pitch was a little high, but Jerry reached out easily with the bat. The ball dinged off the titanium into center and we were up, one to nothing. And that was the final score, with Elise pitching a three-hitter and Jerry taking away a handful of hits from deep in the hole. Jerry walked once and hit another double, but Wheat Bran struck out to leave him stranded in the fifth.

Still, I was pleased with the team effort, and a "W" is a "W," no matter how you get it. The kids gathered around the snack cooler after the game, all happy and noisy and ready to play soccer or something. But not Jerry. He had slipped away before I could pat him on the back.

"Ain't no fair, you playing a slanty-eyed vampire," came a gruff voice behind me. "Next thing you know, they'll allow droids and other such trash to mix in. Baseball's supposed to be for normal folks."

I turned to find myself face to face with Roscoe Turnbull. Sawyer Creek's Mister Baseball. Coach of the reigning champs for the past seven years. He'd been watching from the stands, scouting the opposition the way he always did.

"Hey, he's got just as much right to play as anybody," I said. "I know you're not big on reading, but someday you ought to pick up the U.S. Constitution and check out the 43rd Amendment."

The Red Sox had never beaten one of Turnbull's teams, but at least I could be smug in my intellectual superiority.

"Big words don't mean nothing when they're giving out the Sawyer Cup," Turnbull hissed through his Yogi Berra teeth. He had a point. He'd had to build an addition onto his house just so he could store all the hardware his teams had won.

"We'll see," I said, something I never would have dared to say in previous years. Turnbull grunted and got in his panel truck. His son Ted was in the passenger seat, wearing the family scowl. I waved to him and went back to my team.

We won the next five games. Jerry was batting something like .900 and had made only one error, which occurred when a stray moth bobbed around his head in the infield. He'd snatched it out of the air with his mouth at the same moment the batter sent a three-hopper his way. I didn't say anything. I mean, instincts are instincts. Plus, we were winning, and that was all that mattered.

The seventh game was trouble. I'd been dreading that line on the schedule ever since I realized that my best player was a vampire. Maynard Solar Red Sox versus The Dead Reckoning Funeral Parlor Pall Bearers. Now, no self-respecting parlors were *selling* the blood they drained. But there had been rumors of underground activity, a black market for blood supplies.

And Jerry had slowly been catching the heat anyway. The grumbles from the stands had gotten louder, and whenever Jerry got up to bat or made a play in the field, some remark would come from the opposing bleachers. Oh, they were the usual unimaginative kind, like the old "Kill the vampire," the play on the resemblance between the words "vampire" and "umpire." The other common one was "Vampires suck." And these were the parents, mind you. They wonder where kids get it from.

The cruelest one, and the one that caught on the fastest, came from the unlikely mouth of Roscoe Turnbull, who'd made a habit of bringing his son Ted to our games just so they could ride Jerry's case. Jerry had launched a three-run homer to win in the last inning of one of our games. As he crossed the plate, Turnbull yelled out, "Hey, look, everybody. It's the Unnatural." You know, a play on the old Robert Redford film. Even *I* had to grudgingly admit that was a good one.

Now we were playing a funeral parlor and I didn't know where Jerry got his blood. I usually didn't make it my business to keep up with how the kids lived their lives off the diamond. But Jerry didn't have any parents, any guidance. Maybe he could be bribed to throw a game if the enticements were right.

So I was worried when Jerry came to bat in the sixth with two outs. We were down, four-three. Biff was on second. It was a situation where there was really no coaching strategy. Jerry either got a hit or made an out.

He had made hits in his three previous trips, but those were all in meaningless situations. I couldn't tell if he was setting us up to lose.

Until that moment.

"Come on, Jerry," I yelled, clapping my hands. "I know you can do it."

If you *want* to, I silently added.

Jerry took two strikes over the heart of the plate. The bat never left his shoulder. All my secret little fantasies of an undefeated season were about to go up in smoke. I started mentally rehearsing my after-game speech, about how we gave it all we had, we'll get 'em next time, blah blah blah.

The beanpole on the mound kicked up his leg and brought the cheese. Jerry laced it off the fence in right-center. Dana waved Biff around to score, and Jerry was rounding second. I didn't know whether I hoped Dana would motion him to try for third, because Wheat Bran was due up next, and he'd yet to hit even a foul tip all season. But the issue was decided when their shortstop, the undertaker's kid, rifled the relay throw over the third basemen's head as Jerry pounded down the base path. We won, five-four.

"I never doubted you guys for a second," I told the team afterward, but of course Jerry had already pulled his disappearing act.

Dana was blunt at dinner as I served up some tastiwhiz and fauxburger. I'd popped a cork on some decent wine to celebrate.

"Steve, I think you're beginning to like winning just a little too much," she said, ever the concerned wife.

I grinned around a mouthful of food. "It gets in your blood," I said. "Can't help it."

"What about all those seasons you told the kids to just give it their best, back when you were plenty satisfied if everyone only showed a little improvement over the course of the season?"

"Back when I was just trying to build their self-esteem? Well, nothing builds character like winning. The little guys are practically *exploding* with character."

"I wish you were doing more for Jerry," she said. "He still doesn't act like part of the team. And the way he looks at you, like he wants you for a father figure. I think he's down on himself."

"Down on himself? *Down* on himself?" I almost sprayed my mouthful of wine across the table, and that stuff was ten bucks a bottle. I gulped and continued. "I could trade him for an entire *team* if I wanted. He's the best player to come out of Sawyer Creek since—"

"—since Roscoe Turnbull. And you see how *he* ended up."

I didn't like where this discussion was headed. "I'm sure Jerry's proud of his play. And the team likes him."

"Only because the team's winning. But I wonder how they would have reacted, how their *parents* would have reacted, if Jerry had struck out that last time today? I mean, nobody's exactly inviting him for sleep-overs as it is."

"He's just quiet. A lone wolf. Nothing wrong with that," I said, a little unsure of myself.

"Nothing wrong with vampires as long as they hit .921, is that what you mean?"

"Hey, we're winning, and that's what counts."

"I don't know," Dana said, shaking her pretty and sad head. "You're even starting to sound like Roscoe Turnbull."

That killed *my* mood, all right. That killed my mood for a lot of things around the house for a while. Lying in bed that night with a frigid three feet between us, I stared out the window at the full moon. A shape fluttered across it, a small lonely speck lost in that great circle of white. It most likely wasn't Jerry, but I felt an ache in my heart for him all the same.

At practice, I sometimes noticed the players whispering to each other while Jerry was at bat. I don't think for a minute that children are born evil. But they have parents who teach and guide them. Parents who were brought up on the same whispered myths.

I tried to be friendly toward Jerry, and kept turning my head so I could catch the look from him that Dana had described. But all I saw were a pair of bright eyes that could pierce the back of a person's skull if they wanted. Truth be told, he *did* give me the creeps a little. And I could always pretend my philosophy was to show no favoritism, despite Dana's urging me to reach out to him.

Dana was a loyal assistant regardless of our difference of opinion. She helped co-pilot the Red Sox through the next eight victories. Jerry continued to tear up the league's pitching and played shortstop like a strip of flypaper, even though he was booed constantly. Elise pitched well and the rest of the kids were coming along, improving every game. I was almost sad when we got to the last game. I didn't want the season to end.

Naturally, we had to play the Turnbull Construction Claw Hammers for the championship. They'd gone undefeated in their division again. Ted had a fastball that could shatter a brick. And Roscoe Turnbull started scouting his draft picks while they were still in kindergarten, so he had the market cornered on talent.

I was so nervous I couldn't eat the day of the game. I got to the field early, while the caretaker was still trimming the outfield. Turnbull was there, too. He was in the home team's dugout shaving down a wooden bat. Wooden bats weren't even used in the majors anymore. Turnbull could afford lithium compound bats. That's when I first started getting suspicious.

"I'm looking forward to the big game," Turnbull said, showing the gaps between his front teeth.

"Me too," I said, determined not to show I cared. "And may the best team win."

"What do you mean? The best team always wins."

I didn't like the way he was running that wood shaver down the bat handle.

"You getting all nostalgic?" I asked, tremblingly nonchalantly. "Going back to wood?"

"Good enough for my daddy. And my great-great-grandpaw on my mother's side. Maybe you heard of him. Ty Cobb."

Tyrus Raymond Cobb. The Hall-of-Famer. The Georgia Peach. The greatest hitter in any league, ever. Or the dirtiest player ever to set foot on a diamond, depending on whom you asked.

"Yeah, I've heard of him," I said. "That's quite a bloodline."

"Well, *we've* always managed to win without no low-down, stinking vampires on our team."

"Jerry Shepherd deserves to play as much as any other boy or girl."

"It ain't right. Here this"—he made a spitting face—"*creature* has all these advantages like being able to change into an animal or throw the hocus-pocus on other players."

"You know that's against the rules. We'd be disqualified if he tried something like that. There's no advantage."

"It's only against the rules if you get caught." Turnbull held the tip of the bat up in the air. It was whittled to a fine, menacing point. "And sometimes you got to *make* your advantages."

"Even you wouldn't stoop that low," I said. "Not just to win a game."

A thin stream of saliva shot from his mouth and landed on the infield dirt. He smiled again, the ugliest smile imaginable. "Gotta keep a little something on deck, just in case."

I shuddered and walked back to my dugout. Turnbull wasn't that bloodthirsty. He was just trying to gain a psychological edge. Sure, that was all.

Psychological edges work if you let them, so I spent the next fifteen minutes picking rocks from the infield. The kids were starting to arrive by then, so I watched them warm up. Jerry was late, as usual, but he walked out of the woods just as I was writing his name into the lineup. I nodded at him without speaking.

We batted first. Ted was starting for the Claw Hammers, of course. He was the kind of pitcher who would throw a brush back pitch at his own grandmother if he thought she were digging in on him. He stood on the mound and practiced his battle glare, then whipped the ball into the catcher's mitt. I had to admit, the goon sure knew how to bring it to the plate.

Half the town had turned out. The championship game always drew better than the town elections. Dana patted me on the back. She wasn't one to hold a grudge when times were tough.

"Play ball," the umpire shouted, and we did.

Elise strode confidently to the plate.

"Go after her, Tedder," Turnbull shouted through his cupped hands from the other dugout. "You can do it, big guy."

The first pitch missed her helmet by three inches. She dusted herself off and stood deeper in the batter's box. The next pitch made her dance. Ball two. But she was getting a little shaky. No one likes being used for target practice. The next pitch hit her bat as she ducked away. Foul, strike one.

Elise was trembling now. I hated the strategy they were using, but unfortunately it was working. The umpire didn't say a word.

"Attaboy," Turnbull yelled. "Now go in for the kill."

Ted whizzed two more strikes past her while she was still off-balance. Biff grounded out weakly to second. Jerry went up to the plate and dug in. Ted's next offering hit Jerry flush in the face.

Jerry went down like a shot. I ran up to him and knelt in the dirt, expecting to see broken teeth and blood and worse. But Jerry's eyes snapped open. Another myth about vampires is that they don't feel pain. There are other kinds of pain besides the physical, though, and I saw them in Jerry's red irises. He could hear the crowd cheering as clearly as I could.

"Kill the vampire," one parent said.

"Stick a stake in him," another shouted.

"The Unnatural strikes again," a woman yelled.

I looked into the home team's dugout and saw Turnbull beaming as if he'd just won a trip to Alpha Centauri.

I helped Jerry up and he jogged to first base. I could see a flush of pink on the back of the usually-pale neck. I wondered whether the color was due to rage or embarrassment. I had Dana give him the "steal" sign, but the redhead popped up to the catcher on the next pitch.

We held them scoreless in their half, despite Ted's getting a triple. My heart was pounding like a kid's toy drum on Xmas Day, but I couldn't let the players know I cared one way or the other. When we got that third out, I calmly gave the kids high fives as they came off the field. Sure, this was just another game like the Mona Lisa was just another painting.

So it went for another couple of innings, with no runners getting past second. Jerry got beaned on the helmet his next trip up. The crowd was cheering like mad as he fell. I looked out at the mob sitting in the bleachers, and the scariest thing was that it wasn't just our opponent's fans who were applauding.

There was the sheriff, pumping her fist in the air. The mayor looked around secretively, checked the majority opinion, then added his jeers to the din. Biff's mother almost wriggled out of her tanktop, she was screaming so enthusiastically. A little old lady in the front row was bellowing death threats through her megaphone.

I protested the beaning to the umpire. He was a plump guy, his face melted by gravity. He looked like he'd umpired back before the days of protective masks and had taken a few foul tips to the nose.

"You've got to warn the pitcher against throwing at my players," I said.

"Can't hurt a vampire, so what's the point?" the umpire snarled, spitting brown juice toward my shoes. So that was how it was going to be.

"Then you should throw the pitcher out of the game because of poor sportsmanship."

"And I ought to throw *you* out for delay of game." He yanked the mask back over his face, which was a great improvement on his looks.

I squeezed Jerry's shoulder and looked him fully in the eyes for the first time since I'd known him. Maybe I'd been afraid he would mesmerize me.

"Jerry, I'm going to put in a pinch-runner for you," I said. "It's not fair for you to put up with this kind of treatment."

I'd said the words that practically guaranteed losing the game, but I wasn't thinking about that then. The decision was made on instinct, and instinct is always truer and more revealing than a rationalizing mind. Later on, that thought gave me my only comfort.

I signaled Dana to send in a replacement. But Jerry's eyes blazed like hot embers and his face contorted into various animal faces: wolf, bat, tiger, wolverine, then settled back into its usual wan constitution.

"No," he said. "I'm staying in."

He jogged to first before I could stop him.

"Batter up," the umpire yelled.

I went into the dugout. Dana gave me a hug. There were tears in her eyes. Mine too, though I made sure no one noticed.

Jerry stole second and then third. Wheat Bran was at the plate, waving his bat back and forth. I knew his eyes were closed. Two strikes, two outs. I was preparing to send the troops back out onto the field when Wheat Bran blooped a single down the line in right. Jerry scored standing up.

Elise shut out the Claw Hammers until the bottom of the sixth. She was getting tired. This was ulcer time, and I'd quit pretending not to care about winning. Sweat pooled under my arms and the band of my cap was soaked. I kept clapping my hands, but my throat was too tight to yell much encouragement.

Their first batter struck out. The second batter sent a hard grounder to Jerry. I was mentally ringing up the second out when someone in the stands shouted, "Bite me, blood-breath!"

The ball bounced off Jerry's glove and went into the outfield. The runner made it to second. Jerry stared at the dirt.

"Shake it off, Jerry," I said, but my voice was lost in the chorus of spectators who were calling my shortstop every ugly name you could think of. The next batter grounded out to first, advancing the runner to third.

Two outs, and you know the way these things always work. Big Ted Turnbull dug into the batter's box, gripping the sharpened wooden bat. But I wasn't going to let him hurt us. I did what you always do to a dangerous hitter with first base open: I took the bat out of his hands.

I told Elise to walk him intentionally.

Roscoe Turnbull glared at me with death in his eyes, but I had to protect my shortstop and give us the best chance to win. Ted reached first base and called time out, then jogged over to his team's bench. Roscoe gave me a smile. That smile made my stomach squirm as if I'd swallowed a dozen large snakes.

Ted sat down and changed his shoes. I didn't understand until he walked back onto the infield. The bottom of his cleats were so thick they resembled those shoes the disco dancers wore after disco made its fourth comeback. The shoes made Ted six inches taller. The worst part was the spikes were made of wood.

I thought of Ted's ancestor, Ty Cobb, how Cobb was legendary for sliding into second with his spikes high. I rocketed off the bench.

"Time!" I screamed. "Time out!"

The umpire lifted his mask.

"What now?" he asked.

I pointed to the cleats. "Those are illegal."

"The rule book only bans *metal* cleats," he said. "Now, batter up."

"Second baseman takes the throw on a steal," I shouted as instruction to my fielders.

"No," Jerry shouted back. He pointed to the plate. "Left-handed batter."

Shortstop takes the throw when a lefty's up. The tradition of playing the percentages was as old as baseball itself. Even with the danger, I couldn't buck the lords of the game. Unwritten rules are sometimes the strongest.

I sat on the bench with my heart against my tonsils. The crowd was chanting, "Spike him, spike him, spike him," over and over. Dana sat beside me and held my hand, a strange mixture of accusation and empathy in her eyes.

"Maybe the next batter will pop up," she said. "There probably won't even *be* a play at second."

"Probably not."

She didn't say anything about testosterone or my stubborn devotion to the percentages. Or that Elise was getting weaker and we had no relief pitcher. Or that we had to nail the lid on this victory quick or it would slip away. I knew what Dana was thinking, though.

"I'd do it even if it was my own son out there," I muttered to her. I almost even believed it.

They tried a double-steal on the next pitch. It was a delayed steal, where the runner on third waits for the catcher to throw down to second, then tries for home. Not a great strategy for the game situation, but I had a feeling Turnbull had a lower purpose in mind.

Biff gunned a perfect strike to Jerry at second. The play unfolded as if in slow motion. Ted was already leaning back, launching into his slide.

Please step away, Jerry, I prayed. The runner on third was halfway home. If Jerry didn't make the tag, we'd be tied and the Claw Hammers would have the momentum. But I didn't care. I'd gladly trade safe for safe.

Jerry didn't step away. His instincts were probably screaming at him to change into a bat and flutter above the danger, or to paralyze Ted in his tracks with a deep stare. Maybe he knew that would have caused us to forfeit the game and the championship. Or maybe he was just stubborn like me.

He gritted his teeth, his two sharp incisors hanging over his lip in concentration. Ted slid into the bag, wooden spikes high in the air. Jerry stooped into the cloud of dust. He applied the tag just before the spikes caught him flush in the chest.

The field umpire reflexively threw his thumb back over his shoulder to signal the third out. But all I could see through my blurry eyes was Jerry writhing in the dirt, his teammates hustling to gather around him. I ran out to my vampire shortstop, kneeling beside his body just as the smoke started to rise from his flesh.

He gazed up at me, the pain dousing the fire in his eyes. The crowd was silent, hushed by the horror of a wish come true. The Red Sox solemnly removed their hats. I'd never heard such a joyless championship celebration. Jerry looked at me and smiled, even as his features dissolved around his lips.

"We won, Coach," he whispered, and that word "we" was like a stake in my own heart. Then Jerry was dust, forever part of the infield.

Dana took the pitcher's mound, weeping without shame. She stared into the crowd, at the umpires, into Turnbull's dugout, and I knew she was meeting the eye of every single person at Sawyer Field that day.

"Look at yourselves," she said, her voice strong despite the knots I knew were tied in her chest. "Just take a good long look."

Everybody did. I could hear a hot dog wrapper blowing against the backstop.

"All he wanted was to play," she said. "All he wanted was to be just like you."

Sure, her words were for everybody. But she had twenty-two years of experience as Mrs. Ruttlemyer. We both knew whom she was really talking to.

"Just like you," she whispered, her words barely squeezing out yet somehow filling the outfield, the sky, the little place in your heart where you like to hide bad things. She walked off the mound with her head down, like a pitcher that had just given up the game-winning hit.

So many tears were shed that the field would have been unplayable. People had tasted the wormwood of their prejudice. They had seen how vicious the human animal could be. Even vampires didn't kill their young, even when the young were decades old.

There was no memorial service. I wrote the eulogy, but nobody ever got to read it, not even Dana. There was talk of filing criminal charges against the Turn bulls, but nobody had the stomach to carry it through. What happened that day was something that people spent a lot of time trying to forget.

But that victory rang out across the ensuing years, a Liberty Bell for the living dead in Sawyer Creek. Vampires were embraced by the community, welcomed into the Chamber of Commerce, one was even elected mayor. Roscoe Turnbull has three vampires on his team this season.

That Sawyer Cup still sits on my mantel, even though I never set foot on a diamond after that day. Sometimes when I look at the trophy, I imagine it is full of blood. They say that winning takes sacrifice. But that's just a myth.

Still, all myths contain a kernel of truth, and even a myth can make you shiver.

Scott Nicholson is the international bestselling author of more than 20 novels, 70 short stories, six screenplays, four children's books, and four comic books. His supernatural thriller Troubled *is in development as a feature film. He's also a founding partner of eBookSwag.com. Nicholson's website is www.hauntedcomputer.com, or follow @eScottNicholson on Twitter.*

Protector

Rycke Foreman

A wan smile pulls the corners of my cold lips as my most-hated enemy falls. Ah, but could I be there to see it, its golden rays washing over my face as they become subdued, muted, fading into twilight, swallowed by darkness . . .

Instead of shape-shifting, tonight I take flight, bound for suburbia and its endless supply of fodder. Selecting a house at random, I drop casually to the lawn. No lights are on at this end of the home, but someone is awake—a child. My pulse quickens, listening to her delicate breathing, the faint *lub-dub, lub-dub* of her tireless young muscle.

At the window, I peek in, rather surprised to find the child looking directly at me. Her breath catches in her slender, pale, tender throat, her young eyes widening, drinking in my dark silhouette.

She screams.

Her cry surprises me; normally, once their eyes find mine, I have them.

My body breaks into a fine mist, luminescent under the brightness of the nighttime sun, drifting closer to the gray paneled siding—excellent camouflage—as an artificial patch of yellow light falls onto the lawn.

"What's the matter, honey?" a soothing voice inquires. The mother. I sense her cross the room, hear the quiet squeak of the bedsprings as she sits next to her quivering daughter.

"The bogeyman, Mommy. He was in my window."

"Awww . . . for Pete's sake, Sally." This voice is gruff, impatient. Surely the voice of reason . . .

"But, Daddy—"

"Uh-uh, no buts. Now listen to me, Sally—if you don't get a grip on your imagination, *pronto*, your TV privileges are going to be taken away. I have an important meeting first thing tomorrow morning, and you've got school. So I don't want any more of this foolishness tonight. Got it?"

"Charles . . . do you think it could have been a peeping tom?"

His shadow creeps across the grass, trapped within the lighted square. Casting a brief glance along the block, he says, "I doubt it. If there was one, he's long gone by now." His silhouette disappears; I wish I had a body with which to chuckle.

After a moment, as I begin searching for cracks in the foundation that lead through to the interior and Sensible Father Charles leaves the room, I can only just make out the faint whisper of a smile growing on the mother's face, a sympathetic gesture—she understands.

"Don't worry, honey. It's easy to feel scared in the dark."

For a moment I feel a stabbing pang of melancholia and wicked damnation. My mother whispered such words into *my* ear on a similar night many, many centuries ago. Ah, Mothers . . . the only true noble of the human species . . .

But I have found a suitable entrance, and my luck is in: a rat. The filthy little creature is nervous in my presence, yet an ally, and I am granted entrance to this humble abode, finding myself within the child's closet. I hear Sally's mother slow next to Charles in the hallway. He declares, "That's the last time we let her watch *The Wolf Man* before bedtime."

Sorry, Charlie—wrong species.

Waiting until their footfalls disappear to other parts of the house, I leisurely push the closet door open, ensuring that the hinges squeak loudly enough to get little Sally's attention.

"Uh!" she grunts, her sweet breath now stopped fast within her elegant throat. I lean forward—*Peek-a-boo!*—and her eyes widen and her pulse pounds . . . but she does not scream. Revealing a fang with a grin, my young prey becomes completely immobile, paralyzed in the richness of her own fear.

Rising to my full stature, I glide into her pastel bedroom, keeping my wicked grin full and toothy, drinking already of the terror that radiates from every pore in her tiny, unspoiled body.

Now her baby-blues cannot break free from my unyielding gaze. Oh so wide they are, and so fully aware of her fragile mortality. Like a deer that cannot stop looking at those hateful, blazing headlights . . .

Reaching out, I touch her hand, frozen to the blanket in a death grip. But frozen? Oh no—*my* flesh is *frozen*.

And, sad alas, this affliction seems to snap little Sally from her stupor . . .

I change my focus to a simple yet highly effective trance, but the girl is quick. Too quick. She pulls her sheet up and over her head, covering every delicious millimeter of her body. Her mouth-watering scent fades ever so slightly.

Damn her!

Summoning up my most menacing voice, I chuckle rawly. "Do you really think that thin wisp of cotton threading can protect you from these jagged claws, little one? My fearsome, razor-sharp fangs?"

The girl whimpers—somehow curling into a tighter ball than before—but she does not respond. Could she know that I am at her mercy? That the thin wisp of cotton threading does indeed protect her?

"Sweet little Sally," I say, pausing to sniff longingly at a tendril of fear wafting up from beneath the holy cover, "I will not hurt you if you'll just come out from under there." Now a dramatic pause, during which she remains statue-still. "But if you don't . . ." I lean close, shifting gears with jovial malice, "Well, my dear, my fangs are *razor* sharp . . ."

She begins weeping. The blanket draws tighter around her. Frustrated, I cannot help but roll my eyes. I thought sure she'd scamper out after that . . .

Muttering a silent curse, I then decide upon a different approach. Matters such as this must be handled carefully, delicately—especially if I am to have any of her invigorating fluids warming me like gentle fire from within. "But . . . if you come out from under there right now, you will find I can be quite . . . amicable. Cordial. Yes—really *very* kind." But the quiver in my voice betrays me. A number of seconds slip by,

103

filled with her rapid heartbeat, the pounding rush of her luscious blood. "Little girl . . . sweet little Sally . . . please . . . won't you simply talk to me?"

Trembling, she unleashes a sob. It is her only response.

Resorting to begging is the most humiliating experience my species must ever endure, but my need is desperate—I must! If that delicate morsel doesn't come out on her own initiative— well, her belief in the protection of that sheet is, unfortunately, knit from the same fabric of belief that allows my kind to walk corporeal in the night . . .

"Please. I just want to look at you, young Sally. You are such a pretty girl. We can just . . . talk."

But she is a mere, tremulous bundle of rags on the bed. Completely unresponsive.

Careful not to touch her sacred talisman—with her beliefs so fully realized now, it's surely supercharged like a crucifix on holy ground—I lean closer . . .

"Sally?"

But my senses have become dulled in the heat of the moment. Too late, I realize . . .

The blanket overwhelms me as Sally springs up and flings it off herself, choosing my most vulnerable moment to dart for her door. It folds over like a tidal wave and engulfs me. I tumble and fall and tumble some more, clawing and scrambling to right myself and find that first sweet breath of fresh air, but I am blind in its torrential grip, disoriented, flopping like a fish in a pool of acid.

Growing weak, I collapse fully, just beginning to realize the thick, acrid smoke I am choking on is particles from my own body as it spontaneously combusts under the weight of this tangled sunshine. This damned sheet is a myriad of smoldering ants consuming me, biting, ripping, pinching, burning . . .

Oh—that little bitch!

Alas, I can take only feeble solace in one fact before I am gone: *I know I shall be back to haunt her.* If not as another physical incarnation, then at least as her worst nightmare.

And in this role, I shall live and feed forever . . .

Rycke has published short fiction since the early 90s in magazines and ezines like Marion Zimmer Bradley's Fantasy Magazine, Arkham Tales, Best New Vampire Tales, Red Blood, Black Sky, and 69 Flavors of Paranoia, which he also edits. He's worked in virtually all aspects of independent film, television, and theater for more than 15 years, writing a number of produced short films, one of which became a multi-award winner with the National Film Challenge; Rycke also has three full lengths scripts in various stages of development. During his college years, he was honored with Best Newsletter Editing—regional for Phi Theta Kappa's monthly journal, Honorable Mention.

After the Fall

Paul Fry

September 12th

Day One

We're lucky to be alive. Well, at least I think we are. My wife Sandra is very glad I built this shelter. I'm not so sure. Who knows what will be waiting for us when we surface again? That's if we ever do. We'll have to stay down here for at least two weeks, probably a lot longer. I don't know if we'll last that long. We'll probably go crazy.

Everything topside must be destroyed. It was a huge explosion. We nearly didn't get down here in time. The sirens started at about 11:30 P.M.—I don't think there's any sound in the world worse than an air raid siren. Just thinking back to it now gives me chills.

When the sirens started, we were in the living room watching TV. At first we just looked at each other. I could see the fear in Sandra's eyes. Ever since she was a little girl, she's always been afraid of a nuclear attack. She used to have nightmares about it. That's why she pleaded with me to build this shelter. I didn't really think about it much.

Until now, that is.

Now I can't stop thinking about it. I keep trying to remember all the things I've heard and read about what was supposed to happen after a nuclear attack. But I'm afraid my mind can't recall very much; just the basics. I hope I can remember enough to keep us alive.

It's late now and we're both very tired. I'll continue with this diary tomorrow.

Day Two

We had a very restless sleep. Sandra kept crying. I was awake most of the night comforting her. I'm afraid for her. I don't think she'll ever be the same again. She's changed. She was always happy before, but now, when she's not crying she just sits and stares into space. We don't speak much either. I try to hold a normal conversation—if you can call anything under these circumstances normal—but Sandra doesn't respond. She says the odd word now and again, but she doesn't make much sense. Perhaps she will get better in time. I hope so. I don't think I can bear to see her like this for much longer.

I started to keep a diary because there isn't much else to do. I have to do the daily checks of our shelter: check the air filter, make sure the seal on the hatch is intact, that sort of thing. But apart from that, there's nothing. I can't talk to Sandra, so I'll go crazy if I don't keep busy.

I'm trying to think of things to write about, but my mind's a bit hazy. It's to be expected, though, I suppose.

I'll describe the shelter. That should give me plenty to write about.

I built it about four years ago. As I said earlier, Sandra wanted me to build it. I wasn't all that bothered really; I mean, who wants to survive a nuclear war? What's there to live for? If we had children, then maybe that would give me a reason, but there again, who wants to see them suffer? The world will never be the same again. There's probably nothing left. I bet everything's gone. Still, I suppose somebody's got to survive and carry on. I don't see the point myself, but perhaps it's just me.

Anyway, back to the shelter.

It's one of those underground permanent shelters, made from twelve-inch thick reinforced concrete. It's about 15 feet long, 13 feet wide, and the ceiling's about 10 feet high. Not very big. Not big enough to be trapped in for two weeks anyway. Especially since I'm a bit claustrophobic. I hope I can take it. I've got no choice really; I've got to be strong for Sandra.

The inside of the shelter is very basic. Along one wall there's a bed, a chemical toilet—that's not very pleasant, I'll tell you—and there's a big box of supplies: food, water, toilet paper, first aid kit, can and bottle opener, and knives and forks, that sort of thing, against the opposite wall. I've allowed enough food and water for about two weeks. I hope we don't have to stay down here any longer. It should be safe to go outside after two weeks. Maybe even sooner. It all depends on where the bombs landed.

Next to the supplies we've got a little table—well, actually it's an upturned box—with a portable radio on it. We've also got a spare radio and some spare batteries. I haven't picked up anything yet. Perhaps the emergency broadcast system has been destroyed. But that's its job isn't it? It's supposed to broadcast during emergencies. I'll keep trying, but I don't want to waste the batteries. As soon as I receive anything, I'll write it down.

Oh yeah, we've also got a little box of tools next to our radio stuff. There's a screwdriver, hammer, a small shovel, and a hatchet, just in case we need them.

When I'd finished building the shelter, it looked like a prison cell. Concrete everywhere. The only thing that broke up the grayness of the concrete was the steel hatch in the ceiling, which I'd painted turquoise blue, just to give the place a little color.

Obviously it isn't quite the same as a real prison cell. There isn't any metal bars caging you in, just concrete. But it's a lot worse than any prison cell I know of. In a real prison you at least see some kind of daylight. Not here. This shelter is like a sealed box. No daylight gets in anywhere. Our only light comes from torches that we position around the shelter.

Sandra's put up a few posters on the walls to try and make it look cozier. I'm looking at the one above me as I write. It's a picture of the New York skyline. I've always wanted to go to New York to see the Statue of Liberty. It's probably not there anymore.

I'm starting to feel a little depressed. I think I'll stop writing for today. I'll be back tomorrow.

Day Five

Things are getting worse. Sandra's more withdrawn. She hasn't spoken for days, and I don't feel well. Maybe the air filter isn't working properly. I'll take a look at it. If it *isn't* working correctly, we're fucked. We'll have to take our chances topside. It might not be so bad; there may be people up there. It's got to be better than being stuck in this little box. That's what it feels like anyway, a box. It's starting to look smaller every day. I'd say the walls are closing in, but that's not really possible, is it? I don't think so.

Day Seven

I feel worse. I've got the shakes and my head hurts.

Sandra's dead. She wouldn't eat. I tried to feed her, but she kept spitting it out. I kept shoving the food back in, but I must have shoved in too much. She started choking. Anyway, she was getting on my nerves. She just sat there and stared at the wall all day long.

She's starting to smell a bit.

I don't think I can stay down here much longer.

Day Ten

I can't take the smell any longer. I've got to get out of here.

Day Twelve

I'm back. I had to leave the shelter. I got rid of Sandra while I was up there. It's not so bad down here now. I like it. It's peaceful and quiet, and I can pop up for some fun whenever I feel like it.

I had a lot of fun yesterday. Fell over and cracked my fucking head, though. That wasn't fun. It hurt like shit. There's fucking rubble everywhere. I was right, everything's destroyed. My house is gone.

Everything's gone.

Not everyone's dead, though.

Almost everyone.

I managed to find a nice-looking girl. She was a bit burnt, a little mangled, but not too bad.

I fucked her. Several times, in fact. She didn't put up a fight at all. I was a bit disappointed really; it's not the same when they just lie there. She moved when I stabbed her, though. She put up a fight then. Tried her best, anyway. She kicked and screamed a lot. I couldn't work out what she was saying, though. A bunch of gurgles. That probably had a lot to do with the steel rod I jammed down her throat.

After I'd had my fun with Spike (that's what I nicknamed her), I roamed around for a few hours. I didn't see anybody else. I'll go out again tomorrow. Maybe I'll have more luck then.

Day Fourteen

What a time I've had! I nearly didn't make it back. Some fucking lunatic attacked me. I was scouting around for women, men, I don't care anymore, when this crazy bastard jumped up from a hole in the ground and bashed me over the head with a fucking leg. Can you believe it? He actually hit me with a human limb. It fucking hurt. Left a fucking bump on the side of my head. A fucking leg.

I might try that one myself. I could use an arm (look out, I'm armed) . . . or even better, a head. I could tie some rope around it and use it like a club. I could swing the fucker around and bash the shit out of someone with it.

Hey you, how about a little head?

I could use Sandra's head. She's still up there.

I hope.

It should be easy to cut her head off. She's been up there a couple of days now. She's got to be rotten.

I'll have a look around for some rope; I'll go up and see if I can find her. I'll take the hatchet from the box of tools. I should be able to chop her head off nicely with that.

It's off to work I go!

Day Fifteen

It worked a treat. I managed to find Sandra's body. Some crazy bastard had dragged her away and started to eat her, if you can believe that. Most of her lower body and legs were missing. They probably went first because they were the fattiest parts of her. Saying that, though, her tits were still intact. A bit rotten, but still intact, and they were huge. Loads of fat there, if that's what the crazy fucker was after.

When I found her, she was spread-eagle on top of some rubble. Part of an old table or something. Even though she was rotten and not totally intact, she didn't look too bad. I even thought about fucking her one last time. I decided against the idea, though. Sandra didn't like me to fuck her when she was alive. I could imagine what she'd think if I fucked her while she was like that. I know she's dead, but I still thought better of it.

I positioned myself above her and gave her a final kiss good-bye, then I chopped her head off. It came off easier than I expected it would. Someone had tried before me, I think. God only knows why. There are some sick fuckers in this world.

I'd just managed to get her head off and get the rope tied around it when someone attacked me from behind.

She didn't expect my retaliation, though. I swung Sandra's head at her. She screamed even before it made contact. The first blow didn't kill her, but it knocked her down and dazed her a bit. Gave me time to fuck her.

This one didn't just lie there like old Spike had. She put up a hell of a fight . . . until I buried my hatchet in her forehead.

After I fucked her, I got myself a little idea. The sight of the hatchet protruding from her head is what gave it to me. My first attempt at a 'head-club' hadn't worked so well, so I decided to try something new. I scouted around for some nails or anything long and sharp. It took me a while to find something that would do the trick, but I finally found an old tool kit in the ruins of someone's garage. Some good shit had survived the blast.

I found some six-inch nails. I couldn't find a hammer, but the flat side of my hatchet worked just as well. I knocked a few nails into Sandra's head, leaving about three inches of each nail sticking out. When I finished with her, she looked a bit like Pinhead from that old movie *Hellraiser*.

I was off again.

I got me quite a few people that day. Had some real fun. Lately, though, I've begun to feel sick. I've decided to stay here in the shelter for a few days. Maybe that'll help.

Day Eighteen

I'm not getting any better.

I tried to go out yesterday but didn't quite make it. After a lot of effort, I managed to open the shelter's hatch. I'd just struggled to get my head and upper body outside when I saw a group of people lurking behind a big pile of rubble not far from my shelter. There were about four of them. They were hunched over something that sort of resembled a person. They were tugging and pulling at it. I think they were eating someone. I must have gasped or made some kind of noise. One of them turned and looked in my direction.

I saw blood all around his mouth. It contrasted bright against the unnatural grayness of his skin.

I think he saw me. I mean, I don't know if he actually *saw* me, but he looked *at* me. His movements were slow and sluggish, and as I said, his skin was a very pale gray color. He must have been exposed to a lot of fallout. He looked ill. He looked dead, actually. That isn't possible, though. The dead don't walk, right?

The way he looked at me made me shudder. I returned to the safety of my shelter and locked myself in.

I think they're trying to get me. I've heard muffled voices—more like groans, actually—and strange sounds all night.

It's five in the morning now. They've been at it nonstop for hours.

I just heard the hatch creak.

I've got my hatchet and my 'head-club' ready. Maybe Sandra will help me.

Then again . . . after what I did to her, maybe not.

Paul Fry was born in Birmingham, England in 1971. Ever since he read THE CELLAR *by Richard Laymon he has loved horror stories. It was because of his love of Richard Laymon's books that he got into writing and editing. The first book he edited was an anthology based on the undead called* COLD STORAGE *back in 2000, which included an introduction written by the legendary Graham Masterton. Then in 2001 he created, edited, and published* PEEP SHOW *erotic horror magazine, which ran until 2003. In 2004 he edited and published* PEEP SHOW, VOLUME 1, *the first erotic horror anthology based on the magazine. He then edited a zombie anthology called* COLD FLESH, *which was published in 2005 by US published Hellbound Books. He took a break for a few years but in 2011 re-released* PEEP SHOW, VOLUME 1. *He's currently working on* PEEP SHOW, VOLUME 2, *which is due out the end of 2012. For more details and to purchase his books, please visit Short, Scary Tales Publications at sstpublications.co.uk.*

Beijing Craps

Graham Masterton

Like all professional gamblers whose days are measured only in throws and rolls and hands and spins, it had never seriously occurred to Jack Druce that he would ever have to face death. But that Friday morning at the Golden Lode Casino, at the exact instant when the second-hand swept silently past 1 A.M., he shivered and lifted his head and frowned as if he had been momentarily touched by the chilly breath of impending extinction.

Alert to the slightest tremor in mood at the craps table, the croupier noticed his hesitation and said, "Intending to shoot, sir-r-r?" His r's rolled as hard as dice.

Solly Bartholomew noticed Jack's hesitation too, but didn't lift his eyes from the layout.

Jack nodded and scooped up the dice, but didn't speak.

He had already stacked up eleven thousand dollars' worth of chips in three hours' play. But for no reason at all he suddenly felt as if the layout had gone cold, the same way that (seven years ago) his wife Elaine had grown cold, lying in his arms, asleep first of all, breathing, then not breathing, then dead.

Jack guessed he and Solly could make two or three thousand more. Solly was the only other professional at the table; a neat man who looked like a small-town realtor, but who threw the dice with all the tight assurance of a practised arm. Cautiously, showing no outward signs that they knew each other, or that they were working together, he and Jack were carving up the amateurs between them.

There was money around too. Not yacht money, for sure, but lunch money. They had just been joined by a tall horse-faced over-excited man from Indianapolis in a powder-blue polyester suit who was placing his chips on all the hard-way bets and a redhead with her roots showing and a deep withered cleavage who yelped like a chihuahua every time Jack threw a pass. Divorcee, Jack calculated, splashing out with her settlement. She wouldn't stop playing until every last cent of it was totally blown. It was a form of revenge. Jack knew all about women's revenge. Elaine had stopped breathing while he was holding her in his arms, and what revenge could any woman have exacted on any man that was more terrible than that?

Jack blew softly on the ivories, shook them twice, and sent them tumbling off across the soft green felt. "Nine," commented the croupier, and pushed Jack another stack of fifty-dollar chips.

"I'm out," said Jack, and began gathering his winnings in both hands.

Solly hesitated for a moment, then said, "Me too."

"Aw shit," said the tall horse-faced man.

The croupier's eyes flicked sideways toward the pit boss. Jack said, "Something wrong, my friend?" He had spent thirty years of his life dealing with men who communicated whole libraries with the quiver of an eyelid.

"Pit boss'd like a word, sir. And"—turning toward Solly— "you too, sir. That's if you don't mind."

"I have a plane to catch," Solly complained. Solly always had a plane to catch.

"It's ten after one in the morning," the croupier told him.

"Well, I have to catch some sleep before I catch my plane."

"This won't take long, sir, believe me."

Jack and Solly waited with their hands full of chips while the small, neat pit boss approached them. White tuxedo, ruffled pink shirt, smooth Siamese face, eyes like slanted black olives, black hair parted dead-center. The pit boss held out one of his tiny hands, as if to guide them away from the table by the elbow, but he didn't actually touch them. Players were not to be physically touched. It was bad karma.

"Mr. Newman presents his compliments, sir."

"Oh, does he?" asked Jack, sniffing and blinking behind his heavy-rimmed eyeglasses. Beside him, he heard the redhead yelping again.

The pit boss smiled and went along with the pretense. "Well, sir, Mr. Newman is the joint owner of the Golden Lode, sir. And he would like to see you."

Jack held up his chips. "Listen, my friend, I have my winnings here."

Solly said, "Me too."

"Of course," said the pit-boss. His smile slid out of the side of his mouth like the cottonseed oil pouring out of a freshly-opened can of sardines. "We'll take care of your winnings, sir. Carlos! Here, take care of these gentlemen's winnings."

"Twelve and a half k," said Jack, pointedly, as if it were more money than he had ever possessed in his life.

"Five," said Solly without expression.

"Don't worry, sir. Carlos will keep it in the safe for you."

With a great show of reluctance, Jack handed over his chips. "Twelve and a half k," he repeated. "What do you think of that?"

Behind his well-pumiced acne craters, the stone-faced Carlos obviously thought nothing of it at all. One night's winnings for a mid-Western mark, that was all. The casino would have it all back tomorrow, or the next night.

"Please . . . this young lady will show you to Mr. Graf," said the pit-boss, still smiling. From somewhere behind him, like an assistant in one of those corny Las Vegas lounge magical acts, a Chinese-looking girl appeared in a skin-tight dress of cerise silk, with a split all the way up to the top of her thigh.

"Please follow," she said, and immediately turned and began to walk ahead of them.

Jack glanced at Solly and Solly glanced back at Jack. They could cut and run. But Jack had heard of Mr. Graf; Mr. Graf had a hard, hard reputation. and if they ran away from Mr. Graf, chances were they would have to keep on running for the rest of their natural borns. Whatever had to be faced had to be faced. Jack and Solly had both been beaten up before, more than once.

The Chinese-looking girl was already halfway across the casino floor, headed toward the wide violet-carpeted staircase that led down from the restaurant and the offices.

Solly said, "After you, sport," and Jack shambled after her like an obedient mutt, tugging the knot of his necktie, although it was already too tight. During his gambling career, he had deliberately cultivated the dislocated mannerisms of a Rube, freshly off the Piedmont redeye from the rural mid-West with a billfold crammed with ready money and no idea how to play the tables.

In reality he had been born in Providence, Rhode Island, the son of a high school principal, and he was both well-educated and extensively-traveled. He had lived in Florence, in Aqaba, and Paris. In the 1950s he had spent nine miserable months in London. But in the late 1960s he had spent six weeks living in Bellflower, Illinois, painstakingly imitating the local mannerisms and the local speech. These days, only a fully-bloomed Bellfiorian could have detected his accent wasn't for real. He still said 'grass' instead of 'grayce.'

He had altered his appearance too. He had cropped his hair short and bought himself a vivid chestnut-brown toupee. He had adopted thick-rimmed eyeglasses and sunbathed in his t-shirt so he had acquired that farm-style tan, face and neck and forearms only. Every morning he squeezed lumps of modeling clay in the palms of his hands to give himself cheesy-looking crescents of dirt under his fingernails.

When he was working, he assumed a crumpled seersucker suit in brown-and-white check, a brown drip-dry shirt, and scuffed tan sneakers. At least he liked to think he assumed them and that his 'real' clothes were the clothes that hung in the closet of his suite at the Sands hotel—a single gray Armani suit, three handmade shirts, and a pair of polished English shoes.

In reality, however, the 'real' clothes had scarcely been worn, because Jack was always working. Even the soles of his 'real' shoes remained unscratched. He spent all afternoon and most of the night as Jack Druce the Rube. The rest of the time he spent sprawled on his back on his hotel bed with his sheet knotted around his waist like a loincloth, dreaming of Elaine going cold in his arms and whispering numbers to himself. But he needed the 'real' clothes to be hanging there waiting for him.

If he ever discarded his 'real' clothes, then the 'real' Jack Druce would cease to exist, and all that would be left would be Jack Druce the Rube; Jack Druce the Chronic Gambler. The laughing, sophisticated young college graduate would have vanished forever, along with the husband of Elaine and the father of Roddy, for what that was worth.

On the last day of May, 1961, Jack Druce had been a mathematical whiz-kid, the youngest research team-leader that San Fernando Electronics had ever employed. On the last day of May, 1961, San Fernando Electronics had brought two hundred seventy employees to Las Vegas for the company's tenth annual convention. That night, Jack Druce had played dice for the very first time in his life and doubled his annual salary in four and a half hours.

Jack Druce had woken on the first day of June, 1961, with the certain knowledge that he was hooked.

Now his house was gone and his car was gone. Not because he couldn't afford them. Most days, technically, he was very rich. The simple fact was that houses and cars didn't figure in his life any more. He lived in hotels; he walked to work; he subsisted on free casino snacks and Salem Menthol Lights. His home was the pass line. He never looked at his watch.

The Chinese girl led Jack and Solly through thick suffocating velour curtains and then through double doors of heavy carved Joshua wood.

"I'm not so sure about this," Jack told her, but she turned and half-smiled and said, "Don't be afraid."

Solly said nothing. Solly had an especially sensitive nose for danger. Solly was sniffing the atmosphere, checking it out.

Beyond the double doors they found themselves in a large, gloomy room, ferociously chilly with air-conditioning. In the center of the room stood a gaming-table lit by a single low-hanging lamp of bottle green glass. A dark, secretive lamp that scarcely illuminated the table at all and gave to the six or seven men and women who were hunched around it a ghastly green look, as if they had been dead for several days.

Jack frowned at them. Two of them looked as if they had one foot in the grave for real. Their white hair shone silvery-green in the reflected light from the lamp; their skin was shrink-wrapped over their skulls, thick with wriggling veins.

Three of the players were almost children—a spotty boy of sixteen or seventeen, a young girl of not much more than twelve, and a blond-headed boy who was so small he could scarcely throw the dice.

All of them, however, shared something in common. They all wore loose Chinese robes of gleaming black silk, with fire-breathing dragons embroidered on the back and the name Nu Kua in red silk italics.

"Come," said the Chinese girl, and led Jack and Solly toward the table.

Jack was fascinated to see the dice appeared to glow fluorescently in the darkness, and when they were thrown, they left glowing patterns in the air. Solly watched the game over his shoulder for a while and then murmured, "What the hell kind of craps is that?"

Jack looked around the table. "I'm supposed to be talking to Mr. Graf," he said loudly.

The blond-headed boy left his place and came around the table, smiling and holding out his hand in greeting. He looked no older than five or six.

Jack smiled. "How's tricks, kid?"

"I'm Nevvar Graf," the boy told him in an unbroken but carefully-modulated voice.

"Sure, and I'm Tammy Wynette."

The boy continued to hold out his hand. "You don't believe me?" he asked, tilting his head to one side.

"Nevvar Graf has owned the Golden Lode Casino for twenty years minimum. He's just about old enough to be your grandfather."

The boy smiled. "There are more things on heaven and earth, Horatio."

"Oh, sure," Jack nodded. "Now, is Mr. Graf here, because if not, I intend to leave."

"I told you, Mr. Druce, I'm Nevvar Graf."

There was something in the tone of the boy's voice that caught Jack's attention. Something far too commanding for a boy of five. And how did he know Jack's name? Jack took off his spectacles and folded them and tucked them slowly into his pocket.

The boy said, "I'm Nevvar Graf and you're Jack Druce. I've been watching you for years, Mr. Druce. You're good—one of the best arms in the business. Everybody knows Jack Druce. It's always beaten me why you dress so crummy and talk so dumb when everybody knows who you are. You saw Carlos downstairs? The minute you leave the Golden Lode, Carlos always gets on to the radio-transmitter and warns the doorman at the Diamond Saloon."

Jack said hoarsely, "Young fellow, I don't know what the hell you think you're playing at, but my name is Keith Kovacs and I came here from Illinois for the week to gamble a few hundred dollars, just like I've always promised myself; and when my money's all gone, I'll be gone too. Jack Druce? I never even heard of anybody called Jack Druce."

The boy popped his knuckles one by one. "You see that game going on behind me?"

"I see it," said Jack. "Some kind of fancy dice."

"Beijing Craps," the boy told him with a smile.

Jack shook his head. "Never heard of it."

"Never heard of it, huh?" The boy turned to Solly and said, "Have you heard of it? Beijing Craps?"

Solly nervously sniffed and lowered his eyes. "Sure. I've heard of it."

The boy circled around Jack and took hold of Solly's hand. "Solly Bartholomew," he said in that piping voice. "The greatest arm in the east. The scourge of the Atlantic City boardwalk."

Solly didn't attempt to deny it. He stood holding the boy's hand, his eyes on the carpet, and said nothing.

"Beijing Craps," the boy repeated. "The legendary, magical, mystical Beijing Craps. Banned in China since the revolution; banned in Thailand where they don't ban nothing; punishable by flogging in Japan; punishable by death in Viet Nam. Illegal in every country in the world, with the exception of Pol Pot's Cambodia, and that's where these dice were smuggled in from."

He tugged Solly's hand. "Come on, Solly, come closer. Take a look."

Solly stayed where he was, his head still lowered. The boy tugged his hand again, then smiled. "You don't want to take a look? You don't have to play."

"You know just what the fuck you're talking about," said Solly, his false teeth clenched together. "If I look, I'll have to play."

The boy laughed. "That's up to you, Solly. You're ready for it. You know that you're ready for it. That's why I asked you up here—you and your friend Jack Druce. I've been watching you two lately and you're the cream de la cream. But you're getting bored too. You're too damned good for your own damned good. What's the fun when you don't play the game to the limit— can't play the game to the limit—because the pit boss is going to suss you out and then you're finished at the Golden Lode. Then you're finished at Caesar's Palace and Glitter Gulch and even Sassy Sally's, and before you know it, you're finished in Vegas altogether, then Reno, then Tahoe, then Atlantic City. That's when clever men like you start to play Russian Roulette, hoping you'll lose. But Nevvar Graf here has an alternative for you, a different way out, a new life maybe. Leave the old life behind, all or nothing. Beijing Craps."

Jack said dryly, "You're Nevvar Graf, aren't you? You really are."

The boy released Solly's hand and came back to Jack, looked up at him, his eyes bright with mischief. "I really am. And what you're looking at is proof. Look at me, I'm five years old! And that's the magic of Beijing Craps. You win, you can live your life all over again!"

Solly nodded toward the table where the white-haired men and women were rasping their breath on to the dice. "What if you lose?"

"You won't lose. You're too good. You know you're too good."

Jack stepped up to the table and inspected the layout. "So what's in it for you?" he wanted to know. "Why'd you want me to play?"

The boy smiled more gently now. "Same as always, Jack. The odds favor the house, and I'm the house."

"Explain it to me," said Jack.

The boy came up and stood beside him. "It's pretty much the same as a regular dice game. You pick up the dice, you make your bet, you shoot; other players fade your bet. The only difference is that we use special dice. You want to take a look?"

Jack looked across the table at the withered yellow-faced old man who was holding the dice. He had never seen such an expression of dumb panic in anybody's eyes in his whole life—not even on the faces of trust-fund managers who had just gambled away their clients' investments, or husbands who had just lost their houses.

"Mr. Fortunato, will you pass me the dice for just a moment?" asked the boy.

Old Mr. Fortunato hesitated for one moment, the dice held protectively in the cage-like claw of his hand.

"Come on, Mr. Fortunato," the boy coaxed; Fortunato at last dropped them into the boy's open palm. The boy passed them carefully to Jack.

They were greenish-black, these dice, and they tingled and glowed. Holding them in his hand, Jack felt as if the ground were sliding away beneath his feet—like jet-lag or a minor earth tremor. Instead of numbers, they were engraved with tiny demonic figures—figures whose outlines crawled with static electricity.

"There are six ghosts on each dice," the boy explained. "If you shoot Yo Huang—this one—and Kuan-yin Pusa—this one—that's roughly the same as throwing a seven in craps; and if you shoot Yo Huang and Chung Kuei—here—that's just about the same as throwing eleven. In either case, these are the Beijing equivalent of naturals, okay, and you win. Yo Huang was the Lord of the Skies; Kuan-yin Pusa was a good and great sorceress. Chung Kuei was known as the Protector Against Evil Spirits."

Jack slowly rubbed the dice between finger and thumb. "That's three ghosts. What are the other three?"

"Well," smiled the boy. "They're the bad guys. This one with the hood is Shui-Mu, the Chinese Water Demon; and this little dwarf guy is Hsu Hao, who changes joy to misery; and this is Yama the Judge of Hell, who was the first mortal ever to die—and do you know why?"

"I have a feeling you're going to tell me," said Jack.

The boy smiled. "He was the first mortal ever to die because he traveled down the road from whence there is no return."

Solly licked his lips. "The road from whence there is no return? What's that?"

The boy turned and looked at him slyly. "You're traveling down it already, my friend. You should know."

"Let me feel those dice," Solly demanded.

Jack closed his fingers over them. "Solly . . . maybe you shouldn't."

"Oh yeah? And any particular reason why not? Seeing as how I'm already supposed to be taking the hike with no return?"

There was such a crackling charge of power from the dice that Jack felt as if every nerve in the palm of his hand was wriggling and twitching—centipedes under the skin. He had the irrational but terrible feeling the dice wanted Solly very badly. The dice knew Solly was there and they were hungry for him.

Solly held out his hand and Jack reluctantly dropped the dice one after the other into his palm. Solly said nothing, but something passed across his eyes like a shadow across a doorway. There was no telling what Solly could feel. Jack suspected the dice felt different for everybody who held them. It depended on your needs. It depended on your weaknesses.

"So you place your bet," said Jack, without taking his eyes away from Solly. "What do you bet? Your soul, something like that?"

"Oh, no, nothing as melodramatic as that. Anyway, what's a soul worth? Nothing. A soul is like a marker. Once the guy's dead, how's he going to pay?"

"So what's the stake?" Jack persisted.

"Months, that's what you bet," the boy told him. From the other side of the table, Mr. Fortunato hadn't lost sight of the dice for one moment, and when the boy said "months," he shivered, as if the boy had said "millions."

"Months?" asked Solly.

The boy nodded, and then held out his hand for the dice. "The shooter bets as many months as he wants, and the other players collectively put up an equal number of months. Lunar months, that is, Chinese months. The rest of the players can bet amongst themselves too, whether the shooter comes or don't come, except in Beijing Craps we say dies-a-little or lives-a-little; and there are hard-way bets too, just like regular craps, whether the shooter throws two Yo Huangs or two Chung Kueis, or whether he digs himself a grave and throws two Yamas."

"But if you win, what?" asked Solly hoarsely.

"If you win, you win months, that's what. Two, three months; maybe a year; maybe two years, depending what you've bet."

Solly looked around, found himself a chair, dragged it over, and sat down. His breathing was harsh and irregular. "You mean you actually get younger?"

The boy giggled. "Look at me, Solly! Nevvar Graf, five years old!"

Solly rubbed his mouth with his hand, as if he were trying to smear away the taste of greasy hamburger. "Jack," he said. "Jack, we got to give this a shot."

Jack shook his head. "Forget it," he said, although his throat was dry. "I play for money. Months, what's a month? Who wants to play for months?"

The boy shrugged. "What do they say? Time is money. Money is time. It's all the same. You ought to try it, Jack, you'll like it. I mean, let's put it this way. Keeping yourself in toupees and hotel rooms is one thing, but being ten years younger, that's something else. How about fifteen years younger, Jack? How about twenty years younger? How about walking away from this table tonight the same age you were when you first started gambling, with your whole life ahead of you, all over again? No more crap tables, no more cards, no more cigar smoke, no more shills. How about a wife and a family, Jack, the way your life was always meant to be?"

"How the hell do you know how my life was always meant to be?" Jack retorted.

The boy's eyes gleamed. "I've been working in this business all my life, Jack. You're just one of a million. The International Brotherhood of Optimistic Suckers."

Jack looked at the table; at Solly; at the mean green lamp; at the strange assortment of faces around the layout. He knew with suffocating certainty that he would have to play before he left. Elaine had died in his arms; Roddy had dwindled to a Kodak photograph tucked in his wallet. The chance of starting over burned in the darkness of his present existence like the molten line of the setting sun burning on the western horizon. To go back! To catch up the sun!

He heard himself saying, "Solly and me, we'll watch for a while."

"Hey, you can watch," Solly told him, abruptly standing up, sniffing, and clearing his throat. "Me, I'm going to play."

"Solly . . ." Jack warned, but the boy touched one finger against his lips to silence him.

"We're all playing for time here, Jack. We're playing for life. It's your own decision; it's Solly's own decision."

Jack looked at Solly—tried for the first time in a coon's age to look like a friend, somebody who cared, although he didn't find it easy. To the professional craps player, no expression comes easy.

The boy said, "You'll have to change. There's a Chinese screen in the corner, and plenty of robes."

"Change?" Solly said. "Why?"

"You might win, Solly," the boy smiled at him. "You might win big. And if you win big, you might find yourself ten years old all over again. And how would a ten-year-old boy look, hmh? in a 38-chest sport coat like yours?"

Solly nodded. "Sure. You're right. I'll change. For sure. If I lose, though, you won't take my suit for collateral?"

"You're a kidder, Solly," the boy grinned at him. "You're a genuine platinum-plated kidder."

Solly disappeared behind the Chinese screen; while everybody edgily waited for him, the boy whistled *Jeanie with the Light Brown Hair* over and over.

At last Solly emerged in his black silk robe. He looked like an invalid on his way to hydro-therapy. He smiled nervously, first at the rest of the players, then at Nevvar Graf, then at Jack.

Jack hesitated and then stepped back. He didn't shake Solly's hand. He didn't say a word. He knew he was just as much a victim as Solly.

"All right," said the boy, smacking his hands. "Let's play Beijing Craps!"

From out of the shadows at the back of the room three Chinese and a Burmese appeared, dressed in the Golden Lode uniform of over-tight black tuxedo and frilled shirtfront. The boy said, "Same as regular craps; a boxman, a stickman, and two dealers. In Beijing Craps, though, we call them Tevodas, which means witnesses who can testify to somebody's sins."

It was Mr. Fortunato's turn to roll. Solly stood beside him, watching him with naked eagerness. "Six months," Mr. Fortunato declared, and placed six shimmering gold tokens in front of him—tokens that shone brighter than the bottle-green lamp.

"Two weeks he dies a little," whispered a white-haired old man from the far corner of the table.

126

"One month he lives a little," said the twelve-year-old girl.

Jack looked at her closely for the first time and realized her hair had been permanent waved in the style of a woman who was old enough to be her mother.

"One week he dies a little," said one of the oldest players, a woman whose skull was showing through her skin. Her shriveled hand placed one of her last gold tokens on to the square marked with the face of Yama.

When all the bets had been placed, Mr. Fortunato gasped on the dice and rolled them. They sparkled and bounced, leaving fluorescent after-images of Chinese ghosts melting in the air over the tabletop. Yo-Hang and Kuan-yin Pusa. Mr. Fortunato won his six months.

"Mr. Fortunato lives a little," intoned the Tevoda as he collected the dice and handed them back. Mr. Fortunato breathed a little more easily on the dice this time, but the old woman who had lost a week betting he would die a little had begun to shudder. Jack swallowed and looked at the blond-haired boy, who simply grinned.

Mr. Fortunato bet another six months and rolled again. He threw Kuan-yin Pusa and Shui-Mu. The blond-haired boy leaned toward Jack and whispered, "He's won again. In Chinese magic, Kuan-yin Pusa trapped Shui-Mu by feeding her with noodles which turned into chains in her stomach and locked her guts up for good. Throwing Kuan-yin Pusa and Shui-Mu is like a point in craps; what Mr. Fortunato has to do now is throw them again. But if he throws Yo-Hang and Kuan-yin Pusa again, he loses."

Jack watched every roll of the dice intently—especially the side bets. Some of the players were picking up weeks here and there with easy bets; others lost one month after another with hard-way bets. Live-a-little, die-a-little. Their lives ebbed and flowed with every roll.

Mr. Fortunato bet a whole year, threw a crap, and lost it. Twelve months of his life swallowed in an instant. Who knows what age Mr. Fortunato had been when he started playing this game. Forty? Seventy? Twenty-two? It didn't matter. His age was determined by the dice now; his life depended on Beijing Craps. He coughed and wheezed with stress and badly-concealed terror; he passed the dice to Solly with fingers he could scarcely manage to open. Nobody else at the table showed any compassion. The blond boy had aged by three years since Mr. Fortunato had started playing and was far taller and more composed; the woman with the skull-like face seemed to have shrunk in her black silk robe almost to nothing, more like a bewildered vivisected monkey than a human.

Jack caught Solly's eyes but he remained impassive. They were professionals, both of them. They helped each other on the tables when the dice were rolling, but they never ventured to give each other criticism or personal advice or to warn each other to back off, no matter how cold the table, no matter how vertiginous the bet. You want to fly, you want to die? That's your business. Under the lights, out on the center, there was nobody else but you and Madame Luck.

"Solly," said Jack, but the adolescent Mr. Graf shot him a glance as hard as a carpet tack and Jack said nothing else.

Solly bet six months. He jiggled the dice in the palms of his hands and breathed on them, then he whispered something and he rolled. They had once called Solly the Arm of Atlantic City; his arm didn't fail him now. The dice bounced, glowed, tumbled, and came up Kuan-yin Pusa and Yo Huang. Next he bet a year and threw another natural. He threw again and won again. Roll after roll, he played like a genius; he played like Jack had never seen him play before. With each win, he gradually began to look younger. His gray hairs wriggled out of sight, his wrinkles unfolded like a played-back film of crumpled wrapping-paper. He stood taller, straighter, and played with even more confidence; all the other players bet along with him, hard-way bets, right bets, they shed years and years in front of Jack's eyes. After twenty minutes, he was watching a game played by young, good-looking, vigorous people—attractive young women and smiling young men. Their shriveled skin was plumper and pinker; their hair was thick and shiny; their voices roared with vigor and health.

"How about some champagne?" called Mr. Fortunato. A twelve-year-old Mr. Graf snapped his fingers to one of the girls. "Bring these people champagne."

Jack didn't bet. Not yet. He was tempted to, but he wanted to bide his time. He wanted to see the losing side of this game as well as the winning side. He wanted to work out the odds. And although Solly was winning, and consistently winning, it occurred to Jack that the younger he became, the less experienced he became, the more risks he was prepared to take, the wilder his arm.

"Ten years!" grinned a 24-year-old Solly, shaking the dice in his hands. "I'm betting ten years! Fourteen again, and screw the zits!"

He rolled. The dice glowed, shimmered, sparkled. They bounced off the cushion on the opposite side of the layout, but then they seemed almost to slow down, as if they were bouncing through transparent glue. The ghosts glowed malevolently for all to see. Yama and Shui-Mu. Craps. An entire decade was silently sucked from Solly's body and soul and he visibly shuddered.

After that—as far as Solly was concerned—the table turned as cold as a graveyard. Mr. Graf was shooting, winning a little here and a little there, but Solly was stacking his counters on all the impossible bets, trying to win time, trying to win time, but losing it with every roll. When Mr. Graf finally missed, Solly was white-haired and on the verge of respiratory collapse. He sat hunched over the opposite side of the table, his hands dry like desert thorns, his head bowed.

Jack approached him but didn't touch him. Bad karma to touch him, no matter what affection he felt.

"Solly," he said thickly, "pull out now. You've lost, Solly. Call it quits."

Solly raised his head and stared at Jack with filmy eyes. His neck hung in a brown-measled wattle.

"One more bet," he whispered.

"Solly, for God's sake, you're falling apart. You look about a hundred years old."

Solly wasn't amused. "I'm eighty-seven, two months, and three days exactly, you unctuous bastard, thanks very much. And if I win another thirty on the next roll, I'll be only fifty-seven. And if I bet another thirty after that . . . well, then, I'll be happy to quit. Life was good to me when I was twenty-seven. Twenty-seven is a pretty good age."

Jack said nothing. If Solly bet thirty years and won, then Jack would be happy for him. But if he bet thirty years and lost .
. .

He looked at Mr. Graf, who had lost six or seven years betting on Solly's last roll and was looking much older again. He looked like the Mr. Graf Jack had seen hurrying in and out of the Golden Lode, hedged in by minders and shills and hard-faced accountants. Mr. Graf's eyes turned like a lizard's toward Solly. What could he say? Solly had lost, and those who lost were always hooked. Those who won were hooked too.

"You're not playing, Mr. Druce. It's your roll if you're playing."

"If it's all the same to you, I think I'll stay out of it,' said Jack, although perspiration was sliding from his armpits, and his fingernails were clenched into the palms of his hands.

"Sure thing. It's all the same to me," said Mr. Graf, immediately offering the dice to Mr. Fortunato.

With the unashamed greed of the truly fearful, Mr. Fortunato held out his hand.

"Wait, Jack!" wheezed Solly. He took hold of Jack's sleeve and twisted it, then he bent his head close so Jack could smell his unexpected age—chalk and cloves and geriatric staleness. "Jack, you're the best arm there ever was. If anybody can win back those years for me, you can. Jack, I'm begging you, Jack. We never did nothing for each other, did we? Never expected nothing, never asked for nothing. You know that. But I'm asking you now, Jack. I'm down on my knees. If you let Fortunato shoot next, I'm dead meat, Jack. I'm gone. You know that."

Jack sniffed the way a heroin addict sniffs. He feared this game of Beijing Craps more than any game he had ever come across. It had all the glamor of punto banco and all the fascinating horror of standing in front of a speeding express train. He knew if he rolled those dice just once, he would be caught for good.

Mr. Graf sensed his hesitation, however, and held the glowing dice suspended in the air just two inches above Mr. Fortunato's open hand. Jack could almost see the nerves crawling with anticipation in Mr. Fortunato's palm.

Solly tugged his sleeve even tighter. "Jack, for old time's sake, I'm pleading with you now. I never pled before. I never pled to nobody. But please."

Jack hesitated for one more second. He didn't need to look at his watch. He never did. He knew what time it was. He loosened his necktie and said, "Give me a minute to change, all right?"

He undressed behind the screen. The black dragon robe was cold and silky on his skin. He tightened the sash and reemerged; Mr. Graf was still waiting, still smiling.

Jack approached Nevvar Graf and slowly held out his hand. Mr. Graf smiled secretively and dropped the dice into Jack's palm. They tumbled and turned as slowly as if they didn't particularly care for gravity. When they touched Jack's palm, they felt like fire and ice and naked voltage.

The players gathered around the table again. The lamp was so dim all Jack could see of their faces was smudges of paleness in the shadows. He shook the dice and tiny grave-worms of bluish fluorescence wriggled out from between his fingers. He bet six months and stood back waiting while the side bets were placed.

He threw the dice across the table. They jumped and sparkled with even more brilliance than they had before.

"You see that?" asked Mr. Graf slyly. "Even the *dice* know when an expert is throwing."

Jack had come out with Chung Kuei and Yo Huang. Solly clenched his fists and breathed. "All *right!* You goddamned brilliant son of a bitch!"

Jack threw again—Kuan-yin Pusa and Chung Kuei. He threw them on the next roll as well and picked up a whole year. He didn't *feel* any different, but it was stimulating to think he was a whole year younger.

He continued to win again and again and again, living a little and living a little more, throwing naturals and points as swiftly and confidently as if the dice were loaded—which, in a strange way, they were. The years fell away from him with every win, until he was betting two and three years at a time, and his black silk robe began to hang loosely around his slim twenty-two-year-old frame.

Solly placed numbers to win with almost every throw and gradually won back the years he had lost before. He played cautiously, however, and didn't risk more than a year a time, until he reached forty-five.

Then, just as Jack was about to throw again, he placed a hard-way bet of twenty years.

Jack looked at him sharply, but Solly grinned and winked. "One last throw, my friend, and then I'm going to walk away and never come back."

But Jack felt something in the dice, as if they had shrunk and tightened in the palm of his hand and had suddenly gone cold. The dice were not going to let Solly go.

Jack said, "Twenty years on one throw, Solly? That's a hell of a bet."

"That's the last bet ever," said Solly. "You just do your bit and let me take care of myself."

Jack threw the dice. They dropped leadenly onto the layout, scarcely bouncing at all. They came up Shui-Mu and Hsua Hao; a win for Jack, but Solly had bet Shui-Mu and Shui-Mu and he immediately aged by twenty years.

Jack was only a little over twenty years old now. He stood straighter and taller and his hair was thick and wavy and brown. He took off his toupee and crammed it into the pocket of his robe. Mr. Graf smiled at him. "Hair today, gone tomorrow, huh, Mr. Druce?"

Jack scooped up the dice and prepared to throw them again. As he did so, Solly put down the gleaming tokens that showed he was staking another twenty years.

"Solly!" Jack said. .

Solly looked up.

"Don't do it, Solly," Jack warned in a clear and youthful voice, although he realized he didn't really care too much whether Solly lost another twenty years or not. Look at the guy, he was practically dead already.

"Just throw, will you?" Solly growled at him.

Jack threw and won, but Solly lost yet again, and so did two or three others at the table. Jack heard a sharp, harsh intake of breath from Solly, then Solly staggered and gripped the edge of the table to stop himself from falling.

"Solly? You okay?"

Solly's eyes bulged and his face was blue from lack of oxygen. "What do you care?" he gasped. "Will you shoot, for God's sake? Just shoot!"

Mr. Graf was very young again—a small boy peering over the dimly lit center of the table. He said to Solly, with utmost calmness, "Do you want an ambulance, sir? Or maybe I should call the house physician?"

"Shoot, that's all," Solly insisted, and placed another twenty years on the table.

Jack slowly juggled the dice. Fire and honey in his hand. "Solly . . . you understand what could happen if you lose?"

"Shoot," hissed Solly through false teeth too large for his shrunken gums.

"Go on," urged Mr. Fortunato, although he too was ancient, with sunken, ink-stained eyes and wispy white hair.

Jack shrugged, shook the dice, and threw.

Suddenly the dice crackled with new vitality. They bounced on the opposite cushion and tumbled across the table in a cascade of glowing Chinese images, coming to rest right in front of Solly.

Yama and Hsua Hao.

Solly lost.

"I—" he gargled.

Traceries of light had already crept out of the dice, trembling and flickering like static electricity. They forked across the baize to the tips of Solly's fingers. Silently, enticingly—right in front of Jack's eyes—the light crept up Solly's arms and entwined themselves around him in a brilliant cage.

"*Solly!*" Jack shouted.

But Solly began to shudder uncontrollably. His hair was lifted up on end and white sparks began to shower out of his nose and eyes. He looked as if fierce fireworks had been ignited inside his head.

Jack heard a noise that was somewhere between a sob and a scream, and then Solly collapsed onto his knees, although his fingers still clung to the edge of the table. Twitching electricity streamed out of his body, shrinking down his arms and pouring out of his fingertips, back across the craps table and into the dice. They vanished into the ghosts on the dice like disappearing rats' tails, then Solly dropped backward onto the floor, his skull hitting the polished wood with a hollow knock.

The dice remained on the table, softly glowing, as if Solly's life had given them renewed energy.

"Well, Mr. Druce?" asked Nevvar Graf. "We're waiting."

Jack looked down at Solly's crumpled, dried-up body, and then at Nevvar Graf, then back at the dice. The haunted circle of faces watched him expectantly.

"No," he said. "That's it. I'm out."

"You still have five years on the table, Mr Druce. You'll lose your five years. Rules of the game."

"I'm only twenty-two now. What do five years matter?"

Mr. Graf smiled. "Ask Mr. Fortunato what five years matter. It's an education, Beijing Craps. It teaches you that the time you throw away when you're young, you'll bitterly regret when you're old. Beijing Craps teaches you the value of life, Mr. Druce. What does a month matter to a bored teenage kid? Nothing. He hopes that month will pass as soon as possible. But tell me what a month matters to a man with only one month left to live."

Jack took a deep, steadying breath. "Whatever, I'm out."

"You'll be back."

"Well, we'll just have to see about that."

"All right," shrugged Mr. Graf. "Carlos, will you escort Mr. Druce out of the casino? And make sure you pay him his winnings. Thank you, Mr. Druce. You have a rare skill with the ivories."

Jack changed back into his loose seersucker suit. Before he left, he nodded to the circle of players. One or two of them nodded back, but most of them seemed to have forgotten him already. Carlos took Jack's arm—the first time anybody in the casino had touched him—and led Jack out into the bright, glittering world of the Golden Lode.

When he had cashed his winnings, Jack went across to the *punto banco* table. He watched the game for a while, considering a couple of bets. A bleached-blonde girl standing next to him was screaming with excitement as she won her first hand. After Beijing Craps, the idea of playing for money seemed absurdly petty to Jack. He glanced back toward the staircase that led up to Mr. Graf's private craps game. Carlos was still standing at the top of the stairs; he gave Jack a smile like curdled milk.

Jack knew then he would never escape. He would be back at that table, no matter how hard he tried to resist. Maybe not tomorrow, maybe not next week. Maybe not for years, but he would be back.

No real gambler could resist the temptation of playing for his very life.

He left the Golden Lode and stepped out on to the hot, brilliantly bright sidewalk. He had started playing Beijing Craps at two o'clock in the morning, and now it was well past nine. For the first time in a long time he felt hungry. He decided to go back to his hotel room to shower and change, and then to treat himself to a meal of prime rib and fried zucchini. He could wear his Armani suit—his *real* suit.

135

The sidewalk was crowded with shuffling tourists and squalling kids. Las Vegas wasn't what it used to be in the days of the mob. Bugsy Siegel would have rolled over in his desert grave to see creches and stroller parks and family restaurants, and hookers being turned away from casino doors. But Jack didn't care. He had found himself the ultimate game, even in this sanitized Las Vegas, and he was twenty-seven again. He'd forgotten how much strength and energy he used to have, at twenty-seven—how light and easy it was to walk.

He went up to his hotel room, humming along to the Muzak in the elevator. *Raindrops keep fallin' on my head . . . they keep fallin.' . . .* He boogied along the corridor, chafing his feet on the nylon carpet, and when he reached for the door handle, there was a sharp crackling spark of static.

To his surprise, however, his door was half an inch ajar. He hesitated, then pushed it wide. The room appeared to be empty, but you never knew. There were plenty of scumbags who followed gamblers back to their hotel rooms and forcibly relieved them of their winnings.

"Anybody there?" he called, stepping into the room.

The bed was made and there was no utility cart around, so it couldn't have been the maids. Maybe the door had been left open by accident. He went over to the bureau and tugged open the drawers. His gold cufflinks were still there; so was his Gucci ballpen and five hundred dollars in small bills.

He was just about to turn around and close the door, however, when he heard it softly click shut by itself. A voice said, "Freeze, buddy. Stay right where you are."

He stood up straight. In the mirror on top of the bureau, he saw a young man step out from behind the drapes, holding a handgun—a .32 by the look of it, although Jack didn't know much about guns.

"Looking for some loose change?" the young man asked him.

"Maybe I should ask you the same question," Jack replied.

The young man came around and faced him. He was pale and thin-faced and haggard, dressed in worn-out denims.

"I'm not looking for trouble," he told Jack. "Maybe you should turn around and walk back out of that door and we'll forget the whole thing."

"I'm not going anyplace," Jack retorted. "This is my room."

"Un-unh," the young man grinned. "I know whose room this is. This is Mr. Druce's room, and you sure as hell aren't Mr. Druce.'

"Of course I'm Mr. Druce. Who do you think I am?"

"Don't kid me," the young man told him, raising his pistol higher. "Mr. Druce just happens to be my father, and there's no way *you're* my father, buddy."

Jack stared at him. "Mr. Druce is your *father?*"

The young man nodded. "You sound like you know him."

"Know him? I *am* him."

"Are you out of your tree or what?" the young man said. "You're not much older than me. How the hell can you be my father?"

"How the hell can you be my son?" Jack replied. "My son is three years old."

"Oh, yes? Well, that's very interesting. But right now I think you'd better *vamos,* don't you, before Mr. Druce gets back and finds you here."

Jack said, "Listen, I think we've gotten our lines crossed here. You must be looking for the wrong Mr. Druce. I'm Jack Druce, this is my room, and there's no way in the world you can be my son, because look . . ."

Jack reached inside his suit for his wallet and his Kodak photograph of Roddy by the pool. The young man instantly cocked his handgun and tensed up. "Freeze! Freeze! Keep your hands where I can see them!"

"But if I showed you—"

The young man screamed, *"Freeze!"* again and fired. The bullet hit Jack in the right side of his head and burst out through the back of his skull. Blood and brains were thrown against the yellow flock wallpaper.

He's killed me, Jack thought. *I can't believe it. The punk's gone and killed me.*

He opened and closed his mouth, then his knees folded up under him and he collapsed on to the floor.

The hotel dwindled away from him like a lighted television picture falling down an endless elevator shaft, until finally it winked out.

Shaking, the young man hunkered down beside Jack and reached into his blood-spattered coat for the wallet. He flicked through it. Over ten thousand dollars in thousand-dollar bills. Jesus. This guy must've made some killing.

He found a creased Kodak photograph of a small boy next to a swimming pool. He stared at it for a long time. For some inexplicable reason, he found it disturbingly familiar. Must be the guy's son. It was weird, the way he'd kept insisting his name was Jack Druce.

The young man stood up, unsure about what to do next. He couldn't wait here for his father any longer; he didn't really have to. He'd only come to Las Vegas to ask him for money, and now he had all the money he could possibly want.

He crammed the bills into the pocket of his denim jacket and stuffed his handgun back into the top of his jeans. He took one last look at the man lying dead on the carpet before he left.

He walked along the sidewalk, glancing at every middle-aged man who passed him by. He wondered if he would recognize his father if he ever chanced to meet him. He wondered if his father would recognize *him*.

He passed the Golden Lode Casino. Standing on the steps outside was a young boy, no more than seven years old, wrapped in a black Chinese robe. The young boy was smiling to himself, almost beatifically, as if he were a god.

Roderick Druce smiled at him and the boy smiled back.

Graham Masterton made his fiction debut in 1975 with The Manitou, *the story of a three-hundred-year-old Native American shaman who is reborn in the present day to take his revenge on the white man. A huge bestseller, it was made into a classic movie starring Tony Curtis.*

Since then, Graham has written over a hundred novels—horror novels, thrillers, short stories, historical romances, and sex instruction books such as How To Drive Your Man Wild In Bed. Before he took up writing novels he was editor of Penthouse magazine. It was there that he met his late wife Wiescka, who became his agent and sold The Manitou in her native Poland even before the collapse of Communism—the first Western horror novel to be published in Poland since World War Two.

Apart from five Manitou novels, Graham has also published the Rook series, about a remedial English teacher who recruits his slacker class to fight ill-intentioned ghosts and demons; the Night Warriors series, about ordinary people who battle against apocalyptic terrors in their dreams; as well as many other supernatural thrillers, including Family Portrait, The Pariah and Mirror, which were all published simultaneously in July, 2011, as part of the new book imprint by Hammer Films.

Graham Masterton was born in Edinburgh in 1946, the grandson of John Masterton, the chief inspector of mines for Scotland, and Thomas Thorne Baker, the scientist who was the first man to send photographs by wireless. He was expelled from school at the age of 17 and became a trainee newspaper reporter, joining the new men's magazine Mayfair as deputy editor at the age of 21 and taking over Penthouse when he was 24.

He wrote his first novel in 1967, a highly experimental thriller entitled Rules of Duel, with the encouragement and input of the late William Burroughs, author of The Naked Lunch, whom he befriended when Burroughs lived in London. This was recently published for the first time by Telos Books.

Graham and Wiescka Masterton lived in Ireland from 1999 to 2003. Graham has recently finished Broken Angels, a crime thriller with a tinge of the supernatural set in Cork. He has also finished Community, a sci-fi/ghost thriller set in Northern

California, and Garden of Lies, *the eighth novel in the* Jim Rook series.

A new collection of short stories, Festival of Fear, *was published in January,* 2012, *and a new novel about his fortune-telling heroine Sissy Sawyer,* The Red Hotel, *was published in June,* 2012. *He is now working on a new disaster novel and many other projects.*

Since Wiescka passed away in April, 2011, *Graham's agent is Camilla Shestopal at PFD in London: cshestopal@pfd.co.uk. His website is www.grahammasterton.co.uk*

Shattered Mirrors and Smokeless Flames

Angeline Hawkes

Indeed We created man from dried clay of black smooth mud. And We created the Jinn before that from the smokeless flame of fire.—Surat Hijr 15,26–27; *The Holy Quran*

The sun hung heavy in the sky, sweltering rays beating mercilessly. Rippling waves of heat sizzled from golden sands blowing in swirling crests over the courtyard and against the stone walls of the town home. A lush garden swayed in the gentle breeze—the emerald greens vibrant against the browns of the arid desert that threatened to engulf all in its path.

Janna let the gauzy curtain slide out of her hand and drop into a silky puddle against the crimson carpet on the floor. "It's good that you came to see me then," she said, her full lips curling into a smile.

"Thank you so much for the herbs and the Fenugreek, but I shouldn't have stayed so long. Yusuf will be looking for me," Aisha said, picking up her hijab from the couch and lifting it towards her head. "I should go."

Janna stepped forward and gently grasped the edge of the veil. "Don't go yet. Stay and have tea. This house is so empty and I'm alone. It's too quiet."

Aisha sighed. "How can I leave a friend who's so sad?" She laughed softly. "I'll stay for tea. It's the least I can do after you've helped me with my . . ." she paused. "difficult matters."

Janna nodded in understanding, patting Aisha on the arm. "Just keep those herbs for the next time you find yourself in this predicament. If you take the herbs immediately it'll be much easier and with less bleeding than this time. Yusuf need never know."

"It's not Yusuf I worry about—it's Anwar."

"You have yourself tangled between two webs, my friend." Janna put a pot of water onto the fire to boil.

Aisha sighed loudly and slicked her hands over her ebony tresses. "But what am I to do? I love Anwar, but Yusuf loves me."

"And both Anwar and you will find yourselves a head shorter if Yusuf ever grows wiser. Maybe a baby would be better after all. Anwar doesn't look much different than Yusuf—Yusuf would never suspect."

"Anwar could never stand it," Aisha said. "It would kill him. He loves me so much, but tells me a baby would cost me my life if it were ever discovered to be his and not my husband's."

"Tell Anwar it's Yusuf's babe—and let Anwar go—or you'll be caught in your own web soon enough. How many times have you resorted to the Fenugreek now?"

"I care not to count the number. And each time, I'm not sure if it's Anwar's or my husband's child I kill. Since I don't know, I must not take the risk. I fear Allah will punish me."

"Oh, he *will*. He *always* does when great sins have been committed. It's the way it is. You should let *me* love you instead of *Anwar*—nothing to show for your indiscretions." Janna laughed and poured the water over the tea leaves. "Which sin is greater? Does it matter now? You could find peace in my arms."

Shaking her head, Aisha said, "I couldn't—no, I couldn't."

Janna passed a ceramic cup to Aisha. "I think you could."

Aisha drank, casting shy, nervous glances toward her friend. "I do find you beautiful, but I. . . ."

"Just drink the tea," Janna said. She blew on the steaming golden liquid, drinking in small sips. Setting down her cup, she reached for her instrument and strummed the strings delicately—music filling the air—serenading Aisha with the melody that sprang to life beneath her long fingers. The notes sang, enveloping them, drawing them within the spell of the calming song.

Putting her hand to her eyes, Aisha leaned into the cushions. She moaned as she rubbed her temples.

"Is my playing so poor?"

"No, no. My head. I feel . . . tired."

Janna moved closer to Aisha and smoothed her friend's long hair. Aisha pitched forward—dizzily and off-balance—into Janna's embrace.

"Ssh, you're only emotionally drained from the strain of dealing with two foolish men. Let me help you relax," Janna cooed, cupping Aisha's chin, tilting Aisha's face and kissing her pink lips.

Aisha withdrew slightly. She reclined further on the couch. "Yusuf?"

"Will *never* suspect. The silly man doesn't even know you warm Anwar's bed. He'd never imagine the pleasures I can bring to you. I'm quite certain he isn't capable of envisioning such matters."

Head lulling to one side, Aisha's eyelids fluttered; her breathing slowed. She sluggishly waved a hand. "He's much too trusting."

Janna kissed Aisha's neck and face, pushing her blue and gold embroidered dress off her shoulders, covering her full breasts with more kisses. "As are you, my pet," Janna said, and taking Aisha's hand, led her stumbling into the bedroom.

* * *

When night came and swallowed the sun, a knock sounded at Janna's door. Loudly the pounding filled the courtyard and Janna came rushing to answer it.

When she opened the door, she found Yusuf pacing on her steps. "Yusuf, it's late. What is it?" She held the lantern higher, engulfing him in the beam of the single flame.

Yusuf looked through the street and back at Janna. "Have you seen Aisha?"

"Not since last week."

"She said she was having head pains and was seeking help from Ta Rekhet," Yusuf persisted.

"I'm not the only healing woman in this town, Yusuf."

"Yes, yes, I know. I just thought that since you were friends that she'd come to you."

"Not this time. How long have you been looking? You look exhausted," Janna said, opening the door wider.

"Since night fell. I haven't had dinner and I'm beside myself with worry over her failure to come home. The goat needs milked and there are other chores. She's never let me go hungry before."

"Come inside. I'll make you something to eat. Aisha's probably visiting with friends and time has escaped her. It's easy to do when in good company." Janna laughed. "Come inside. You still need to eat, even if Aisha isn't home yet. You're right, it isn't like her to forsake her responsibilities. A good wife would never allow her husband to go hungry while she chatters like a magpie with her friends."

"Thank you, it's kind of you. I'm sure you're right. Aisha loves to talk." Yusuf came inside, crossing the splendid courtyard with its fountain and garden, and followed Janna into the house. He'd been to visit before, but always in the company of his wife.

"I have harisa and goat cheese. Is this acceptable?"

"Of course. Whatever you wish to serve. I cannot thank you enough. You should be blessed with a fine husband as dutiful as you seem." Yusuf sat on the couch as Janna left the room. He looked through the window into the dark courtyard, but without the lantern he could see nothing beyond the narrow slice of light coming from the window.

After a few minutes, he smelled the meat and the wheat frying—the aroma wafting through the house. Janna brought out a platter heaped with fresh fruit, cheese, harisa, and wine.

Yusuf took a fig from the platter and bit it, juice spurting over his chin.

"I've already eaten or I'd join you. I'll have a little wine, though," Janna said with a smile. She poured wine into two cups.

Yusuf returned her smile but glanced nervously at the floor, unaccustomed to being in a room with an unveiled woman not of his family. "Yes, do share the wine." He fidgeted with his napkin and studied his fig closely.

Janna laughed musically, causing Yusuf to look up and into her green eyes, which she had fixed upon him.

"I make you nervous, don't I?" she asked.

"No, it's just, I, you—"

"I can put on my hijab if it would put you at ease."

"No. It's your home."

"Are you certain?" Janna asked, sipping her wine. She ran her tongue over her lips seductively—purposely tormenting the handsome Yusuf.

He cast his eyes to the floor once more. "I'm certain," he said in a voice that made it clear he was indeed uncertain and uncomfortable with her behavior.

He ate his food hurriedly, as if he couldn't wait to be finished and out of Janna's presence.

Drinking his wine, Yusuf looked around the room. Rich carpets decorated the walls and floors. Shelves displayed beautiful pottery intricately painted with geometric designs.

"That must have cost a pretty dinar," he said, looking past her.

"What? The floor?" she asked, following his eyes to the blue and white mosaic tiling on her bedroom floor, visible behind the open velvet curtains hanging from the doorframe.

"It's exquisite. Did a local artisan do it?"

Janna shook her head. "No, a traveling artist crafted it for me in exchange for his life."

Yusuf choked momentarily, wiping his wine-dribbled chin with his napkin. "Was he ill?"

"Oh, no, quite the contrary. He was the picture of health."

"But you said he crafted it for you in exchange for his life. You must've healed him from something terrible."

Janna smiled. "No."

"You're being modest. Your talents must be great."

"Oh, they are. That's why I don't live in one place for too long. I feel it's my duty to Allah to heal as many as I can. There are so many in need of ministrations. Man is such a frail creature and the powers of the wicked threaten to weaken him further with illness and misery of all sorts. So I travel and share my talents. I think I've enjoyed my time here best of all."

"That's good. What brought you here?" Yusuf drank from his goblet, finally relaxing under the wine's effects.

"Beauty."

"What's so beautiful about our dusty town?" Yusuf asked with a laugh. "The merchants camp outside of it, filling the air with the stink of their camels' dung."

"Oh, not the town. The people. Aisha . . . you."

"Aisha? How has news of her beauty traveled?" Yusuf raised his dark brows inquisitively. "She's rarely without her hijab."

"Your beauty too, Yusuf. I didn't come just for Aisha alone."

Yusuf frowned. "You're talking in riddles."

"Great beauty draws me as honey draws flies," Janna said with a flirtatious smile.

"So you're a fly now?" Yusuf laughed, reaching for more wine. He almost knocked over his goblet with the wineskin. A fig fell from the plate and rolled under the low table.

"Here, let me help you," Janna said, pouring the wine with a steadier hand. Quietly, but in plain view, she reached inside her dress and pulled out a small, draw-stringed brocade pouch. She unknotted the gold metallic cord, opening it. Tapping the pouch over Yusuf's goblet, a black powder streamed into the purple wine, making it fizz.

"What's that? What did you put in my drink?"

"Just a little poppy to calm your nerves."

"My nerves are fine," Yusuf said, drinking the wine anyway. "I'm sure you're right about Aisha visiting her friends. I shouldn't have gotten so upset over such a trivial thing. Your wine has calmed me. I'm fine, really."

Abruptly, Janna pulled her dress over her head and tossed it onto the couch beside Yusuf. "I'm sure you're frazzled. A wife shouldn't make her husband search for her. It must be upsetting as a husband to be faced with a quest throughout town just to have some dinner. So I've given you a little poppy. And I've other plans for you."

Yusuf stared at the naked woman standing before him in a state of mingled shock and dismay. His knees knocked. His hands trembled. He wanted to feel outrage, but all that washed over him was desire. Never had a woman been so bold.

"Do you like what you see, Yusuf?" Janna purred, moving closer, swaying seductively, like a dancing serpent. Her hennaed hands brushed his beard delicately and he smelled her perfume.

"I, I," he stammered; his eyes refused to look away. His manhood hardened, forming a tall tent beneath his striped robe.

"I'm lonely, Yusuf. Aisha's been busy this week and my other friends were unable to visit. I've no family. No husband to fulfill the desires of a wife's heart—and hidden places." Her bottom lip grew pouty. "If *you* were *mine*, you'd never hunt for *me* in the streets at night. You'd never be forced to eat in the homes of others. Your bed would always be warm and your sons many."

Yusuf watched his hands explore Janna's naked body. He felt as if his arms were separate from his being, roaming the sacred places of this enchantress before him. He leaned forward and pulled Janna to her knees, catching her stiff brown nipple between his teeth, tweaking it gently. She groaned.

Janna ran her fingers over Yusuf's chest, pushing at his robes until he shrugged them off. Her fingernails raked over his back as he slipped two fingers into her. She gasped. Leaning into him, she moaned loudly.

Yusuf gripped her buttocks and lifted her onto his erection—somewhat startled that she didn't even feign resistance. She held onto his shoulders, plunging herself up and down, gyrating over and over with wicked abandon. Janna panted as waves of orgasmic pleasure cascaded over her trembling body. She flung her head backward, long hair streaming across her back and Yusuf's legs. He dug his fingers into the flesh of her backside and thrust into her. Spent at last, he collapsed into the cushions of the couch.

Peeling her sticky thighs from his, she moved next to him and whispered into his ear, "I want to show you something."

Yusuf laughed. "Go on then, you beautiful temptress. Show me what you will."

Kissing him on the lips, she looked deeply into his black eyes. "Watch closely, lover," she said and, one leg draped over his nakedness, suddenly called out:

"By wind and by air,
By the smokeless flame of fire.
Open, open, open for me . . .
Open, Rub al Khali!"

Yusuf stiffened, his eyes transfixed on the glowing rectangle forming in front of him. It hung in the air, pulsing with a golden light. Hinges and a door handle shimmered into existence.

"What's *this?*"

Janna, still naked, pulled him to his feet, guiding him toward the magic door. "Come," she commanded, holding firmly to his hand, her face radiant with happiness.

Fighting the effects of the poppy and wine, Yusuf was unable to resist her tugging. He allowed himself to be drawn through the pulsating door, holding tight to Janna's hand.

As effortlessly as he had stepped into the door, he stepped inside the room on the other side of the golden light. The door faded away in a silvery shower of sparkles.

Naked, Yusuf realized he was standing in another house—this one far more luxurious than Janna's previous one. "Is this a palace?"

Janna smiled. "Yes! This is *my* palace." She playfully yanked him to a balcony made of gleaming gold. It was daylight outside and brilliantly bright. "Behold: The Lost City of Irem!"

She waved her arm before the vast city that lay far beneath her golden balcony.

"Irem?" He looked puzzled. Confused. "Not Irem zhat al Imad?"

"Yes! It *is* the *city of the old ones* in all of its glory!" Janna leaned toward a climbing rose bush whose scarlet blooms snaked their way up the stone wall, and she inhaled deeply.

"I don't understand. *How? What?* How are we here?"

"I opened the door to Irem—Rub al Khali—this is my home. I travel far to bring my healing gifts to man."

Yusuf grew more perplexed. "I don't understand."

Janna handed him a robe of soft fabric of which he'd never felt. "Here. Put this on."

He clumsily grabbed it and slipped it over his head. He continued to stare at the amazing city below. They were so high that the city looked the size of a child's toy.

"Do you want to see the city?"

He nodded mutely.

With a wave of her hand, they descended in a quick blur of motion into a street made of white marble and began to walk.

"Janna?"

"Yes?"

"You're naked," he said, as if this thought had slowly formed in his bewildered mind and had just made its way to his mouth.

Janna laughed. "That's of no matter here, but if it'll comfort you . . ." She moved her hand up and down before her and a silver gown covered her naked body.

Yusuf stared in shock. "I don't know what you are or from where you came."

Janna giggled, leaned into him, placed a hand over her sacred place, and laughed louder. "I know where you came."

Yusuf frowned, continuing to follow her. She showed him colossal statues—elaborate pillars holding up enormous buildings. Marble. Gold. Rubies and diamonds. The splendors of the city grew as they traveled each street.

"Where is everyone?"

"Busy. There's much to do," she replied, and led him toward a high tower painted in brilliant hues.

His legs began to tire after hours of touring the great city. Before he could tell her how tired he was, they were back in the palace where they had first arrived.

Janna pushed him into a pile of velvet and silk-tasseled cushions and, saying nothing, ran her tongue over his face and into his mouth. Hungrily, he kissed her, removing the silver gown she'd adorned herself with and shoving his own robes from his body, then he drew her into his arms.

Entwined within her arms and legs, he rolled her over onto her back and found her hidden temple once more with his hardness. All of his confusion and apprehension was drowned in her rapture as a cloud of elation filled his mind and removed all misgivings. When he had spent himself, he lay on her heaving breasts. She smiled and laughed. "You have got a babe on me this time."

Yusuf's head bolted upward and he pushed himself up on his arms. "How do you know this? Oh, Aisha!" His voice revealed the acknowledgement of his betrayal. "What have I done?"

Janna's laugh took on a wicked ring. "*Aisha?* Aisha, who murdered so many of Anwar's babes before they could take root within her womb? Think not on *her,* but on the *son* that grows now in *my* belly."

Yusuf rolled to his side. "*Anwar?* What do you speak of? How do you know these *abominations?*"

"I give her the herbs to rid herself of the bastards growing in her. Your sweet Aisha loved you not."

"Loved? Past tense? What's happened to her?" Yusuf shouted, growing afraid.

"She's well. You should be overjoyed! *I* would never kill a child—*our* child." Janna took his hand and placed it on her soft belly. "I'll give you the children you richly deserve."

Horrified, he wrenched his hand from her grasp. "I must go. I must find Aisha." The spell broken, he jumped up from the cushions and frantically sought the robe he had cast off.

Janna's face distorted with anger. "You don't want to stay with *me?*"

"I must find Aisha!"

"But she's fine. I've told you this."

150

"People will be looking for me. I can't be gone long. I have many responsibilities." Yusuf looked for the door. Any door. He found only smooth walls and no exits.

"Our son will go back and fill your shoes. It's how it's done. No one will know it's not you."

"Our son?"

"He can't stay here after all. He's half human. It would be difficult for him in Irem." Janna's voice sounded sorrowful.

Yusuf backed against the wall, his expression growing more terrified. "Half? What *are* you?"

Janna looked sad. "I'd hoped you'd be different."

"Different than *what?*"

"Than the others. They never want to stay either." She sighed. "I thought you'd be different, that you'd want to stay after you learned what an adulterous whore you possess for a wife."

He turned to the wall and groped it, feeling for an indentation, a crack, anything that would show him the way out.

"You're a liar and a devil! You've bewitched me somehow. None of this is real! It's the result of the poppy you put in my wine! You've drugged me and forced me to lie with you!"

"It's been a long while since you drank the wine. You're not drunk. You weren't coerced to sin with me. And, you don't make love like a drugged man." She reached for his hand.

"Stay away from me, devil!" Yusuf darted from her reach, shouting. "I must go home! I won't stay here! I must find Aisha!"

Janna's face twisted and darkened. She flew into a rage and smashed a vase against the wall in a crazed frenzy. She screamed, tearing at her hair, clawing at her flesh—her features contorting in fury.

"Do you want to see Aisha, you stupid fool? I would've given you anything your heart desired! Anything! But you'd rather pine for the false love of your harlot wife!"

Yusuf cowered against the wall as the woman before him shucked off the flesh husk of her humanity in a screaming fit.

151

"I'll give you Aisha!" Janna's voice rumbled low. The walls of illusion around Yusuf crumbled away as Janna grew in size. Eight. Nine. Ten feet and more. She twisted and changed; snakes coiling where silken ebony locks had been moments earlier.

Her eyes flashed red as she scooped Yusuf up in an immense hand. Her curled talons twitched precariously around him, capable of slicing through him like the sharpest scimitar.

Yusuf screamed as he was held aloft over the giant room. Shelves lined the stone walls. On each shelf were rows of huge blown glass jars—blue, red, green. And in each jar, he could see a person—a human—pounding noiselessly against the glass walls.

Janna grabbed a green jar with her free hand. "Here's your *harlot!*" she shouted so loudly that the walls quaked with the echoes.

She held the jar in front of Yusuf. Aisha was inside, struggling to stand; each time Janna flinched, the movement would send Aisha flying across the jar, sprawling her against the bubbled glass.

"Aisha!" Yusuf cried, further provoking Janna. He turned to look at her, staring up into her hideous face. "I should've *known* what you were!"

Janna's deep bass laughter filled the room. Yusuf clutched his ears in pain. "And *what am* I?"

"*Janna* means to conceal. You've hidden the truth from me long enough! I *know* what you are! You are *Jinn!*"

The laughter boomed through the cold stone room again, causing all of the unfortunate captives in the jars to drop to their knees, hands clasped tightly over their ears in agony.

"Very good! See, Aisha? He's much smarter than we gave him credit for! Maybe you were right to destroy all of Anwar's bastard seed. Our Yusuf is a smart one after all!" Janna said to the terrified woman in the jar.

Raising the green jar to her mouth, Janna chomped down on the cork, popping it out. Turning the jar upside down, she dumped the screaming, flailing Aisha onto the floor and stepped on her, silencing her with the sickening snap and crack of bones. She kicked the dead human underneath the bottom shelf, leaving behind a slick, crimson stain, and plunked Yusuf into the now empty jar, corking it.

Janna set the jar back in its spot on the shelf.

"I love beautiful humans, Yusuf. I have many—some a century or two old. You don't age in Irem as you would in your world, which is a good thing, as I'm very selective about the pieces in my collection and I hate having to replace them." Janna smiled, her yellow jagged teeth bright against the black of her face. She peered into Yusuf's jar through the bubbled glass, her red eyes glowing. Yusuf lay on the bottom weeping and beseeching for a merciful Allah to deliver him from the hands of the Jinn.

"Don't be sad! I'll bring our son to see you soon!" She smiled a ghastly smile and then conjured up the magick door, the music of a thousand tiny screams tinkling against glass, chiming in her ears.

Angeline Hawkes holds a B.A. in Composite English Language Arts from Texas A&M University-Commerce. Her collection, The Commandments, *was a 2006 Bram Stoker award finalist. Angeline's story* In Waters Black the Lost Ones Sleep *appears in the 2007 Origins award-nominated Chaosium anthology,* Frontier Cthulhu. *Recent fiction includes* Sorrow Creek *and* Black Mercy Falls, *Delirium Books novellas, co-written with Christopher Fulbright. Bad Moon Books published Angeline's sword and sorcery collection* Out of the Garden and Other Tales of the Barbarian Kabar of El Hazzar *in March 2012.* Scavengers, *a novel from Elder Signs Press, is another Fulbright and Hawkes collaboration. Angeline has seen the publication of novels, novellas, collections, fiction in 40 anthologies, and over 100 short fiction publications. She is an active member of HWA and former member of the Robert E. Howard UPA. Visit her websites at www.angelinehawkes.com and www.fulbrightandhawkes.com.*

3:33

Randy Chandler

3:33 PM

The sun comes back, trailing stringy clots and haloed with crimson fog. Dense silence gives way to metallic ticking and a dry hiss of escaping air that reminds you of the old steam engines you worshiped as a child, your father warning you not to get too close to the tracks and yanking you back by the scruff of your jacket when you ignored his keen counsel. You blink your eyes: kaleidoscopic mosaic of swirling patterns framed by shards of glass. The sun goes dark again.

The smell of warm asphalt and dirty motor oil are somehow as comforting as your mother's hot oven on those cold winter days when she did her holiday baking in preparation for the big feast for the gathered clan. You lick your lips and taste coppery liquid salted like seawater, sacramental and vital to the disposition of your assumptive soul. You waste no time pondering your dubious assumption. You know such things are out of your hands now.

Buffeted by unnatural winds and lashed by a pungency of burned petroleum, you give yourself to an image of aeons-old giants lumbering overland in search of provender. "Boys love dinosaurs," whispers a phantom of memory, "Lord knows why."

Warm rain falls. Seasons wheel across the heavens. The circus comes and goes, comes again. A taste of peanuts. Cotton-candy bliss. Clowns frighten you with their painted mouths and sinister eyes. A girl slips her hand into your loose fist. A sticky kiss. A surge of fledgling lust. Leaves die colorful deaths. The carnival comes to town and you wander the midway, haunted by the sad-eyed freaks and the two-headed monster preserved in a cloudy pickle jar. The carnival moves on and the world summons you. No longer chasing carnivals, you go with loins ungirded into the freak-haunted world at large.

The sun burns a hole through the cloudwall's battlement, flares briefly, then is gone for good.

"Oh, my God," someone cries.

Fear now the frailty of existence. Feel life's tenuous connection to this world, and see your destiny writ small in sinew and bone and muscle, all unraveling with dead certainty, leaving you untethered and at ultimate loose ends. The pain and sorrow of a lifetime are drawn together, then honed to a single focal point like sunlight through a magnifying glass, burning away the horror and finally making you fearless and absolutely numb. Now you understand your hold on life was illusory. Life was holding you. The clawing and scraping to get ahead, the psychic turf wars, loves lost or won, the blood spilt on wrong battlefields, the moral choices made in the name of expediency and self-preservation—the whole of it comes to nothing at this unfortunate locus on the teeming infrastructure. You had a pretty good run, you see, at least as good as a gerbil running in its plastic wheel. Hearing echoes of divine laughter, you finally get the joke.

Come now the ghosts.

Old Blue breaks off his fanciful romp and bounds toward you across fields lost to time. His sad eyes betray the happy lashings of his debris-matted tail. You can almost feel his rough tongue on your face. He wants you to follow him somewhere, but you're in no condition to go traipsing off into your boyhood on a doggie frolic.

"Call nine-one-one."

An old man shrunken in withered skin smiles as he extends gnarled fingers with yellowed nails, and you think you may know him, but you can't be sure at this particular time with that peculiar gray light shining through the slanting rain. He sheds his desiccated skin and wraps himself in a cloak of mist, his skull gleaming beneath a numinous cowl.

Your father hangs back a little at the edge of the black road. He wears an expression of concern, the antipode of the hollow, rouged face he wore when you last saw him in his coffin. Were he to speak, you know what he'd say. Old Dad—who fancied himself a man of science, though he invested his almighty numbers and formulas with near-supernatural properties—would say, "It's all about the numbers, son. Civilization is built on numbers. Your age, your income, your whole identity—it's all numerical. Simple as pi, eh? And don't forget the number of the beast."

Your mother hovers above you, her milk moon face reddened in the penumbra of eclipsed radiance. You catch the fleeting scents of hot pies, sun-dried linen, and fresh-squeezed lemons.

"Can you talk?" asks a stranger, his solemn face blocking your vision of your mother.

But there is nothing to say, even if you could.

In the dimming distance a siren wails, and your impulse is to answer the forlorn cry like a lone wolf howling for its companions, but you have moved beyond mundane exertions. Your tongue is stilled, your vocal cords slack and superfluous.

The old man cloaked in mist raises an arm and points a starry finger at the gray sky.

Seconds strobe/wink at you from your bloody wristwatch.

The shimmering sky pulses like glistening viscera.

The earth begins to release you from its gravitational field. You are suffused with an extraordinary lightness of being.

The sky opens like a ruptured membrane, revealing a red-walled channel filled with cool light. Unborn souls gather to witness your passing.

"It's time," someone whispers.

What time is it? you wonder. If it really is all about the numbers, then this very instant might have meaning of considerable import. Riding inescapable currents, you glance down at the broken, bloodied body falling away from you and you read the numbers on the face of the dead thing's wristwatch as the last digit changes from 3 to 4.

3:34

The number means nothing to you.

Your progenitor was wrong.

It's simpler than pi.

Death Comes Calling

Randy Chandler

Death came for Reginald Summerfield much in the manner of an unexpected houseguest; Reggie deeply resented the unanticipated intrusion upon his orderly life, but he was bound by tradition and folkloric convention to receive the unwelcome visitor into his society, no matter how greatly he detested the distasteful fact of Death's arrival.

When the grimmest of shadows darkened his door, he had little choice but to meet it with decorum befitting a gentleman and a scholar of no little renown. If some cosmic mistake had been made, it would be foolhardy to engage Fate's emissary in hostile debate. Better to play the proper host and greet the dark envoy with equanimity. Begging for one's life, Reggie knew, was out of the question.

"So this is it, then," Reggie said as he gazed into the impenetrable darkness within the cowl veiling Death's face. Then he glanced at his own cooling corpse on the floor before the fireplace and added, "I can't tell you how long I had to lie there in limbo, wondering, as it were, if this was really *it*."

"My apologies," Death said in a mellifluous voice and with a slight nod of the hood. "I was unavoidably delayed. Terror bombings invariably throw me behind. I trust that you used your extra time wisely. So many of my transients have little or no time for personal reflection."

"Rather more like torture, really," said Reggie. "Lying there in terror and pain, wondering if your time has come or if it's merely an episode from which you might recover and then go on with a renewed appreciation of living . . . if not as a mindless radish."

"Acceptance is no easy thing," Death intoned. "Especially for one accustomed to drinking so deeply from life as to be in a constant state of drunkenness."

"Drunkenness! See here, I resent your implication. No, I do more than that. I deny it!"

Death made a rumbling noise that might've been deep laughter. "Deny you were drunk on life? You? Reginald Summerfield, philosopher and professor of aesthetics? You *are* Summerfield, aren't you? I rarely make mistakes, but they do happen."

"Of course I'm Summerfield. This is my house, this is my study, and those are my books. You'll find my picture on the back flyleaf of each one of the baker's dozen."

Death glided over to the books and pulled down a copy of *In Defense of the Aesthete*. Holding the volume with elongated digits of a shimmering black bone-like substance, Death opened the book, studied the author's photo, and then snapped it shut and set it back on the shelf.

"It would appear that you had a productive life, Summerfield." Death again gave a slight nod.

"You may as well call me Reggie. It's what my friends call me, and though you are certainly no friend, it would seem that my relationship with you is destined to be of the most intimate nature."

Death projected a brooding silence.

"As to my productivity, well, I hate to quibble, but you certainly cut *that* short. And rather rudely, I might add. I was just entering the most productive phase of my life. I don't mean to sound sullen, but my greatest contributions to the world of letters and reflective thought were ahead of me. Hardly seems fair. Or even wise."

Death made no response.

"I'll go so far as to call it a grave injustice," Reggie couldn't stop himself, though he realized he probably sounded like a petulant child to the dark spectre. "Grave indeed. I don't know how you live with yourself, if you want to know the truth."

"Death doesn't live. A man of your learning should know better than to make such an oxymoronic statement."

"I was speaking metaphorically. Or aren't you capable of grasping such abstract concepts? I mean, what *are* you really, but a workman. A journeyman working the slimy bottom links of the Great Chain of Being, *that's* what I suspect you are. A cosmic scavenger, feeding on befouled corpses and broken lives. No offense."

"None taken. It's a bit more complicated than that, but you needn't concern yourself. I am your escort out of this plane of existence. What happens to you after that isn't my affair."

"I see. You're just the ferryman. Analogous to a modern taxi driver with a terrible fashion sense."

Death hovered by the hearth in deepening silence.

Reggie stared at his vacated cadaver. "I had no idea it would happen so quickly. The mortification, I mean. The changes are subtle enough now, but I see them quite clearly. I hate it that my wife will be the one to discover me this way. She'll be scarred for life, I'm afraid."

Death shrugged within the rippling folds of its flowing black cloak. "Your earthly concerns will slough off soon enough."

"And my dear daughter. God, I can't bear to imagine how she will take the news of my death. Megan is such a sweet girl. Always was. Too gentle for this world. I fear she'll be devastated."

"Gentleness is often a sign of great inner strength."

"I suppose that's true. Still . . ."

"Stillness is the seed of spiritual expansion and increased inner activity."

"You're beginning to sound as platitudinous as one of my first-year philosophy students. Conjectural thoughts don't thrive in concrete brains. And believe me, I knew a great many blockheads in my time."

"You're calling me a *blockhead?*"

Though Reggie couldn't see Death's face, he could hear the mocking smile in Death's deep voice.

"What if I am? What are you going to do, kill me?"

"I have certain discretionary powers," said Death. "You would do well not to incur my wrath, Summerfield."

"Really. So you *are* more than a mere taxi driver. I suspected as much. What sort of powers?"

"Not your concern."

"Come now, sir. Don't be modest. Tell me what you can do. I won't take it as idle boasting."

"You are becoming tedious. I know what you're up to. It won't profit you in the least."

"Forgive me, but I believe you are misjudging me. I am—or *was* a scholar. My hunger for knowledge didn't die with that pathetic body there. Indulge me. It's not every day a man gets to have a conversation with the angel of death."

"I am no angel."

"Figure of speech. It is one of your many colloquial names. I didn't make them up. Won't you allow me to pick your brain, so to speak? What could it hurt?"

Death came forward, cloak billowing.

Reggie stood his ground, or more accurately, he floated a foot or so above it. "For a being that has become a cliché, you might be overrating yourself, you know. I mean, look at you! Who knew you would actually appear in this cartoonish guise of the Grim Reaper? This can't be what you really look like. You're about as frightening as Count Chocula."

"Count . . . ?"

"Cultural reference to crass commercialism. Never mind." Reggie knew he was doing all the things he'd told himself he shouldn't, but he couldn't stop. He pressed on, knowing full well that his persistence might indeed incur the wrath of Death. "What *are* your discretionary powers?"

Death waved him off with a black hand. "I will not restore your life."

"But you could. If you wanted to."

"Had I arrived in a more timely fashion, then perhaps I could have, but now it is too late. Your brain is irreparably damaged. Your biological systems are degraded beyond redemption, your mortal husk well on its way to becoming waxy soup. None of which is to say I *would* have restored your life."

"So you're saying that your belated arrival doomed any chance I may've had of resurrection."

161

"See here," said Death, now on the defensive, "those Dead Sea bombers are a notoriously tardy bunch."

"The fact remains, my friend: You bungled my death. You and you alone are responsible. I want to speak with your supervisor. I wish to lodge a formal complaint."

Death laughed; his laughter was the sound of thunderous black waves crashing on a rocky shore. "So you wish to go over my head, is that it?"

"Yes."

"I am completely autonomous. There is no higher authority."

"Careful, sir. You are very close to blasphemy."

A new volley of laughter broke against pitch-black rocky crags. "For all your fine philosophizing, you have no grasp of the ineffable entity you call God, Summerfield. If you did, you wouldn't make such a moronic statement."

Reggie scarcely heard Death's blunt indictment. He was all at once in the grip of an intense longing for—"My God," he blurted, "I'm hungry! How can I be hungry? I'm dead!"

"Ah, that would be soul hunger. Your spirit is giving up the ghost, so to speak. Your soul is . . . evaporating. You experience the loss as a kind of hunger. Nothing to worry about."

"Losing my soul? I don't like the sound of that!"

"Soon you will be pure spirit, all traces of your mortal identity gone. Only then will you be able to know the elusive truth you spent a lifetime seeking, as the knower becomes the known. It's quite a humbling experience, I'm told. The apotheosis of humbling."

"Humbug! I don't want to lose my identity."

Death seemed to shrug within the darkly shimmering cloak, which appeared to have a mysterious life of its own.

A world away, a door slammed with a hollow bang. The sound waves hollowly resounded within Reggie's ethereal form. "Good Lord! What day is this?"

Death said, "I don't go by your calendar's arbitrary blocks of time."

From another part of the house came a sweet-throated song, bringing with it a diffusion of feminine light, airily emotive.

"My housekeeper Camilla," said Reggie. "It must be Tuesday. I don't want her to see me like this."

"She has a good voice. A pity it's wasted on a domestic."

"*Wasted?*

Listen to her. She sings for the sheer joy of singing. She *is* the song. I would trade places with her," Reggie said with a bitterness born of deep sorrow. "A singing housekeeper trumps my sad heap of dead flesh any day. What I wouldn't give for just one more day of life! Then, my grim friend, then you would indeed see me drunk on the beauty of life. I would drink deep and fill my soul one last time."

"It wouldn't be as you expect. Knowing of your impending demise would cheapen the experience and make you desperate. I find mortal desperation particularly repulsive."

"You are mistaken. I would make the most of it, and not out of desperation."

The door opened and the frumpy young housekeeper entered, tentatively calling, "Mr. Summerfield? Are you—" Then she saw his body on the floor, quickly recognized the unmistakable pallor of death, and recoiled with a gasp. Camilla clutched at her full bosom, swayed dizzily, and thereupon collapsed on the floor.

"My God, I think she's had a heart attack," said Reggie.

Death hovered over her, making a humming noise. "It would seem so. She is dying."

"Can't you do something? If our bodies are found together, there will be no end to the malicious rumors. I say, didn't you know this was going to happen?"

"Certainly not. She's a drop-in. Not every death is scheduled in advance. Usually, it's just the more significant ones."

"A drop-in? You mean—"

"Domestics are not priority collections."

"I find that offensive, sir. She deserves the same consideration as I."

"That's not the way it works."

"You mean to tell me that even in death the caste system persists? I would've hoped for classlessness in the afterlife. I don't think I'm going to like being dead, not one little bit."

"What's to like? As I told you, soon you will lose your *I*. You won't be *you* much longer."

As soon as the idea came into his mind, Reggie gave it outward expression: "Put me into her."

"What?" asked Death.

"Use your discretionary power and do whatever it is you have to do to put my soul in her body. While there's still time. You owe me that much. It would make up for the torture I had to endure due to your late arrival. You should've been here as midwife to my passing. You've as much as admitted it. If you're the plenipotentiary you claim to be, then do it."

"I owe you nothing." Death's cloak bristled with a green-black sheen.

"There *must* be consequences, even for *your* actions. You have to be accountable."

"You're talking nonsense."

"Am I? Put me into her body and we'll forget your little slipup. And I'll prove to you that I can drink life's beauty without mortal desperation or regret. One day is all I ask. Twenty-four hours. One rotation of the earth on its axis. What could be the harm in that? Unless you don't actually have the power to do it."

"I could destroy your soul this instant if I chose."

Reggie drifted with a will over to his supine housekeeper. Her eyes were glazed, her jaw slackened. "I think she's expiring this very moment. Now is the time, sir. Do it!"

"You would regret it," Death told him.

"I won't."

"You are a stubborn soul, Summerfield." Death's cloak began to expand, swelling as though filled with stormy winds. "Very well. But you must not say I didn't warn you."

Reggie studied Camilla's vacant face. He took in the fine cheek bones, full lips, and smooth skin. She wasn't an unattractive woman. Not beautiful by any stretch, but passably pretty even with the plumpness fostered by a starchy diet and a sluggish metabolism. And such a fine singing voice!

All at once, Death's cloak expanded to fill the room with surging darkness, and he was drowning in black fire. *The bugger tricked me,* he thought. *He's destroying my soul.*

A screaming whirlwind took him deeper into unfathomable darkness, but then the wind became a ragged breath, and he opened his eyes, which were now *her* eyes, and he knew he presently inhabited Camilla's corporeal form. He sat up and looked around for Death, but Death was not there.

He reached up and felt his (Camilla's) heart beating behind an ample bosom. "By God, you did it!" he said, and was startled to hear himself speak with a feminine voice. He stood slowly and then took several tentative steps, in hopes of becoming accustomed to carrying the extra burden of voluminous womanly flesh.

He addressed his corpse there on the floor in front of the fireplace: "Thank you for the years of faithful service, old fellow, but I'm thirty years younger now and these female hormones have made me more alive than you ever were, even in your prime. I had no idea . . ."

He looked at the grandfather clock in the corner and saw that he still had time to reach his wife at the art museum, where she served as curator. He phoned her, cleared his throat when she answered, and then said, "Mary, I . . . this is going to be difficult for you to believe, but . . ."

"Camilla? What is it? Is something wrong?"

"Perhaps you should sit down."

"Camilla, *what is it?*"

"That's the thing, you see. I'm not Camilla. Well, I am, but not really. This is Reggie. I wanted to prepare you before you came home. I'm afraid I've died. Fell out right there on the floor of the study. When Camilla discovered my body, she had a heart attack. I prevailed upon the . . . uh, Grim Reaper to put my soul into her body for twenty-four hours. You see? I'm still myself, but I've borrowed her body."

"Have you been drinking?"

"Ask me something Camilla couldn't know."

"This isn't amusing, Camilla. I'm afraid I'll have to terminate your employment."

"For God's sake, Mary, *ask me*. I can't afford to waste time."

"This is ridiculous."

"Please, lambkins." He hoped his using his pet name for her would begin to convince her that he was telling the truth.

Mary sighed into her mouthpiece. "All right. If it will end this sick charade. Where were we the first time we kissed?"

"Your family's gazebo, in a December snowstorm. You were huddled in your furs and I was too hot with passion to feel the cold."

"Camilla, put my husband on. I know he's there with you."

"He's dead, I tell you. *I'm* dead, but only physically."

"I'm hanging up now."

"Wait! Mary, please. I'm only trying to spare you the shock of finding my corpse. I'm calling for the ambulance so if you take your time, you won't have to see me that way. I swear I'm telling the truth. I wouldn't joke about this."

"Camilla, as of this moment you no longer work for us. I'll mail you your last paycheck. And you can tell Mr. Summerfield he's in very deep do-do." Then she broke the connection.

"Damnation," he said. This was going to be more problematical than he'd imagined.

* * *

Mary arrived as the ambulance attendants were loading the remains of her husband into their vehicle. The coroner met her at the front door and Camilla (Reggie) waited in the foyer with a snifter of cognac. Then Camilla was placing the drink in Mary's hand and guiding her to the study.

"I know this is hard to accept," Camilla said, "but I *am* your husband in Camilla's body. Please believe me."

"I want you out of my house."

"Mary, I . . ." Reggie felt an intense cramp in Camilla's lower belly. He (she) lifted the skirt of her pink maid's uniform, stuck two fingers between the cotton panties and the puff of wiry hair and into the fleshy groove where the wetness was. He withdrew and examined a finger smeared with bright red blood. "Oh my."

"If you don't leave right now I'm calling the police," Mary said.

"I'm having a bloody period." He smiled with Camilla's lips. "I wonder if Camilla has something in her purse. You don't . . . no, of course not. You're post-menopausal."

Mary started for the phone. He seized her arm and said, "Hear me out. Then I'll go."

Mary jerked her arm out of his grasp, then crossed her arms over her chest.

In Camilla's soprano he said, "I'm grateful for the wonderful years we shared. I'm sure I didn't deserve you. I should've told you every day how much you meant to me. The best I can do is to tell you now. You and Megan were the world to me. Of all the scholarly books and passable poetry I wrote, Megan was the finest thing I ever had a part in creating. Please tell her for me that Daddy loves her very much and is very proud of her. I . . . love you both. Deeply."

A tear trickled down Camilla's cheek. Mary's eyes, too, were wet with emotion.

Reggie kissed his wife's lips and embraced her. She didn't resist. After a long moment, he released her and said, "Now I've *got* to do something about this little blood tide in my drawers."

"In the bathroom cabinet," she told him. "Megan keeps a box of tampons there."

"Of course. How does one . . . ? Never mind, I'll manage."

And manage he did, though not without a certain amount of queasy embarrassment. When he emerged from the bathroom, Mary was sitting in her husband's favorite armchair before the fireplace, where a fledgling fire was feeding on carefully stacked logs.

"Oddest thing," Reggie said. (Camilla's voice had a lilting quality to which he wasn't yet accustomed.) "I'm beginning to have access to Camilla's memories. And emotions. I know what killed her. She had a faulty heart valve. I can feel its nervous little flutter."

"Please leave," Mary said in monotone as she stared into the fire.

"Yes, I suppose I should. See here, I know you can't believe any of this, but someday when Death comes for *you*, you'll know the truth of it. For now, if you must grieve, grieve for the end of our life together, but don't grieve for me. I'll be fine. Death is not the end. Goodbye, love."

He used Camilla's plump lips to give his wife a final kiss, and then he left his home for the last time.

* * *

As he walked Camilla's voluptuous body along the gritty sidewalks of Manhattan, he began to know what a mystical creature a woman truly is. The lunar cycle tied her blood tides to the larger world in alchemical sympathy. Could there be any doubt that a woman's spirit was endowed with the ability to use this metaphysical nexus as a receptacle of Heavenly vibrations? Seen through a woman's eyes, these ordinarily drab sidewalks were invested with a silvery glow suggesting paradisiacal destinations whose auras must surely be golden. The vast sapphire-blue dome of twilight hung so low over the jagged skyline that it was easy to imagine the taller skyscrapers actually making scratches in the deep blue gemstone of the sky. Pedestrians making their way through the cold city were anything but pedestrian; the dullest passersby possessed a portion of the magic—even if they were unaware of the mystical gift they carried. He saw it shining in their eyes.

As he waited on a crowded corner for a green light, he inhaled such a rich mix of pheromones arising from so much humanity pausing in one place as to become dizzy with life itself. When he exhaled, he realized that death and life were in every cycle of breath. Death lurked in each moment of life. The miracle of simply being alive while knowing that time was the only thing keeping him from death, touched his (Camilla's) heart with such poignancy that he feared the awestruck heart might simply stop. It did skip several beats when its valve went aflutter, but then it quickly caught up to its own rhythm and to the cacophonous rhythms of the city, and he crossed the street, turned another Lower West Side corner, and dashed into a SoHo art gallery, driven by a deepening hunger to catch visionary glimpses of worlds beyond this one, extraordinary though *it* was.

Looks of disdain cast from beneath bridges of snooty noses didn't touch the Rubinesque woman in the pink maid's frock as she moved from painting to painting, entranced by the framed "windows" upon idiosyncratic worlds—-worlds captured in swirling colors and frozen celestial light. The sheer vibrancy of the artworks filled her breast with indescribable emotions that could only be expressed in song. So she began to sing.

A sublime aria from Rossini's *The Italian Girl in Algiers.* The other patrons were stunned by the warmth and power in her voice and stood with mouths agape as she sang. A security guard came toward her, a scowl riding the prow of his sharp face. Camilla sang on until the guard grabbed her arm and hustled her toward the exit. The others in the gallery applauded her, then booed the guard when he shoved her out onto the sidewalk.

Camilla giggled at the spectacle she had made, and then bowed to the art gallery crowd watching her through the glass. A well-dressed man stood in the doorway, removed a carnation from his lapel, and tossed it at Camilla's feet. She blew him a kiss, picked up the flower, and went merrily down the sidewalk.

When Reggie caught Camilla humming a country & western song, he knew his soul was conforming to the contours of her bodily vessel. The biochemical memories imprinted on his soul were fading and were being replaced by Camilla's. Very soon, he surmised, Reginald Summerfield's identity would be usurped. *Evaporated,* as Death had said. This realization caused a brief moment of panic, but it quickly passed because the soul inhabiting the maid's body was taking such joy in being Camilla.

She moved through the sidewalk throngs with remarkable agility for a woman of her size. She paused in front of a storefront window to study her face's reflection superimposed on a slim manikin in a slinky evening gown. She laughed at her own folly and then buzzed on like a thick-bodied bee to the next flower, humming all the way. She'd forgotten to put on her coat before leaving the Summerfield townhouse, but the pleasant bite of winter air was a crisp reminder that she was gloriously alive. Soon enough she would not be able to feel any physical sensations. In less than twenty-four hours—was that right?—she would die again and leave this body and this world, presumably forever. She couldn't precisely remember how she knew this, but she felt the truth of it in her bones, particularly inside the ribcage and within the skull. She was sharing her body with . . . another. Some sort of marriage, perhaps made in Heaven. She was on a dreamlike mission to experience the joy of being alive and to . . . drink deeply of the world's wonderful symmetry. Tired as she was, she couldn't waste the night sleeping. She didn't have to worry about getting up in the morning to go to work because Mrs. Summerfield had fired her. She was *free.* Her overweight, overworked body would run on beauty and holy light. She was, she now realized, a creature of light. That light would not be extinguished when this body's clock-spring finally wound down to a stop. That certainty was itself exhilarating.

She ducked into a cozy diner and sat at the counter. She ordered a slice of apple pie and a cup of coffee. The pie was the best she'd ever tasted, the coffee piping hot and full-bodied. The little diner's warmth elicited nostalgic memories of her grandmother's kitchen back in North Carolina.

An angry voice upset the pleasant din of low conversations and musical clatter of silverware. "You got no business bringing your disease in here," said a male voice. "We shouldn't have to see this. I look at you, I see slow death."

Camilla turned her head to see a burly red-faced man in a turtleneck sweater leering at a skeletal young man with leeches attached to his face. She did a double-take and saw that the black things on the malnourished young man's face weren't leeches but were ugly eruptions in his skin.

The counter waitress came over and whispered to the afflicted young man: "I'm sorry, but you see how it is. My customers look at you and lose their appetites. You're hurting business. Now I can't refuse to serve you. I'm just asking you to please eat someplace else. Okay?"

The young man stared at the waitress with his sunken eyes, then nodded and slid off the stool and walked with an old man's gait toward the door. Camilla shot a scorching look at the waitress, but the waitress ignored her and moved down the counter to refill the burly man's coffee cup and spout placating apologies.

"Wait," Camilla called after the banished young man. He glanced over his shoulder and gave her a weak smile and a shrug, then walked out the door and into the frigid night. Camilla slapped a ten on the counter and went after him.

She caught up with him and tugged on the sleeve of his black overcoat. "Let me buy you something to eat. I'll get it to go."

"Thank you," he said with labored breath. "You're kind, but I'm really not hungry."

"You have AIDS, don't you?"

"Yes. I'm sorry if I ruined your dining experience."

"You didn't. Those other people did. I couldn't believe how rude they were."

"I'm used to it." He shrugged inside his coat. "I just wanted to sit down in there one last time. For sentimental reasons. That's where I met my boyfriend."

She nodded. "Is he . . . ?"

"Six months ago. But not before he gave me something to remember him by. I'm sorry, I don't mean to sound bitter. I do still love him. I only wanted to feel close to him again, but . . . it didn't work. That man back there was right. I'm a walking advertisement for disease and death."

"You have beautiful eyes," she told him.

He smiled sadly. "I used to be quite handsome. Now . . . I'm a monster."

"No you're not. You're sick. But what's inside will go on to a place where there is no disease. The same place your boyfriend went, I would imagine."

171

"You must be freezing. Did you forget your coat?"

She shook her head, teeth chattering. "I don't mind the cold. I'm going on too. I probably have less time than you do."

He looked puzzled but said nothing.

"I have an appointment with Death. I'm literally living on borrowed life."

His eyes smiled. "I know the feeling."

"I mean it. It's really true."

"I don't know why exactly, but I believe you."

She smiled. "Do you mind if I walk with you?"

"I'd be honored." He gave a slight bow that obviously pained him. They didn't bother to tell each other their names. They were both beyond given names and knew it.

She took his hand and they began to walk slowly, almost casually, down the sidewalk. She felt like singing, something from Verdi's *Rigaletto*, but she couldn't remember the words or much of the music, so she started singing *On The Wings Of A Dove*, one of the many country classics she knew by heart.

They drew curious stares from other pedestrians, but they walked as if on the stage of a Broadway musical—seemingly carefree and light of heart.

"That was the most beautiful singing I've ever heard," he said when she reached the end of the song. "Do you sing professionally?"

"Goodness, no. Just for myself. And now for you."

"You're an angel, aren't you?"

"I think we're all angels, adrift in a mad world. But you and I are on our way home."

He squeezed her hand. "I think I want to believe that, whether it's true or not."

"It's true enough," Camilla said.

"I live in that brownstone there. Would you like to come up? I'm very tired, but not at all sleepy. Your singing energized me. I would be grateful for the company."

In his austere flat, they drank wine and filled the hours with effortless camaraderie. She learned that he was a poet and playwright of modest success (only one of his avant-garde plays had ever made it to the stage). They took turns reading aloud some of his darkly romantic poems, and she was moved by them; for all the poetry's wrenching horrors, a life-affirming light shone through their inherent darkness.

They talked the night through and then quietly watched the sun rise over city. In the cold warmth of the sun's early rays he revealed to her what he took to be the secret of life: *love life to the fullest and you will not fear death.* "I wanted with all my heart to believe in God and the afterlife, but I just couldn't do it," he confessed. "I did see Jesus, though. He was dying of AIDS. I thought at the time that He was taking on my suffering, if not my sins, but then I realized I was only hallucinating. We each have to die alone. But that's okay." They talked awhile without words, communing with their eyes and what lay behind them, and she finally kissed him goodbye and went out into the bright winter morning to meet Death.

* * *

"I suppose now you'll issue pathetic pleas for more time," Death said.

"Not at all. I'm ready." She glanced back at her estranged body. It remained in the gloom of an alley, slumped against the back wall of a Chinese restaurant, where she'd sat down only moments ago to die.

"What, no desperate last attempt to hoodwink me?"

"No."

"Yours is the rare soul."

"No, it's not, not really. I met a beautiful young man last night, doomed to die hideously, but his was the most sublime spirit I've ever known. I know now that the most beautiful thing in this world *is* the human spirit. What a wonder it is! Life should be about uncovering that spirit and opening our hearts to it."

"It was your heart that killed you," Death reminded in a decidedly smirking tone.

"But I'm not afraid of you now, Mr. Taxi Driver. My heart and soul are open to what lies beyond. I'm done clinging to life."

A bass string thrummed deep within Death's black cloak.

"Now step on it, driver," said Camilla with a gay laugh. "And don't spare the horses. I think I hear the angels singing."

Death rumbled. "If you hear anything it's the wailing winds of the void. You and your lot drove God to a far corner of the cosmos, so don't imagine he will save you. You lived your life in illusion and now you come to your end in delusion. Beauty is your decomposing corpse. *Nothing* is the only thing that matters. And I am delivering you into an eternity of nothingness. No spark, divine or otherwise, will fill the void in the center of your soul. Nothing is sublime."

"Then I will embrace that nothingness. Embrace it sublimely."

"The worm swallows itself."

"You've never had the gift of life. That's why you don't get it. You will never understand what it means to live and die. You're the *illusion* at the end of all things. You're the shadow on the wall of the cave. And I'm going through the holy fire to a place you will never know."

Death suddenly threw off the hooded cloak, which swirled and then sank to the ground, forming a dark circular pool. Attired in a black clawhammer frock coat, the skeletal creature began to dance around his whirling pool of midnight.

She lost herself in Death's sidewalk-gray face.

Just before the black whirlpool drew her down, she clearly heard the angels screaming.

It would take an eternity to find the harmony hidden within that awful sound.

But harmony was everything.

Randy Chandler is the author of the new novels Dime Detective *and* Daemon of the Dark Wood, *and of two previously published novels* Bad Juju *and* Hellz Bellz. *He also co-authored* Duet for the Devil *with t. Winter-Damon (God rest his soul) and has contributed short stories to numerous anthologies. He also wrote the novellas* Dead Juju *and* Howler.

Live Better

Steve Voelker

Marcus heard the familiar ding and headed outside. He didn't remember hearing a car pull in, but he had been lost in a dog-eared copy of the *Aenied* he was reading for a grad class when the bell rang. He tucked the book into the back pocket of his faded blue coveralls as he opened the door. After so much time in the station's dreary interior, the brightness of the world induced a painful squint. As his eyesight adjusted, Marcus was surprised to see it was not a car that had triggered the bell at all, but rather a man on horseback, followed closely by three others.

The large white stallion standing on the air hose next to pump number three carried a tall, lean man with a shoulder-length mane of unkempt dark hair and a full, wiry beard. Perched atop his head was a tarnished crown. The well-used hunting bow slung across his back made him look to Marcus like an extra from a Tim Burton adaptation of Robin Hood. Everything about the rider seemed dull and listless until their gazes locked. Marcus was shocked by the fierce intensity and at once felt the strength drain from his limbs like air from a deflating pool toy.

The figure raised a gloved hand and pointed a finger at the rack of AAA maps and brochures by the gas station door. He said not a single word, yet Marcus felt the push of the stranger's instruction insinuating itself inside his own head, urging him to comply. Marcus grabbed an Arkansas state map and tentatively approached the group of riders. He handed it over, thankful to avoid direct contact with the man. As soon as the map left his hand, the mental press of compulsion vanished and Marcus' mind immediately cleared.

The first rider opened the intricately folded paper as another sidled up to get a better look. This second rider, atop a fiery red mare half again the size of the first, was easily the largest man Marcus had ever seen. One gargantuan arm rested on the handle of a massive sword. Marcus was reminded of an interview with Andre the Giant that showcased the shocking portions the Eighth Wonder of the World consumed in a typical meal: two-dozen eggs, a pound of bacon, a loaf of toast. He wondered how it was possible for a single human heart to pump blood through that much real estate. The man pointed to something on the map. The first rider only shook his head and pointed somewhere else.

As the two horsemen debated, Marcus felt his attention drawn to the third. This one rode a horse that seemed to be made entirely of shadow, its features shifting any time Marcus attempted to focus on them, somehow staying just beyond the edge of his mental grasp.

The rider's hyper-anorexic gauntness and sunken eyes gave the impression of a living skeleton. The emaciated figure raised a hand and pointed, as the first rider had done, only not at the map rack. Marcus followed the line of the gesture to the other side of the station door and the flickering light of the battered Coke machine. He dug deep into the pockets of his coveralls, anxious to be rid of his uninvited guests. He extracted a crumpled dollar bill and inserted it into the machine, surprised to find it was accepted on the first attempt.

Marcus punched a large plastic button that had been repaired with a strip of blue duct tape and labeled with black Sharpie ink. A series of internal thuds and whirring sounds emanated from the machine's bowels. Marcus gave it a practiced shove and a dented can of Diet Coke was ejected into the tray at the bottom, joining the company of three dead June bugs and a wad of neon green chewing gum. Without bothering to collect his change, Marcus relayed the beverage to the waiting rider, who drained it eagerly without stopping for air, then dropped the empty can to the dusty macadam.

Marcus wiped the condensation from his hand on the front of his coveralls, leaving a dark streak behind on the light blue material. For the first time, he noticed the last of the four riders sitting a full three lengths behind the others on a sickly yellowish horse. His features were completely obscured by the hood of a dingy gray cloak. Marcus felt an unexplained chill run down his spine when he looked at this unassuming figure. He quickly averted his eyes, suddenly terrified this last rider would notice him. Some primal instinct assured him that it would be bad indeed. Marcus understood this horseman was here on business, and that business was Death.

The first two riders finished with the map and set it free to drift on the light autumn breeze. The paper slowly skittered away as Marcus watched the horsemen head in the direction of US-71. Relieved, he headed inside the gas station to get back to his reading.

"What was that all about?" Bob asked from behind the counter.

"Just some out of towners looking for directions to the Wal-Mart headquarters over in Bentonville," Marcus replied.

Steve Voelker is a writer who lives in Pennsylvania with his three young children and his implausibly supportive wife. His work can be found in Daily Frights 2012, Frightmares! *and* Slices of Flesh *from Dark Moon Books. Follow him on Twitter @Voelker58, where he will keep you informed in the very likely event of a zombie apocalypse.*

I Was Yet Another Teenage Vampire

Chris Hugh

Vera wanted exactly two things in life: to look good and to never get old. In her mind, they were one thing, although some might argue that technically they were two. She also cared a little about environmentalism, but only because all her favorite stars did.

"My mirror's broken!" she shrieked as she skipped into the girls' restroom.

Madison, Vera's best friend forever, squealed as the girls jostled their way into the gloom. "You'll have like seven years bad luck! You're gonna be unlucky until, like, two thousand . . ."—she scrunched up her eyes and did the math—" . . . whatever!"

Courtney, Vera's other bestest friend ever, snatched the pink compact away. "It's not broken," she said, checking her lipstick.

Vera slathered on sunblock. Her belly and back—everything below her tight Forever 21 t-shirt and above her straining low-rider pants—was pink with sunburn. Madison and Courtney rolled their eyes at Vera's belly, which was spilling over her sturdy jeans.

Madison fake-coughed and mumbled "muffin top" just loud enough for Courtney to hear. They giggled.

Vera was five feet six inches tall and one hundred thirty pounds, with wavy shoulder-length brown hair and a sweet, pale face. She had a charming figure and would have been lovely if she wore clothes that flattered her figure. Vera, however, despite being acutely aware of fashion, did not have a sense of aesthetics. If it were fashionable to have a powdered wig, a monocle and bound feet, Vera would have happily hobbled on the bandwagon.

Courtney looked at Vera's sunburn, gave Madison a significant look, and started humming the tune to Rudolph the Red-Nosed Reindeer. She tried to think of appropriate funny lyrics but couldn't.

Vera grabbed her compact back. She was annoyed that the girls' restroom didn't have a mirror. She tried the mirror in the compact again; it reflected everything except Vera herself. She found this disturbing because it would hinder her ability to apply another coat of makeup during class. "It's not *broken* broken," she explained. "It's broken!" She gave it a couple shakes, tried again, and gave up. She didn't want to remove her sunglasses to apply eye makeup anyway. Ever since that sparkly guy in Biology drank her blood, the light hurt her eyes

Madison watched Vera put the compact in her backpack. "Whatever."

Courtney agreed and the three girls went to the cafeteria.

* * *

The girls stood in line and bought their soft drinks and pizza, then they walked to a table with an uneven gait, occasionally skipping and walking backward and laughing loudly at nothing.

Vera unwrapped her pizza, took a bite, then screamed, clawing at her throat. "Garlic!" she gasped.

"What is your problem?" Morgan asked.

Vera gave a guilty start. "I'm so fat!" she finally cried. "I'm not going to eat anything for the next six months!"

"Oh, me neither!" Madison and Courtney said together. None of the girls were fat, although they probably would be when they got older, since their mothers were.

They threw their food away and decided to walk around campus, screaming, squealing, and making quick, random movements in order to look sexy. Vera saw a boy wearing a Marilyn Manson t-shirt with a crucifix on it. Her hands flew to her mouth, she shrieked, doubled over, and turned away. Madison and Courtney thought it looked cute and started doing the same thing. Later they went to the gym where the school was holding a blood drive.

Vera fainted when she saw the Red Cross symbol.

* * *

She woke up in a curtained-off area of the gym. A beautiful young woman in a traditional nurse uniform was attending her. "What's wrong with me? Who are you?" Vera asked.

"Gaetane." The nurse's voice was sweet and sophisticated, like blue cactus agave syrup from Trader Joe's.

"But, but . . ."

"Shhh, little one," Gaetane continued. "I will be your guide, your mentor."

The mysterious woman talked and Vera grew to accept her special destiny. Now she understood. She had known for some days that she was changing. TV reality shows were losing their charm. Her parents didn't seem like such pathetic losers anymore. Texting and talking on the phone no longer seemed to be the sole purpose of her existence. There was even a nagging thought that her appearance could bear improvement. Gaetane was much older than Vera. Maybe she could learn something from her. *Hmm,* Vera thought, *learn something from someone older.* She was changing, indeed.

"Why are you being so kind to me?" Vera asked.

"All vampires must guard each other, take care of each other, so we will not be persecuted." Gaetane replied. "I have a stake in your future."

A *stake?* Vera stiffened at the pun, then shrugged. "I'm glad I've got someone to go to *bat* for me."

"And do you understand now why the sun has been bothering you and why you reacted so badly to the garlic pizza and the crucifix on the t-shirt?"

"Yeah, that kinda . . . *sucks.*"

The mysterious woman looked into space for a moment, distant memories floating behind her crystalline eyes. She turned to Vera and quietly said, "Whatever you do, don't go to a Madonna concert."

Gaetane suddenly smiled, and Vera found herself laughing, really laughing. Not laughing-squealing like she did with her friends because they were putting someone down or trying to get attention, but laughing with pleasure because she'd finally found a friend who shared her creepy sense of humor.

"Would you like to come live with me in my large house on a hill?" Gaetane asked. "I have a subterranean vault to keep us out of the sun."

"I don't know . . ."

Gaetane continued in the same vein: "Jacuzzi, high-speed Internet access, a PlayStation . . ."

"*Count* me in!"

The two left for the parking lot, having some difficulty crossing storm drains and underground water lines because vampires cannot cross running water, but eventually getting to Gaetane's van, recognizable for its super-tinted windows and the fix-it ticket under the windshield wiper.

As they sat in Gaetane's kitchen, Vera had a terrible thought. "Wait a minute. I'm a vampire. I can't see myself in the mirror any more. Is there a way I can get around the mirror prohibition so I can still check my appearance and apply my makeup?" Normally, she would get hysterical and enjoy a drama queen act when she had a problem. Now she thought in terms of problem solving. Vera's bloodless reaction surprised her, but she was pleased at her growing maturity. She chuckled.

Gaetane led Vera to an elaborate walk-in closet. "Here you go," she said, and flipped on a closed-circuit TV. Vera saw herself on the monitor and had the most significant revelation of her life.

"I look like crap in low rider jeans."

Together Gaetane and Vera picked out clothes for Vera. Vera tried them on and used the closed-circuit TV to see which ones were becoming. Later, they went shopping.

* * *

As time went by, Vera acquired a flattering wardrobe, and she never grew old, maintaining her appearance naturally, by sucking blood, a renewable resource, rather than by injecting manufactured chemicals and potentially harming the Earth's fragile ecological balance. Thus it came to be that Vera fulfilled her dream of looking good and staying young.

And she was undead happily ever after.

By night, Chris dances through the universe on a web of light, gathering the strange and creating the humorous through the dark filter of a warped imagination. By day, Chris haunts the darkest halls of Silicon Valley's law firms, battling the evil dragon known as Million of Pages of Documents Need To Be Reviewed So Let's Hire Some Lousy Temps. At least it pays the vet bills. Enter Chris' world through many portals. Visit soon, while Chris Hugh remains sane. www.chrishugh.net, www.chrishughblogs.com, www.CeilingCatIsBlack.com, www.TheGadgetTree.com.

Resurrecting Mindy

Joe McKinney

The big Christmas tree in front of the Dayton Mall had fallen down sometime during the last year. Kevin's gaze drifted over the faded tinsel and mud-encrusted ornaments and wondered when it had happened. Probably during the rains back in early September. Those had been bad. A lot of the area had flooded, and the winds that came with the rains must have done that damage to the tree as well.

Of course, he really didn't know for sure. The only time he ever came back here was at Christmas time. The world had ended three years before, just before Christmas, and the inside of the Dayton Mall still had a lot of decorations hanging from the common areas and inside the shop windows. Every year right around this time he made the trek back to the mall and scavenged whatever he could carry to decorate wherever he was living at the moment. These days it had become a ritual, just like keeping up his calendar, and keeping his hair trimmed, and making sure his food stores were well stocked. The rituals, in fact, were about all he had left. That, and the soul-sucking loneliness that came with being the last man left alive.

It made him wonder if there was any reason to keep going. After all, did it matter when he died? Tomorrow, or thirty years from now, the results would be the same. After he was finished, humanity was finished. Wasn't he just postponing the inevitable?

Could be. But he wasn't quite ready to throw in the towel just yet.

For now, he had a mission.

Kevin got down on his belly so he could squeeze between the front tandems of an 18 wheeler. From there, he watched the parking lot, mentally charting a safe route over to the doors.

It actually didn't look like it'd be very difficult this year. The zombie hordes that had swarmed the area in years past had thinned. He didn't know if the majority of them had moved on or decayed away to the point they couldn't function anymore. Maybe they'd started to eat each other. Who the hell knew?

He supposed it didn't really matter.

Fewer zombies meant it was easier to stay alive, and that was all that mattered.

There were fewer than fifty of them out there walking the parking lot now, and it didn't take long for a wide gap to open up in the crowd. Kevin tensed, ready to run. Another few seconds and it would be wide enough for him to go.

And that's when he saw her.

Mindy Matheson.

Holy shit, he thought. He stared at her for a long moment, watching her curious, clumsy movements. That really was her. *That's Mindy Matheson.*

And she's faking it.

* * *

It'd been a while since he'd seen a faker.

Most didn't last long. Right after the outbreak Kevin and some of the other survivors he'd hung out with back then had seen one or two a week. The fakers tried to make themselves look like zombies. They smelled like zombies, moved like zombies, had flies swarming around their eyes and mouths like zombies. But they weren't zombies, and sooner or later, they messed up. They slipped out of character for just a second.

And that was all it took.

One tiny slip, one momentary distraction, and the zombies they moved with swarmed them.

Usually, at least as far as Kevin was concerned, it wasn't much of a loss.

The only reason a person ever decided to fake it was because they had given up on their humanity. Surviving among the ruins of what the world had once been was hard. It sucked, in fact. In order to survive, in order to stay sane, you had to work at it. Every day was a fight. Every breath was bought with tears and sweat and loneliness. And sometimes, living free didn't seem much of a pay back.

The fakers couldn't hack it.

But they didn't have the courage to end it all either.

They were the real walking dead, not the zombies, and Kevin had never felt anything but disgust for them.

Until now, of course.

He and Mindy Matheson, they'd dated right after high school. She'd never said two words to him during school. Neither one of them had been all that popular, but it had been a big school, and she had her friends and he had his. But afterward, when they found they were working at the Home Depot together, neither one of them with the foggiest notion of what they were going to do with their lives, they sort of fell together.

For about eight months.

They didn't end on an obvious note. No cheating, no fighting, nothing like that. They just drifted apart. At the time he'd figured they just weren't right for each other. That explained why they hadn't noticed each other back in school. What happened while they were working together was just the natural gravity of two lonely people. And so, just as their orbits brought them together, those same orbits carried them apart. She grew distant, he grew irritable. She stopped calling, he stopped caring. Soon they were basically strangers again. The brief interlude was forgotten, and the two of them went back to their lives of uncertainty and quiet desperation.

He gave himself a self-deprecating chuckle.

For all that the world had changed, they hadn't. The two of them were still living their half-lives, midway between life and death.

But he had laughed louder than he wanted to, and she had heard him. He saw her cock her head to one side. She turned toward the truck where he was hiding, her shifting, searching gaze the only thing that separated her from the wandering corpses nearby.

Kevin whistled faintly, just loud enough for her to hear.

She staggered forward.

For a moment, he thought of running away from there. What did he think he was doing anyway? What could he do? It wasn't like they were going to run off together or anything. Not now. To fake it for any length of time at all, she had to go native in a mighty convincing kind of way.

And that she certainly had.

Kevin looked her up and down, from the stringy, matted mess that was her hair to her bare and blackened feet, and tried not to grimace at the stench that came off her. Her face was filthy, her lips cracked and flaking. Her clothes were so filthy and ratty he couldn't even tell what color they had once been. Flies swarmed about her face.

But she was standing right in front of him now, watching him. She swayed drunkenly, her mouth hanging open slightly. He wanted to hate her, but her eyes were over bright, pregnant with the suggestion of pain, and despite his loathing, he felt his heart breaking out of pity.

He could, after all, still see the girl under all that grime and slathered gore. She had gotten skinny as a crack whore, but the curves were still in the right places. And she still had that cute little upturned nose that used to drive him wild when she smiled.

"Hi, Mindy," he said.

She just stared at him, no expression on her face.

"Hey, you know why they put fences around graveyards?" he asked her. He waited a beat. "Because people are just dying to get in."

Again, he waited.

Her expression didn't change. She just stood there, swaying.

"You heard that one, huh?"

She might have nodded, but if so, it was faint and he couldn't be sure.

"How about this one? A guy finds out he only has twelve hours to live. He goes home to his wife, determined to live it up for his last night on earth. So they have sex, and it's great. An hour later, they do it again, and it's even better. And then, a few hours after that, he tells her he thinks they can go at it a third time. 'Easy for you to say,' she tells him. 'You don't have to wake up in the morning.'"

He beat his index fingers on the truck tire in front of him like he was firing off a rim shot. He smiled at her, and then the smile faded. Why in the hell was he doing this? There was no reaching this girl.

And was he really so lonely that he was talking to a faker?

But then he saw a flicker at the corner of her mouth, the faintest trace of a smile, and that brought a huge grin to his face.

"Are you doing okay, Mindy?"

The smile disappeared. He saw what looked like a tear forming in her eyes.

He almost reached up for her hand then, and had one of the real zombies not let out a moan at that very moment, he might have thrown her over his shoulder and carried her away from there.

But a few more real zombies had spotted him. Several were moaning now, staggering toward him. He'd been careless and now it was time to go.

"I'm staying in an apartment at Woodlawn and Spruce," he said.

A zombie dropped to the pavement and started crawling under the truck toward him.

"I gotta go," he said. "Remember, it's the Bent Tree Apartments. Woodlawn and Spruce, number 318."

More zombies had gotten under the truck now. The lead one held up a mangled, handless arm, the blackened tips of its ulna and radius extending from rotten flesh.

"Gotta go," he said.

* * *

Several days later, with Christmas, by his count, less than a week away, Kevin was putting up ornaments on a fake tree. There had been a Hallmark in the Dayton Mall and he'd made good use of the Snoopy ornaments piled on the floor. Growing up, his mom had waited out front of the local Hallmark in order to scoop up whatever was new that year. At the time, he'd thought it stupid. They're collector's items, she'd said. Or they will be. Which, to his way of looking at it, hadn't made it any less stupid.

But now, hanging the Snoopy with the little typewriter and Snoopy as a World War I ace ornaments on his tree, he sensed a flood of painful memories trying to surface.

Christ, he thought. He didn't need this. Not now.

He heard moaning coming through an open window and he jumped to his feet to take a look. There was no point in it, really. The zombies keyed off of what they saw and heard. Those were about the only two senses that seemed to work, and as long as he stayed out of sight and kept quiet, his little hiding spot up in this third floor apartment was as safe as any spot on Earth.

But he crossed to the window anyway, because checking out the zombies kept him from his memories.

And that's when he saw Mindy Matheson for the second time.

Her group had wandered from the mall over to here, probably in search of the pack of wild dogs Kevin had heard baying in the night the last few days. The group wasn't especially large. He counted about thirty, though there were almost certainly a few more somewhere out of sight. They wouldn't be much of a threat when he needed to go out, but even still, there were enough of them that they would probably be sticking around for a few days at least. They hunted collectively, he'd discovered, so the bigger groups tended to stay in one place longer.

Just as well, he thought. It would give him a chance to talk with Mindy again.

He slid out the window and into the chilly evening air. It looked like it would probably rain later. There was a ledge just below his window that led over to another building's roof. From there, he climbed onto a billboard that looked down on the intersection, where Mindy and the others were wandering around, moaning.

He kept a can of spray paint up here just in case.
He gave it a shake and wrote:

Hey Mindy! I'm in 318 over to your right.
Come on up.

He'd gathered quite a crowd. At a glance, he noticed that he'd underestimated the size of the group by at least half, probably more. Their mangled, upturned faces and ruined hands were all pointed at him, their moans taking on an urgent, pulsing quality that he had come to think of as their feeding call. He saw quite a few of them down there.

But Mindy wasn't with them. She was drifting away from the group, stepping back toward a screen of shrubs at the far side of the intersection while the others surged forward.

"Good girl," he muttered.

Moving quickly, he went back to his apartment. The zombies wouldn't be able to follow, and besides, he had some quick cleaning up to do.

* * *

She wouldn't sit down. He offered her a place on his couch, at his table, on the floor. She just shook her head every time he offered.

Kevin tried small talk, but she wouldn't answer any of his questions, and after a while, he began to feel foolish and stupid, like he was wasting both their time. He jammed his hands into his pockets and looked around the room for some glimmer of inspiration.

Nothing.

"So," he said. "You know what they call a fast-moving zombie?" He waited a beat, hoping for another of her half smiles. "A zoombie."

She just stared at him, and the cold, lifeless emptiness there sent a chill through him.

"How about a hockey playing zombie?" he said, forcing a grin. "A zombonie. What do you think, huh? I got a million of

189

them. How about this? A zombie, an Irish priest, and a rabbi walk into a bar—"

"This was a mistake," she said. "Coming here. I'm sorry."

She spoke quietly, her voice cracked and hoarse, as though she'd almost forgotten how to use it.

"I'm going, Kevin."

"What? No."

He took a step toward her, but stopped when the smell hit him. He tried not to let his surprise and his disgust show on his face, though it probably did anyway.

"Please, Mindy, don't. It's Christmas."

She didn't answer. But she didn't turn to leave either.

"I've got some food. Are you hungry?"

She nodded immediately.

He went into the little kitchenette and slid a cube of Spam out of a can. He cut it into four big slices, then handed her the plate.

"I'm sorry I don't have—"

Mindy snatched it from his hands.

She ate with her fingers, jamming the meat into her mouth, barely chewing. Several times she nearly choked. Bits and pieces fell from the corners of her mouth.

She stopped eating only once, long enough to look at him over her plate.

"Don't look at me while I eat," she said, her words about as close to a snarl as any he'd ever heard a girl make. And then, more quietly: "Please. Don't look at me."

He nodded. "Sure. Okay."

Kevin went to the cupboards and took down some more cans. He had Vienna sausages, some fruit cocktail, applesauce, a jar of sauerkraut. Better take this stuff out of the can, he thought, remembering the way she'd jammed her fingers into the pile of Spam. Last thing he wanted was for her to cut up her fingers on the sharp edges of the cans.

He went to work putting the meal onto paper plates and then setting the plates onto the table.

When he turned around, she was standing right behind him, watching his neck. Seeing her made him jump.

"Shit," he said. "You scared me."

The look in her bloodshot eyes was inscrutable and he didn't like it.

Her gaze drifted down to the food on the table.

"Go ahead," he said. "I have tea and water, whichever you'd prefer."

She fell on the food without answering, without bothering to sit in the chair he pulled over for her, so he got her a cup of water and set it down next to her plates.

She had asked him not to watch her eat, which was okay with Kevin. The wet, slurping noises she made were enough for him to know he didn't want to watch. He went over to his couch and looked at some of the magazines he'd left there. A bunch of old *Playboys* he'd found at the used bookstore over by the mall. He gathered them up and hurriedly stuffed them under the couch, but not before catching a glimpse of the sleepy-eyed brunette on the cover of the top magazine. *So much had changed,* he thought sadly. *So much has been lost. The good and the bad.*

Eventually Mindy's eating noises stopped.

Kevin walked over to the kitchen. Mindy was still at the table, looking around at the cupboards with a bovine-like vacuity.

"Are you still hungry?" he asked. "I have more. You can have anything I have."

She shook her head.

"More water, maybe? I can make you that tea I promised."

Again she shook her head.

A joke about Little Johnny, a bucket of nails, and a zombie hooker came to mind, but for once his internal filter was working and he cut it off before it had a chance to get out.

Instead, he let the silence linger.

She had turned to face him, and now she was swaying drunkenly, same as she had done in the mall parking lot. It occurred to him that she had probably internalized so much zombie behavior that, even now, when she was completely safe, she was unable to turn it off.

But the silence was murder. He had never dealt well with uncomfortable silences. It was the main reason he told so many bad jokes. Better to fill up the void with inane nonsense than let a painful silence grow.

He said, "Listen, there's no need for you to go back out there. You're welcome to stay as long as you like. I've got some Sterno. We could heat up some water, let you take a hot bath maybe . . ."

All at once the tears started. One minute she was watching him, quietly and vacantly, and the next she was crying. Big, muddy-colored tears ran down her cheeks.

"Ah shit," he said. "Mindy, I . . . I'm sorry. What did I say . . . I—"

"I shouldn't have come," she said. "This was a mistake."

She moved hurriedly to the door. Every impulse in him told him to go after her, hold the door closed, take her in his arms.

But he didn't do it.

He just watched her go without a word

* * *

Mindy shuffled through the rain, her mind a blank.

Or at least she tried to make it a blank.

Right now that wasn't working out so well.

It was cold, windy, and rainy. Her clothes were little more than rags; they offered no protection whatsoever. For too long now she'd wandered, mindless, emotionless, denying all pain and shame, a true ascetic. The rain tore at her skin like icy razors and chilled her to the bone, but she did not tremble, nor did she cry. She let her arms swing limply by her side, her fingertips grazing the ice that formed on her clothes, as she kept pace with the horde of dead things brushing against her.

Thought was the enemy, not the dead. With thought came fear, and pain, and a memory of all that was gone. If she thought too long—if she thought at all—the dead would see it in her eyes and she wouldn't last long after that.

192

But the mind was like a flood. It could be contained for a while, even a long while, but it could never be truly silenced until it had run its course.

And right now her mind was turning toward shame.

But it wasn't the shame of what had happened to her—*no, strike that*, she thought, *of what you have* allowed *to happen to you*—that bothered her so.

It was that damn Kevin O'Brien.

When she was by herself, she felt no shame for what she was doing. She was surviving. And she was doing it in the face of a universe that didn't give a rat's ass for what happened to her. Or the rest of humanity, for that matter. She was surviving, damn it.

But so was he.

And he hadn't given up anything. He hadn't debased himself like this. He hadn't sacrificed every last scrap of his self-respect just to draw another breath.

She hated him.

She hated him because he was still human.

And because his charity reminded her that she was not.

Not anymore.

So she turned off her mind and wandered. Damn him. Damn the world. Damn life. There was nothing of the world left for her anymore. Nothing but emptiness and the slow, relentless crawl of time.

One foot in front of the other.

Forever after.

* * *

The billboard came as a surprise to her. For a moment, just a fraction of a second, she stopped.

And she stared.

She hadn't realized where she was. But up there, up above the mindless crowd, was a message written just for her:

Hey Mindy, it's cold. Come on up.
I've got a warm bed.

A memory floated up into her mind, unbidden. The two of them, finishing off their shift, her letting him walk her out to the parking lot. He had a joint in his pocket and she didn't have anywhere to go. They went around back to the loading dock and passed it back and forth, talking about random shit, nothing either of them really cared about.

He was nice. A little dorky, but all right.

She could tell he was getting interested. It was in the way he cracked his lame jokes when he should have let the quiet grow, the way his fingers twitched when they touched each time she took the joint from him.

She could have shut it down right then. He was the scared type. He'd back off and nothing more would ever become of it.

But she didn't have anywhere else to go and they both knew it.

She went back to his place.

Sitting on his couch, her hand on his thigh, he actually asked if he could kiss her. That had never happened to her before. Most guys went straight for the tits. After that it was a wrestling match to keep her pants on.

"You don't have to ask," she'd said.

And before she knew it, they were some sort of couple.

But he wasn't wasting that kind of time now. The apocalypse, it seemed, had made him a little bolder.

Come on up. I've got a warm bed.

Yeah right, she thought, I bet you do.

But she'd been careless. She'd thought too long, dropped out of character.

One of the dead ones a few feet to her right had turned her way, and now his dead, vacant stare was locked on her. She tried to clear her mind, to stumble forward, but the zombie's gaze never wavered.

He raised his hands like he was trying to take something from her and staggered after her, a moan rising above the wind and the cutting rain.

194

She pushed his hands away and looked around.

This wasn't going to work. Every moment she lingered, more and more of them turned her way. She scanned the crowd, and in the dark, the only way out seemed to lead around the corner, where she had taken the stairwell once before up to his apartment.

A limp hand fell on her shoulder and that was enough.

She ran for it.

* * *

She stopped in front of 318.

Jesus, she thought, had she really sunk this low? Getting torn apart by the walking dead almost seemed a joy compared to coming to him like a penitent. She'd thought she was done with guilt, with shame. But it hurt now more than ever.

Utterly demoralized, she knocked.

* * *

He couldn't sleep.

In the dark, he rose and put on his boxers and went to the kitchen to light a candle.

Enough light filled the room that he could see her sleeping in his bed. The rain had washed away a good amount of dirt and grime from her body and hair, but her breath had still been enough to turn his stomach. And even in his sleep he couldn't quite hide his disgust. He had dreamt of a zombie forcing her face into the soft part of his neck; when he awoke, he'd found her, pressing her cracked and ulcerous lips into the well beneath his chin.

Half-asleep, he'd recoiled from her, almost falling out of the bed before realizing it was only a dream.

Now, fully awake, he watched her sleep and tried to hate her.

But he couldn't.

Who in the hell was he to judge anyway? She was desperate. She was lonely. She was scared. Wasn't he all of that, and more?

In fact, the only thing he had on her was the appearance of normalcy.

The truth was, he was drowning. His life was an act. His jokes; the Christmas decorations; his calendar keeping; all of it was a terrible, useless, stupid joke. He drifted from one empty apartment to the next, from one false front to the next, like a ghost blown on the wind, and he called it a life.

Were they any different, he and Mindy?

He couldn't answer, not truthfully anyway; and eventually, he blew out the candle and crept back to bed and reluctantly put an arm around her as he drifted off to sleep.

When he awoke the next morning, he was alone, the only sign she had been there a muddy stain on the sheets.

He sat on the side of the bed, asking himself why he even bothered.

She had left him, again, and this time it was because she knew he was the one who was faking. He was the hypocrite. He was the disgusting one.

And she had found him out.

* * *

Mindy stopped in the doorway as she left Kevin's apartment building and scanned the street.

There were no dead in sight, but that didn't mean they weren't there. She'd seen it happen a few times over the last year. She'd be shuffling along with the others, absolutely nothing going on inside her head, and suddenly there'd be a scream. Another careless person had wandered into their midst, completely surprised by the sudden appearance of a zombie horde that, in reality, hadn't been trying to sneak up on anybody. Most of the group's kills were made that way, completely by accident, people caught by their own carelessness.

Without realizing it, she had assumed the awkward shuffle of the dead. Her bare feet, no longer sensitive to heat or ice or even broken glass, slid across the cracked and weedy pavement as though on autopilot.

She tried to turn off her mind as well, but she found that much harder.

She kept thinking of Kevin.

196

What, exactly, had happened last night?

Not *what*. Not really. She knew *what* had happened. That had actually been quite pleasant. Better than she remembered it, anyway.

No, what she really wanted to know was *why?* And why *now?* She'd seen others before him. She knew they weren't the only ones. She suspected—and she believed this without reservation—that there were more normal people out there than she'd seen. There had to be. The world couldn't simply be empty. That wasn't possible.

But none of the others had managed to arouse her pity. She'd watched them die, and in some cases rise again, and she'd felt nothing.

And then—Kevin.

He'd told her his stupid jokes. He'd offered her a place to stay, all the food he had, even a warm bath. In the few days since she'd first seen him she hadn't been able to stop thinking about him. Before him, walking around being dead was no trouble at all. She could go days at a time without a single thought passing through her mind. The world was one unending parade of nothingness.

And then he came along, and she couldn't take three steps without falling out of character, without thinking of the life they'd once shared.

That's what it was, she told herself. He was a window to the world that used to be, a shipwreck from her past that had mysteriously surfaced to haunt her mind. There was nothing more to it than that. He was nothing but a ghost, and she was merely lonely.

But a voice at the back of her mind kept prodding, questioning.

What if this was more?

What if this was . . . love?

Maybe, she thought. It was Christmas day, after all. She'd seen the calendar—the days gone by dutifully crossed out with a big red X—right before she'd walked out of his apartment. Christmas had a way of warming even the coldest heart.

Wasn't that the secret to Scrooge's redemption? She'd never paid much attention to books in school, but she thought she remembered that much. For Scrooge, it hadn't been fear of the grave, but fear that the heart would no longer love again, that made it possible for him to accept the spirit of Christmas into his life.

She stopped then, a sudden alarm causing her pulse to quicken.

She had fallen out of character again. She'd stopped walking like the dead. Like her mind, her feet had started to wander. If she'd happened upon one of the dead while walking like that, they'd have torn her to ribbons.

But, for now, she was alone on the street.

Turning, she happened to see her reflection in a shop window. And at first, that one quick glance threatened to send her over the edge of reason. She looked horrible. In a word, she looked dead. And she played the part well. Her hair was stiff with mud and probably blood too. Her face, which hadn't been that bad back in the day, was discolored with God knows what; attractive, it seemed, only to flies. Her body was a bony jangle of sticks. She looked like a crack whore, though she imagined that even the crack whores of the world gone by had more self-respect than she did at that moment.

She had nothing.

But then her gaze shifted beyond the window, to the sexy elf costume in the display. For a moment she experienced an odd sense of displacement. It was her face, her gaunt, exhausted face, but her body was draped in the red velvety finery of the elf costume. Her fingers reached for, and could almost feel, the cotton candy fringe at the edge of the playfully short skirt.

She smiled.

Kevin O'Brien, you wonderful bastard. I'm gonna blow your mind.

* * *

It was Christmas morning. He had hoped to wake up late and spend the day with her, hopefully draw her out little by little. The two of them had been pretty good, he thought, back

198

in the day. And they were certainly good last night. When they were good, it seemed, they were really good. He'd hoped it could be that way again.

But she'd left him sometime in the night.

His attempts to draw her into his world weren't fair, he supposed. Why would she want to join him anyway? Hadn't she found him out? She knew he was faking it. He knew he was faking it.

And he was tired of faking it.

The choice, once he'd given it voice, was surprisingly easy to make. The only hard part had been accepting *that* as an option. But once he opened his mind to it, it actually made a lot of sense.

He went to the billboard and spray painted a message for her. Then he went down to the street and climbed on top of a brick wall and waited for one of the dead to come along.

He thought he'd be scared, but for the first time in a long time, he felt relaxed, at ease with himself and the world in which he lived. You can settle in quite comfortably to even the most horrific of circumstances, given enough exposure to it. All horrors lose their immediacy, their nastiness, sooner or later. The nerves can only be slashed and cut and shredded so many times before they deaden to the pain.

No, he was past horror. What he was feeling now was worse than that. In the time before he met her, his world had been filled with zombies. The horror they represented was a shallow, fast moving river that beat him down and cut him on its jagged rocks.

He had gone beyond that now.

Here the waters ran far slower, but they were deep, endlessly deep, and what lurked down there was something he could not fight, for what lurked down there was love.

A zombie was at the base of the wall, its hands clumsily racking at the bricks just below Kevin. Kevin stared into the thing's eyes and saw the emptiness he'd fought against for so long, but had never truly understood. That would all change now. He had tried to get Mindy to live in his world, and that had failed. So now, he would live in hers.

And only love could allow him to do this.

He jammed his left hand down into the zombie's face. It shook its head, as though to shoo away an insect, and then realized what was in front of it.

The zombie grabbed Kevin's forearm and clamped its teeth down on his wrist.

"Motherfu—"

Kevin pulled his hand away, holding his wounded wrist in his right hand while blood oozed between his fingers. It hurt so badly he nearly rolled off the top of the wall. Already he could feel the virus creeping through his blood stream, racing for his heart. It felt like somebody was jamming a red hot copper wire up his veins.

He didn't have much time. Maybe thirty minutes, but probably less.

Kevin rolled off the wall and trotted back to his apartment. Once inside, he washed the wound with hot water and wrapped it in a towel. It was already starting to smell like death. His head was soupy, and walking to the chair in the center of the room was hard.

But he made it.

He dropped down into the chair and turned it to face the door, waiting for the pain to stop.

* * *

This felt absolutely glorious. Mindy had spent the day cleaning herself up, scouring off the stain of more than a year of living down among the dead. Now her hair was washed and brushed. Her legs were shaved, her skin soft and fragrant from cocoa butter, still a little pink from her bath. The sexy elf costume showed a lot of leg and a lot of bruises and cuts, but those would heal. If her heart could heal, her legs certainly would.

She felt better than she had felt in a very long time. She couldn't remember a time she'd felt this good, even before the world died. Mindy Matheson had come back from the dead, and love had done it for her.

And it was glorious.

Now she picked her way carefully through the rubble-strewn streets. The dead were out—the dead were always out—but there weren't many of them around at the moment.

Then she saw the sign and she smiled.

It's all for you, Mindy Matheson.

I love you.

I want to be with you forever.

She couldn't hold herself back any longer. She sprinted up the stairs and down the hall to his door.

Slightly out of breath, she knocked on the door.

No response.

Maybe he was out getting stuff, she thought. More candles, maybe. Or, God help her, even a bottle of wine.

She turned the knob and swung the door open slowly . . .

"Kevin?"

Joe McKinney has been a patrol officer for the San Antonio Police Department, a homicide detective, a disaster mitigation specialist, a patrol commander, and a Bram Stoker Award™-winning novelist. His books include the four part Dead World *series,* Quarantined, Lost Girl of the Lake *and* Dodging Bullets. *His short fiction has been collected in* The Red Empire and Other Stories *and* Dating in Dead World and Other Stories. *For more information go to http://joemckinney.wordpress.com.*

The Bride of Frankenstein Dances with Celebrity

Chris Hugh

The pale woman's flowing white gown dragged across the marble floor. Her wiry black hair, bound up in a strange cone-like style, was shot through with two streaks of white which had been fashioned into lightning bolts. Outside, the lashing rain made the afternoon gray and dangerous. The woman lurched to the reception desk.

"Welcome to Forever Pretense, Los Angeles' Premier Beauty Destination!" the receptionist chirped. "How may I help you?"

"How beautifully dramatic!" the woman said conversationally, looking out the window. Lightning flashed bright, as if someone had momentarily switched on a strobe light, and a clap of thunder shook the building. The customer smiled, exposing a collection of yellow teeth that seemed not to match each other. "The cruelest savage exhibition of nature at her worst!"

"It certainly is unusual to see weather like this in L.A.!" the receptionist agreed, her smile undimmed. "What can we do for you today?"

"I am here for a Transformation." The woman raised her arm high and lighting struck as she spoke. Thunder rolled.

"Whew!" The receptionist leaned over and looked outside. "That sounded close!" She turned back to the customer. "A makeover, did you say? Wonderful! May I ask your name, please?"

"My last name I take from my creator, the greatest scientist in all of Prussia, Viktor Frankenstein. My Christian name, dare I call it so, I take from Mexico's Saint of Death, for my body, though animated by lightning and the spirit of science, was created from the plundered corpses of the most heinous criminals who ever gave lie to the lofty title woman. I am the Bride of Frankenstein. I am Santa Muerte Frankenstein!"

"Um, Sandy," the receptionist said, running her finger down the appointment list. "Here you are. If you'd like to follow me, Sandy, I'll show you our waiting room. May I get you a water or some tea?"

Santa Muerte Frankenstein followed the receptionist and thumbed through a copy of Bride magazine as she waited for her appointment.

***

Later that week, she appeared on the *Maury Povitch show*. Her grizzled mane had been traded in for a playful, shoulder-length flip in a light auburn. Her flirty green miniskirt complemented the color of her veins.

"So, Mrs. Frankenstein," Maury was saying, "I understand that you have reached a financial settlement with a number of movie studios and publishing houses that have been making money from your story for the last however-many years."

The Bride remembered the joke her new agent told her to make. "Mrs. Frankenstein sounds so old," she said. "I'm only one hundred and ninety eight!" The audience laughed. "Please call me Sandy."

"Okay, Sandy. Tell our audience, how does it feel to be vindicated after all these years?"

The Bride opened her mouth to answer and then remembered she wasn't supposed to say *vengeance is mine.* She smiled. "It just feels good to know that America's legal system works, Maury. Now it's time for me to get on with my own reanimation." Maury stared at her a moment. "I mean life."

Maury stepped into the audience. "Here's a man with a question, Sandy." He thrust the microphone under the chin of a tall, rough-looking man. "What's your name, sir? And what is your question?"

"People just call me Grease," the man replied, an ugly smirk on his face. "Here's my question, Sandy. You seem like you're gonna be a big celebrity, like all those other chicks I see. So when am I gonna see a sex tape from you?" He leered.

The Bride's agent hadn't covered that question. "Sex tape?" she stammered. "I have the strength of ten men." Steam started

203

coming out of her ears. "Tape? *Mere tape?*" she shouted. "Even iron manacles cannot hold me if I want—"

Her head exploded.

***

After she was repaired, she continued with a manic schedule of interviews. Larry King asked, "So, it is true that you and your husband are separated?" She looked at him mutely with large eyes, afraid to say anything. He repeated, "Are you separated?"

She silently touched her neck bolts, looked at her hands and feet, and counted her fingers. "No, everything is attached, Larry. I'm not separated," she said, relieved. Waves of uncharitable laughter froze her smile.

And her head exploded.

***

The Bride learned to meditate to try to improve her patience.

***

On Fox, Bill O'Reilly asked, "What is it like to be the Bride of Frankenstein?"

Another guest, Ann Coulter, broke in before the Bride could reply. "Excuse me, Bill. But *Frankenstein* was the name of the monster's creator. If you've read the book, which I recommend, although Mary Shelley does not have the extensive footnotes that my books have, which prove the scholarship of my books as well as the correctness of my opinions." She tossed her sheet of golden blonde hair and rolled her eyes. "What was I saying?" The Bride started to answer Bill O'Reilly's question, but Ann Coulter butted in again. "Oh, yes, Frankenstein was the creator. His creation is referred to by conservative people as *Frankenstein's Monster*. And by conservative, I mean informed, intelligent, God-fearing, decent people, like the ones who watch Fox." The studio audience clapped.

The Bride spoke through gritted teeth. "My husband is not a monster!"

Ann glanced at her and back to Bill. "There's no need to get pedantic, Sandy. I learned the word pedantic in law school,

204

which is where I learned to be a lawyer. That's why I'm so lawyerly."

The Bride started to say something but Ann talked over her and Bill ignored her because he was looking at Ann Coulter's body and wondering if he'd saved enough money so he could pay a settlement if he sexually harassed her. "I've got a bone to pick with the whole mad-scientist label." Ann continued. "Did Frankenstein set up an actual experiment? Did he have a control group of other cadavers that he did *not* reanimate? Were his results peer reviewed or published? Hmm?" Her lips turned down at one corner and she lifted her chin, looking at the Bride. "Well, did he?"

"Herr Frankenstein was my creator! He created life!"

"Of course. I'm not arguing that he didn't create you. I simply take issue with him being a mad scientist." She turned to the camera for the punch line. "He was more like a mad engineer!"

The Bride's ears started to steam.

"Actually, Ann," Bill O'Reilly said, "the problem I have is that Mary Shelley wrote the Frankenstein novel as some sort of new-age, women's lib, feminazi rant. She seemed to want to make the point that new life is something that comes from women, and when men try to usurp that and create life the result is monstrous."

The Bride clenched her fists while the other two chuckled over Mary Shelley.

"Well, Bill," Ann said, "I've given that aspect quite a bit of thought. As you might know, Mary Shelley's mother was Mary Wollstonecraft, who wrote a ridiculous piece of claptrap called *Vindication of the Rights of Women* back in 1798 that asserted women were rational beings. Oh, that's right, Bill, now stop laughing."

The Bride slammed her fist onto the table, pulverizing it and finally gaining everyone's attention. "Mary Wollstonecraft wrote that women should be educated! She said that women were essential to the nation and should be viewed as human beings with the same fundamental rights as men! What's wrong with that?" She turned to Ann Coulter and pointed her long finger. "You are a woman. I can tell because your first name is feminine and you don't have an Adam's apple. How can you—"

Then her head exploded.

***

"No more interviews for you," the Bride's agent told her. She was glad. She was almost starting to miss life back in her Prussian village. Every time she saw a pitchfork or a flame-engulfed barn, she felt nostalgic. Her agent seemed oddly happy, though. "Look at this, kid!"

She went to the computer and the agent played a YouTube video. Someone had spliced together footage of her head exploding and set it to a Jewel song called *Pieces of You.* "Eighty million hits, kid! You're a star!"

***

The Bride's last television appearance was the worst. *Dancing With The Stars.* She tried her very best, but she could tell she'd be the first contestant to leave the show. Her Cha-cha was dismal and the judges let her know it.

Len Goodman said, "Sandy, I could not even tell that was a Cha-cha. You lurched across the stage, your footwork was terrible. You need to bring Doctor Frankenstein in here to reanimate your dancing because it was literally dead!"

The Bride's patience had worn thin.

Her head exploded.

Host Tom Bergeron looked down at the corpse, then turned to the main camera. "Viewers, have we got a surprise for you!" With a sudden orchestra sting, the ABC NASCAR team pit crew ran onstage. There was a quick whir as the tire changers' impact wrenches removed the Bride's lug nuts. The tire carrier pushed a new head into position and, with another whir, the nuts were tight again. The crew chief did a rapid defibrillation as the gas man handed the Bride a Red Bull. The jackman pulled her to her feet and slapped her butt, then the pit crew ran off stage. The whole operation took 6.5 seconds.

Bruno Tonioli jumped up and watched the departing men with naked admiration while the audience cheered. "Now *that*

206

was dancing!" he drawled. He turned to the Bride and sat down as the applause died. "But you! You daanced." He stretched the word out. "You daaanced as if you had two left feet! Maybe Herr Frankenstein made a mistaaake. Perhaps you do." He leaned over extravagantly and looked at the Bride's feet. There was a roar of ugly laughter. "Well, there is a right one and a left one, but Herrrr Frankenstein did not take those feet from a graceful garrotter or a pirouetting poisoner! Noooo. He must have taken them from a boxy bludgeoner!"

The Bride's head exploded.

After the pit crew left again, Judge Carrie Ann Inaba said, "Now, now, Bruno," in her usual, conciliatory tone of voice. Then she addressed the Bride. "Sandy, I think you did some things very well. Your Cha-cha had a lot of excellent lifts. It's just that it's usually the man who lifts the woman, so I'd like to see more of that if you make it to next week. Overall, you're not the best contestant we've had on the show, but you're not the worst either." Everyone nodded uncomfortably, remembering Kate Goselin. "I'm really looking forward to seeing what you do next."

The Bride was so touched she ran up to Carrie Ann and hugged her, as so many female contestants had done before. Unfortunately, none of those contestants had the strength of ten men. Carrie Ann snapped in two. As the famous judge and choreographer slowly slipped to the floor, the Bride staggered back in horror. Seeing what she had been driven to, the Bride shook her fists toward the overhead studio lights. Lightning flashed, thunder rolled, and the Bride's face was a river of tears. And, in her grief, all her pent-up rage, alienation, and longing burst forth. She flung herself across the stage, tore the judges' table from the floor, and hurled it into the orchestra pit. Sobbing, she grabbed a twelve-foot potted palm and smote the famous mirror ball, then she smashed through the studio audience, leaving a trail of B-list actors and reality stars in her bloody wake.

It was a rampage. A dance of death on *Dancing With the Stars* (immediately followed by a rampage on *Jimmy Kimmel Live*).

***

A month later, the Bride and Frankenstein's Monster were back at their remote castle in the Austrian Alps. They stood at a window, hand in hand. "I am so glad that you have come home to me," the Monster said.

"I went crazy in L.A.," the Bride said. "But I've learned this is where I truly belong." She looked up at her husband and smiled. She lifted her hands and tenderly touched the Monster's face. "These are the hands of a Prussian governess who was executed in 1808," the Bride said. "They were not meant to do graceful extensions during a ballroom dance. They were meant to strangle young students."

The Monster gently kissed her. "And your lips were not meant to speak on television."

"No, indeed, my love," she said softly, touching her bottom lip. "These lips were meant to falsely accuse people of witchcraft, leading them to be tortured to death. And they were meant to scream anguished death cries when their owner's own perfidy was unmasked and punished." The Bride sighed happily and leaned against the Monster.

An angry mob of villagers suddenly appeared, carrying pitchforks and torches.

"Are you worried, my love?" the Monster asked.

"No." She squeezed the Monster's hand. "They can't be any worse than the people in L.A."

When the Earth turns its face from the sun, the night finds Chris in lonely darkness, the cold light of a computer monitor playing upon tortured-but-finely-wrought features as Chris spins a diseased soul into tales of myth and legend, along with various articles on gadgets, humor, health, and cats. By day, Chris earns a living playing piano in a fancy house. Well, actually, Chris is a lawyer, but how do we tell the children something like that? Many are the paths that descend to the shadowland of Chris

Hugh's mind. Visit, if you dare, and see if you can be the one to lead Chris Hugh into the light. www.chrishugh.net, www.chrishughblogs.com, www.CeilingCatIsBlack.com, www.TheGadgetTree.com

Dead Run

Frank Larnerd

"We're gunna have to keep that arrow in 'im." Marcus told me.

I didn't argue. I didn't wanna have to help him tug it out.

Marcus helped me get the man in the white plastic body bag. We had to pull the bag around the arrow and even then the nock pushed against the bag, stretching the plastic, making a tent shape by the man's chin.

We scooted him onto the gurney. I loaded him into the van. I smoked a cigarette with Marcus and a deputy. Then, buttoning my coat, I said goodbye, got into the, van and cranked up the AC.

I'm a night runner, a transporter. Late at night I wander country roads in a windowless black van. I wear a thick winter coat and always keep the air conditioning goin' full blast; it helps with the smell. Don't transport nothing illegal or anything like that. I transport people . . . dead people.

See, if you should die under unusual circumstances and the medical examiner decides you need yourself an autopsy, you get sent to Charleston. Transporters are the ones that make sure you get there. Day or night, every day of the year, we run. I work for Netty Funeral Home and we're one of two funeral homes contracted by the state to transport for the medical examiner.

In the old days we would just use hearses. Now days we all use vans. Some white, most black; they all got air conditioning.

It ain't a job for just anyone. You can't have a bad driving record and you can't get the willies. If you work the third shift like me, sometimes you might not get a call at all, but sometimes you'll run the whole night long. Just depends on how lucky folks is. I've had five loaded at once.

I had gotten the call to Gilbert, deep in Mingo County, that Saturday night. Nothing unusual about that, I suppose. But this was the first body I had that got killed by an arrow. That was all I knew when Mr. Netty called me about three in the morning.

Knew it weren't bow season, so I figured some good ol' boy was playing himself a drunken version of William Tell, only with beer cans. Or if it had been a full moon that night, I might even imagined some eight point buck was out getting poetic vengeance.

The truth was, as it tends to be, just tragic and sad. He had been drinkin' with some friends and jumping around on his bed. He was dancing and swaying, beer in one hand, cigarette in the other, having himself a time as music blared from the radio. He had 'im a quiver of arrows on the bed and came down wrong. The arrows spilled out of the quiver. He tried to keep his beer upright as he come down and landed on one of them arrows. It got 'im under the right collar bone and the weight of his body pushed it diagonal, right though the lung and into his heart.

You get a lot of overdoses nowadays. Folks get to drinking after taking a fistful of pills and the next thing you know, they're calling me to come get 'em. Get a few murders too. Jealous husbands, angry friends, bitter feuds that boil over in harsh words and bullets. I've seen all kinds, from 3 days old to 99. Fat bloated green ones pulled up from the river, charred black ones from smoking plane wrecks, red as an Indian, and white as a ghost. Every one of 'em smells bad.

You never get used to that smell. Something 'bout it—part rot, part warning that says, I'm dead, stay away. Something powerful and primal in its warning. The air conditioner helps make it tolerable. After a hot shower you can almost forget it.

My trip back to Charleston started easy enough; I made a right at the light and started up the mountain. I had my window halfway down, smoking a cigarette. *Hotel California* was playing on 105 and I wondered what song had been playing on the radio when my passenger had his problems with that there arrow.

Rain started coming down so I flicked on my wipers. A coal truck pulled up behind me, his lights filling up my mirrors. I gave the van more gas and started snaking my way up the mountain. The coal truck tailgated me, his lights blinding as the rain came down in sheets. Lighting would cross the sky and Don Henley's voice would crackle in the dark.

I threw my cigarette out the window and used both hands to keep the van on the road. Left and right I yanked the wheel, squinting into the rain. I felt a little better at the top of the mountain when the coal truck finally turned off. Letting my eyes readjust to the darkness, I began the descent down the opposite side of the mountain.

Now, don't matter if you're going into or out of Gilbert, the fastest way is 44 over Horse Pen Mountain. The mountain gets its name from the Shawnee Princess Aracoma, daughter of great Chief Cornstalk. After her father's death, her tribe had been driven into the wilderness. They were starving when winter came. The Shawnee stole some horses from the white settlers and brought 'em to the top of the mountain. The settlers tracked 'em and ambushed the starving Shawnee. When it was finished, it was pretty much the end of Princess Aracoma and the rest of her people, but it was the start of the legends surrounding Horsepen Mountain.

Now, folks like to tell how Cornstalk had cursed the whites as he lay dying on the banks of the Ohio River. I don't know if Aracoma was as vengeful as her daddy, but I reckon Horse Pen Mountain is 'bout a top contender for haunted Indian spots. It's 'bout the curviest road you'd ever see too, and narrow as a stick o' gum. It's so steep I can barely understand how it's legal or sane. The whole stretch is dark and lonely, save for the thunder of overloaded coal trucks that run over it day and night.

Because the incline is so steep, my seatbelt was the only thing keeping me from driving with my face against the windshield. The rain started to come down harder. Thunder boomed around me and the radio went silent. The display was still lit up, just no sound. It was quiet except for the sound of the rain and the rattling air conditioner. Pressing the brakes, I slowed the van and twisted the knobs of the radio.

Nothing.

I was considering the idea of not driving the van until Netty could get a new radio. Suddenly the headlights went out. The dash still glowed green, but other than that, I was in darkness. I pulled the van to the curb and put it in park. I switched on the hazard lights, but they didn't even blink.

Figured it was something electrical, so if I restarted the engine, maybe I could reset the problem. I turned the key and the engine and air conditioning went silent. Sitting there at pretty much a 60-degree angle toward nothing but black, I prayed the van would start again.

Taking a deep breath, I started to turn the ignition when I heard a sound from the back. I was startled, not scared, mind you, just startled. Sometimes bodies will wheeze, move, and even break wind hours after death. Still, my hand went to my breast. I looked over my shoulder into the back of the van.

The body was still there, still covered, and still had the shape of the arrow protruding. Taking a deep breath, I turned away and lit up a cigarette.

The van began to fill with light. Wasn't sure what it was at first—either another electrical glitch or a holy vision. I got kind of hypnotized for a moment, watching the dust dance in the smoke from my cigarette as the light cut through it. By the time I knew what was happening, it was too late to do anything. A coal truck was almost on top of me.

I could hear the brakes groan over the sharp splitting sound of the air horn. There was no time to pray, let alone see my life flash before my eyes. Throwing up my hands to protect myself, I imagined being ground into a blood and metal smudge. The van shook as the coal truck missed my vehicle by inches. Opening my eyes, I saw the truck's brake lights and the dust and dirt where it had run onto the shoulder of the road.

The truck roared down the mountain and out of sight like an angry ghost.

I'd accidentally bumped the gear shift when I flung up my hands. The van began to roll forward, slowly at first, then picking up speed. I panicked, stomping my feet around to find the brake pedal. I jerked the wheel and hit the guard rail, rocking the van on its axles. There was a popping sound from the back and a screech of metal as the gurney, body and all, slid between the seats, slamming to a stop at the console.

I may have screamed at that point. Not ashamed if I did.

Finally got my foot on the brake and slowed the van down to a stop. My heart was pounding in my chest; I didn't want to look down but couldn't resist.

When the gurney shifted, the arrow had pushed through, splitting the body bag open. It was torn from the top down to the chest of the dead man. He was in his 30's, about 200 pounds, had a week's worth of beard, and was chrome-dome bald. His skin was grey and looked cold. His mouth was slightly open, as were his eyes, and he was looking right at me. I might have been tired, it might have been the shock of almost being crushed by 50 tons of truck and coal, but I swear to God, he reached up and took my cigarette out of my hand. He took a long draw and let the smoke out slowly, like a country fog. A thin trickle of smoke drifted from his bloody arrow wound.

"You like pancakes?" he asked, taking another drag, his brow wrinkling as if the question were a serious one.

Backing against the door, I could still smell the beer on his breath. The hair on my arms stand on end, even now when I tell the story.

"Go to Rita's" he told me. "They got 'em some mighty good pancakes. Just take a right once you're off the mountain."

I just stared at him, lying there in the body bag, smoking my cigarette, unable to find the words to say anything.

"You go get some pancakes. If you don't, you'll be sorry" After he said it, he reached up and passed me back my cigarette.

I took it from him, my hand shaking, and put the damn thing to my lips—a cigarette from a dead man's mouth.

Coughing and gagging, I tossed the cigarette out the window and spat. When I turned back to the corpse in the bag, he was just lying there stone dead. Didn't look at all like he could have ever spoken a sound, let alone like he could smoke one of my cigarettes.

"Are you OK?" I asked, wincing at the idea of him givin' me an answer.

But none came. He was surely dead; I had never wanted out of that van so bad in all my life.

I tried the key again and the van came alive. I nearly jumped out of my seat as the radio blared Jim Morrison's voice at top volume. I quickly shut the radio off.

I needed to get off of that mountain. Things in the van seemed to be running all right. My head lights and radio were working proper, so I put the van in drive and headed down the mountain.

Stealing a moment, I looked down at the body. Against all gravity and natural forces, the gurney slid itself to the back of the van. It snapped into place with a metal clank.

I lit up another cigarette.

By the time I came down from Horse Pen Mountain the sun had begun to peek over the hills. My hands had finally stopped shaking. The rain had stopped and I hadn't heard a peep from the back of the van. I was beginning to think I had dreamed the whole thing.

Until I saw the roadside sign for Rita's Little Diner.

I made a right and in six minutes I was at a little red diner. It was full of miners going to or coming from work. Got me some coffee, sausage links, and two of the best pancakes I've ever eaten. It might have added forty minutes to my time, but it was worth it. When I left, I felt a world better, but knew I hadn't dreamed the talking, smoking dead guy at all.

I sat on the bumper of the van and smoked three cigarettes in a row. The morning sun pulled the cold and fear out of my bones. Spring warblers sang, and country music floated from a pickup across the parking lot. It rallied my courage; I buttoned my coat and climbed back into the van.

Listening to the radio on my way back to Charleston, I knew about the accident before I reached it. Sitting there in the traffic, looking down at the bent steel, blood, and wood chips, I realized had it not been for the dead guy and the pancakes, I might have been in this accident. A logging truck had over turned and spilled its load over the four lanes. Seven cars were totaled. Sixteen people went to the hospital and five people died. I ended up hauling the driver of the truck myself.

I still work for Mr. Netty. I still wander the roads in the middle of the night with my winter coat and my air conditioning. I don't get the willies, but I make sure to stay clear of Horse Pen Mountain.

Frank Larnerd is a writer, filmmaker, artist, and poet. Currently, Frank studies Professional Writing at West Virginia State University, where he has received multiple awards for fiction and non-fiction. His first anthology as editor, Hills of Fire: Bare-Knuckle Yarns of Appalachia *will be released in the fall of 2012 from Woodland Press. Frank lives in Putnam County, West Virginia.*

Coda

Walt Hicks

Detective Mack Coda slipped past the crime scene tape surrounding the rubble of an abandoned shotgun house in the Lower Ninth Ward, New Orleans. Despite sporadic rebuilding and the highly publicized best intentions and efforts of government, non-profits, and Hollywood celebrities, there were sections of the Ward that were still in utter mildewed and weed-choked shambles seven years after Hurricane Katrina. Coda had been in Darfur during that fateful August in 2005 and had avoided that particular catastrophe. Specifically, he had been an unwilling guest of a brutal Janjaweed tribal leader for the majority of that year, and still bore the scars to prove it. All things being equal, he thought he probably would've preferred the 'natural' disaster.

"Coda, Homicide Section." A young, jump-suited crime scene unit officer was dusting a moldy, water-marked door jamb for prints as a familiar coroner's assistant gingerly combed over a corpse just inside. Coda startled the attractive young redhead at the door, although that hadn't been his intention. Since Coda blocked the doorway and the rising sun, she slid her sunglasses to the top of her head to look him over.

Coda was a large black man, around six-five, two sixty, well-muscled and quietly intense. He was dressed in immaculately pressed khakis and a form-fitting PD-issue grey polo embroidered with the NOPD 'star and crescent' logo on the left, Coda's name, rank, and district on the right. He was wearing a Blackhawk tactical holster slung low on his right thigh, housing a big Heckler & Koch Mark 23 .45 caliber semi-automatic handgun. The combat belt the holster was attached to held three additional 12-round magazines, handcuffs, and other necessities of his trade.

The young crime scene tech had never met Coda before, but his larger-than-life reputation had certainly preceded him. The big, handsome, two-fisted war vet who seemed held together by unbending determination—and scar tissue—had become something of a legend at the PD in a span of just five years. Most of the other cops secretly envied or outright feared him; even the most ruthless gang lords made it a wise business policy to stay out of his way.

"Detective," she said, not so subtly sizing him up. "This is a bad one. Never seen anything like it." She stepped aside. "Go on in. Crime scene's a DNA nightmare anyway. Just watch where you step. There's pieces of the vic everywhere." He took off his sunglasses as he crossed the threshold, just as she'd hoped he would. His striking emerald green eyes seemed to pin her to the door.

The odor of mold and mildew paled beside the sudden stench of rot and corruption. Coda had smelled the reek of death in nearly every possible permutation, but nothing quite like this. Medical investigator Chase Peyroux from the Orleans Parish coroner's office was taking digital photos of what could only charitably be referred to as human remains. Peyroux was pale and wiry, a slightly displaced Cajun the detective had known since his childhood in the Lower Ninth.

"Mack. Figured they'd send you on this un."

"Chase. What we got here?"

"Got called in as a possible dead homeless dude . . . but . . ." Peyroux pushed the New Orleans Saints visor further up his bald head and slid the dust and mist respirator from his nose and mouth. He inclined his head toward the multi-colored ruins of what formerly comprised a human being. "Well, near's I can tell, something et a person, then puked 'em back up."

"Nice. So, what're you telling me—a gator?"

"Nope. Know how a python swallows somethin' whole, squeezes the holy shit out of it, then regurgitates the remains? More like that. No teeth or tool marks, though. Everything was crushed. Including the skeleton."

"Shit. How long?"

"With insect predation, heat and humidity, I'd say round twenty-four to thirty-six hours, topmost. I'm fixin' to get whatever this used to be over to Doc Whelan. Should know more in a few days. I'll give you a shout."

Seeing nothing else telling on the inside of the crumbling structure, Coda walked the perimeter of the small, ruined house. He had grown up near here, gone to high school at nearby Lawless just before joining the Marine Corps. His father had been driving for a wrecker service when he was killed collaterally in a gang shoot-out over on Decatur Street the day after Coda's eleventh birthday. Even before that, Coda and his white mother had experienced quite a rough time of it in the Lower Ninth. In addition to his dominant African ancestry, Coda had inherited his father's muscular build, rugged good looks, and two-fisted drive; from his mother, a quiet, steely resolve—and his striking green eyes. His mother had been murdered in their home just after Coda graduated from boot camp.

At the western corner of the shotgun house, something caught his eye. A small wooden carving lay propped against the foundation. He retrieved a clear evidence bag from his belt and carefully secured the item inside. He held the bag closer to his face and whistled softly.

The crime scene tech appeared behind him, several shades paler than before. "Detective, uniforms found three more vics. Three different houses, this same street."

The three additional scenes were nearly identical; three more corpses, crushed beyond recognition, no obvious forensic evidence, no tracks in or out, and similar odd wooden carvings located at the western corner of each house. Now that it was evident that some homeless squatter hadn't died of natural causes in an abandoned home, swarms of police and coroner's personnel had been called on scene. Coda had all he could get from the scene, so he met Peyroux at the coroner's van.

"Jesus Henry Christ," Peyroux said, loading a covered gurney into the van. "Some zeerah shit all up in here. Looks like Dahmer dropped acid and tried to make hisself some jambalaya. Ain't sure what it is yet, but the remains are coated in some kinda gloppy corrosive goo. We'll have to use hazmat procedures up in the morgue. Hopin' the bodies might actually have ID on 'em too. Well, in there somewheres. I'll call you once we find out."

Coda nodded, distracted. "Can you send a few pics of the bodies to my phone?"

"Yeah, sure, Mack. You got it. What in the hell's goin' on here, anyhow?"

"Not sure, Chase. Not sure what we're dealing with here."

Peyroux stared at his old friend with concern. "What you gone do, podna?"

"I aim to find out who—or what—is behind all this. And then I'm gonna stop it."

Peyroux nodded gravely. "That's what I's 'fraid of."

Coda jumped into his worn-out PD-issued Ford Crown Vic, radioed in his intended destination, and left the Lower Ninth, heading west on St. Claude Avenue to North Rampart and into the French Quarter. He thought he recognized the bizarre carvings he found at the crime scenes from his time in Africa. He needed verification of origin, as well as their meaning and possible significance.

Not so far from the Riverwalk, on the Quarter side of Canal Street, and somewhat off the beaten path from the numerous tourist destinations, was Lady Simone's. Jammed between newer and aging architecture, the columned façade of the double-gallery two-story was iconic yet nondescript; a flowing cursive neon sign in the central second story window was the only indication of a business housed within.

While she was widely known as Lady Simone, Coda had known her for years as Paulette Métoyer—five-foot-one, ninety-five luscious pounds of sexually voracious Créole goddess. She was also the most knowledgeable person he'd ever known on the subject of all matters arcane. The front of her small shop contained more mainstream, touristy occult items such as customizable gris-gris bags and voodoo dolls with frames in the faces where one could place the picture of a loved one or acquaintance as a joke. Deeper into the shop and further along the dark rows of mystical esoterica could be found some quite startling religious and magical artifacts, along with a variety of dark arts paraphernalia. For those who were true believers, Lady Simone was the real deal. Coda also knew that from the back room Paulette sold a little weed, bongs, and other smokers' paraphernalia from time to time. The PD generally overlooked her minor sideline because she was an occasional and accurate source of information regarding some of the city's criminal heavy hitters.

Paulette was standing behind a glass counter, gazing at a spread of tarot cards. She was dressed in opaque black tights, barely covered by a clinging multi-colored top that was off the shoulder and made a sharp V-line to her alluring cleavage. Her hair was pulled up in a red do-rag, a burst of dreadlocks spilling out the back. She was wearing a pair of elaborate red cat-eye glasses and her skin was exactly as he remembered it: porcelain-smooth and dark cinnamon in color.

"As I live and breathe," she said, her voice satin with a smooth Créole lilt, "Look what the ol' cat dragged in. Mister Mack Coda."

Coda managed a half-smile. "Paulette."

She seemed to stretch seductively, as if it were second nature, Coda noticed. "What brings you to my humble shop? Oh, I bet you must've forgot my number, since you never, ever call. Probably figured you'd catch up on old times, right? Card I just turned over said I was gettin' a visit."

"Justice?"

"The Fool."

Coda needed a diversion quick. He figured the best one would be the actual reason he was there. He held up one of the bagged carved statuettes from the crime scene. "Actually, I was wondering what you could tell me about this."

"You boys and your wood, is that all you can think—" Paulette's eyes widened; the diversion had worked. "Holy . . . where'd you get this li'l fella?" She took the bagged carving from Coda's hand and examined it appreciatively.

"Crime scene. Found it outside an abandoned house—real mess of a corpse inside."

"West side of the house, right?"

"Yeah. Oh, and there's three more just like it out in the car, with three more corpses at the morgue."

Paulette depressed a button hidden within the framework of the glass counter. The front door locked with a loud click and the neon 'open' sign began flashing 'closed.' She slipped off her glasses and the do-rag. The dreadlocks had evidently been sewn into the do-rag because the whole fashion statement now lay on top of the counter like a dead animal. Paulette's actual hair, a severe, jet black pixie cut, framed her lovely face. She stepped from behind the counter, settling uncomfortably close to Coda.

"What do *you* think this is?" she asked.

"That's why I'm here, girl." He shrugged. "To me it looks a little like a miniature version of an Easter Island mo'ai. Voodoo, maybe?"

"Not bad, big boy, not bad." She rotated the sculpture around, carefully examining it. "Actually it's African in design, not Polynesian. And a whole helluva lot older than voodoo, Santeria, or even Yoruba. Looks to be from an ancient animist religion, maybe Orexalta. The wood itself isn't very old, but the technique is. See the primitive cuts? Made by a sharpened piece of stone instead of a modern cutting tool. Takes forever to do it right."

"What's it for?"

"The Shalgbalatá, a priest or shaman—or in this case closer to 'conjure man'—uses this particular talisman to call and control an elemental spirit or deity, usually for lust, revenge, or something disgustingly human like that. It usually makes for a really bad ending."

"I can vouch for that."

Coda's phone chirped an abbreviated version of *Taps*. "That's Peyroux, I gotta take this," he said.

Paulette waved her hand absently. "Tell the Cajun wonder boy I said hey." She gently placed the carving on the counter and retrieved a massive leather bound volume from the bookcase behind the counter.

"Hey, Mack. Where you at?" Peyroux's voice was muffled, distant.

"Lady Simone's."

Peyroux barked a gruff laugh. "She swingin' off your pecker yet?"

"Not yet. You sound like you're calling from a men's room stall."

"Nah. I'm still in a goddamn Tyvek moonsuit cause of that corrosive shit. Ain't nothin' left of them bodies 'cept piles of crunched-up bones, man. And some blue-black-red lookin' gooey shit. Was able to find three wallets and a purse inside the wads of human paste, though. Fished 'em out and cleaned 'em off before they melted too. Not positive ID's, you understand, but might get you started."

"Can you text me the info?"

"You got it, brother. Also, before all the inside goodies turned into human soup, we noticed they was all ridden with cancerous tumors, plaque-filled, hardened arteries, and so many other disease markers, we couldn't count 'em all. None of us ever seen the like. Hey, you be careful, hear? This here is some boo-coo weird shit. Oh, and since you hangin' with Paulette, best tell your pecker to watch out too."

"Yeah. Thanks."

Coda looked down at Paulette, who stood scarcely chest high to him. "You said a spirit or deity. What's that mean, exactly?"

Paulette shrugged. "Each religion had hundreds. Some overlapped. Impossible to say for sure."

Coda pulled up the crime scene pictures on his phone. "Peyroux said the remains were eaten up with cancer and other diseases. Plus, it did *this* to them." He held the screen facing her, an unrecognizable smear of blood, organs, muscle, and gore in the picture.

She whistled softly. "That might narrow it down some," she said, consulting the dusty old tome.

Coda grinned a little. "Can't you just Google it?"

"A lot of books aren't on the Internet yet." She looked him squarely in the eye. "Some books should *never* be."

As Paulette researched, Coda glanced through the tentative vic ID's on his phone, then found himself pondering the realism of a shrunken head in the glass case, the stitching securing its eyes and mouth seeming to squirm a little. He shook the cobwebs away just as Paulette said, "Think I may have your bad boy. It's called the Oómùlarè. A particularly nasty specimen that was considered to be the embodiment of disease and death. The name more or less translates to something like 'between light and dark, he walks' since it can be called from the realm of death over to our reality by a particularly knowledgeable and practiced Shalgbalatá."

"Know of such a fella around the Easy?"

"I heard about a really small splinter cult in the Lower Ninth, back before Katrina. Led by a dude by the name of Dunsimi Akinsanya. Best I remember, he was an illegal, but the Orexalta church's nonprofit was held by one of the members who was here legally. The church and several homes were in the church's name, so nobody got harassed or deported. Katrina either scattered or wiped them all out; I haven't heard anything of them since."

Coda nodded. The bizarre pieces were beginning to fall into place, if forming a nightmarish, insane puzzle. The vic had been a code enforcement official for the Lower Ninth, a district councilman, a real estate agent, and a wealthy construction developer. Coda didn't claim to understand the mechanics of what was happening, but he knew for certain he had to find Dunsimi Akinsanya.

"How do I kill it?"

"What? A mythical being from a nearly extinct religion?" Coda nodded as Paulette approached him, running her hands across his broad chest, then up and across his shoulders. "What's it worth to you?"

"I'm serious, Paulette."

"Me too. I'm just asking for dinner at Commander's, a few drinks maybe? Bet I could make you remember what being a man's all about."

Coda recalled the wanton frenzy, the fevered clawing and biting all too well. "If this is extortion, I have to admit to liking it. Dinner? Sure. Why the hell not? Now, how do I kill this Oómùlarè?"

Pursing her full lips, Paulette slipped behind the counter and unlocked the front door remotely. She donned her uniform of glasses and dreadlocked do-rag, returning to her tarot cards, all business now.

"You can't."

* * *

From his car, Coda used his Smartphone to narrow down a possible location for Dunsimi Akinsanya. A probable illegal, he was not listed in any directory. However, a quick search of court house records showed that his church currently owned—and had recently paid property taxes on—an industrial property not far from Lakefront Airport. He waited for the sun to set and the dazzling lights of New Orleans to come on. He radioed in, reporting himself 10–10: off duty. What he planned to do next was far outside the blurry confines of procedure, policy, protocol, or *law*.

Within minutes, Coda pulled his tired Ford into a deserted parking lot. The industrial area was crowded with old, squat buildings; the brick fronts and stucco were broken by aluminum garage bay doors, barred windows, and entrance doors, displaying varying degrees of peeling paint and neglected signage. In a half-hearted attempt to keep the roofs from leaking, some buildings were topped with ubiquitous blue tarps, torn and faded from nearly seven years of thankless service. Coda quickly found the bay number associated with the Orexalta church's listed ownership. The building was on an isolated corner, seemingly empty, but with heavy chains and big padlocks on the doors.

He popped the Ford's trunk and retrieved his Bushmaster AR15 modular carbine assault rifle. He checked the 30-round clip then slung the throw and go rig over his shoulder. He also readied the HK .45 and returned it to his TAC holster, then he took a deep breath and walked toward the building.

The chains securing the entrance were rusted but sturdy; the big padlock seemed new. Coda was trying to figure out how to quietly access the building when the padlock abruptly fell open in his hand. The chains clattered to the cracked concrete. Coda toed open the door.

Inside, the place was nearly empty except for random pieces of old derelict machinery covered by dusty tarps. Concrete columns supported the sagging ceiling at close intervals and at the middle of the large bay, two 55-gallon drums spouted lazy flickers of flame. Toward the back of the room seemed to be a small office, maybe a restroom. In one corner, a silent generator sat with three five-gallon jerry cans next to it. There was a humid, musty smell with the putrid fetor of illness and rot hovering just beneath it. Coda unholstered the .45, holding it combat-style low as he approached the center of the still room.

The gut-slamming stench was first; a slaughterhouse in summer, a nearly palpable odor of death, despair, sickness, and loathsomeness. Behind him, Coda heard a slimy bursting sound; instinctively, he ducked, shoulder rolling across the concrete slab floor to his right. From where he had been previously standing, he heard a wet slap against the floor then an even sloppier pop—the sound a suction cup makes detaching from a moist surface. He rolled quickly to his feet, pivoting the .45 toward the movement. In his peripheral vision, he thought he had seen something that looked like a tall, ragged tree trunk hit the floor and then somersault away . . . into nothingness.

The walker between worlds? Between light and dark?

A gelatinous puddle roughly the size and shape of a manhole cover covered the spot Coda had occupied moments before. The deathly rank stench had dissipated somewhat, but now the pungent tang of a corrosive filled his nostrils.

Coda figured remaining stationary was most likely a death sentence, so he moved from post to post, systematically rotating the cocked and locked .45 around the room. He realized just before he had heard or seen the Oómùlarè, he actually *smelled* it.

Maybe he could—

The retch-inducing odor punched his nostrils once again and he ducked and rolled, this time left. He heard a thudding crash as the concrete load support beam he had been leaning against shattered and exploded outward in a violent shower of dust and debris. Coda scrambled away just as part of the ceiling collapsed. He fired two quick rounds into the thing's center of mass and it disappeared again. He thought he heard a high-pitched squeal as it vanished, and he saw something on the floor where it had been. It looked a little like a sliver of gnarled brown-green bark from an ancient, diseased tree. It smoldered with the corrosive substance and rapidly withered.

"If I can hurt it, I can kill it," Coda whispered.

"You really are quite the fool, aren't you?" a voice behind him boomed.

Coda whirled and very nearly shot the old man peering at him from behind the concrete post's rubble. Coda raised the muzzle slightly.

"Hands up, Akinsanya, New Orleans Police."

"I'm well aware of who you are. *I'm* not what you should be most concerned about."

Akinsanya was a tall, bent man, perhaps in his mid to late seventies. His flesh was ebony black and his hair was starkly snow white and closely cropped, matching his beard. He was wearing some sort of multi-colored ritual robe festooned with feathers, along with the claws and bones of small animals draped about his waist and across his chest. Rounding out his bizarre ensemble was a purple felt fedora and matching Nike running shoes. He was holding another of the wooden carvings in his gnarled hands.

He moved between the concrete pillars like a ghost.

"Let's talk about this, Akinsanya. I don't want to have to kill you."

The booming laughter echoed throughout the empty space. "I guess the only alternative left for you is to murder me, since you can't very well arrest me."

"No, you'll not be going to trial in this world. Look, you got your revenge, made your point, or whatever the hell it is you're trying to do. Just leave the Oómùlarè where it belongs. Put down the potato head and let's call it a day."

The old Shalgbalatá sprinkled something into one of the flaming barrels and fire shot to the ceiling, illuminating the room. From the shadows of the far wall, Coda could see shelf after shelf of the iconic carvings—dozens of them.

"Oh, I'm just getting warmed up, Detective," Akinsanya said, indicating the statues. Closing his eyes, he held the one in his hands high above his head. "And this one belongs to you!"

The Oómùlarè burst into existence once more, crashing through the wall behind Coda this time, bounding end over end, again narrowly missing him. It leapt over his head, gobbled up an old machinist's rotary table, and vanished in a hail of .45 slugs. Seconds later, a mangled version of the rotab seemingly fell from the ceiling with a crash and the misshapen metal sizzled.

"How the Oómùlarè dances! It wants a dance with you!" the old man yelled.

"Why are you doing this, Akinsanya? If you're making a point, I'm not getting it." Coda realized that whenever the Oómùlarè made an appearance, the old man seemed to be chanting, concentrating hard with eyes closed intently.

"*They* kill or scatter my people, *they* steal my land, and *they* think they will go unpunished? Of all people, *you* should understand that."

Coda continued his diversionary tactic, even as he cautiously circled the crafty old man. "All my people are in urns on my bookcase. Who are 'they'?"

"My flock drowned like rats because of *your* government. Those who didn't die were scattered to the winds like animals. My properties were condemned by your so-called code enforcement, eminent domain declared so my land could be stolen by the corrupt and greedy." His dark eyes flared and he licked his lips. "The night of the big storm, I *heard* the explosions on the Industrial Canal. *They* figured to keep the Quarter from flooding, by drowning the Lower Ninth, driving us out."

Coda had heard similar street whispers before. "Don't suppose you can actually *prove* any of that?" He edged closer so he could see the old man's face. "Hell, if you could, I'd shoot 'em myself."

"Look for the craters under the Industrial Canal levees. Still there," the old man remarked sadly, closing his eyes.

Coda reached behind his back, grasping the AR15's pistol grip with his left hand. He trained the .45 on what he could see of the old man's face, covering the other side of the bay with the AR15. "Don't push this, old man. Don't make me—"

Akinsanya murmured, "You cannot kill it . . ."

From his left, Coda could see the Oómùlarè's dreadful shape burst through thin air, somersaulting inexorably toward him. The thing was stunningly, grotesquely simple: an oozing blood-red sphincter on either end of its tubular length enveloped unfortunate prey, crushing with powerful, undulating contractions, finally unceremoniously depositing the grisly remains out the other end.

Coda emptied the AR15's 30-round clip toward the relentlessly advancing shape, and at the point the creature vanished with a blood-curdling shriek, he fired one round at the old man from the .45. The hollow-point round caught the edge of a concrete post, mushroomed, and took off the top of the old man's head just above the eyebrows, in a gruesome spume of scarlet, white, and gray.

After the echoes of gunfire faded, the bay was as still as a crypt. Coda stood over the shaman, whose rheumy, angry eyes stared up at some fixed point far beyond Coda—the ceiling and the heavens outside. "Maybe I couldn't kill the conjure," Coda said quietly, "but I could damn sure kill the conjure man."

Quickly gathering his expended brass into an evidence bag, Coda next piled the wooden carvings around the old man's body, dousing them and the entire bay with the contents of the jerry cans: fifteen gallons of gasoline. From outside, he tossed a makeshift Molotov cocktail through the doorway, feeling the hellish *whoosh* blast past him as the interior exploded into a cauldron of white-hot flames.

The fire was a bad one, and shortly after Coda drove his unmarked cruiser through the gate, New Orleans FD was already responding—units from Squrt 4, Engine 12, Engine 6, and Ladder 3 piling on scene in a sort of loosely choreographed chaos.

Coda drove around his city, waiting for the adrenaline high to finally wear off. As he navigated the familiar streets, he could feel the kinetic and diverse lifeblood pulsing through New Orleans and it revitalized him. As he knew he would, he ended up back in the Lower Ninth. He slowly drove by the empty lot that used to house his alma mater, Alfred Lawless High School. Only a few blocks away, he shined his car's spotlight on the now-deserted crime scene from earlier that day. A humid breeze fluttered a forgotten shred of crime scene tape; nothing else stirred as all ghosts slept.

Coda parked near the Industrial Canal. An unimaginable pile of cash was being spent to preclude a repeat of 2005's disaster. He could see new structures intermingling with the old, failed levee. *Old scar tissue still trying to hold everything together,* he thought. He didn't see anything resembling an explosion's crater, though.

Monsters weren't all that hard to find, he knew. They were everywhere, lurking in the dark or walking the world, cleverly hiding in plain sight. They might be outwardly hideous, or worse, glowering behind a beautiful face with perfect teeth and a deceptively warm smile. Unlike the old black and white horror movies his mom and he had watched in their darkened home all those years ago, evil had blurred into so many sizes, shapes, colors, and singularities it was nearly impossible to keep track.

Coda wondered—not for the first time—if madness and hatred spawned the monster. Or, was the monster actually the *source* of madness and hatred? He realized his causality dilemma was irrelevant.

Coda could only hope that by thwarting the monster at hand, he hadn't allowed an even worse evil to abide.

Walt Hicks has authored hundreds of "weird" short stories, and is founder, publisher, and editor of the now-defunct HellBound Books Publishing Co. He is also the author of DeathGrip: The Collection *and co-author (with HORNS) of* Exit the Light.

In a Fit of Jealous Rage

Ray Garton

His thumbs pressed down hard. Whatever was beneath them—it was hard but pliable—gave beneath the pressure.

Skin. He was touching skin. It was something beneath the skin that was hard.

Thirty-one-year-old Samuel Mason, Sammy to all his friends, opened his eyes and found himself looking down at his wife Kaylee. Her narrow eyes were open and bulging and her swollen tongue stuck out of her mouth. Her face had a bluish tint, especially around her lips.

"Kaylee?" he said, and he hardly recognized his voice, it was so cracked and hoarse.

Sammy realized he was out of breath, as if from a great deal of physical activity, and his heart was pounding overtime in his chest and throat. He looked around and found that he was in his bedroom, on the bed, his knees straddling Kaylee's naked body, his hands on her throat, thumbs pressing hard.

He released a broken cry of shock and pulled his hands away from Kaylee's throat, which was badly bruised.

"Kaylee? Kaylee, please," he said. He touched two fingertips to her throat. He tried to find a pulse, but there was none.

The window shades were all down and the room was dark. Sunlight seeped in around the edges of the shades, giving each window a halo of light.

"No," Sammy said. He spoke the word flatly, almost coldly. He pulled away from Kaylee and got off the bed. His foot hit something on the floor. He looked down at the body stretched out a few feet from the bed. It was a naked man who lay on his back. There was blood everywhere—it seemed to be mostly on the left side of his head, but it had gotten on his shoulder and all over the carpet around his head.

He looked around at the clothes on the floor, his and hers. They'd shed them and let them drop where they stood before getting into bed. He imagined them quickly undressing, fumbling with their clothes, maybe fondling each other in the process, unable to get naked and into bed fast enough.

Sammy did not recognize the naked man on his bedroom floor. Beside him lay a bronze figure of a posing woman that normally stood on Kaylee's nightstand. Now it lay on the floor with a clot of tissue and hair stuck on the woman's sharply-bent elbow.

He frowned, thinking, trying to reach back with his mind. Was he dreaming? It certainly *felt* like a dream. He closed his eyes tightly and concentrated on waking up.

The smell of feces made him wrinkle his nose.

No, he was awake, wide awake.

He looked down at the bronze figure again. The posing woman had her left hand on her forehead, elbow sticking out. As he stared at it, he could feel its weight in his hand, and he flashed on a memory of swinging it. He closed his eyes and he could feel it hitting its mark in his hands. The man's head had been that mark—the side of the man's head. Sammy had swung the figure like a bat and it had connected with the naked man's head, and down he'd gone, and the blood had begun to flow.

Sammy opened his eyes, bent down, and felt for a pulse in the man's throat.

He was as dead as Kaylee.

"Oh, god," Sammy said in the same flat, cold way he'd said, "No."

He turned to the digital clock on his nightstand and read the glowing green numbers: 2:41. He looked down at himself and found he was wearing a suit.

He wondered what day it was. He thought back to that morning. He remembered breakfast. He'd eaten a banana sliced up in a bowl of Corn Chex and had a couple cups of coffee. He decided it must be a weekday because he'd gone to work. He remembered kissing Kaylee goodbye. It had been a warm, lingering kiss—it had been a silent lie, he now knew. Then a janitor at Halden Software had accidentally hit an overhead fire sprinkler nozzle in the operations center with a broomstick. The sprinkler had gushed for almost an hour before it was cleared with the local fire department and shut off. Most of the cubicles had been soaked, including Sammy's. Everyone was sent home early.

Home. That's where he had gone, straight home. He'd noticed a dark SUV parked at the curb in front of their house, but thought little of it. People commonly parked there to go to other houses, so it didn't seem strange. Sammy parked his Lexus in the garage. He would've liked to surprise Kaylee, but he figured she'd probably hear him pull up, hear his car door shut. He'd gone inside through the door in the garage, which opened on the kitchen.

Kaylee usually had the radio or TV on, but the house had been oddly quiet, he remembered that much. There had been one sound somewhere deep in the house. It was a familiar sound, but he couldn't place it. He stood in the kitchen listening to it closely, intensely, wondering why it disturbed him so. He was feeling a growing anger even before he recognized it as the sound Kaylee made while having sex. It was her low, throaty, "Oh, oh, oh, oh."

He stood there a while longer, just listening, as the anger became a rage.

He had no memory of going upstairs to the bedroom—one moment, he was standing in the kitchen, and the next, he was standing in the bedroom's open doorway.

Kaylee had been on top of the man, moving up and down, saying, "Oh-oh-oh, oh-oh-oh."

Sammy had stood in the doorway watching them as the rage grew in him, as it pressed at the backs of his eyes and constricted his throat. Adrenaline surged through him like a freight train racing through a tunnel.

After that, things got very murky. He remembered swinging the bronze figure. He remembered shouting something at Kaylee, but he couldn't remember what he'd said. Maybe he'd said nothing—maybe he'd simply shouted his rage, or made some kind of animal-like growling sound. She had shouted, too, he remembered. She had shouted for him to stop.

Stop what? he wondered. He looked down at the man on the floor again. The left side of his skull appeared to have caved in. Sammy wondered how many times he had hit the man with the bronze figure. Maybe that was what Kaylee had wanted him to stop doing.

It didn't matter. Nothing mattered now, he realized, looking at Kaylee with her bulging eyes and tongue.

"Kaylee," he said in his broken voice. His chest rose and fell with his breaths. He paced beside the bed and tried taking a few slow, deep breaths.

What now? he thought. Should he call the police and turn himself in? Would they be more lenient with him if he were to do that? *Temporary insanity,* he thought. It was risky. A lot of people simply didn't believe in the temporary insanity defense. Would his jury?

He could say they were dead when he got home. Maybe he could try to make it look like a robbery, take a few things, do some damage in a few rooms, throw things around. He could say he came home and found the front door not only unlocked—they routinely kept the front door locked at all times—but standing half open.

No. He watched *CSI*, he knew what they could do. They'd nail him for it in no time.

Sammy bent down and picked up the man's pants. He found the wallet in the right back pocket, opened it up, and looked at the driver's license. Maury Linders. He looked down at Maury. He looked to be in his early fifties, tall and fit, with brown hair shot with silver. Sammy noticed two little indentations on Maury's nose, one on each side of the bridge. He wore glasses. Sammy looked at the nightstand and saw them there, a pair of wire-framed glasses folded up and lying by the base of the lamp.

Sammy's hands shook at his sides and he could not quite catch his breath. His scalp tingled as a chill passed over him.

He left the bedroom and went downstairs to the liquor cabinet in the dining room. He opened the cabinet and removed the bottle of Black Velvet, took a glass from the shelf, and poured himself a drink. He knocked back the first, then poured a second. He put the bottle down on the sideboard and paced the dining room. The warmth of the Canadian whiskey started in his stomach, then spread slowly. He did not want to get drunk, he just needed something to warm him, to stop the shaking in his hands. As he paced, he looked down and saw blood on his red-and-black tie. There was some on the lapel of his jacket too. He would have to burn the suit.

That was when he realized he'd already made up his mind. He was already thinking about the spot at Shasta Lake near his friend Bobby Kris's cabin—a deep, still cove where the shore dropped off sharply.

Sammy finished his drink and set down his glass. He went out to the garage and opened a large cupboard in the back. He had a few black tarpaulins rolled up in one of the tall cupboards. He took two of them back to the bedroom with him. He unrolled one of the tarps beside Maury Linders. He took the glasses from the nightstand and put them on Maury's face, then rolled Maury onto the tarp. He slowly rolled Maury up in the tarp. He spread the other tarp out on the floor, then lifted Kaylee from the bed and placed her on it, face up. He rolled her up in the tarp as he had Maury.

The rolled-up tarps lay side by side on the bedroom floor.

There was a chair against the wall between the bedroom's two walk-in closets. Kaylee's robe was always on that chair, draped on the seat or over the back. It was there now. Sammy went to the chair and picked up the robe. He sat down and looked at it. He slowly lifted the heavy terrycloth to his face and breathed in Kaylee's scent.

An ache blossomed in his chest. It spread as it grew worse.

"Oh, god, what have I done?" Sammy whispered into the robe.

* * *

By the time he discovered Kaylee in bed with Maury Linders, Sammy had been worried for about a month because something wasn't right. A sudden distance between them had sprung up, a distance that hadn't been there the week before, or even the day before. She hadn't stiffened when he touched her, nothing like that—she'd simply not responded at all. Just a few weeks ago, he'd taken her to the City Grill for dinner, her favorite restaurant, and asked her what was wrong.

"What makes you think something's wrong?" she said.

"C'mon, Kaylee, *some*thing's wrong," Sammy said. "Are you unhappy?"

A smile grew slowly on her face. "We've been married eight years and that's the first time you've ever asked me that."

"Really? Well . . . maybe I should ask it more often."

She said nothing, just held his gaze, smiling.

"I want you to be happy, Kaylee," he said.

After a moment, she said, "Do you want me to be happy? Really? I mean, are you sure?"

Sammy frowned as he reached across the table and took her hand. "Of *course* I'm sure."

Kaylee squeezed his hand. "Yeah, I know. You're a good man, Sammy. Don't ever let anyone tell you any different. Let's order, okay?"

He should have said more, he should have pressed it. But after that, she seemed somewhat warmer, more herself. When they got home that night, they made love for the first time in over a month, and it almost had been the same as before. But only almost.

He'd decided to say no more about it; he wasn't going to *beg* her to tell him what was wrong. She'd tell him in her own time, sooner or later.

Of course, it all made sense now. She'd been seeing Maury that whole time, possibly falling in love with him.

Do you want me to be happy? Really? I mean, are you sure?

Kaylee's words took on new meaning now. They made *sense* now.

Sammy took his glass to the dining room and poured some more Black Velvet. There were a few hours of daylight left. He figured he could afford one more drink. He'd be sober come sundown. But now, he needed the drink.

He was glad they hadn't had children. What would he tell them if they had?

Sorry, kids, but it looks like I killed your mom in a blind rage.

He decided he'd load his bicycle into the SUV. He could drive the SUV into the lake, then ride back on his bike. That meant he'd be spending most of the night on his bike, but that was okay. He rode a lot and he was in good shape.

Sammy walked back into the bedroom and returned to the chair, sat down.

They'd met at Costco. Kaylee had been handing out samples of cheddar cheese at a little table with a red paper tablecloth on it. Sammy had been unable to take his eyes off her. He stepped up to her table and she handed him a little cube of cheese on the end of a toothpick. Then he went through the store shopping. But before long, he made his way back to her little table for another piece of cheese.

He couldn't take his eyes off her. She had shiny black hair that fell long and thick over her shoulders. He found out later she was Korean, but at first, all he knew was that she was Asian. She had a voluptuous figure—her breasts generously filled her shirt and the jeans she wore were tight on her curves.

The fourth time he stepped up to her table, she said, "You must really like this cheese, huh?"

"What?" he said. "Oh. The cheese. Well. Actually. Uh, I'm Sammy."

"Hi, Sammy."

"Would you like to go out with me? To dinner? Any kind of food you want."

She laughed, but it was a pleasant laugh, not at all mocking. It was a *pleased* laugh. "When?" she asked.

"Tonight?"

"Tonight, huh?"

"Is tonight good for you?"

She thought about it a moment, then: "Yeah, tonight's good."

"What's your name?"

"Kaylee."

"All right, Kaylee. Can I have your phone number? I can call you this evening and you can tell me how to get to your house."

He was a nervous wreck the rest of the day. He couldn't wait to see her again, but was worried he would somehow blow it, that he would end up making a fool of himself. His luck with women was spotty at best, and part of the reason was his shyness. He spent some time rehearsing what he would say at her door when he picked her up. He tried complimenting her on how nice she looked. He decided he didn't like "nice" and tried to come up with some other words. Lovely? Too fancy. Beautiful? Because she was, there was no doubt about that. But maybe that was a little too forward.

"How about great?" he said to the mirror over the bathroom sink. "You look *great*." But that sounded too much like something you'd say to someone who's just lost a lot of weight. He toyed with "pretty." It was good—not too forward, but direct and honest. "You look very pretty."

When she opened her door that evening, she wore a beautiful black floral-print dress under a long red coat with black lapels.

"Hi, Kaylee," he said, smiling.

"Hello, Sammy."

"You look . . ." He stalled. *Pretty*, he thought, *You look very pretty*. But what came out was, " . . . beautiful. You look beautiful."

Kaylee had one of those mouths that always looked like it was smiling a little, but her smile grew much bigger. She gave him an odd look, like she was assessing him, sizing him up. Then she nodded once and said, "Thank you."

They went to Jade Gardens, a Szechuan restaurant. Over dinner, they talked about work—her job at Costco and his at Halden Software—and about what they liked to do in their spare time. Sammy found himself warming up to her, feeling more comfortable. He never stopped looking at her.

When he took her home, he told himself he was going to kiss her. He told himself this very firmly, as if he were going to tolerate no bullshit from himself. He walked her to her door and they stood on the porch of her little house and he smiled and realized he had no idea what he was going to say. He feared the possible rejection that might come from trying to kiss her. *Kiss her,* he thought, *Kiss her, dammit!*

He couldn't do it.

"I had a nice time," Kaylee said. "Thank you, Sammy."

"Yes," he said, "I did, too."

Then he did it, so suddenly he couldn't stop himself. His lips lingered on hers for a few seconds. Sammy was tempted to say, *Whew,* afterward, but he didn't.

He said, "I'd really like to see you again if—"

She put an arm around his neck and kissed him. This one was longer, and their tongues met.

"You're a good kisser, Sammy," she said. "Did you know that?"

"Uh, no, I wasn't aware of that."

She laughed. "How would you like to come in for a glass of wine."

But they never got to the wine. They kissed in the small living room and she led him down the short hall to her bedroom, where they undressed and got into bed.

The evening had gone far better than he'd expected.

Two weeks later she moved in with him. Four months later, they'd driven to Reno and gotten married. Sammy considered himself the luckiest man in the world.

That had been eight years ago.

What had he done wrong? Why had she been unfaithful? Was Maury the only one? Had there been others he didn't know about? What had she gotten from Maury that she wasn't getting from him? Thinking about it just made the ache in him worse.

Sammy finished his drink. He put the glass on the floor. He leaned forward and put his elbows on his thighs. He put his face in his hands and sobbed. He stumbled to the bed and stretched out on it. He cried himself to sleep.

* * *

He awoke at a little after five. He'd wait another hour, maybe ninety minutes. He wanted it to be good and dark.

He went to the kitchen, opened the cupboard under the sink, and got some cleaning materials. He went back into the bedroom, moved the two rolled-up bodies, and started cleaning the blood on the carpet. On his knees, in his suit, he scrubbed furiously. It took most of an hour.

When he was done, he put the cleaning materials back.

He picked up Maury's pants again and took the keys from the right front pocket. He went out to the garage and backed the Lexus out, parked it at the curb, and took from the visor the clipped-on garage door remote. He went to the SUV, got in, started it up, and backed it into his garage. Then he closed the garage door.

He opened the back of the SUV, went into the house, and picked up Maury. He carried him out to the garage and put him in the back of the SUV. Then he got Kaylee and put her next to him. He gathered up Maury's clothes and threw them into the back of the SUV. He took his bike from its hooks on the wall and placed it on top of them. He closed the back of the SUV and went into the house.

He took off his suit and put on a sweatshirt and a pair of sweatpants and sneakers.

Sammy was frozen in place when his eyes fell on their wedding picture on the wall.

He began to sob again. He said her name over and over. He sat on the bed, then fell back and put his hands over his face.

When it finally passed, he sat up, then stood. He told himself he had a lot of thinking to do—he had to decide what he was going to tell the police. That she'd just run off with someone? He wasn't sure yet. But he'd figure something out.

He made sure the doors of the house were locked, then he went to the garage and got into the SUV. He pulled out of the garage, hit the remote, and closed the garage door, then he got back into the SUV and pulled out of the driveway.

Sammy headed for the lake.

Ray Garton is the author of more than 60 novels, novellas, short story collections, and movie and TV tie-ins. His novels include the erotic 1987 Bram Stoker Award-nominated Live Girls, *which changed the face of vampire fiction,* Crucifax, Dark Channel, Shackled, Sex and Violence in Hollywood, Ravenous, Bestial, *and more recently the thrillers* Trailer Park Noir *and* Meds. *In 2006, he received the Grand Master of Horror Award. He lives in northern California with his wife Dawn and is currently at work on multiple projects.*

Charles

Steve Rasnic Tem

The night before Charles' wedding, his mother took the long bus ride from her small house in the suburbs to the run-down apartment building downtown where he had been staying for many years. She had never visited him in this place, and although she missed him terribly, she didn't at all look forward to the meeting. Off and on during that day she had such spells of absentmindedness—misplacing her keys, forgetting why she had gone in to this or that room, walking out to the clothesline with her blouse all undone, finally losing the worn-out slip of paper with her son's scribbled address—she eventually just had to sit down and have herself a good long cry. She really hadn't thought she'd been sad and wondered if sadness was really the right word for what she was feeling. Sometimes her body seemed to feel things she herself had no knowledge of.

Eventually she did find the piece of paper with the address—she'd put it in the canister with her teabags—and she managed to get herself dressed. It was one of the outfits she regularly wore to church, and it bolstered her. But even with these improvements in her condition, she discovered that her hands weren't working properly. They trembled so badly she dropped her fare by the bus driver and he had to pick it up for her. Maneuvering her feet down the narrow moving aisle proved difficult, her shoes feeling oversized and full of stones.

Her son's building was shabby, but not as bad as she had expected. A sharp odor of urine in the lobby made her clasp a tissue over her nose and mouth. She was relieved to find that the odor did not follow her up the stairs. She stood outside her son's door, sniffing self-consciously, then made herself stop. She rapped the door. It wasn't a very loud knock, but it was the best she could manage.

He didn't say anything when he first opened the door and looked down at her. He was wearing the kind of baggy shorts he'd always liked, except much bigger, of course, man-sized. And a t-shirt—it had always been hard to get him to wear anything but t-shirts. This one had some logo she did not recognize, whose jagged lines and garish colors made her uneasy. When she looked away from it she found herself following his long, sturdy legs down to the floor, to the huge, dirty gray, and almost disintegrated tennis shoes. She stopped there, staring, somewhat sickened by the look of the rotting canvas and rubber, and wondering if the tennis shoes were exaggerated, or if his feet were actually that big.

"Hi, Mom." His voice had a phlegmy sound. She looked up into his expansive face, the tall forehead, the soft doughy cheeks and chin. The eyes buried inside that face appeared tiny, dark, and feverish. "I didn't know you were coming." His oversized head bobbed unsteadily on the thin neck when he talked.

"I'm sorry," she said, her eyes tearing. "I should have come before."

His eyes blinked rapidly before focusing. "Do you want to come in?"

"Oh. Of course, honey." The *honey* was meant, and deliberate, and caused her pain.

He stood awkwardly aside to let her by. He seemed not to know what to do with his hands, like he didn't know how to invite someone into his apartment. He didn't know how it was done, so he raised his hands above his head and allowed them to hang and flutter there. Before his mother had a chance to step inside, he asked, "Are you coming to the wedding?"

She stared up at him, feeling very much a small woman. It seemed to her she had always been a small woman alongside her son, even when he was a little boy. She did not say anything for a time but watched his face intently.

"I will be there," she finally said, "because I think that's the right thing for me to do. But you must not get married, Charles. You really mustn't."

He blinked and looked away, and she thought about how raw and sore his tiny eyes appeared. When he was small, he'd get these terrible colds and eye infections, and it just seemed like they would never go away. "Mom, my name is *Charlie*. I want to be called Charlie now."

"I apologize, Charlie. That's a very nice name and I will call you that from now on. But Charlie, you just can't get married. That's something you must not do."

"I'm old enough."

"Yes, you are old enough, but that's not the point."

"She says she loves me, and I told her I love her, too. I promised. So did she."

"Oh, Charlie, I'm so glad someone said that to you. Really, I am. But you can't do something like this."

"We have to now. Everything's all ready. There's a party after, but you can't come if you keep saying things like that."

"I have to be honest with you, Charlie. I loved you when you were a little boy and I love you still. I have always loved you and I will always love you. You will always be my son. Forever, but you just can't get married."

"Why?" He said it looking around the room, looking everywhere but at her. She looked down at his feet wrapped in those terrible tennis shoes. He was rocking back and forth on those two huge feet, lifting one and then the other.

"You can't marry, honey, because you passed away. You died when you were just six years old."

He blinked his eyes a couple of times and then started rubbing them with the swollen mitts of his hands. Soon he was rubbing them so hard she was afraid he might hurt himself—a genuine but ridiculous fear. She thought she knew now why his eyes were so raw, so red, so small. He let his hands flutter up above his head, stretched, and yawned deeply, with all his body, like someone awakening from a long and extraordinarily deep sleep, unable as yet to muster the power of speech. He stared at her, frowning. Finally she looked away, not knowing how to interpret the look in his eyes.

"We never talk about that," he finally said. "It's just too silly."

"Charlie," she said with a sad smile, "that's my fault. At first, well, of course I wanted it that way—I wanted to pretend. The alternative was just unacceptable. But then when I couldn't pretend anymore, I still couldn't talk to you about it. How could I? I suppose I thought if we didn't talk about it, it would, well, take its own course, and that things would evolve as they were intended, in a more natural way, if natural means anything at all in your case. Charles, oh Charlie, do you understand what I'm trying to say?"

He looked vague, or bored, or perhaps he was trying to pretend he was bored. "You think I'm stupid." His lips contorted in an ugly way. "A lot of people think I'm stupid, but I'm not."

"No, of course you're not, honey. It's all my fault, this whole thing. I'm your mother. It was my obligation to help you adjust to this in some way. I just thought that, well, I always assumed you did not know you were dead."

He scratched his belly absently. He wasn't skinny, he had a bit of a bulge there, and she wondered how that could be when, as far as she knew, Charles did not eat. And if he was eating now, she did not want to think about what he might be eating.

"I dream sometimes I'm dead, I think. Or maybe I just remember it. And sometimes when I want to care about something I can't. It's like some things I think about are just movies, and I'm not in the movie, I'm just watching it. Sometimes I lean on one side when I walk and I think I'm going to fall over, but I don't, and I always think about that, but I don't want to. It makes me scared and mad."

"When you were six years old we were having the downstairs recarpeted. I was in the kitchen and you had wandered away from me." Her face felt suddenly wet, but she didn't try to wipe away her tears. "We had a conversation pit, they called them back then. They were somewhat popular in the seventies. They had put the huge roll of carpet down on the edge of it and gone back to the truck for something or other.

246

We never found out exactly what happened, but when we found you, you were at the bottom of the pit, the end of the carpet roll on top of you."

All through his mother's explanation, Charlie felt around his head, his fingers finally settling into a particular spot three inches above his left ear. "I have this place here."

"Yes, Charlie. That was one of the results of . . ."

"Couldn't you have gotten it fixed? I don't like it at all. My cap never fits right and my hair grows funny."

"Charlie, you were *dead*. There seemed no *reason*."

"It's not *your* head, mom. You don't have to comb your hair over and over again until it looks right." His mouth suddenly seemed like this uncontrollable thing. He turned his head to the mirror just inside the apartment, and she watched as a sneer spread across his face in the glass. He turned back and frowned at her. "You should have watched me better. When Ellie and I have kids, you better bet we're going to watch them better than you did me."

His mother trembled. "I made a *mistake!*" she cried. "And I have paid for it every day since then. You have been a constant reminder and a knife in my heart! But I never complained—I never even told you. I have only loved you."

He backed up a few steps. It pained her to see. "You let me die," he said, his hands held up between them.

"I'm your mother, Charlie, and I've always loved you. And I know it's sad, it's terribly, terribly sad, but you just *can't* have children. Just think of what they would be like. Something like that was never meant to be. My own grandchildren."

"They'd be like me, Mom. Maybe they would look like me. What's so bad about that?"

She gazed up at him, drying her eyes on the edge of her sleeve. "Oh, nothing, nothing, sweetheart. I'm sorry I got so upset."

"Do you want some tea? Ellie likes it, so I have a lot of it. You can see my place. That's what Ellie calls it—'Charlie's place.'"

"That would be very nice, Charlie. Thank you for inviting me."

He held the door open for her as if he were a doorman at attention. She stepped inside carefully, watching her feet. Once inside, she sniffed. It was a bad habit. Her son had no smell, virtually none. He never had. But the mind plays tricks, and after he'd died, she'd found herself attributing almost every unknown smell to him.

There were also no cooking smells, or smells of garbage, or unwashed clothing, or unwashed body smells—the smells she generally associated with young men. There was a strong aromatic mix of soaps and disinfectants. Her son was no corpse. He was something else. He was his mother's son, and no son of hers could be referred to as a corpse.

Charlie's apartment was profoundly neat. The area appeared completely without clutter, the rug well-vacuumed, spoiled by not even a thread of lint, her son's few personal items (if an empty vase, a stapler, and a battered dictionary could be termed personal) equally spaced on a single white plastic shelf mounted on the wall. There were a few toys—some cars, a plastic soldier, a yo yo—scattered by the bed. While she was looking, he walked over and nudged them under the bed with his foot.

"I don't play with those," he said. She gazed at the neatly-made bed. "I have some cookies here, Mom. I used to like cookies. Ellie likes to have a cookie with her tea when she stays over. Would you like a cookie with your tea, Mom?"

"That would be nice." She noticed his politeness and his politeness pleased her. She went over to the bed, trying not to look at it too directly. On a small table beside the bed was a young woman's photograph. She picked it up gingerly, as if it might go off. In her experience the most innocuous things sometimes had a tendency to go off, ruining everything. She stared at the image of the creature who chose to "stay over" with her dear, dead son. She didn't like to think of these things, but how could she avoid it? The young woman in the photograph had a shy smile, and the saddest eyes she had ever seen. She put the picture down quickly.

"Here, Mom." Charles walked awkwardly into the room with a cup of steaming tea on a small metal platter, along with what appeared to be a spotless plastic ash tray with a single cookie resting inside. He went over to a large chest in front of the single window and set it down. "You can feel the wind when you sit in front of the window. I always like feeling the wind on my face. I don't have any chairs. Do you want to sit on the floor?"

"That will be fine. Your floor is very clean." She sat down on the floor by one end of the chest and he sat down at the other. She started sipping her tea, which had a dry, dusty flavor. Nevertheless, she smiled and nodded at her dead son as she drank. The cookie was stale and hard, but at least the ash tray it sat in appeared quite sanitary.

Charles watched her as she consumed these things, occasionally peering out the open window, his eyes fixed and distant. Finally he said, "Mommy." He stopped, closed his mouth, began again. "Mom, why aren't I . . ." He closed his mouth again.

"Why aren't you lying in some grave somewhere?" she prompted.

He nodded. "I want to know. Do you know?"

She was grateful for an excuse to put down that awful tea, even though her hand was shaking as she returned it to the platter. "I can't tell you exactly," she began, "because I don't exactly know myself. We had the funeral and it was very sad. I thought I would die too, or that at least it was what I deserved." She paused then, looking for some reaction from him. As there was none, she continued. "For the next few days I stayed in bed while your father went to work. I knew he was suffering greatly, but I was in no condition to help him.

"At the end of a week, perhaps two—I really have no idea—I got up and made breakfast. Your father joined me at the table. No words were said, then after a few minutes, you walked in, much slower than normal, as if you had awakened from a hard sleep, and sat in your usual chair." She stopped and looked at him. "Do you remember any of this?"

Without pause he replied, "I don't remember. Was Dad surprised?"

"I thought he would have a heart attack."

"Were you surprised, Mom?"

"No. No, I was not."

"I think I knew you weren't surprised. Were you happy to see me?"

His mother did not know how to answer that question, and so she said other things she knew to be true. "For the first half hour or so your father cried and hugged you to him and told me how wonderful this was and what a joyful, joyful thing it was that had happened to us that day, a true miracle. You, however, acted as if there was nothing unusual going on. You looked from one of us to the other, as if you hadn't the faintest idea what we were talking about. Your father wanted to call your grandparents and all our friends and even neighbors who we didn't even know all that well."

"Did they all come?"

"I wouldn't let him call anyone. And just as I knew it would happen, over the second half hour or so your father stared at you and stared at you, until he became terrified of the sight of his own son, and he wanted to call the police and the doctors, but most of all he wanted to call our parish priest. But again, I would not let him. And though he said he could not bear it, he agreed to do what I wanted and he did not make those calls."

"What happened when our neighbors saw me?"

"The next day I got you up before dawn. I had packed some essential things, including a bag of your toys, even though you appeared uninterested, suddenly bored with everything you had had before. We left just before daybreak. I left your father a note telling him the city I would be taking you to, to start a new life. He was welcome to come join us later, I said, but for the time being I didn't trust him."

"Did he come?"

"He did. After three months he got himself together, and one night there he was, on our doorstep. But he was never the same. We were never the same. Nothing was ever the same again. That's not your fault, I want you to know that. That's just the way it is sometimes. He couldn't live with the change, and so he died."

Charles didn't ask how, as she had known he would not. Some things she understood instinctively, but there were so many things she did not understand at all.

Charles stood quietly and took the tray with the cup and ash tray into the kitchen. She could hear water running, the sounds of vigorous scrubbing.

She looked at the trunk they'd been eating on. It was spacious and sturdy—she thought she recognized it as one they used to have at the house. Everything in the room was plainly displayed. There appeared to be no other containers than this.

She pushed up the lid of the trunk. She recognized most of the few toys and books he'd owned when he died. All these toys for a child who would no longer play. But she thought about the toys shoved under the bed and knew he had been playing, in secret perhaps, but playing just the same. She gently shut the lid, determined not to think of these toys again.

Charles returned and stood looking down at her. "I'm getting married tomorrow, Mommy. Are you going to be there?"

"Do you remember any of these things I have told you about?"

He was looking out the window again, distant, as if they were in two separate locations, but he said, "I remember riding my tricycle down a long sidewalk, except it was longer than just long. It never stopped. And I was thinking, *I can't ride a trike. Mommy says I'm too little.* You said I couldn't have one until I was at least five, remember? But there I was, in my memory, riding the tricycle better than any boy ever rode a tricycle before, down that brand new sidewalk and by the trees and these great big houses, these huge houses that I'd never seen before. But that's all I remember, Mom. Did I ever go to elementary school?"

"You went to elementary school and junior high and high school—you did all of that."

"Did I have many friends?"

"No, I'm afraid not."

"Did I have girlfriends?"

"No, but you did lots of things. You watched television and you took the dog for walks—remember Corky, that Spaniel I got you?—and we sat on the porch and I played records for you. So many records—we had so much *music* in our life. And I told you so many things—I *encouraged* you. I told you how you would have a great career one day, and get married, and that you'd have many children of your own. You'd be a wonderful father. You'd make me a *grandmother*. I—we—talked about all that. Tell me you remember at least some of that."

He looked at her with what might have been a smile—it was hard to tell in that soft, doughy face of his in the failing light. "All I remember, Mom," he said, "is riding that tricycle, and how good I was driving the tricycle, and how good it made me feel. That's all I remember."

She looked down at her hands. She'd been picking at her nails. It was a terrible habit. Now her fingers were bleeding. "I'm sorry."

"Don't be sad, Mom," he said, but she didn't think he really meant it, or *knew* how to mean it. "I'll have kids. That means you'll have grandkids. You wanted that, didn't you? Isn't that great?"

And she did smile. She said, "That's great, honey. Sometimes we do get what we wish for," and closed her eyes. She went to that place where she had not been in many, many years, and when she opened her eyes again, her lovely boy Charles was gone.

She sat alone in a dusty dry box of a room with no furniture, with much of the window boarded, with trash on the floor and the remnants of numerous fires set for warmth or cooking or perhaps just for mischief. The door was off its hinges, lying in the corner, smeared with a variety of dark substances. She had never been in such a place in her lifetime, although she had heard of such places, seen them in movies and on television. One thing she did know about them was that a woman such as herself did not belong there.

On her slow journey down the stairs, she passed a young woman with dark eyes, so terribly sad. They nodded but did not speak.

Steve Rasnic Tem's most recent novel is Deadfall Hotel *(Solaris Books). This fall New Pulp Press will be collecting the best of his noir crime fiction in* Ugly Behavior. *In 2013 Chizine will publish his slipstream fantasy collection* Celestial Inventories.

Cut

Alex Bledsoe

The color cartridge in the DHS office printer had run out, so the client information he'd printed was barely legible. He parked on the street outside the tract home belonging to Dave and LeeAnn Blazer and their two children. Six weeks ago, Blazer, a former soldier who'd served two tours in Afghanistan, had threatened to cut up his wife in front of their kids. She'd called 911, officers arrived, and the Department of Human Services subsequently took the kids. "Dave Blazer," the initial investigator stated, "shows signs of dangerous mood swings and a preoccupation with knives." Dave had even spent the entire interview sharpening an Asian sword, not the least bit concerned with getting back his children.

Knowing the other DHS workers like he did, he was amazed the investigator hadn't run like a spooked rabbit. Their workload was too horrendous and their pay far too low for this kind of confrontation. Now, though, it was time for the follow-up, which had fallen to him in the rotation. No one answered his phone calls, so he used the excuse to take the afternoon off. He'd do the interview right after lunch. It would take no more than thirty minutes, then he could start the weekend early.

He walked up to the low, crumbling frame house, past the rusted tricycle and scattered toys on the sidewalk, and knocked on the screen door. He cupped his hands around his eyes and saw someone seated at the kitchen table.

"Hello? I'm with the Department of Human Services. Is that you, Mrs. Blazer?"

The figure at the table did not move or answer.

"Is your husband here?"

Silence.

"Your door's open. I'm going to come in, if that's okay."

No answer.

254

Inside the dark and silent house, his footsteps creaked across the uneven floor; something smelled of garbage and decay. Somewhere flies buzzed. It couldn't be the children because they were still with their aunt.

"Mrs. Blazer?" he called to the woman in the kitchen.

A slight whisper from the immobile figure reached him. He stepped closer.

"Help me," the small, hoarse voice said.

He tried the kitchen light switch, but it didn't work. He saw the small woman clearly now, seated with her hands folded on the table. She did not turn to look at him, but her eyes and lips moved when she said, "Please help me."

He got chills down his neck. The smell grew stronger. "Is, um, your husband here?"

"He's in the bedroom. Please help me."

He'd glanced down the hall on his way to the kitchen, but saw nothing obvious. Now he crept backward and peered carefully into the dimness. The clutter resolved into a grim tableaux.

A man huddled on the floor beside the unmade bed. Two dozen knives and swords, each with the point outward, lay in a neat semicircle around him, like the rays of the sun. A sword blade protruded from his back and his hand still gripped the hilt. Dried blood blackened the rug. Low-rent harakiri—it explained the smell and the flies.

He felt queasy. This was not the first suicide he'd found, but none of the others took such care with the presentation. He went back to the kitchen. "What happened?"

"The a-army wouldn't t-take him back," the immobile woman said. "He didn't make the cut. Please help me."

"Calm down. Did he kill himself?"

"Yes. He spent three days sharpening his kitana until it could split paper. Please help me."

"I will, I will." He took out his cell phone, but got no signal. "Does your phone work?"

"No. Please help me."

"Okay, let's get you out of here." He reached for the woman's arm.

"No!" she screamed, with more intensity than actual volume, like a vivid whisper.

He pulled her to her feet, intending to get her out of the house. When he did, her head fell from her shoulders, so cleanly severed that it had remained in place, allowing continued circulation. Great gouts of blood shot from the arteries. He screamed as the twitching, decapitated body seemed to attack him. His foot slipped in LeeAnn Blazer's fresh blood and he fell backward. His head struck the tile floor.

As he lost consciousness, he saw LeeAnn's severed head lolling beside the refrigerator.

She blinked sadly one last time.

I grew up in west Tennessee, an hour north of Graceland and twenty minutes from Nutbush. I've been a reporter, editor, photographer, and door-to-door vacuum cleaner salesman. I now live in a Wisconsin town famous for trolls, start writing at five in the morning, and try to teach my two sons to act like they've been to town before.

Harlots of New Chapel Row

Terry Horns Erwin

My eyes were burning and I couldn't force back the cough I knew was going to bring me to my knees. Its punch rippled through the entire sinewy stretch of my being like a mad surgeon's scalpel, slicing through flesh and nerve with an intensity wicked enough to numb my brain's functions. I wasn't lucky enough for the numbing, though. I felt everything. All the agonizing pain. I smelled blood, tasted it, was blinded by it.

My blood.

The blood of all my pals.

It was Leroy Miner, the campus custodian, who found me close to dying and struggling to stand back up. He pulled me from the hedges and put me in his car.

"Who did this to you, boy?" he asked.

I looked over at him as I slouched in the seat, seeing only a blur I accepted as Leroy, who was now sitting behind the driver's wheel. Whatever I said must've made little sense, meaningless sounds like the babble of a baby, because he said, "You save your breath. We'll get help."

I felt the car rumble, its engine spark to life. Its energy was overpowering considering my life force was tipping near empty. Suddenly I imagined her face, the dark-haired one, and got a jolt.

The car moved.

"Just stay down," he encouraged, setting his hand on my shoulder.

I had to tell him.

Needed to find some way to get the words out.

To warn him.

"You've lost a lot of blood, boy. You're gonna want to keep what you got left inside of you. And moving around like that will undermine that aim, I'd think."

I wrangled the pain off long enough to feebly say, "The chicks killed them." He cautioned me against using what little strength I had left, but I kept going. "They're monsters. They murdered my friends. She tried to waste me."

When I stopped speaking, I listened, waiting anxiously for his reaction.

The car seemed to slow considerably.

"The New Chapel house . . ." I continued, but quit when the brakes squealed and the car jerked to a stop.

With one eye strained open, I caught the quick shifting of a hazy shape just before a surprising blow to my head.

What the hell had happened?

The question lost its urgency as soon as I heard Doug's voice asking me if I wanted to go with them. My heart thumped fast. I started to shake.

"Well, *douchebag,* you comin' or not?"

This had taken place earlier. Something wasn't right. I couldn't remember what was coming next, but I knew in my gut it was crucial to remember.

"Okay, fine. It's your loss."

My collegian buddy bustled for his dorm room door.

What *was* it I so imperatively wanted to know?

"The guys are gonna say you're a fairy," he called, hanging partly in the doorway. "Maybe you are."

Then he swept away, leaving me staring foolishly at the wall in the hallway.

I wanted to go.

And Doug likely knew I would go, which was why he'd left the door open.

My phantom concerns dissolved; I dashed to catch up.

The car was ready and running.

Doug jumped into the back.

I was skipping down the steps when I heard Daniel shouting, "Come on, Winfall, the ladies aren't going to wait for you to reach puberty!"

I shook my head.

Laughter sounded from the car where Marc and Ryan also waited.

When I reached the sidewalk, Daniel, popping his head out the window, jokingly asked, "You didn't forget to bring your pecker with you, did you?"

I grinned naughtily and stepped toward him. "Yep, wanna see?" I clutched the crotch of my jeans and jiggled my bulge.

He lurched back, laughing.

"Just get the hell in," he said.

I opened the door and slipped into the back seat.

Daniel was driving. After all, it was his car. Ryan sat beside him. Me and Doug, with Marc in the middle, took up the back. A tight squeeze.

"You got the goods?" Daniel asked Ryan.

Before answering, Ryan fidgeted, rooting in his pockets. "Got 'em!" he said at last, holding up a chain of packaged condoms.

"Good," Daniel said.

"And the brewski?" Doug asked.

"The chicks will provide," Daniel assured us.

"How do you know?" Doug challenged.

With a sore glance, Daniel said, "Because I said so."

I saw Doug and Marc exchange doubtful looks. It went without saying Daniel was running the show. Without him, none of us would be getting laid. He'd met the girls. He'd set it up. Most of all, he had the car. If the girls he described were really waiting for us, truly willing to let us have our way with their luscious bodies, then for the time being Daniel was God, in my mind at least. And as the Good Book illustrates, you *don't* want to piss God off.

I leaned forward and patted Daniel on the shoulder.

"You're the man!" I praised.

He smiled with pride.

"Let's tap some tail!" he cried.

The rest of us hollered and howled.

The car jerked into motion. It carried us through the campus lanes. Everyone was worked up and chatty. We were about to have sex with beautiful girls we didn't know, with the exception of Daniel, who knew all of them. As I understood it, he'd only gotten together with one of them, and just the previous night at that. The details as Doug had informed me of them were sketchy at best.

As we were passing the grand Vanderberg library, it clicked with me Marc was the only one of us who had a girlfriend—a serious relationship of three years—and I began to wonder if our raunchy pleasure trip was at all weighing on him. From my observation, he seemed at peace with his decision.

I was shaking and my heart was pounding, but not from some dreadful anticipation. Now stemmed purely from lust. I, like my fellow mates, needed a release of sexual desire. End of term studies and athletics had us pent up.

"So look, how much are these hookers going to cost us?" Doug mouthed off.

"They're not hookers . . ." Ryan said.

"You saying I paid for sex?" Daniel broke in. "These girls are *not* whores!"

I reached around Marc and flicked Doug, indicating he should drop it.

"But I was hoping they were at least sluts," Marc whined.

Laughter.

"You know what I mean," Daniel said, grinning.

"Hey," Doug asked, "what was the name of the chick you hooked up with again?"

"Alarice," Ryan answered for him.

"What the fuck!?" Daniel said.

Ryan jumped back like a bratty kid expecting a swift, overdue backhand from one of his parents.

"Are you my damned spokesperson?" Daniel said.

"So, where they live again?" Doug pressed.

Shaking his head at Ryan, Daniel continued. "Her name's Alarice. She's fucking hot. I don't know her last name or the names of her friends. They stay on New Chapel Row and live in the big old church."

New Chapel Row.

I knew it was close by and it was where you could find sorority houses. The big old church had been converted long ago.

"Wait," Marc said. "Do we have any classes with these girls?"

I didn't know anyone named Alarice.

"Probably not," Daniel replied, and after a moment of silence said, "I don't know. What do I look like? A wizard or something? You guys better not embarrass or cock block me. You've got more questions than a census taker. I'm getting you laid, man! Thank me later."

I began to rethink the situation. College girl cuties, not salacious town chicks or starved MILFs. *What's the catch?* My excitement waned. I suspected Daniel might not be the god I thought he was and had placed my faith in.

"What does any of it matter," Daniel griped. "They're horny chicks, and they like jocks. We're in college, they're in college. Haven't you ever heard stories?"

He had a good point.

"Okay, okay, man," Doug said. "Just get us there."

"I dated Destiny Brewer my senior year of high school," Ryan stated. "I heard she's an Alpha Delta Kappa."

"Aww, how sweet," Daniel taunted. "Thanks for sharing with us, girlfriend."

The snide remark drew a humiliated frown from Ryan.

I smelled a strengthening aromatic woody fragrance, but Doug was the first to say, "Whoa, what's that dang smell?"

"Crap," Marc muttered.

"What?" I asked, watching him thrust his hand under his bottom in an agitated hurry.

"My cologne bottle spilled," he said.

He raised up in an exaggerated fashion, unintentionally knocking me in the head with his elbow. I heard Doug tell him to watch it, which meant he'd probably gotten hit too.

"Just great!" Daniel complained. "My car's gonna smell like you for weeks."

"Sorry," Marc said, reluctantly sitting back down.

"You will be," Daniel grumbled.

My nostrils started to tingle.

Every window in the car suddenly came down.

"Good thing we're here," Daniel said as the car turned a corner.

We were all silent as we drove past large homes—commodious residences on land leased from the college way back when they were likely regular places for regular families. Lights were on in most of them, but the last house with its distinctly different structural church design, looked dark and unwelcoming. Traditional Roman Catholic architecture. *A kinky setting for sex-crazed coeds and an orgy*, I thought to myself.

"They home?" Ryan asked with a tone of dejection.

"Alarice said they would be," Daniel responded. "And I believe her." He laughed and then added with a voice that hinted he was thinking about his first encounter with her, "I *definitely* believe her."

The car stopped.

We spilled out.

The air helped clear away Marc's cologne.

Gathered together on the sidewalk, Daniel led our pack up the stone stairs.

I tried to spot some sign of a light through the windows but found none.

When we assembled on the deck, Doug punched me in the arm and whispered with a smile how excited he was.

As I looked up at the oversized, arch-topped mahogany door, a feeling of strange recognition struck me again.

Déja vu.

A troubling spirit without explanation.

Daniel pressed the buzzer.

I heard nothing.

Marc was smelling himself and Ryan just looked plain nervous.

The door slowly opened.

I admit I shied away when I heard Daniel say, "Hey, Alarice! We made it."

I heard her before I saw her.

"We?" she asked.

The alluring sound of her voice roused me to nudge Marc out of the way enough so I could see her.

Daniel stammered as he introduced us. I'd figured he hadn't been entirely honest with us. I eyed Alarice up and down as I listened to Daniel bullshit.

Daniel hadn't lied about her looks. She was beautiful. Wavy dark hair with bangs teased back. Big hoop metal earrings sticking out on both sides of her gorgeous face. And the kicker, a white cotton spandex dress, decorated with an all-over pattern of tiny stars, tightly hugging every single inviting curve of her mature body.

My mouth watered.

I focused in time to hear her say, "I didn't warn the girls."

So there are more girls!

A quirky, bored kind of smile floated on her face. At least, that's what I saw.

"We're great guys, really," Doug said, sounding half convincing.

Marc and Ryan both agreed.

I felt compelled to say, "We're sorry if we came at a bad time."

I could feel the surprised looks and glares from all my pals. Daniel, already perspiring, shot me a fixed dirty look. I gave him one back and he backed off by turning away. He knew I knew he was full of it.

Her catching jade-green eyes centered on me when she said, "You're all wrestlers?"

Daniel laughed. "That's us."

I smiled.

God, she's hot!

There was an awkward space of silence that was so hush I could hear the restless breathing around me.

Then she smiled and said, "Let's have a party."

We all cheered.

Alarice stood back as we poured into the house, or church, or sorority, or whatever the place was supposed to be.

A pleasant, sweet scent was adrift in the air. Apples and cinnamon, reminding me of a bowl of Cheerios of the same flavor. I ate them a lot. Of course, Marc's thick cologne clung to it like wet mud on the bottom of a gym shoe.

When I went by Alarice, my arm accidentally slid across her breasts. I could feel the contrast of their spongy soft forms against the unexpected hardness of the nipples. A twinge of embarrassment came over me, but then it dawned on me there was more than enough room to have gotten by without trouble, and I was confident she had deliberately put herself up against me. I blushed and, in the same moment, glanced back to see if the same thing would happen to Doug, who was a few steps behind.

It didn't.

For some reason that made me proud.

Once inside, our group huddled together in a giant room. Alarice closed the door. From what I could see in the dim light, the room was a mixture of old and new things. Blackout curtains explained why from the outside the place had appeared so stygian. Modern furnishings were laid out within the immense skeletal structure of what once was a church rich in design. Broad rafters sloped out of the darkness settling in the highest points of the roof. I noticed we were standing on a circular pink area shag rug—one of many. Where long ago there was a vestibule and a nave that would've been crowded with pews, today two flat screen TVs, a PlayStation, a sectional couch, regular and beanbag chairs, coffee tables, and other ultramodern objects were present. Next to a pair of rainbow-colored pompoms, I spotted a bra and panties.

Alarice's movement drew my attention. That's when I noticed she was barefoot. To my surprise, her feet were rather unattractive—somewhat crooked and perhaps wrinkled. A downright contradiction to the rest of her dazzling beauty. If it was a birth defect or a deformity caused by an injury, she sure didn't seem to have any insecurities or shame about it.

264

"Where's the babes?" Daniel asked in a cocky tone.

Alarice puckered her lips then cupped her hands under her titties, lifting, squeezing, and gently shaking them. "Aren't I enough?" she asked in a pretend-sad voice.

Daniel rushed her and began groping and kissing.

She wasn't being receptive. She cleverly slipped out of his clumsy hug, stiff-arming him for good measure. "My sisterhood," she announced, signaling direction by extending a slender arm upward, much the same as a *The Price Is Right* model would.

Daniel shuffled to catch her but cooled it. His demeanor instantly changed when he aimed his gaze at what she was pointing to. His face became rife with strong sexual intent.

Where the transformation of the old church had undergone the most construction, at the area where I guessed the sanctuary might have began (my parents hauled me to our local St. Mary's on occasion in my younger days) I saw the staircase again, but now it was in use. A group of girls had come onto them. Six girls. One more than us, not including Alarice, of course.

"Oh man, oh man," Doug cried happily.

I watched Marc quickly pimp up his hair.

Ryan looked scared.

The girls were all very pretty, but not quite like Alarice. For me, she had that something extra. An exotic advantage that couldn't be defined. I couldn't pin it down, but that's the way I felt.

The girls, dressed in stylish, sexy pajamas that were all pink with flairs of white, curiously walked in a single file down the stairs. The peculiarity of the situation was understated by the distraction of their sexiness. I especially liked the way a couple of them had their tops open, letting their bras (pink also) show. The flash of flat tummies and cleavage made my blood flow faster. Though their hairstyles were each different, all six of them were blonde.

I wondered if some sorority house rule was at play.

And did that make Alarice president?

With the pleasant aromas of apples and cinnamon and the titillation of being around so many hot, curvaceous girls, my senses scrambled. My self-control was in danger of giving into wild desires. And I wanted it—wanted it *bad*.

The girls trotted down the stairs.

I loved watching the little white drawstrings on their pajama pants bounce just above their, what me and my pals liked to call, *cave of wonders*.

There was an embroidered lettered design on the pocket of each of their tops, which I assumed to be their club insignia.

Like a choreographed scene, Alarice introduced each girl precisely as she sprang down off the last step in fluffy pink and white slippers.

"Kenzie."

The first one, Kenzie, smiled and said, "Hiya!" Her blond pigtails whipped every which way as she hop-skipped by us with a lot of energy.

Then there was . . .

Sophia.

Perla.

Rene.

Savannah.

And lastly, Buffy.

The girls were rowdy, whereas we, normally loud and reckless to our educators and elders horror, stood there dumbly like boys finally granted their most fantastic sex fantasy and then not knowing what to do with it or where to begin.

Put-up-or-shut-up time.

Kenzie exclaimed, "We need some beats!"

She disappeared into an adjoining room on the other side of what I guessed was the living room. A light flashed on. Seconds later, thumping music blared out around the room.

Rene grabbed a TV controller and clicked off two screens that'd been projecting images without sound. Her fine ass pleasingly tightened each time she bent over.

The other girls got comfortable, plopping down on the couch and chairs, playing with pillows, laughing, and wrestling with one another.

Suddenly Daniel faced us, standing before us like a coach speaking to his players right before the game. "What are you waiting for, assholes?" He chopped Ryan in the gut. "This is it! Don't wuss out!"

Kenzie skittered back into the room and encouraged everyone to dance.

I had my eyes on her. She was the one I would try to get with.

Doug was the first to go and mingle. The rest of us followed.

I started to make my way to my preferred sorority babe, sidestepping Alarice and Daniel, but Alarice grabbed me by the arm.

"Hey, Winfall, get your own chick," Daniel snapped.

"He has," Alarice said sharply.

Daniel grumbled something. An unkind expression refashioned Alarice's elegant face. Rejected, Daniel waved his hand dismissively and walked away.

"I like your muscles," Alarice said, lightly squeezing my arm before letting go.

"Thanks," I replied.

Now I was nervous.

"Would you like something to drink?" she asked.

"Sure."

She spun around and told the girl snuggling with Daniel to get some beers, and he didn't look happy when she abruptly left him.

I made sure to get a good look at Alarice's well-proportioned derriere before she turned back around. My love muscle swelled, crowding my drawers a bit.

Alarice leaned in against me. I felt the moistness of her lips bear upon the side of my neck. This was heaven.

"You taste good," she whispered into my ear.

I'd never been with a female this hot and my nerves were starting to ruin the moment, so I kissed her before I did or said something lame. I felt her tongue slowly twirl around mine, our lips joined for what seemed like forever.

I looked over her shoulder and saw Daniel give me the finger.

When Alarice and I came apart, she said, "Wow, now I know why I liked you from the start."

I smiled, feeling my cheeks turn red.

The girl—Savannah, I think—returned and handed Alarice two beers from a full tray.

"Here ya go," Alarice said, offering one to me.

I took the bottle and didn't waste a second before gulping some down. Its bitterness coated my throat. I'm not much of a drinker, so I tried to hide my face while I fought it down.

"You live on campus?" she asked.

I shook my head, swallowed again, and said, "No."

"With your parents?"

"Yeah." I felt ashamed.

She smiled.

"I'm glad you came tonight."

Taking the bottle from my lips, I said, "Yeah, me too. Daniel told us—"

I stopped myself. What was I thinking? I couldn't tell her what Daniel had told us, or at least what I'd heard.

With a lustful gleam in her eyes, she admitted, "It's been a while since we've had company like you . . . strong, virile . . . should I say, men?" She grabbed my hand as she glanced at my family jewels. "Come with me."

As I walked with her, I looked around and saw the other guys and girls all making out. My mouth dropped open when I spied two of the girls rolling on the floor together, fondling and kissing each other. The last thing I saw before Alarice pulled me down on top of her on a large round cushion was Doug's head just before it disappeared between the naked thighs of his partner.

Alarice moaned beneath me. She twisted and flexed, rubbing her pussy rhythmically against my knee. I dropped the bottle, and we made out for a long time. I was on the verge of coming as my hard member slid back and forth inside my underpants, even though the restriction of the waistband caused some pain.

Was this all? I had the hottest chick I could ever hope to score with in my arms and I was going to finish myself off with a dry hump.

I pulled away from her. There was a flash of surprise in her captivating eyes.

I needed to find Ryan. He had the rubbers. I discreetly searched the dimly lit room. Alarice began to caress my chest. I prayed her hands didn't stray too far south. At least not yet.

Doug had his girl's legs high in the air as he pumped her in the missionary. It was the sight of her bare feet that caused me to startle. To a pair of lovely legs belonged god-ugly feet. Much like Alarice's. Were they biological sisters as well?

Then I began to notice—those of which I could see—all the other girls had unattractive feet too.

I was mystified. I mean, feet were feet, but something wasn't at all right here.

Ryan was far from my spot, but I saw him only because his girl was giving him head at the moment. He started screaming before I could call out to him.

"Fuck! Fuck! Fuck!" He bucked.

It was Kenzie who jumped up. I wasn't sure what I was witnessing. She turned around, pigtails swinging, with a face smeared in blood. Her tits were exposed and they looked to be catching what substance was dripping down.

"I couldn't help it," she whined.

Ryan continued screaming while he rushed at the big door. He tripped and fell and I caught a glimpse of a dark pocket of horror between his blood-soaked thighs. Of something missing. I ripped my eyes away at once.

I suddenly heard Alarice laugh. I felt her body vibrating with her laughter. I stared down at her. "Guess the party's over for the boys," she giggled.

The atmosphere changed, like a biting cold leak from a morgue freezer, and the stinking smell of decay began to surge out from the foundation.

I leaped off Alarice, but she just kept laughing.

By the time I turned to look, Ryan was dangling way up in the air, being held there and choked by a creature baring the distinctive features of the sorority girl who'd given him an emasculating BJ. Blond pigtails appeared ridiculous in contrast to its large leathery serpentine head. It licked at the blood running down its arms, then it shifted on incredibly long legs and threw him into the front door.

Marc went down under the force of three other similar-looking beasts. I knew without really knowing that these *things*, these unimaginable fiends, were the sorority sisters—monsters they had transformed into; monsters they had deviously hidden from us to ensure our exploitation.

Their clothing had been symbolically shed, much the way a serpent sloughs.

I ran through a shower of blood to try and rescue Doug from the same grisly fate. He was fighting his monster with some success, but my attempt to help was prevented when another one struck me in mid action and knocked me across the room, where I landed at the bottom of the staircase.

The blaring music and screams were now less loud, since it felt as if cotton had been stuffed inside my ears. Only a dull pulse remained.

I saw a pair of ugly feet coming my way. Alarice's feet. They'd not changed.

I scrambled up the stairs, stopping halfway up when I saw Daniel emerge, his naked body slashed and covered with blood.

The creature following him on the landing growled, "Get back here!"

His terror-filled eyes pleaded with me to save him.

There was nothing I could do. The instant before the creature snatched him, I turned and found myself face to face with Alarice.

Except for being covered with blood, she still looked human, then she flashed her long fangs.

"Having fun?" she jeered.

She moved to bite my neck and I pushed her, but I was the only one affected. Her strength was staggering. By my own muscle, I was propelled backward and went crashing through the handrail, falling in a rain of broken wood that ended when I hit the floor.

"Look what you've done to our house's decor!" Alarice screamed, hanging over the edge where I'd busted through.

I squirmed in pain.

With no warning, she changed into one of them and dropped on top of me, her repulsive nude form now showing off what seconds before had been desirable parts, complete with plump breasts and a lush tangle of hair lovingly trimming her genitalia.

One of her hoop earrings popped me on the forehead. The weight of her altered body threatened to crush me outright.

I was no match against her.

"Our house!" she shrieked, and with lethal claws began slicing away at me.

In a desperate act, I twisted and grabbed hold of a split piece of wood bar, which she must not have noticed in her mad frenzy. Each one of her rakes into my flesh burned as if I were being torn open by a heated poker.

I took the bar and stabbed her with it as hard as I could. Not quite able to see where I'd hit her, I heard her roar in agony, then the attack suddenly stopped.

A stream of syrupy fluid doused my face and, because I was suffering to breathe, a lot of it I had to swallow. The overly strong taste of apples and cinnamon and something foul singed my taste buds.

"Alarice!" someone cried.

Then another. "He hurt Alarice!"

"Help her! Help her!"

It seemed I was momentarily free.

"She's really hurt," one of them wept.

I escaped toward the front door in a daze, expecting at any time to be stopped and killed, but I wasn't. I got out.

I made it out *alive*.

I took to the street and began running raggedly through yards, overcome suddenly by the strange feeling this had all happened to me before. When my battered body fell into some hedges, a fleeting trance of darkness came over me. When I opened my eyes (if they'd even been closed at all), I saw clearly. No blurriness, instead sharp, crisp images of indoors.

I was sitting upright in a cushiony chair and I felt extraordinarily good.

Someone commented, "Well now, don't you look a ton better."

I knew that voice, but whose?

The voice belonged to Leroy Miner.

He came around through an open doorway and stepped into view.

Curious enough was the low lighting, but more strange was the unknown reason why I was sacked down in a blanket of chains. They didn't hurt, didn't feel heavy at all actually, despite the fact the links were huge and plainly metal, but I couldn't budge them. I felt as though I had the strength to lift them to the ceiling, but with all my effort, I couldn't disturb them.

Leroy must have seen this. He said, "The blood made you better than better, but you won't be able to get free of those, I'm 'fraid."

"What is this?" I demanded.

He chuckled first, then explained, "Vampire hunter's security. From Old Rome, so I've been told."

"What?"

"Though they belong to the college now. A gift in good faith."

"Mr. Miner, tell me what's going on, please." I strained to move the chains again, but came up short.

"Settle yourself down, boy, and focus on your surroundings. You're almost like one of them, you'll see. You downed a lot of their sweet stuff . . . magical stuff."

I saw him lift a tiny clear vial to his mouth and stick out his tongue. Then he touched an end of the vial to it and moaned right after. "Mmm, tasty stuff, but I never cared much for cinnamon really."

He hid the vial in one of his pockets.

"She'll surely give me more of it for nabbing you. I'll show her I used up my last."

I was getting angrier by the minute.

"Get me out of this." I demanded.

"Oh no," he said, "them vamps aren't gonna want that. You and your pals screwed up *big* this time. Them girls probably smelled your all's kind of testosteroned blood a little bit too close for even them to resist it. This kinda thing isn't supposed to happen. It's in the contract. Alarice has never been this reckless. The head dean and the others won't like this when they hear about it. And that's what I'm counting on. Alarice should reward me well to keep this played down, I'm a bettin.'"

Oh my god, I could hear his heart beating in my ears and could pick up on the swoosh of his blood as it flowed through his veins. Another heart, a nonhuman one, drummed nearby us. I heard a cat's meow miles away from where I was sitting. It was true. Everything had happened. All the ungodly horror before the campus custodian had found me, knocked me out, and brought me to his place. I was different.

Leroy, as old as he was and out of shape, suddenly did a handstand. He held it for quite some time.

"Wahoo!" he called out, standing once again.

I needed to get out of this. Maybe I could learn something from him that'd help me do just that.

"How is this all possible?" I asked. "Why are they here? And what will happen to me?"

He stared at me with a look of disgust, or maybe indifference, it was hard to tell. Then he walked over to a cluttered up old bookcase and picked out what seemed to be a photo album. He brought it over to me and showed me a bunch of aged pictures. I spotted a girl who looked exactly like Alarice in one of them; she was wearing old-fashioned clothes, maybe late eighteen hundreds, early nineteen hundreds.

"It began more than a century before I was a squirt in my mammy's pussy," Leroy began.

He flipped through the last of the photographs.

"Don't ask me nothing about how those girls became what they are, 'cause I don't know. But Alarice is the oldest of 'em. Her and Hubert Vanderberg himself, the father of this fine educational institution, as you should know, came to an understanding way back when my great grand pappy's pappy worked here." He lowered his head and said, "Jesus rest his soul."

"What kind of understanding?" I asked.

"Well, it's kind of a tradeoff. See, Alarice and her girlfriends were given a sanctuary, a safe hold from those seeking to destroy them. Hidden right here in our little campus world. We bring 'em their feed too. Always from the outside, though, and never from our own, like you and your pals. And in return the ones in the know, like Vanderberg, his administration, my dear blood relative, and the ones that've taken their place when they gave up the ghost, like me, well, they all got and *get* to live a long, healthy life. A life without sickness and not that much pain. I imagine I'd've been down with diabetes by now, or even dead and gone. Diabetes runs in my folk."

I had to ask, and I didn't care if he took offense either. "You're just a custodian. Why do *you* have a part in it?"

Mimicking me, he repeated my words, "*You're just a custodian.*"

He stuck out his tongue, then said, "You don't want to hear my story?"

I kept mum.

He continued anyway. "They—*we*—didn't and *don't* get eternal life. No. But just a single drop of their blood can do wonders. There's a monthly fix is all. But that means no illness and no bullshit. Heck at my age, I can work over any of you jock college brats. I knocked *you* out a good'n. Well, sorry 'bout that. I had to do it before the blood started really working in

274

you, or else I wouldn't've been able to. Why you think this institution has some of the sharpest minds teaching in the nation?"

"Why the church?" I questioned.

"Don't know." He went and put the album away. "Alarice has some secret reasons for wanting it. All I know is she wanted it at the cost of murder and her own suffering. Just one glance at her feet will testify to it." He chuckled. "Vampires in a *church*. Good hiding place, I guess. Something holy still tarries in that chapel's roots, I'd say."

Those ugly feet!

I could see a depth of unhappiness in his face.

"My forefather and the others had to spill the blood of its parishioners. Alarice said it had to be done. An abomination had to transpire on holy ground." He shook his head. "Well, that's their sins to bear."

Now was my chance. I laughed.

He looked puzzled.

"And I'll be your sin to bear," I said. "If you keep me like this." From his words, I believed he was a spiritual man. "Is not getting sick till you die really worth an eternity in Hell?"

Silently he turned his back on me.

I waited uneasily for him to react.

At last he said, "I don't believe in a Hell, boy."

My heart sank.

He moved over to a window and barely drew back its thick curtain. "It's close to daybreak," he said. "I was kind enough to keep the place lowly lit and curtains shut tight just in case the amount of blood in you makes you susceptible to things like that."

"Gee, thanks," I said sarcastically.

He disappeared into another room.

From the same direction, a dog yapped. It was a small breed.

I was panicked.

Doug and the rest of them.

Could one of them have survived?

Would I ever know?

Daniel.

All his fault.

All his *goddamned* fault.

I started to cry.

All at once a brilliant light disorientated me, then it was gone, leaving me with flash blindness, though the spots gradually faded and the room became clear again.

Leroy's front door opened up.

There was an eerie silence; No one entered.

Had it opened by its own volition?

A familiar cold flowed into the room; the smells followed— apples and cinnamon laced with festering death.

A cloaked figure strolled inside. A hood guarded the identity of whomever was wearing it.

The mysterious chains kept my body prisoner.

Two more cloaked shapes entered; one of them closed the door.

The first one in faced me.

I tried to peer inside the blackness shrouding the face.

A female hand pulled open enough of the front of the garment to reveal a shapely naked thigh. Seductively she slowly unveiled more. Under normal circumstances, I would have gotten erect the instant I saw the fabric raise high enough to show the puffy pink crease and lips within.

That was the end of it. They stopped the strip show and threw back the hood.

It was Alarice who glared at me with a thin smile.

Again the odd feeling of what I thought was hopeless recurrence came over me.

Time displaced.

"You don't have to do this," I told her.

She yanked aside her cloak to show me a gruesome puncture wound caked with a pus-like substance that was just above her breast.

I got the message. This was what I'd done to her.

She shot a look to the side. Leroy had slipped into the room. "See to him," she instructed her cohort. Her voice sounded raspy.

I would have liked to have bashed in his gray-haired skull, and if given a chance, that's what I would have done.

The rest of the girls followed him out of the room. Alarice directed her attention back to me. With a devilish grin, she completely disrobed. The cloak fell and lay about her feet, covering them, encircling her au naturel self.

"You wanted it," she sneered. "So now you're *fucked!*"

"Make me like you," I pleaded, one last hope.

"But first . . ." She leaned forward. " . . . give me back what's mine."

A tremendous force shifted my insides, and as if by some incredible magnetic pull, I felt an upsurge. My gut and then throat expanded seconds before a river of blackish matter ejected out of my mouth.

The nightmare ended when I reopened my eyes.

A zesty odor of cooked buffalo wings was hanging in the air.

Leroy wandered into the room, nestling his pooch under one arm.

I was still under the restraint of the chains.

He crossed in front of me and stopped at the window, peeking past the curtain. "Almost nightfall," he observed.

His pet growled. "Hush now," he told it, gingerly scratching it between its ears. He turned to me and said, "To answer your last question."

I waited.

And what will happen to me?

He continued as he walked by me again. "I think you ain't gonna make it, boy."

"You'd better hope I don't!" I screamed.

Immediately after he was out of the room, I sensed, with a prickling sensation, Alarice's creeping approach.

I had to find a way to live.

HORNS writes from his birthplace haunt on the urban outskirts of downtown Cincinnati, Ohio. He slithered into the world of literary horror in 1999. From this genre of darkness, he's penned one novel, Chophouse, *which celebrated scream queen Linnea Quigely (Return of the Living Dead) declared "[Chophouse] makes me scream!"*

Animals

Kody Boye

"Are they still here?" Tricia asked.

"Yes," Clive said. "They are."

From their place within the kitchen, in which they were shrouded from view by black curtains, they watched the moonbeam eyes pierce through the darkness and light their whole world. Even from such a vast distance away they could be seen—watching, waiting, salivating. They'd been here for a week now and so far showed no signs of going back.

Directly opposite Clive stood Tricia, his wife. Her arms were crossed and her face was painted in a mixture of fear and pain. She locked her eyes on the farthest window on Clive's side of the room and let out a sigh that made the hairs on Clive's arms stand on end.

Poor Tricia, he thought.

It was no secret she was troubled, as such were her eyes that, in looking at them, Clive felt weak—nothing like the strong man whom, on the second night, had boarded up their doors and tried to do the same with their windows. To know the animals were there placed upon the air an apprehension that rang in tunes of shivers and sighs, but to actually *see* they were still watching—that in itself was a cold monstrosity that sucked all happiness from life and all sense of security from his heart.

"Have you checked on the baby tonight?" Tricia asked.

"I haven't," Clive said, only managing to tear his eyes away from the window when his wife spoke. "Do you want me to?"

"No. I'll go do it."

"All right."

Clive watched his wife flee the kitchen in a few short steps until she disappeared down the hall off the living room—to the room he, she, and their son had been sleeping for the past week. He heard first the doorknob clicking, then the door opening, groaning in anticipation. Shortly thereafter, the bedroom door was closed and their connection once more broken.

If only I could do something.

To think that he could do *anything* right about now was ridiculous, preposterous to the point where he might as well open the door and invite the things outside in for tea. His gun had been loaded, his bullet set, his sights locked in, and when tasked to bring down one of the creatures, he found he could do nothing—that, somehow, some way, they were invulnerable to such displays of violence. Understanding that simple form of logic would have made any man break, Clive felt, especially a man who had a family.

"And a baby boy," he mumbled.

Blinking, he looked at the window nearby, only to find that the eyes had moved forward a few steps. No longer did they appear to be across the backyard and in the woods. Now, it seemed, they were on the freshly-mowed grass, attempting to slink forward and once again asked to be let in.

No. Don't think about that.

First the doorknob began to tremble, its light brass makeup clicking like a dog's untrimmed nails, then the knocking began anew. It came once, then twice, a third then a fourth, each in a soft pitch that would have been similar to a child knocking upon the door. The fifth and sixth, however, were much more violent, and when it stopped, only to begin anew, Clive hugged himself and took several steps back.

They always do it three times, he reminded himself. *Only three times.*

It was one to six a second time, each in low pitch, then again, this time in a fevered monotone that Clive felt for a moment might break the door down. He had to keep inspiring the urge to realize that whatever these things outside were, they couldn't get into the house, especially not since he'd boarded the front door up so well.

"If only you would leave," Clive whispered.

When the third and final set of six knocks ended, he turned and began to make his way into the living room.

Before he could reach the hallway, he stopped to look back at the window. One of the animals stood just outside, its bright moonbeam eyes staring in at things it could not see.

* * *

In the quiet sanctuary of their bedroom, Tricia watched the TV as a news anchor continued to talk. "There are no confirmed reports," the anchor said, "as to why the world has gone dark, nor have there been any breakthroughs in determining just what these creatures are."

"Why are you watching that?" Clive asked, careful to close the door as softly as possible to avoid waking the baby.

"There might be news," Tricia said.

"There *might* be?"

Tricia ignored his comment. Instead, she turned the television set up a few decibels and leaned forward, one hand poised on the cradle beside the bed and the other wrapped around the remote control.

They're never going to tell us anything new, Clive thought, *because there* isn't *going to be anything new. It's not even worth—*

"And now," the anchorman said, "we turn our attention to Natalie Crimcraw, professor of biology at the University of Texas in Austin. Tell us, Natalie, what exactly are the things we're dealing with?"

"Well, Brandon," Natalie said, adjusting a light on a shelf in front of her. "As you and most of the continental United States already know, we have been dealing with creatures we are simply referring to as 'Animals' for the past week now."

"Is there any word on what exactly they are?"

"Confirmed reports of individuals who have been in close proximity of the creatures say that they are tall, about six to seven-feet in height, and they resemble something of an upright-walking canine—most specifically, a jackal."

"Can you confirm whether or not we are dealing with a terrestrial or an earthly threat?"

"I cannot confirm that," Natalie said.

"They don't even know what the fuck they're talking about," Clive said, settling down on the bed beside his wife before reaching forward to attempt to take the remote from her hand. When Tricia pulled away, he exhaled through his teeth and shook his head. "They think we're dealing with aliens."

"What do *you* think they are?" Tricia asked.

"I . . . I don't know. Animals, maybe, but—"

"But what?"

"I don't know what to tell you, hon. All I know is that we're dealing with something bad."

"At least the power is on," Tricia sighed. "At least we don't have to worry about being in complete darkness."

For now, Clive thought. *Maybe later, but—*

Their son began to stir in his cradle.

"Shh, shh, shh," Tricia said, lifting the baby into her arms and holding him against her chest. "It's ok, Colton."

"We still have formula for him, right? We don't have to worry about him going hungry?"

"I would go hungry long before I even considered letting him."

Nodding, Clive reached over, cupped the back of his baby son's head in the palm of his hand, then looked up—where, on the screen, the anchorman had switched cameras to display the station's expansive back parking lot. Distantly, eyes could be seen piercing through the darkness, though unlike in the real world and through a real set of eyes, these appeared green, an after effect of a night-vision security camera.

"We shouldn't be watching this," Clive said once more.

"But, Clive, shouldn't we—"

Clive pushed the POWER button on the remote before his wife could finish. "We should sleep," he said. "Besides, the white noise might be bothering him."

You pansy-ass pussy, he thought. *Why not tell her the truth and let her know what you're really worried about?*

To state that he was afraid electronic equipment might draw the animals was to instill within his wife a sense of dread that, as of now, lay restrained only to him. His panic was enough—a beast rolled up in a cage, it could be said—but his wife, who bore not only the difficulty of wondering if her distant family was safe, but also the burden of a child still breastfeeding? He wasn't sure just how she was getting along, but by God she was a strong woman.

Exactly what I married her for, he thought, then reached forward to push her dark hair away from her high cheekbones.

In the brief moments of silence that followed, Clive stood, pulled the comforter hanging over the single computer chair in his wife's bedroom-slash-office into his arms, and brought it back to the bed.

Tricia pushed the cradle a few short inches away.

Clive threw the blanket over the bed.

In his cradle, Colton slept.

When he and his wife crawled into bed together, Clive prayed for safety.

Please God, he thought. *Let us all be all right.*

* * *

He was pulled from bed by the gravitational force of curiosity later that night. Having just risen from a troubled sleep in which he'd tossed and turned, Clive crawled from beneath the covers and began to make his way to the attached bathroom before something drew him out into the hallway, then to the living room, where, in the far corner, the stairs leading up to the second floor stood.

What the hell are you doing? he thought, still inching forward without much conscience.

Of course, had he been honest with himself, he would have said that he was going upstairs, to where, in the bedroom on the hallway above, the windows looked out at the forest, providing ample and more than beneficial opportunity for him to see what these things truly were.

At the top of the stairs he paused, craned his head back to make sure his wife had not followed, then walked the few feet to the end of the hallway before letting himself into the guest bedroom. Once inside, he was perpetually frozen by terror.

You work up the gall to come up here only to stop halfway? What the fuck are you doing, Clive? Get a hold of yourself.

"I am," he whispered. "I have."

The looming series of windows encompassing the northern half of the room stood tall and gargantuan, their curtains only partially closed and their surfaces marred by rainwater. Here they waited for his approach, beckoning him with kind, simple eyes, and here they would stand the test of time until he stepped forward to look through them.

Only one thought struck him in the moments leading up to what would soon be his first true revelation.

Do I really want to do this?

Would, by looking out the window, he risk not only his own life, but his wife's and son's? Unable to know, and not willing to risk the ignorance he held in regards to these creatures, Clive stood proud, took a long, deep breath, then began to step forward, all the while staying to his left in order to conceal his presence.

He reached the side of the room.

His heart beat a thousand times more in his chest. *By God,* he thought. *Am I going to have a heart attack?*

Rather than risk the implications, Clive leaned forward, took the curtain in hand, then pulled it slightly away.

Below, they lurked—not in the thicket of trees, as he'd imagined they would, but out in the cold and open.

Clive braced himself for the revelation which was to come. When it finally struck him, his sense of reality was lost.

They resembled something like jackals stripped of their coats and allowed to roll carelessly in the dirt. Tall, emaciated, with a pair of glowing white eyes that pierced through the darkness and more—hunched over at the shoulder, they looked to be something akin to hunchbacks who once upon a time had walked without care. Perhaps the most terrifying feature, however, past their smiling, open mouths and their devilish rows of crocodile-like teeth, were their hands. Not paws, as many would have expected, but a series of five fingers which lay forward, they carried them limp-wristed with the nails hanging to the ground and the flats of their palms curled and depressed.

Standing there, hidden to the world and the monsters it offered, Clive could barely believe his eyes.

They're . . . he thought, then swallowed a lump in his throat, unable to complete the thought. What was he to have said? Smart, agile, regretful, inappropriate? What should have come out of his mouth in order to describe the very things that were lurking in his backyard below?

Clive drew back a step. His hold on the curtain shifted. The three animals who'd been stalking together instantaneously turned their eyes up, their stares instantly stabbing daggers in his heart.

Did they see me? he wondered, attempting to breathe whilst he stood there trying desperately not to panic. *Did they? Did—*

The things below began to make a grating, chuckling noise, a sound which could have been compared to a lifelong smoker's laugh unsupplied by proper oxygen but fueled by ulterior intent.

After taking a few steps back, Clive was finally able to gain the breath he'd so desperately wished to inhale.

They didn't see me, he decided, nodding if only to give himself better support. *They just saw the curtain move. That's all.*

That, however, did not answer the question that rang strong and clear in his mind. Could they determine the movement of objects within a dwelling and therefore deduce that someone was inside?

Trembling, Clive turned, wrapped his hand around the doorknob, then let himself out of the room.

A few short minutes later, he crawled back into bed beside his wife and closed his eyes.

No matter how warm it was beneath the covers, he couldn't help but feel cold.

* * *

It was seven AM and there was still no light. A thought unwelcome, a burden all but carried, Clive opened his eyes to find that the nightlight in the corner of the room—which, until just now, had been dead—had miraculously come back to life.

What did you expect? Clive thought at the notion of light and what it could signify. *Sunshine? Maybe even a rainbow?*

At his side, Tricia slept peacefully, her arm sprawled out, her body cupped in his. Directly opposite him, their baby son continued to sleep without a care in the world—Colton's light, almost-inaudible snores a chorus to the peace Clive felt within this very house. It was enough, for just one brief moment, to make him disregard the world that existed outside—that the monsters, so frail and old, had all but disappeared. Unlike miracles, however, and unlike the sweeping hand of God coming forth to push all the sand away, that feeling soon disappeared. With its absence came a sense of apprehension that, within the air, seemed tangible enough to cut with a knife.

Stirring, guided only by the nightlight that rested on the outlet in the corner of the room, Clive threw his legs off the bed, rose, then began to make his way out into the living room, dressed in only a pair of boxers and a short-sleeved shirt.

So cold, he thought. *So very, very cold.*

Near the threshold that opened into the living room he stopped to consider what it was he was actually doing. There, between two walls and the entrance to a gateway called hell, he contemplated just whether or not it was worth going out into the kitchen to make him and his wife something to eat, as no more than a few feet outside, the animals would be watching. While that notion was all but clear, it did little to disarm the hunger that snaked through his stomach, wrapping about his gut and creating an almost-unbearable lightness.

With little more than a sigh, Clive took his first step out into the living room.

He turned to look at the windows.

He braced himself for what was to come.

He saw, distantly, the moonbeam reflections piercing in through the windows—watching, waiting, hunting.

Don't worry. You've got a four-inch wooden door between you and them.

Added to that realization were a series of several wooden two-by-fours, which, in their current state, made the entryway resemble something of a final threshold between them and death.

"You're getting yourself in over your head," he whispered. "Stop."

While most thought within his head ceased to exist, the cat-shaped clock hanging above the stove continued to tick—tail switching, sound egressing. Each individual vibration that came from its insides sent trembles of unease throughout his heart. *Hello,* it would have said as it looked down and upon him, its bobble-head eyes jumping up and down, left to right. *Come to get yourself something to eat there, Clive boy? Well, let me tell you something, good sir—you are quite the work of art, coming out here all by yourself. But you're not alone. You know you're not.*

Of course he wasn't. *No one* was alone in this world—not anymore, not after this . . . *calamity,* if it could be called that, had struck them.

Rather than face succumbing to the devils of insanity, Clive instead decided to partake in the pleasures of the human landscape before him. He crossed the break in the carpet and the beginning of the tile in a few steps and opened the fridge to find that, inside, the remnants of last night's chicken noodle soup lay in plain and bold sight.

Can't eat it cold, he thought, then sighed, pulling the pot from its place inside the refrigerator. Oh well. He could care less whether or not his food was warm or cold. The fact that they had food to eat was enough to put him at ease.

While he poured himself a small bowl of soup, taking care not to give himself too much for fear he would deprive his wife and infant son of nourishment, he tried to keep his focus on his food rather than on the window. That, however, was impossible. It seemed their presence alone was mandated—that their appearance, though slight and grim and almost invisible in the darkness, was of the utmost degree—and no matter how hard he tried to keep from looking out the corner of his eye, his peripheral vision continued to send shards of reality into his brain, directly connecting to the optic nerves in his head a horrible image of something standing directly outside the window.

No.

"No," he said.

The doorbell began to jingle on the opposite side of the room.

I think it's time to leave now, he thought, taking several steps back.

"Clive?" Tricia asked.

Something bumped into him.

Clive released his hold on the bowl.

It fell, shattering upon impact.

A chorus of laughter began outside the house.

"Is that . . . *them?*" Tricia asked, beginning to retreat back toward the hall as the doorknob continued to jingle with increased intensity.

"That's them," Clive replied. He pushed a hand back to position his wife behind him. "Stay back, Tricia."

"But—"

A heightened pitch of laughter began once more.

In the bedroom, the baby began to cry.

Fuck.

"Go get him," Clive said.

"What are you—"

"Just go get him!" he hissed, turning, then taking her by the shoulders. "He can't keep crying. They'll hear him."

"I know, but—"

"Go, Tricia! I'll make sure the two of you are safe."

Tricia turned and bounded down the hallway without a word in response.

Clive paced his way to the couch.

The laughter continued. The cat clock clicked. The doorknob jingled.

At the loveseat, Clive bent down, took several deep breaths, then began to pull the cushions from their place.

288

Come on. Come on! Where the fuck are you?

The rifle, complete with its trigger locked, came into view a short moment later.

Clive grabbed the gun.

Something began to pound against the door.

"Clive!" Tricia called out.

"Stay there!" Clive called back, taking the gun into his hand and removing the lock in but a few short moments. "I've got the gun!"

"Are you sure it won't—"

A bout of laughter so loud it drowned out Tricia's voice echoed throughout the house.

Please God, he thought, pulling the fully-loaded cartridge out to check it one final time. *Please, just let me protect my wife, my son. Grant me the strength to—*

All sound disappeared instantaneously.

Trembling, Clive pushed the cartridge back into place and checked the chamber to make sure there was a bullet in it.

Thank God.

A single bullet lay in the chamber—waiting, it seemed, for its chance to declare justice.

Raising the gun, Clive trained it on the door and waited for something to happen.

Outside, the creatures continued to shift back and forth along the windows, their glowing eyes the only presence that he could see.

"Clive?" Tricia asked.

Clive lifted his head, looked down the crosshairs, then shook his head, lowering the end of the rifle to the floor before raising a hand to keep her in place.

If they break in, he thought, *there's nowhere for them to run. Maybe they should go upstairs. Maybe if they were up there, I wouldn't have to worry about—*

The doorknob began to jingle again.

"Tricia," Clive said, raising his voice as once again the knocks on the door began. "Take the baby and go upstairs. You'll be safer there."

"But what about—"

"I'll come when I make sure we're safe."

Tricia said little in response. Instead, she lifted the baby into her arms, walked carefully out into the hallway, then stood directly beside him, where she waited but a moment to kiss his cheek before turning and making her way up the stairs.

Please don't let anything happen, he thought. *Please, God, don't let my family die. Kill me if you want, but don't let my wife or my baby suffer.*

As had happened before, all sound ceased to exist.

Outside, the creatures laughed.

Their eyes, once pressed close to the window, began to retreat back through the yard, into the tree line where their presence diminished until nothing could be seen.

Rising to his feet, Clive sighed, took a deep breath, then expelled it before turning and making his way upstairs.

Only one thought ran through his mind.

They were safe for one more night.

* * *

In the upstairs master bedroom, where, in past days, he had come to view the progress of the animals outside, Clive pulled the curtains across the window and fell to his knees. Exhausted not from lack of sleep or a slight of his body, but the emotional integrity that was the possibility of death, he allowed the gun to slide from his grasp and onto the floor, where, once flat on the ground, he pushed it up against the wall until he felt the distance between it and everything else in the room appropriate.

"Are you all right?" Tricia asked.

Clive didn't respond. It wasn't that he didn't *want* to so much as he *couldn't,* as no more than a few minutes beforehand he'd seen his whole life flash before his eyes. To know he was so mortified he could not speak stirred tears from his eyes and made clever trails of oceans along his face.

Am I all right? Clive thought, still staring at the carpeting below the window.

What could he say to such a question? Could he lie, grieve, mourn, rant, and scream and yell at the top of his voice, despite the animals outside, that he was *not* all right, that he was *not* ok? To do anything in and at that moment would possibly cost him everything. His wife, his life, his son—just *what* was he supposed to do in the aftermath of such a horrendous moment without breaking down and succumbing to tears?

You're stronger than that, Clive. Get a hold of yourself.

"Clive?" Tricia asked. "Are you ok?"

"Not really," he managed, "but at least the two of you aren't dead."

Rising, Clive turned and took the short few steps it took to get to the bed. Once there, he sat down, sighed, then reached up to run a hand through his unruly, curling hair.

"You really thought they were going to get in that time," Tricia said, "didn't you?"

"I don't know what to think, Tricia. They're . . . they're just . . ."

"There?"

"Yeah. *There.*"

"I'm fairly sure we're safe in this house, Clive. I mean, look at what all you've done—you've boarded up the front and back door and moved us into a room where they won't know where we're at."

"I sure hope to God that's the truth."

"I guess," Tricia said, crossing her arms over her chest, "we have to decide something here and now."

"What would that be?"

"What we're going to do if they break in."

The silence that followed played cruel symphony to an apathy neither of them had discussed since the animals had appeared. A broken harp, a withering cello, a series of whistles played from a crystal flute whose surface had been cracked time and time again, until it could no longer make noise. The wind whipped around the house and screamed hellfire at their plight, and the sound of Colton's breathing drew cold the reality in plain and bold colors across his vision. It was in these moments, during which time not a soul or a monster spoke, that Clive looked into Tricia's eyes, and within their blue surfaces, he saw the weight of the world and then some, a warm blue planet that had since been shadowed over by darkness.

Ok, he thought. *What're we going to do about this?*

"What do you mean?" Clive finally asked.

"What we're going to do," Tricia said.

"I get that, but . . ."

"But . . . what, Clive?"

"I'll shoot them if they come in."

"You know good and well that if those things get in we're all going to die."

"I won't let that happen."

"You're not a one man fighting machine."

I'm not? he thought, then laughed before reaching up to paw at his face.

His laugh was not reciprocated with one of Tricia's own.

Ok . . . she's serious.

"What do you suggest we do?" Clive asked.

"What I think we should do," Tricia said, "if in the event they get in . . ."

She's playing with your head, Clive. She's trying to mess with your thoughts . . . No she isn't. She would never—

Listen to what she's asking!

"Clive?" Tricia said, raising her voice just to the point where he could hear its whispered pitch. "Clive, are you even listening to—"

She wants to kill you. She wants to kill herself. And you know what's worse? She wants to kill your little boy.

No she doesn't.

Yes she does!

No she—

The hand waving before his face brought him back to reality. "Clive," she said.

"Yuh-Yeah," he managed. "I'm here."

"Why aren't you listening to me?"

"I am listening to you."

"No you're not."

"Yes, I—"

"What did I just say then?"

Clive remained silent and merely stared as a dumbstruck smile crossed his wife's face. "You weren't even listening to me," she said.

"Yes I was."

"Then what did I—"

"You're absolutely mad if you think I'd ever agree to anything like that."

"Anything like *what?*"

"I *would never* hurt you or our son," Clive said, standing.

"Is it better to be torn apart," Tricia asked, "Piece by little piece? And what about after we're dead? Huh? What do you think they'll do to us?"

"I don't know."

"You don't *know?*" Tricia laughed. "Clive, you saw it on the news. You saw what they did with the *bodies.*"

"That doesn't mean anything," Clive replied. "Just because we saw something on the news doesn't mean that—"

"They're harvesting us."

Harvesting? Clive frowned. *Why would she—*

The notion struck him shortly thereafter, when, upon staring into his wife's eyes, he realized the intent of her words. It'd been reported not too long ago that the animals dragged people's bodies off into woods or heavily-concealed places of the land. What they did with them afterward was, and would probably remain, a mystery, but the series of lights usually accompanied by such 'stealing' gave life to a thought that many would rather have not had.

To think, he mused, *that this would be the way it would happen.*

"Our first contact," he whispered.

Tricia crossed her arms and made a noise that resembled something between a grunt and a sigh. She stood there for several more moments, likely internally debating what it was

293

Clive had said, before turning and making her way toward the door.

"Where are you going?" Clive asked.

"To get us something to eat," Tricia replied. "Crackers, at least."

"All right then."

At the door, Tricia paused. She turned her attention first to the baby lying on the bed, then to Clive, before turning the doorknob and stepping out of the room.

When she closed the door behind her, Clive thought a part of him had died.

It was almost unbearable to think his wife would really prefer death as a way out.

* * *

He lay in bed for a long while alone and without the company of his wife. To his side the baby lay, wrapped in several layers of loose-fitting blankets, though what sounds Colton made were barely audible above the low hum that droned in Clive's ears. Where this sound was coming from he couldn't be sure, as no electronic devices existed within this room and no electricity was currently lighting any object within the room.

Tricia, he thought, then sighed, reaching forward to cup a single hand around their son's body.

How could she have been reduced to thinking such things— killing her child, asking him to kill her, and then expecting him to kill himself. Had she fallen so deep down the rabbit hole that she could not even dream of crawling back up, or was there something else at play here—something that, while weak to begin, had since festered and grown stronger?

She wants release. You know that.

Humankind could succumb to such simple desires far too easily. To draw a blade, to wring a noose, to take a pill, or to hold a gun to your head or chin or neck or heart and to pull from its interior a bullet that would open the portal to one world and close another—it was said that men and women, as deeply set into their evolution as a whole, harbored failures within their consciences that they could not control. It was not of the fox's intent to eat a number of pills, as with its curiosity it would find that such things tasted quite nasty, and it was not of the owl's good will that it would arrange from the arm of a tree a noose in which it could hang itself, as they believed such things to be much too geometrical for their own intent. Animals, as a whole, did not harbor the regret that humankind felt. For that, it could be said humans were weak, that, without purpose, they would simply collapse in and onto themselves. To know that reality was to expose a fallacy within all of humankind—to reveal in the flesh and blood the inner makings of what it was to be alive—and in that moment, while lying there next to his baby son, Clive began to understand slowly why his wife would consider an easy way out.

Is this what you really want? he thought. *For all this to go away?*

The door opened.

Clive pushed his elbow down under him to prop himself up before turning to look at the open doorway. "Tricia?" he said.

She gave a slight nod, then entered the bedroom, balancing on her arm a platter of various meats, cheeses, and crackers. "I figured you hadn't eaten," she said.

"No," Clive said. "I haven't. Thank you."

"Clive," she sighed. "I . . . Can we talk about something?"

"We can," he said.

"I didn't mention what I did earlier to upset you, and before you say it, I know it doesn't change the fact that it did. However . . ."

Always the key word, Clive thought.

"I'm just . . ."

"You can say what you want," Clive said. "I'm not stopping you."

"It's not you that's stopping me. It's . . . well . . . *me* that's stopping me. And Colton. He's stopping me too."

"Say what you need to say, hon."

"I only mentioned suicide," she said, "because . . . I don't want anything to happen to any of us, especially not you or Colton."

"I feel the same way."

"So . . . you understand where I'm coming from, right?"

"Sort of," Clive said.

"Good." Tricia set the snack platter on the bed beside Colton before taking him into her arms. She watched for several minutes as Clive arranged and ate the crackers, meats, and cheeses, then she sighed and settled down on the bed beside him, taking into her hand a small sandwich which she immediately put into her mouth. "Clive."

"Yes?"

"The military might come."

"You think?"

"I think."

We can only hope, Clive sighed. *We can only hope.*

* * *

They were trying to get into the house again. This time, however, they had a plan.

"Clive," Tricia said. "What're we going to do?"

"I'm not sure," Clive said.

Along the walls they skittered, to the left and right they went, up and down they jumped in a feeble attempt to latch onto the shingles of the lower areas of the roof and around the house they stalked—they were without abandon, attempting to find each and every way into the house, and while they had yet to succeed in exposing any flaws that may exist within the structure, the fact that they were restlessly seeking refuge from the outside world was enough to put Clive over the edge.

It's ok, he thought. *Deep breaths, deep breaths.*

"One," he said. "Two . . . three . . ."

"Clive? Are you all right?"

"Ah-asth-mah."

Tricia ran to the doorway and let herself out before Clive could even attempt to say more.

Don't worry. She's just going to get your inhaler. She's not going to do anything else.

But how was he to know whether or not the sound of her running through the house would draw attention to them? They had not run in many, many days, had not spoken above a whispered pitch, and had not turned on anything that would make too much noise. They could, metaphorically or not, have been compared to a police state, where, in every room, on every faucet, and on every surface there were cameras watching everything they did; the Big Brother of the future determined in a few microscopic electronic bugs.

You're getting ahead of yourself.

Either way, the panic strumming through his heart was enough to make him pray for his life.

Tricia flew through the open door.

Clive jumped.

She thrust the inhaler into his hand and sighed as he took his first breath off it.

"Thank God," she breathed.

"Thuh-thank you," he managed, pounding his chest with the curve of his fist before taking another hit off the inhaler.

"I wasn't sure if I would find it."

"Well, you did. That's all that matters, right?"

Tricia nodded.

Outside, a chorus of chuckles went up into the air.

"What're we going to do if they get in?" Tricia asked.

"We have guns," he said.

"We've only got the—"

"Did you forget about the revolver?"

Tricia stared blankly, blinking every few minutes, as if she were a doe caught in the limelight of an oncoming truck. "What?" she asked.

"I bought you that revolver for your birthday so I wouldn't have to worry about you while I was on my trips."

"Do you think a revolver would . . . *kill* them?"

"We can't say it won't if we haven't tried, right?"

"I guess."

Pocketing his inhaler, Clive stood and began to make his way for the door. "I'm going to go get the guns," he said. "Stay here."

"I will."

"If something happens, *do not* come running for me. Push the vanity in front of the door and pray they don't find you."

"Oh God, oh God, oh God. I can't believe this is happening."

"Neither can I." He stepped forward and pressed a kiss against his wife's mouth before taking her hand and squeezing it. "I'll be back," he said.

Tricia nodded.

When he was sure he need not worry about anything else, Clive exited the room, took the short route to the stairs, then began to descend them as quickly as he possibly could.

God, please don't let anything happen to her or Colton. Please don't—

A pair of moonbeam eyes stared directly at him the moment he stepped off the final stair. For a moment he was paralyzed— frozen with fear over what stood before him—then he realized it was nothing more than a face pressed up against the window.

"Thank you, Lord."

Clive took off into the hallway that led to he and Tricia's room. He pulled the bottom drawer of their cabinet open and began to fling clothes out of it as fast as he could.

Where the fuck is it? he thought, fuming, his cheeks swelling red with anger and his heart trembling with fear. *I know I put it in here. I know it!*

A brush of something smooth came under his touch.

Clive threw the final item of clothing away. Before him lay the revolver—old, cold, and filled with the five bullets its chamber allowed.

Reaching forward, he locked his hand around the grip and removed the weapon from its mortal prison.

Outside the room, in the dark place where nothing could be seen and where their hopes for the future lay in easy access, the sound of glass falling to the floor echoed throughout the house.

No.

They'd never tried using the windows before, only doors. How could they have gotten in?

Standing, Clive opened the chamber, checked to ensure all five bullets were inside, then flicked it back into place and pulled the hammer toward him.

The sound of glass being crushed filled his ears.

Clive stepped forward. Holding the revolver before him, he braced himself for whatever was to come.

The creature stepped into view.

Please, he thought, trembling, his arms shaking from the reality that they were no longer safe in their very own home. *Don't you hurt them. Don't you dare. They didn't do anything to you.*

The animal stretched its elongated body out as high as it could—ribs contracting, emaciated form lengthening. With its hands and its head full of crocodilian teeth braced forward, it tilted its nose up and sniffed at the air before turning its head to look at him.

The moonbeam eyes shined directly into Clive's.

Momentarily blinded, he lifted his gun and held it steady before him.

When his vision finally began to clear, he saw the animal was stepping forward, knee bent as its foot rose, setting back into place when it fell once more.

I can't believe it, Clive thought. *I can't fucking believe it.*

Such a comical display should have only existed in a cartoon, where the world was allowed to operate on the absurd notions of reality and the heightened realms of fantasy. The thing should have been chasing Roadrunner down the road, across the deserts, over the seas, but despite that fact, the thing continued forward, one leg up, one leg down. Its eyes broadened and the scope of its moonbeams became so targeted that the hallway appeared lit in light, almost to the point where Clive felt blinded by that act alone.

"You can do this," he whispered. "You know you can."

The thing's mouth, which up until now had only been slightly revealed, opened to expose the rows of needle-sharp teeth that existed between its jaws.

Clive raised the gun.

The animal laughed.

Clive fired.

The shot connected with the thing's head. Shot directly between the eyes, it could only stand for moment before it fell to the floor—dead, it seemed, as no longer did it breathe or move.

Stepping forward and around the body, Clive leaned around the corner and looked out into the kitchen, where he saw the door had been knocked from its hinges and now lay lopsided with its lower half still connected and the upper half all but splinters.

The rifle, though. *Go.*

With hate that he could have never imagined, Clive stole across the room and threw himself to the sofa. He flung the cushions off the loveseat and grabbed desperately for the rifle lying just beneath his touch.

Something laughed from the doorway.

Clive raised his rifle and trained it directly on the creature. "Get away," he said. "Go. Now. You don't belong here."

The thing laughed before snapping its jaws together and stepping into the house.

Behind it, two more animals appeared, both in varying stages of height and hunger.

After shoving the revolver into his pocket and making sure the grip would remain in place, Clive rose, made his way around the couch, then stood with his back to the stairway, taking extra care not to take too many quick steps back for fear of falling and shooting himself.

The creatures advanced slowly, with the cunning intent of wolves who had just cornered a baby fawn in a thicket of trees. He knew he would not serve as an ample meal, for upon his frame was merely a thin layer of skin, but it was common knowledge these things would do anything to get what they wanted, even if it meant killing him to get to his family.

Clive stepped back. His foot hit the first step.

"Get away from here," he said, stepping up onto the stairway, hands braced along the rifle and eyes set directly ahead. "You don't want us. You don't."

The lead animal tilted its head to the side and let out a brief chuckle, its sound deep but resembling something like that of a song bird. It raised its hands and sniffed the air once more before stopping in place.

As the two behind it stopped in turn, Clive took a deep breath.

No.

The animals charged.

Clive fired his rifle. The bullet tore through flesh and bone along the front creature's shoulder and sprayed its fellow companions in blood.

In a few moments they would be upon him.

Reaching down, Clive took the revolver in hand, set the hammer back into place, then screamed, *"Tricia! The gun!"*

Overhead, the door opened.

Clive threw the revolver up into the air and over the banister.

"Clive!" Tricia cried.

"GO!" he screamed. "GO! GO, TRICIA! *GO!*"

The three animals broached the stairwell.

It took but a moment for Clive to realize his fate.

He was going to die here, alone at the foot of the stairs, with his wife and baby son no more than a few dozen feet away.

God, he thought. *Use me as your vessel. Do what it is that needs to be done to keep my wife and son safe.*

He fired the rifle again.

One of the animals went down.

Another came in its place.

He fired again.

A creature knocked his rifle aside.

The rifle fired again before it was torn from his grasp.

Clive could only watch as the creature pounced on him.

It sunk its claws in.

It bit into his neck.

Blood sprayed the air as his carotid artery was ripped from his body.

In the few brief moments at the end of his life, in which he could only stare at the ceiling as his body went numb and the creatures continued to tear him to pieces, he thought of only one thing as he heard the upstairs window break.

She has the keys, he thought. *She can get away.*

Tricia and Colton were safe.

Kody Boye was born and raised in Southeastern Idaho. Since his initial publication in the Yellow Mama Webzine in 2007, he has gone on to sell nearly three-dozen stories to various markets. He is the author of the short story collection Amorous Things, *the novella* The Diary of Dakota Hammell, *the zombie novel* Sunrise *and the first book in* The Brotherhood Saga, Blood. *His fiction has been described as "Surreal, beautiful, and harrowing" (Fantastic Horror), while he himself has been heralded as a writer beyond his years (Bitten by Books). He currently lives and writes in the Austin, Texas area. You can visit him online at KodyBoye.com.*

Beach House

William Cook

Patrick pulled the black Lexus into the narrow driveway, the coarse hedge scrabbling down the side of the company car as it came to a halt next to the old cottage. He switched the ignition off, yawned, lit another cigarette, and gathered up his things before stepping out into the fresh morning air. A two-hour trip up from the capital with a southerly tailwind had blown Patrick into Paekakariki just before dawn.

The morning was cold, but the sun was on the rise, the crisp air thick with the salty smell of surf and dew-sodden shrubbery. Patrick didn't bother to look over his shoulder at the Ocean lapping the shoreline a mere stone's-throw away. Instead, he contemplated the bleak clouds billowing from behind the eastern hills, threatening to covet the sun's slow ascent. He took another drag on his cigarette and depressed the alarm tab on his key ring. The car simultaneously omitted an electronic fart as it blinked its park lights.

Patrick looked at the overgrown shrubs and the tall unruly hedge that fenced the beach house and provided shelter from the ocean's buffeting winds. *A job for the weekend,* he thought as he ground the cigarette butt into the grass and made his way down the narrow path to the rear of the property.

He turned the northeast corner of the cottage and stopped short. Two dead sparrows lay in the centre of the gravel path that led to the back door. Patrick carefully stepped over them, noting the puncture wounds in the small bodies as he continued toward the rear of the house. He made another mental note to himself to get rid of the small corpses at a more amicable hour.

The key turned with force and he was greeted with the musty smell of enclosed months. He made his way down the dark hall to the bedroom, the silence pervasive save for the soft murmur of the sea outside. He flung his business jacket and overnight bag onto a chair in the corner and pulled the curtains, wincing as hard light flooded the room. Loosening his tie, he changed into an old pair of jeans and a t-shirt and set about airing out the bungalow. He began to feel more relaxed, the coastal ambience and fresh air already seeming to have somewhat reduced his peaked stress levels.

Patrick opened the lounge window. A crow swooped from nowhere and arced within an inch of the pane, blasting him with song and disappearing as quickly as it had appeared. He gathered himself together, breathing hard. "*Bloody bird,*" he cursed out loud as he held his hand to his chest, his heart beating quickly. 'Creepers,' his old man used to call them, and Patrick felt compelled to agree. They gave him the creeps all right.

He had noticed that the longer he spent in the city, the more phobic he had become about 'natural' things, birds in particular. He didn't like the way their eyes seemed to follow his every movement, the abrupt shift of their wings, or the way they tilted their heads to one side as they peered mercilessly into what felt like his very soul. He shivered, lit a smoke, and turned the stove on to boil a pot of tea.

Patrick opened the latch on the French doors that faced out toward the coast and sat on the top step in the sun, admiring the clarity of the morning vista as he finished his cigarette. Inevitably, he thought about work. He was a broker for a large multinational and had enjoyed the challenge of the first five years, but the long hours had driven a wedge between himself and his wife Daphne. They had been separated for three months and the phone call he had been dreading had come last night, cementing the inevitable divorce.

Finishing off a bottle of Chivas he'd seconded from the staff drinks cabinet in the boardroom, he had packed a bag and steered the Lexus toward the coast at four o'clock that morning. The old family bach had always afforded some sort of security for him—from his parent's death, now to his impending divorce. He had fled to a reliable peace of sorts, albeit temporary, at least until he could think about what to do next.

The creeper chortled violently from the hedge next to the house, waking Patrick from his thoughts. He remembered the pot on the stove and hurried inside. It was cold to touch. The element was switched on. He remembered the power board and flicked the main switch on. Dull yellow light illuminated the hallway as the dusty stereogram tucked in next to the sofa-bed in the lounge crackled to life, Dave Dobbyn singing about being 'loyal.'

Patrick touched the element just to make sure the power was really on and burnt the tips of his fingers. Cursing his stupidity, he turned the cold tap on, stepping back as it spluttered and shook, spraying rust-coloured water out of the faucet 'til it ran clear.

Cooling his fingers, he looked out the small kitchen window into the yard. The old clothesline pole leaned limply against the frayed line, a few stray wooden pegs, scattered flax against the hedge, the grass a good foot-high . . .

Another dead bird lay on the pipi-shelled path under the clothesline. It looked like a fantail with a sizeable chunk removed from its small body. Patrick leapt back from the sink as the crow alighted on the sill in a flurry of obsidian wings and mocking stares. It rapped its glistening black bill aggressively on the glass as if it was trying to break the windowpane.

Tap tap tap.

Tap tap tap.

Patrick quickly filled a glass with water and slowly opened the side window, ready to douse the malicious protagonist. The creeper seized the opportunity to retreat to the clothesline, where it perched on the swaying line, chortling and tilting its head madly as it puffed its plumed breast, its white collar displayed like a proud priest uttering last rites over the body of the crumpled bird below. Patrick drew the blinds angrily, disbelieving the bird's audacity.

He knew he'd been hitting the bottle a bit hard since Daphne left him, and he knew his drinking was part of the reason she left him in the first place. He knew it was the reason he was strung out now, letting some pugnacious bird freak him out, of all things. He also knew he had to stop his self-destructive habit, which was one of the main reasons he'd retreated to the beach house.

So many reasons. So little motivation.

Cold turkey.

He'd done it before and knew he could do it again, for good this time. He pushed his anxiety aside and decided to get some much-needed rest, despite the fact the sun was rising steadily outside. Sleep came quickly as he lay on the wire-frame single bed. It had always been the most comfortable bed he'd ever slept on, despite all the expensive hotel and design-store brands that had been a part of his adult life for so long now.

There's a lot to be said for simplicity and maybe, just maybe, for being alone, he thought while slipping into sleep.

* * *

It was dark when Patrick woke to the sound of the Kowhai tree scratching the side of the house. It sounded like a set of long fingernails being dragged across a blackboard. He lay awake on his back with the moonlight streaming through the window and the sound of the approaching storm gathering momentum outside. The old bach creaked as the wind pushed its weight against the corrugated iron roof. Patrick heard the power lines moan outside his bedroom window as the wind whipped through the small community, just as it had done when he was a small boy curled up in bed against the cold.

There were roughly twenty or so baches in the small cove, surrounded by ancient Pohutukawa trees, a carnivorous ocean, and a jetty in dire need of repair. One road in, one road out, and a small store that sold fishing supplies and over-priced canned food and cigarettes.

At least half the residents still lived in the dwellings. The rest were like Patrick—out-of-towners who lived in the city and headed north in their SUVs and European cars for the occasional weekend away. Daphne had whined at him to buy a more elaborate bach elsewhere—somewhere with restaurants,

306

golf courses, and a marina—so he had. Most of the time they would travel across to the other coast and spend a few days hob-knobbing with the people one would usually be trying to escape by going to the beach in the first place.

The new bach on the east coast had set Patrick back a cool half million and an extra year of overtime at the office, but it had kept her happy and that was the main thing. He had drawn the line when she tried to suggest he should get rid of the old bach. It was handed down through the family and he was damned if he was going to get rid of it on a whim from her. His thoughts slipped away again as the house started to shake with the force of the wind and the rain that now lashed the outside with a vengeance.

Patrick shivered and pulled the blankets up under his chin. He fumbled in his bag beside the bed and produced a hip flask of whisky. After a few sips, he felt the chill evaporate from his body and a sense that everything would work out all right. Not just with the storm raging outside, but within himself. There were plenty more women out there and he was rich, successful, and good-looking. He would fall flat on his feet again shortly.

"Patrick Tripp always bounces back," he reassured himself out loud as he took another long swig. He checked his cell phone and, discovering there was no coverage, threw it disgustedly on the floor.

A tremendous crash sounded from the kitchen—the sound of glass breaking, followed by loud thumping noises.

Patrick threw himself out of bed, unsteady on his feet from the whisky, and fumbled for the light switch, stubbing his toe on the corner of the dresser as he did so. There was no power. Not knowing what to expect, he grabbed an old oak walking stick off the coat rack in the hall and made his way tentatively toward the horrible banging noise emanating from the kitchen. The cane extended in front of him like a swash-buckler's rapier. The house was unbearably cold and his breath came in short gasps of fog as he advanced nervously, rubbing roughly at his eyes as he tried to distinguish shape from darkness.

Moonlight illuminated a chaotic scene in the kitchen. The door was wide open, the wild wind blowing sheets of rain into the room, along with leaves and debris that swirled amongst the puddles of water on the linoleum.

Patrick dropped the cane and rushed forward to barricade the entrance against the storm, letting out a piercing scream as broken glass from the smashed pane in the door cut into his bare feet. He fell to the ground and tried to cup his lacerated soles in his cold hands, blood running as freely as the rain blowing on to the kitchen floor. Taking his t-shirt off, Patrick tore it in half and applied a tourniquet to both feet, effectively stopping the blood flow.

After gathering his strength and securing the kitchen door with the back of a chair, Patrick scrambled on hands and knees through the cupboards looking for the earthquake kit Daphne had given him for Christmas last year. He entertained the idea that it was almost as if she had known he would befall a disaster such as this at some point or other.

Disregarding the mice that scampered across the backs of his freezing hands, he breathed a sigh of relief when he found the plastic case which, amongst other things, housed two candles and some safety matches. After much fumbling and striking, Patrick managed to ignite a match and subsequently the candles. He found a couple of empty whisky bottles under the sink and after hauling himself up on his sore knees, he placed the candles strategically on the mantle above the coal range.

After managing to heave himself up onto a chair, he rummaged through the earthquake kit at the kitchen table and found a small first-aid kit with a pair of tweezers inside. Unwrapping his tender feet, he was pleased to see the lacerations weren't as bad as he first thought and had already begun to coagulate nicely. One cut on his instep was particularly nasty and looked as if it would require a few stitches.

Patrick removed a sliver of glass the length of his finger from the cut, releasing fresh blood from the wound. He reapplied his makeshift bandage and proceeded to remove the rest of the glass from his other foot under the light of the flickering candle. All the while, the storm howled and shook the small bach with a fury he hadn't witnessed for a long time.

Patrick blew out one of the candles and hobbled back to his bedroom, candle in one hand and in the other what he now recognised to be his deceased Grandfather's walking stick. He heard ghostly drips in the spare room on the bare floorboards, mimicking the tap of the cane. He felt cold drips on his head and shoulders from where the rain crept in under the iron and leaked through the roof. The small cottage was in need of repair, and as he slumped back into bed, he resolved to spend some money on the place and get it back to new. After all, the bach was in a family trust and Daphne wouldn't be able to get her greedy hands on it when the divorce settlement came through, so he may as well make it as comfortable as he could.

His feet were starting to throb with pain. He would have to go into town to the doctor tomorrow and get some help. In the meantime Patrick self-medicated with the rest of the whisky. He lit a cigarette off the candle, now perched on the small table next to the bed, and inhaled deeply. He couldn't believe his bad luck. "They say things happen in threes," he mused to himself. "Wonder what the third piece of *good* luck will bring with it?"

He lay as still as he could, watching the smoke from his cigarette drift up toward the ceiling, where it was swirled away by unseen drafts of cold air. The curtains fluttered in the breeze creeping through the cracks in the old window frame. Moonlight flashed across the small room as the clouds parted for brief seconds and then rendezvoused, bringing more torrential rain and wind to beat against the small west coast settlement.

After a handful of cigarettes and the last drops of whisky from the hipflask, the wind began to subside, but the rain became heavier on the old tin roof. Patrick began to slip into unconsciousness, the drink taking its course. He drunkenly imagined he could hear that infernal crow warbling its haunting refrain, hidden in the wet shrubbery, camouflaged somewhere in the darkness. The flame of the candle flickered. Patrick slipped into another dream, the tapping of the rain on the roof lulling him to sleep.

* * *

Patrick sat in the drizzling rain on what was left of the veranda step and smoked a cigarette as he looked out at the expansive view. The ocean was slate grey and flat as glass. Patrick's clothes were as sodden as his heart was weary. After the fury of the previous night, he couldn't believe the calm of the day. He had stuffed things up once again. The fire engines had gone half an hour before, with the officer in charge recommending Patrick follow them to a small hospital in the next town to get his feet attended to.

Behind Patrick, blue smoke twisted sluggishly from the soaked remains of the charred bach. He hadn't realised how small the section was until now. A clothesline lay like a dead thing on the grass. The hedge still stood strong, although gaps from the thrashing it had taken the previous night were evident. The wind-strapped Kowhai tree, which had scratched away at the side of the house, still splayed its sinewy limbs defiantly, though slightly scorched.

Patrick felt sick yet somehow relieved. He guessed it was just something less he had to worry about now, and he was feeling rather lucky to have escaped the inferno he had inadvertently created.

He forced himself to look over his shoulder and tried to suppress the tears that welled up inside as a flood of good and bad memories came over him. He picked himself up and managed to hobble toward what was left of the company car, a blackened key clutched in his dirty fist.

He stopped in mid-step, knowing what he'd stepped on— the dead fantail lay flat on the path, looking peaceful in death. Patrick looked around the property again, and there amongst the blackened limbs of the Kowhai sat the Tui, its head tilted to one side, its beady black eye focused intently on Patrick's passage.

Patrick took the last cigarette from the packet and lit it, crumpling the packet and throwing it at the bird. The packet fell well short of the mark.

The crow didn't budge.

Patrick turned and walked gingerly past the smoking wreckage of the car, dropping the keys in the wet grass as he went. He regretted parking the Lexus so close to the cottage. He hadn't used public transport in years and wasn't looking forward to catching a bus back into town.

Despite his charred and slightly hung over state of dishevelment, Patrick couldn't get over how calm he felt. Last night's rain should have prevented the fire from being worse than it was, but somehow not a timber was left free from its burning rage. The bach was gone. A lifetime of memories tangibly incinerated and yet Patrick felt free for the first time in his adult life. He knew he was covered by insurance, but he also knew the insurance company might not be so forgiving for this culmination of recent indiscretions. He pried his melted Gucci wallet open, the expensive nappa leather peeling back to reveal a relatively unblemished sleeve full of cash.

The rain had become a soft drizzle and Patrick's clothes could get no damper. He hobbled the short distance to the village centre and stopped at a store to purchase a fresh pack of cigarettes, a new ten-dollar flannel shirt, and a cheap tracksuit. The store's clothing selection was limited, but the old codger gave Patrick a pair of his son's well-worn gumboots in exchange for a slightly charred twenty-dollar note.

Patrick looked at the assortment of hipflasks on the shelf behind the balding proprietor and opted instead for the more sensible purchase of an over-priced set of bright yellow wet-weather gear.

Oblivious to the chimes of the doorbell and the accusatory but somehow sympathetic stares of the local shoppers, Patrick bundled himself into his ill-fitting garb, selected a hot pie from the warmer, left the appropriate cash on the counter, and made his way back out onto the quiet street.

The gumboots sucked at his bare feet, tugging the raw wounds as he hobbled to the bus stop. He ate his pie in silence and stared at the slick grey road in front of him. There wasn't even a motel he could camp out in for a few days. He would have to head back to the city. Back to his expensive suits, his serviced penthouse apartment, and all the other trappings he had geared himself toward over the last twenty years.

He lit a cigarette and checked the timetable. Another half hour and he would be on the bus, heading south toward the capital. He looked across the road at the rows of hedges and the small roofs of the cottages. He could see both ends of the street, one of which opened out toward the coast and flat grey ocean. He could still see faint drifts of blue smoke rising from the remnants of the beach house in the distance.

He turned and looked the other way, watching for the bus as he smoked his cigarette, trying hard to ignore the prying gaze of the crow insolently perched on the gable of the cottage directly opposite the bus stop.

He couldn't remember the last time he'd seen such a bird in the city . . . and somehow he felt the better for it.

William Cook lives in Wellington, the small wind-blown capital city of New Zealand. He has been writing weird stories ever since he was a kid. His first published works were poems in various literary journals in NZ and a few in the States. He is the author of a collection of verse entitled Journey: The Search for Something. *His work also appears in the 2010* Masters of Horror Anthology. *William's novel* Blood Related *was published by Angelic Knight Press in December 2011. His art work has appeared on numerous book covers. Find William online at http://williamcookwriter.blogspot.com/, or for a look at his macabre art, visit http://nzartist.blogspot.com/. Find William's poetry at http://williamcookpoet.blogspot.co.nz. You can also look him up on Facebook and Twitter.*

It Sounds a Bit Like . . .

Gary Fry

I think there's something wrong with my Dad, but it's worse than that. I think it's spreading to *all* of us . . . Sorry, I'm a bit nervous. Let me provide a bit of background information.

My Mum died about two years ago: cancer of the spine. The hospital didn't spot it early enough, even though she'd had some routine tests after complaining about back pain. She'd always been a smoker, so we were naturally concerned. Still, when the results came back clear, we were happy, despite all the problems we'd always suffered between us. Bloody NHS! Then again, it wasn't the authorities' fault that we were a . . . yes, I guess you'd call us a *dysfunctional* family.

I was an only child. I secretly think my Mum had wanted a boy, or maybe a girl who matched her ideas of what a girl should be. But I was always more of a tomboy. It wasn't that I'd associated more with my Dad or anything, because he worked a lot and I rarely saw him, but as far back as I can remember, I'd always preferred climbing trees and playing with noisy toys and other stuff. I liked sports, too, and at school I was always the best, particularly in athletics—running, mainly.

Anyway, my Mum didn't like this, was kind of embarrassed by it. But my Dad, he was proud. Despite his long hours, he used to come to all the track events and cheer me on. However, I was never really allowed to get *close* to him. Whenever I tried, my Mum would intervene. If I asked him to come into my bedroom to kiss me goodnight, she'd always be standing there; the same whenever I phoned home—*she'd* always answer, and only reluctantly pass me on to him.

If it was jealousy, I couldn't understand why—she was probably neurotic or something. She was an edgy sort, whereas Dad and I were calmer. Neither of us smoked and we hated the habit; she was a forty-a-day woman. Her influence was like an invisible force over me. Even when I did well in school tournaments, I could hear her voice at the back of my head saying, "That's not what women *do*, Jenny." I hated her calling me 'Jenny.' *Hated* it.

It got worse. When I was sixteen, whenever I looked in the mirror I saw *her*. We were alike in appearance, if poles apart in outlook. I'd just discovered boys, or rather they'd discovered me, and for many months I was juggling my sporting aspirations with my social life. Yeah, feminism and all that stuff has allowed women a chance at doing whatever they wish in the modern age, but it's still not easy. My first boyfriend always moaned whenever I had to train first thing in the morning and then last thing at night. So I chucked him. But guess what? My Mum had *liked* him. When I was on a date, Mum could have my Dad to herself, though what did they ever do together? *Nothing*. Still, that was obviously enough for both of them.

Dad loved Mum; he's a simple man, not very good at dealing with people. He'd always worked alone, on building jobs. He was forty-seven when they had me; Mum was thirty-eight. There were certainly some strange family dynamics going on, but I never understood them. Maybe they'd struggled to have a child when they were younger—I don't know. I might have been a late decision or a mistake . . . I don't know that either.

Anyway, I got rather sick of coming between them all the time. I had a chance at getting in a UK running team for a tour of the Far East, but by then I'd taken the softer option. My second boyfriend—Alan, my husband now—had his own flat, and I'd spend as much time there as I would out training. He's a decent, attractive man whose own family is comparatively stable and straightforward. Of course I was drawn to this. Even though family was important to him, and he couldn't understand the issue I had with mine (I kept most of it to myself), he finally persuaded me to marry him, planning children and a mortgage—the *usual* stuff.

Well, I put the athletics career on hold. Mum was delighted. However, at this point she'd had begun to complain of those back aches. Dad was frantic. I think he feared, now that I was gone (Alan and me moved into a nice, small terrace about four years ago), that he'd be left alone in the world; remember, he was then in his sixties, just a few years off retirement. So he insisted on Mum going to the doc's. It was quite a fight—one of the few occasions I've seen him so wound up. He even had a go at me because he thought I wasn't expressing enough concern. But it wasn't that I wasn't worried, rather that I'd had enough of Mum's malingering—she'd always used it to get the better of me, to attract Dad's sympathy. I thought I knew her better.

The next time I saw them, she was hunched over terribly. Dad was walking with her in the park while I was out jogging (I'd decided to give the running another shot, despite the fact that Alan and his family kept harping on about kids). I was shocked. This time, I joined in with my Dad's demand for a medical assessment. Mum was still smoking heavily, and her face, when I examined it in broad daylight, was all wrinkly. It scared me. I imagined my face like that in thirty years or so, perhaps as a consequence of the pressures of bringing up children, and it didn't appeal at all. So I took her to the hospital. "No, no, I've just slipped a disc or something," she protested, her voice hacking on smoke. "It'll pop back in. This happened before, when I was younger; I did it when I . . . I . . . ."

We never did find out how she hurt herself because that was when she collapsed. I called Alan on my mobile and he came straightaway—he liked my folks. And here's the ironic thing. When we drove my Mum in to the hospital, I also had a funny spell—fainted or some such. All I know was that when I came to, my husband was there, beaming down at me, and he'd also brought his own parents. And they were all smiling.

Yep, you got it: I was *pregnant.* I was stunned. However, all I could think about was whether my Mum was okay, or rather how my Dad was coping with this episode. I kept my news to myself and made Alan's family promise to do so too.

My parents were simply waiting to leave. A few tests had been done. Results pending, nothing to worry about, the young male doctor told me—he looked about twelve. Still, perhaps that's the state of the country, isn't it? You'll see that it *certainly* is when I tell you the rest.

Excuse me, this is the hardest bit for me to explain. Give me a second, will you . . . ? Right, thanks. Let me go on.

Time seemed to pass too quickly. Before I knew it, I was already *showing:* two months of morning sickness and bad moods had led to Alan working even longer hours at the supermarket where he's branch manager. Anyway, one day I went round to my parents because I fancied a walk as much as anything else. I couldn't have run if you'd paid me! My own back was hurting, but I still couldn't imagine what Mum must have been going through.

I already knew the tests had come back all-clear (just a little swelling around the vertebrae or something, easily treatable by tablets), so I was reasonably unconcerned when I entered their bungalow, which is situated in one of the nicer areas of Leeds. By now, they knew about the baby, of course, and Mum had been delighted, despite her obvious pain. Dad's response had been more—what's the word?—more *ambiguous.* He'd certainly smiled when Alan and I had related our news while driving them home from the hospital, though I'd also sensed a kind of . . . oh, I don't know . . . a kind of *regret.* Maybe he was still concerned about Mum.

And soon I realised he had good reason to be.

She looked *horrible.* She could barely stand up straight. Her voice was like it was full of dirt, and she'd clearly neglected the housework. Since Dad had retired, perhaps he should have helped out with chores, but he didn't have a clue. She'd always done everything for him. Bloody men!

Anyway, I called Alan who—bless him—skipped a meeting and drove us to the hospital at once. My Mum couldn't even walk from the car park; her back seemed to have locked; she was in agony. When we got inside, I demanded to see a specialist, since Dad had never been any good at asking for anything. Mum was taken to a room and they did stuff to her— God knows what. And *then* the devastating news.

It was cancer.

The doctor who told us could only assume some test results had got mixed up. In response to this, Dad had another of his rare tantrums; he called the NHS every dreadful name he could think; he got so bad that even I started to think I should leave in case my unborn child absorbed any of it! The things you think about when you're under stress! Dad said that he'd paid his taxes all his life, and was this his reward? I think he went a little *mad* that afternoon. You'll see in a moment what I mean . . .

Mum never came out of the hospital. The tumour had spread to her blood, and then to her brain. She died at about midnight the same day. Dad just sat in silence while Alan rubbed my back.

Things were rather subdued for a while. It took me a long time to come to terms with our loss—I mean, my Mum and I had never really got on, but she was still my *Mum,* wasn't she? Alan was supportive, but it was my Dad I was worried about. Whenever I'd go round there, as my belly grew bigger and bigger, he'd take only a cursory interest in his future grandchild, while paging through old photo albums and handing me pictures of Mum, as if to say, "Don't forget her, Jennifer. And make sure your girl or boy knows where she or he comes from too." Of course, I nodded at the right moments. In the past, we'd become adroit at communicating via gestures, and even now, without interfering Mum around, we still did this. It was like a habit. Weird, eh?

But not as *weird* as the few years that followed . . . oh, good God, not at all! And this is the main bit of my story, so let me start by outlining what happened after my son—Harry, we called him: a beautiful, healthy boy—was born.

Things were okay for a while. I got back into shape by running of an evening after Alan had stumbled in from work. Whenever I returned, I'd see him stooping over our child, showing him photos and repeating the names of the people in them again and again. I think he was determined for Harry's first word to be 'family.'

I used to call in to see my Dad, now in his late sixties, about twice a week, and he'd generally be sullen and quiet, though always ready to greet his grandson with a childish prank or a daft comment or some silly language of his own devising. This cheered me, but I didn't realise that *these* might have been the early signs . . .

After a year had flashed by (*don't* they just?), I became a bit worried by Harry's eating habits. The only thing he'd entertain with any enthusiasm was bananas. He'd turn his nose up at proper food, while dribbling cereal or toast or whatever down his chin. But with bananas he'd just sit there, munching for hours. I wasn't sure this was healthy. I read books on the subject. I consulted Alan's folks. I even asked my Dad, who I'd somewhat neglected since becoming such a fretful mother . . . and *then* I realised what I was up to.

I was being as fussy and neurotic as my own Mum had been! *That* couldn't be good, could it? I didn't wish to repeat *those* patterns; I wanted Alan, Harry, and me to be happy together, and not to bear any of those strange complications my family had suffered.

Is that natural? Do all parents go through this? Trying to make sure their own efforts at bringing up kids are better than their predecessors until surely one day the perfect family is produced? I mean, are we always trying to strip away the bad influences of previous generations? Well, perhaps that's partly true. But I also know that it's never as simple as that.

My first realisation that matters were very wrong was when I received a phone call one morning, about a month ago now. Alan had the day off and was talking to Harry, who'd yet to say his first word and who wouldn't eat the mashed meal I'd prepared. Exasperated by this, I told my husband to give him a banana while I escaped for a moment to shut up the ringing, which was pricking my nerves.

"Hello?" I said, possibly a bit sharply—but the reply didn't seem concerned about that at all.

"It's your Mum," the person at the other end of the line said.

Imagine what I thought then. There I was, up to my neck in the inevitable problems of motherhood, and now I was hearing a voice from beyond the grave! Except that it was no such thing; in fact, if anything, the truth was far *worse*.

Once I'd calmed down a little, closing the door to silence Alan (who was again going through a photo album and naming every person we knew), I recognised the harsh tone, which had indeed sounded like a woman's voice after a lifetime of cigarettes.

It was my Dad.

"What do you mean?" I asked, suddenly very uncomfortable. I hadn't been jogging in weeks, and I felt tired and rundown.

"She's come back!" Dad told me, his tone so bright it might indeed be a woman's . . . or a child's.

Of course I went round there immediately. I asked Alan to look after Harry, and I ran the short distance across the village in which we all lived.

Dad had just got up. What little grey hair he had left was all spiky and his eyes had a sad, rheumy look. He'd obviously been dreaming and had called just after waking.

I was able to settle him, even though he still insisted that my Mum *had* visited him. By this stage, I'd begun to suspect that this behaviour might not just be senility . . . that he might be getting seriously ill. Dementia? Alzheimer's? Something like that.

In light of what happened with the NHS last time, it's easy to understand why I was reluctant to phone a doctor. In the event, however, I got in touch with Social Services, whose male representative suggested that my Dad might be best off selling his home and moving in with us . . . Yeah, *sure*. In a two-bedroom terrace and with a baby. I mean, my husband was doing okay at the supermarket, but with house prices the way they are lately, we were stuck there for the foreseeable future. So thanks for nothing, authorities.

Instead, I decided to keep an eye on my Dad . . . not always face-to-face, since I had Harry to look after (who, at twenty months, still hadn't spoken and still had that annoying eating habit), but I'd phone Dad at least once a day, making sure he had everything he needed.

The next creepy episode occurred about a fortnight later. To be honest, racing over to my Dad's that day had given me back the running bug. I was keen to return to my former aspirations. Oh, I don't mean in any professional capacity—I was way past that—but there are various amateur organisations for less ambition people, and after spending all my time at home with Harry, I was keen to get out there, have some kind of life of my own.

I'd said all this to Alan the night before *that* call. We'd argued, and I hoped our son hadn't overheard. I didn't want his first word to be 'selfish' or the phrase 'bad mother.' Still, these are what my husband had called me, so I was extremely wound up when I rang my Dad to make sure at least *he* was okay.

Someone answered, and when I said, "Hi, Dad . . . *Dad?*" the line went silent for a moment. Then I heard my Dad say, "All right, love, I'm coming," but his voice was faint, as if . . . as if he was speaking from the other side of the room. But how could that be when he would be holding the handset? I heard footsteps approaching, and then my Dad replied, "Hello, Jennifer? Sorry. Your Mum answered first—just like she used to. Still, it's so nice to have her back, isn't it?"

I felt as if she *had* returned. I was going crazy at the time. After exchanging a few carefully worded pleasantries, I got Harry out of bed and fed him his usual banana. "Say 'banana,'" I instructed, almost by rote as this stage. "Say 'banana'—come on, say it! *Say* it!" I was hardly in my right mind. Once I'd settled him in front of the telly, I phoned Social Services about the possibilities of residential care.

I was so frantic that I initially dialled the wrong number and got put through to the employment office. Mind you, the woman there used to work in housing, and she was able to explain a few details. Apparently, if older folk had savings (and my Dad did; he'd always been careful with his money), then they must live on those savings, since they weren't entitled to benefits or a relocation to sheltered accommodation or whatever. I was also told a load of other stuff too complicated for my tired brain to take in.

I just needed a *run,* to blow out the cobwebs. I'm afraid I lost my temper with this woman, who I later realised was simply toeing the line of government policy. She'd told me that the law had just changed, that care of the elderly was no longer an entitlement for all, that each case was means tested, and blah, blah, blah. I hung up angrily.

When Alan came home from work, I left at once, having strapped on my trainers to take several laps of the nearby park. This overlooked my Dad's house, but I didn't have the confidence—or I was too scared—to visit. So as soon as I felt more collected, I trudged home, resolved to talk it all through with my husband.

He had Harry on his lap and another photo album open. I was dismayed to see that the picture both he and our son were staring at was one of my Mum, just before she'd become ill. Perhaps it was the resemblance between her and me that attracted Harry's attention so lengthily; he'd even flung aside his second banana of that day. Alan had been just about to repeat the names of the people on the pages—I'd have called her 'Grandma,' but his family used another term of address—when he turned to me to say, "We've got to talk."

We did, for several hours. We decided that we couldn't afford to look after my Dad in our current circumstances, though if we re-mortgaged the house and combined the cash with my Dad's savings, then we might be able to get him a place in a nice rest home, where he'd be cared for "by professionals." These were Alan's words, and naturally I was sceptical, yet come the next day—a Saturday—we visited the nearest home for the elderly. I felt bad about doing this behind Dad's back, but he'd always been led by other people and had never protested—my Mum had seen to that . . . *when* she'd been living.

The place impressed me, even though I experienced several unsettling episodes with some of the residents. I rapidly felt as if I was surrounded by children—the old folk were all so simple, so innocent, so carelessly jolly . . . Did I really want to leave my Dad here? However, maybe he was headed the same way; perhaps that's what awaits *all* of us. Anyway, after I'd instructed my husband to take Harry into the garden to play, someone called me by name.

It was an aged woman who I vaguely recognised. Once I'd crossed to her seat, she grinned up at me, bearing immaculate dentures, and introduced herself as Mavis Hall, an old friend of my Mum's. I smiled back and then became engaged in various reminiscences which almost brought a tear to my eye until I remembered how much of the really strange behaviour in my family had been kept behind closed doors. It's the same with all families, I imagine.

But then Mavis made me *scream.* She said, "Your Dad hasn't wasted much time, has he?" I asked her what she meant.

Every fortnight, I was told, the old dears were taken to the local park, the one in which I jogged, to see the ducks and to get a bit of fresh air. It was during one of these trips a few weeks earlier that Mavis had seen my Dad . . . with another woman.

"Still," Mavis finished, "I dare say he's being charitable as much anything else. The poor lass! Stooped over like *that*—I didn't get a good look at her. the sun was in my eyes. Tell me, dear, does his new lady-friend have something wrong with her back?"

I didn't stop shaking until Alan drove me home, and then not for another few days. We argued again, my husband and me, and on this occasion Harry *did* overhear. Alan grew so infuriated (I said some terrible things, such as that my marriage had stopped me doing what I'd always wanted to do, and that I regretted having become tied down: I was very confused) that he drove off to work on the Monday as if our relationship was over. It wasn't, of course, but the voices in my head wouldn't let me get the whole situation into any perspective. When Harry cried, I just gathered him from the floor in front of the telly, spilling the photo album he'd been holding open, and then grabbed one of his precious bananas from our fruit bowl before charging out of the house; I was determined to put an end to all this mess.

I didn't stop running until I reached my Dad's bungalow. It was still early. He'd forgotten to pull on the curtains in his bedroom and I could see only the headboard; weak April sun made the glass all waxy. Shamefully, I was terrified to enter the building.

"Dad!" I called, almost waking the street, whose residents were mostly elderly. "Dad! *Dad!*"

And then he appeared . . . or *someone* did: a figure bent upward, as if from a severe back injury. What with the light on the pane, this person was just a hazy shape. When I squinted, with my son's arms wrapped around my neck to prevent a good view, I saw . . . I saw *my Mum* sitting up in the bed.

Oh, but *no*, I was mistaken. What I was actually seeing was my own reflection projected onto my Dad's face, his wrinkles making mine look older. Still, I jumped on the spot, so severely my son looked at what had caused the fright.

"Nana," he said as the image disintegrated or my vision refocused, and indeed there was just my Dad staring dreamily, forlornly, out of the window. "Nana, nana, nana," my son went on.

Just then I was too delighted by Harry's first word for much thought. I gave him his usual feed—you've guessed what: the thing I believed he'd asked for—and then went inside and spent several hours crying in my Dad's arms.

It was only later, after I'd gotten home and started to tidy the house before my husband returned from work, that I began to wonder what my son had *actually* meant. The family photograph album had been left open on the carpet, bearing a picture of my Mum. In Harry's company, Alan had never referred to his own Mum as 'Grandma,' but the one alternative—the word I can't bring myself to write here.

It sounds a bit like . . .

Forgive me, my son's hungry; I must go and feed him.

That's what mothers do, isn't it?

Gary Fry has a PhD in psychology but his first love is literature. He's had several short story collections published (including the first in PS Publishing's Showcase range), a couple of novellas, and two novels. His latest book is the cosmic horror novella The Respectable Face of Tyranny *(Spectral Press) and his next* Shades of Nothingness, *a collection from PS Publishing. None other than Ramsey Campbell has described Gary as a "master". He can be found online here: www.gary-fry.com*

Conversations Kill

Tim Waggoner

She became aware of motion first, a steady rhythmic jostling that caused her to sway from side to side. Next the rumble-growl of a hard-running car engine, felt as much as heard. Heated air blowing on her skin, seeping into her flesh, penetrating her bones until it felt as if her body was filled with warm, golden honey. So soothing, so peaceful, so tempting to remain swaddled in darkness, warmth, and comfort. She almost gave in, surrendered herself to the safety of nothingness. Instead, she opened her eyes.

She saw a splash of garish yellow light surrounded by velvet blackness. Her vision cleared a little, and she realized she was looking at headlights illuminating a patch of asphalt. Blackness meant night, asphalt meant a road, headlights meant a car.

"Don't worry. Everything's going to be all right."

A man's voice, familiar. She turned to her left, saw him sitting at the steering wheel. He didn't turn to look at her, kept his gaze on the road ahead. In the soft blue glow of the dashboard lights, she examined his features. Lean face, prominent cheekbones, strong chin. Short, straight hair, neatly trimmed beard. There was no way to tell for sure in this light, but she felt certain that his hair and beard were both reddish brown. He wore a brown suede jacket, faded jeans, and ratty running shoes that desperately needed to be replaced. His expression was impassive, almost as if he were wearing a mask, or was perhaps a mannequin someone had buckled into the driver's seat of the car as a bizarre joke. She knew that face—knew it better than she did her own.

"Walter . . ." Half statement, half question.

He didn't answer, but his gaze flicked toward her for a brief instant before returning to the road. In that moment she thought she saw a resigned sadness in his eyes, mingled with a touch of anxiety that bordered on fear.

Why would he be afraid of me, of all people? I'd never . . . The thought trailed away as she realized she couldn't move her arms. Her seat belt was on, but surely she should still be able to move them, at least a little. She looked down at her lap and saw the reason for her immobility: her wrists had been wrapped together with duct tape. She also saw that she wore a sleeveless green dress—a garment she didn't recognize—along with a black belt around the waist, and no shoes. No bra or panties either. She tried to move her legs and discovered her ankles were also bound with tape. An icicle spear of cold panic lodged in her heart, and her first instinct was to scream at Walter to let her go, to thrash about in an attempt to break free of her bonds. But she forced herself to remain quiet and still. She was a slender woman, not weak by any means, but even though she was in good shape, she knew she couldn't tear the tape apart with sheer strength. In the end, it was confused disbelief that helped her maintain control more than anything else. She simply couldn't conceive of any reason why Walter would tape her wrists and ankles together like this. Walter loved her; he'd never hurt her. This was all too weird, like something out of a nightmare. It couldn't possibly be real.

"You're probably wondering what's going on." He sounded almost apologetic.

She glanced out the windshield. For the last few minutes since she'd wakened, the road had been winding gently uphill, with large pine trees on either side, so high that the car's headlights couldn't illuminate them fully, leaving their tops shrouded in darkness. She had the impression the trees might continue upward forever, without end, that perhaps they were holding the heavens themselves aloft, the stars nothing more than bits of frost clinging to their branches, glittering with reflected light from the nearly full moon.

"I know this area," she said. "It's Krahling Hills. We come up here every summer. We rent a cabin, go hiking, fishing, swimming in the lake . . ."

"That's the thing. We don't. We never have." Walter's tone held a measure of pity now, and for some reason that frightened her more than anything else since she'd awakened.

"How can you say that? I remember—"

"I'm trying to tell you!" he snapped.

The sudden intensity of his words scared her, and without thinking, she scooted away from him, closer to the passenger door.

He turned to give her a sheepish smile. "Sorry. It's just . . . this isn't easy for me, you know?"

"No, I *don't. I'm* the one who woke up with duct tape around my ankles and wrists, not you." She was surprised by her own bravado, wasn't sure where it had come from. But the words, and more importantly the attitude behind them, felt right.

"I know. And I'm sorry." Walter turned his attention back to the road but continued to talk. "It's just that I didn't know how you were going to react, and I thought restraining you would make things easier. For both of us."

"What *things?*" Her confusion was quickly becoming replaced by anger. She loved Walter, but his stubborn reluctance to directly answer her questions infuriated her. "I don't remember getting in the car, and I don't understand why I'm dressed like this." She sat only inches from the passenger side window, but she could feel the outside cold seeping in through the glass. She guessed it was late fall, maybe early winter, but why couldn't she *remember?* "Where are my shoes? Why don't I have a coat? Why am I your prisoner?"

"You're not. Well . . . not exactly." He took a deep breath and let out a shaky sigh. "This is going to sound weird, but try to hear me out, okay? This is . . . well, it's therapy. For me."

She felt her body pressed back against the car seat as the road's incline grew steeper. *We're getting closer,* she thought. But closer to what, she didn't know.

"Therapy." The word came out flat, toneless. Nothing more than a nudge to keep him talking, like the single swift hand motion of a juggler trying to prevent a spinning plate from falling off the stick.

A nervous laugh, pitched high, an almost feminine sound. "This is probably going to sound weird . . . hell, forget *probably*—" another laugh—"but I've been seeing a psychologist for a while now. Her name is Dr. Naislund, and she's been working with me on, as she puts it, my 'issues' with the opposite sex."

She frowned. She didn't remember any Dr. Naislund, but she decided to keep quiet. Now that she'd gotten him talking, she didn't want to interrupt.

"Dr. Naislund thinks that my problems stem from my inability to relate on a fully mature level with the women in my life." He paused, shook his head. "I sound like a parrot mindlessly repeating psychological terminology, don't I?" He glanced at her, gave an apologetic shrug. "What do I know? I'm just a heating and cooling technician, barely a step or two up from a Mr. Fix-It. Dumb as a box of rocks."

The bitterness in his voice as he said this last bit didn't surprise her, though it did make her heart ache. Walter had always suffered from low self-esteem. It was what had kept him from taking more than a couple quarters' worth of college classes, what kept him from starting his own business instead of working for Builder's Depot.

"Honey, I know things haven't always gone smoothly for us, but I think we get along pretty well." *At least, we did up until the point that you duct-taped my arms and legs together.*

He pursed his lips and wrinkled his nose—actions she recognized as signs of frustration.

"You just don't get it, do you?" His voice was tense, and he gripped the steering wheel so tight his hands shook. The car edged into the opposite lane for an instant, before he corrected and pulled back.

Sudden anger flared hot and bright within her. "Maybe I'd *get it* if you'd take this goddamned tape off me!" She raised her bound wrists and shook them for emphasis.

He turned to look at her then, and she saw cold hatred in his eyes, so intense that seeing it hit her like a slap to the face. She knew Walter could get angry sometimes, but this . . .

"You're not real."

Of all the things he might've said at that moment—*Fuck off, bitch; shut your damn mouth, cunt*—she hadn't expected Walter to negate her very existence. This whole situation was already way too bizarre, and this last comment of Walter's only served to push it over the edge into total insanity. She couldn't help it; she laughed.

Walter faced forward and kept driving, his hands continuing to grip the steering wheel so hard they trembled.

"What's your name?" he asked softly.

Her laughter died. "What?"

"Tell me your name." He sounded calm now, though his hands still shook on the steering wheel.

"Are you kidding? Have you gone completely—" She was about to say *nuts,* but then a horrible realization struck her. She didn't know her name. She struggled to recall it, wondered if Walter had drugged her in addition to binding her arms and legs. That would explain why she couldn't—

"Joy." The word popped out of her mouth of its own accord. "My name is Joy."

Walter half turned to look at her, a small, sad smile on his face. "That's my ex-wife's middle name. Kind of a joke on my part, since the women in my life haven't brought me much. Joy, that is. She's the one I used to come up here with, not you."

She felt like a vast chasm had just opened up in the pit of her stomach. "Ex-wife? But you've never been married to anybody but me . . . we met in high school, for godsakes. We got married the August after we graduated."

"That was Laurie Hissong. And I didn't marry her after we graduated. She broke up with me and started going out with Darrin Weidemann. They eventually got married and had four kids. Darrin's the manager of a grocery store now. Doing pretty well for himself too. Well enough to afford a better car than this old beater Chevy of mine, that's for damn sure."

Laurie . . . Darrin . . . The names meant nothing to her.

"A few years later I met Susan. I was working on the air conditioning at the car parts store where she was a cashier. We got to talking, and she told me she was separated from her husband. We started going out, but it didn't last. She went back to her husband six months later. He was in charge of loans at a bank, made a lot more money than I did. With women, it always comes down to money in the end, doesn't it?" Before she could respond, he shook his head as if to clear away that last thought. "Sorry. Dr. Naislund says I shouldn't generalize about women like that. She says it's a sign of displaced anger."

"I don't understand . . . I used to work at a car-parts store years ago, you know that. But you never told me about any Susan. Are you telling me you had an affair?" Her stomach clenched tight at the thought that Walter could have betrayed her like that.

He went on as if she hadn't spoken. "I met Karen a year or so later. Karen *Joy*. She was a massage therapist. I strained my back on the job, and my doctor sent me to do some rehab at the hospital. Karen helped my back heal, and then when she agreed to be my wife. She healed my heart." His laugh was self-deprecating. "Sounds cheesy, huh? But that's how I felt."

"Walter, honey, I don't know why you're so confused, but *I'm* a massage therapist. Remember? I got tired of being a cashier and went back to school. I've worked at the hospital for almost five years now."

"After Karen left me—for a goddamned radiologist almost twice her age—I got depressed, started drinking pretty heavily, messing up on the job . . . My boss told me if I wanted to keep working for Builders Depot I had to get my act together. So I made an appointment to see Dr. Naislund. This was all *her* idea."

Her hands and feet were starting to go numb. The tape was too tight, cutting off her circulation. "You're not making any sense, Walter. Something's wrong, *really* wrong. Please, stop the car, get this tape off me and let's go home. In the morning I'll call the hospital and we'll find someone who can help you."

"I'm already seeing a therapist, *Joy*. And what's wrong—really, *really* wrong—is *you!* In case you haven't guessed by now, that's the whole reason for our little late-night drive!"

The sudden fury in his voice frightened her, but not as much as the expression of sheer hatred that twisted his features.

She fought to keep her tone calm as she spoke, but she couldn't keep a quaver of fear out of her voice. "Walter, sweetheart, whatever it is, we can talk it out. I love you."

"Don't you fucking GET IT? There *is* no YOU!" He practically screamed this, eyes wild, spittle flying from his lips.

Ice water sluiced through her veins as she realized her husband was gone and a madman had taken his place.

They drove on in silence for several minutes after that, Walter taking deep breaths, letting them out slowly. When he spoke again, his tone was even, his words controlled.

"I told you earlier, *you're* . . . *not* . . . *real* . . . There is no Joy. You're . . . I don't know how to put it . . . a combination of the women in my life. The women I have *issues* with. Laurie, Susan, Karen . . . You look a little bit like each of them. You have Laurie's eyes, Susan's figure, Karen's long black hair . . . and you're wearing my favorite outfit of Karen's. She wore that dress when we went to Mexico on our honeymoon. She had no bra or underwear on either. Said it made her feel sexy to go commando."

She felt dizzy, her chest felt tight, and she thought she might be on the verge of losing consciousness. Maybe it was because of the tape, maybe it was because she was trapped in a car with a lunatic that was wearing her husband's face. Most likely it was both.

"Dr. Naislund says my resentment toward women is the cause of my drinking problem, that I'm turning my anger inward and punishing myself. What I need to do is get my anger out, to release it and let it go once and for all. Dr. Naislund's one of those new-agey types, into all sorts of weird stuff. One of the things she's big on is role-playing. She uses it a lot in therapy sessions. She suggested I . . . what's the word she used? *Personify* my resentment and deal with it in a *symbolic* way. That's what you are, a personification."

Her fear edged a notch closer to outright terror. "You can't be serious! Are you saying that you . . . *imagined* me?"

"Yep. I have a good imagination, Joy. *Really* good. Have ever since I was a kid. I just never did anything with it." A pause. "Before now, that is. To be honest, I'm surprised at how well you turned out. It's almost like you're really here. It's pretty amazing, actually."

She stared at Walter for a long moment. "So if I'm real, I'm just a . . . what? A voice in your head? An image in your mind?"

"That's about it, yeah."

"And you imagined me bound in duct tape?"

He gave her a smile that turned her already chilled blood to ice. "Like I said, I have problems with resentment toward women."

"You're insane." The words slipped out before she could stop them. She doubted it was a wise move to tell a crazy person you knew they were crazy, but it was too late now.

"Am I? Then let me ask you one simple question: what were we doing tonight before we started our little"—he smiled—"*joy* ride?"

"We . . ." She hesitated. She figured they'd probably had dinner, watched a movie on DVD, maybe made love before turning in for the night . . . but she had no specific memory of doing any of these things with Walter tonight. In fact, the memories she did have were hazy, generic ones . . . almost as if they weren't real memories at all, but someone else's, memories that had been told to her but which she'd never actually lived.

It's the after-effects of whatever drug he used to knock you out, she told herself. *That's all.*

"You can't, can you?"

She wanted to smack the smug smile off his face, and she might have too, if her hands hadn't been taped together. "Let me make this clear: I don't believe you, and while I probably should humor you, right now I'm too pissed off to do it. But, assuming that what you're saying is true, why don't you tell me how this little psychodrama of yours is supposed to play out?"

"It's all very symbolic. We're going to drive to Stephens Watch, the place where—"

"You asked me to marry you."

"Where I asked *Karen* to marry me. And then I'm going to do exactly as Dr. Naislund suggested. I'm going to release my anger, every goddamned bit of it, once and for fucking all."

In her mind, she saw Stephens Watch—the most scenic spot in Krahling Hills. The area had been shaped thousands of years ago, when the great glaciers moved southward, molding the land during their tortuously slow passage across what was now Ohio. Most people thought of the Midwest as nothing but dull, flat plains, but here in southwest Ohio the countryside consisted of deep, lush valleys and beautiful tree-covered hills that, if not quite mountains, were nevertheless breathtaking in their own right. Stephens Watch was located at the top of the largest hill in the area, the highest point of elevation in southwest Ohio. People came from all over Ohio, Indiana, Kentucky, and even further to park at the observation point, get out of their vehicles, walk over to the safety railing, and gaze upon mile after mile of verdant forestland spread out before them, feeling as if they were gods looking down from the heavens. It was a prime spot for taking photos and video, and she remembered doing that very thing, snapping pictures with her digital camera, when Walter tapped her on the shoulder.

She'd turned around, irritated because Walter had caused her to muff her latest shot, but she forgave him instantly when she saw the diamond ring he held out to her. It wasn't a huge diamond by any means, but it glittered in the sunlight like a stone five times the size, and she instantly fell in love with it and, without waiting for Walter to formally ask her to marry him, she'd said, *"With all of my heart,"* and then leaned forward to kiss him.

But according to Walter, it was someone else's memory, not hers. She wasn't *real*.

She was about to ask him how she could have any memories at all if she wasn't real, how she could possibly feel or think. But before she could speak, a terrible thought occurred to her. She remembered what Walter had said.

I'm going to do exactly as Dr. Naislund suggested. I'm going to release my anger, every goddamned bit of it, once and for fucking all . . . It's all very symbolic.

At Stephens Watch.

She remembered what he'd said about the duct tape around her wrists and ankles.

It's just that I didn't know how you were going to react, and I thought restraining you would make things easier. For both of us.

"You're planning to kill me, aren't you? You're going to park at Stephens Watch and then throw me over the safety railing." She surprised herself by how calm she sounded. There was a damn good reason the state had installed the railing there. Though most of the hills in the area possessed gradual slopes, at Stephens Watch it was a sheer drop straight down to a rocky outcropping below—nearly two hundred feet, according to a helpful information sign the Ohio Park Service had erected at the site.

Walter didn't answer right away, and when he spoke, his tone was apologetic. "It's nothing personal, Joy. I just need to get on with my life, you know? My unresolved feelings about my past relationships are holding me back . . . dragging me down. I can't get anyone to go out on a date with me, and I may lose my job because I'm a fucking drunk. My life is in the toilet, and the only way I can crawl out of it is to . . ." He trailed off.

"Kill me," she finished for him, her voice soft, tone hollow.

"Look, I've already told you, it's just symbolic. I'm role-playing in my imagination, acting out both parts—yours *and* mine. You're not really here, not really real, so there's nothing to worry about. Everything will be okay once it's over. You'll see." A sideways glance, a snorting laugh. "Well, maybe you *won't*, but you get the idea."

The road began to level off and she knew they were drawing near Stephens Watch. There was no question in her mind that Walter was insane. That he'd never shown the slightest sign of madness during their entire marriage didn't matter. Maybe he had a brain tumor or something, or maybe he'd just snapped for no reason at all. That happened sometimes, didn't it? How many times did you read it in the newspaper: *He was such a nice man. Quiet, polite . . . You'd never in a million years guess he'd do anything like that.* However it had happened, whatever the cause, Walter had gone 'round the proverbial bend, and she was going to be forced to take a fatal swan dive off Stephens Watch as part of her husband's twisted "therapy"—unless she did something fast.

But what? Lunge across the seat and slam into his shoulder, hopefully causing him to lose control of the car? What good would that do? If they wrecked, she'd be just as likely to get hurt as Walter. And with her hands bound as they were, she wouldn't be able to work the release on the seat belt fast enough to surprise him anyway. He'd know what she was trying to do and he'd be ready.

Walter eased off the accelerator and the car slowed. The headlights passed over a metal sign, raised letters spelling out STEPHENS WATCH; behind it, curving along the edge of the hill, the thin green metal bars of the safety railing.

The car had slowed enough that she might be able to jump for it. But even *if* she could undo her seatbelt, *and* unlock and open the door, *and* not break too many bones when she hit the asphalt, her legs would still be bound with duct tape. What could she do? Make a *hop* for it?

Walter pulled the Chevy into the empty gravel parking lot, rocks crunching and pinging beneath the tires. Brakes squealed as he brought the car to a stop, put it in park, and shut off the engine. The beater's ancient motor knocked and sputtered a couple times, the car rocking slightly from side to side before finally falling silent.

Walter sat staring straight ahead for several moments, expression unreadable. He'd left the headlights on, the wash of light making the safety rail's green paint look sour yellow. But though the light continued past the railing, it did nothing to illuminate the darkness beyond.

"Walter, honey, you have to listen to me." She fought to keep the desperation she felt out of her voice. She wanted him to think she was speaking out of love and concern, not simply out of fear for her own life. "Whatever's wrong, we can deal with it together. I'll do anything to help you, sweetheart. I-I love you." Her voice broke on the word *love,* and she prayed he hadn't noticed.

He turned to her then, his expression cold and dispassionate. "Love? What do *you* know about love? What do *any* of you know about it?" He turned away from her, unlocked the car door, and shoved it open. He got out and walked around the back of the Chevy, shoes crunching gravel, tread fast and determined. Then he was outside the passenger window, grabbing the door handle, yanking the door open, and reaching inside for her.

"C'mon, *Joy.* Our little play has just about reached its climax." He pressed the button to release her seatbelt, then grabbed hold of her bare upper arm. His fingers sank into the soft flesh of her slender arm, and she drew in a hissing breath as he tightened his grip. She imagined she could feel the tips of his fingernails scraping against her bone.

He pulled her out of the car and she gasped as the cold night air sank icy teeth into her skin, slicing through the sheer fabric of her dress as if it wasn't there. She winced as her bare feet pressed down on sharp gravel. Bound as her ankles were, she couldn't shift her weight to find a more comfortable stance, but sore feet were the least of her problems right now.

Walter half-carried, half-dragged her across the gravel toward the safety rail, muttering beneath his breath the entire way. "Fucking bitches, goddamned cunts, oozy-coozies . . ."

When they reached the railing, he stopped, grabbed her shoulders, and turned her around to face him. They stood in the wash of the Chevy's headlights—a spotlight for the final act in Walter's theatre of insanity—and though she expected his

336

eyes to be dancing with madness, she was startled by how calm they were. No, more than that: how *serene.*

"I'd like to say that this is going to hurt me more than it does you, but you know what? This isn't going to hurt me at all. In fact, if this works like Dr. Naislund says it will, I should be feeling pretty fucking good in the next few moments." His grip on her shoulders tightened, his muscles tensed, and she knew he was preparing to shove her over the railing to tumble down, down onto the jagged rocks far below.

A memory flashed through her mind. Karen . . . no, she—*Joy*—kissing him right here, on this very spot, seconds after he'd asked her to marry him. She remembered the words she (Karen-Joy) had spoken just before the kiss and she said them now.

"With all of my heart."

A look of confusion passed across his face, and before he could react, she leaned forward, opened her mouth, pressed her lips against his, gently sucked his lower lip between her teeth, and bit down as hard as she could.

Walter shrieked and pulled back at the same time he shoved her away. Unable to maintain her balance with her ankles duct-taped together, she fell backward onto her rear, a sizeable chunk of Walter's lip clenched between bloody teeth. She saw Walter stumble backward—blood streaming over his chin, pattering onto his jacket—then he turned as if to run and lunged forward . . . straight into the waist-high safety rail. Disoriented and in pain, he'd turned the wrong way.

It happened fast. He smacked into the railing, pitched forward and over, and then was lost to darkness. Walter released an inarticulate cry that might have been at attempt to say "Joy" but which could just as easily have been a try at "fuck you, bitch." That sound was followed by several solid, meaty thuds as he bounced on the way down—evidently the drop wasn't quite as steep as the park services sign made it out to be—and then all she could hear was her own ragged breathing.

She turned her head to spit out the bloody piece of lip, then flopped onto her side, rolled over onto her elbows and knees, and managed to maneuver herself into a standing position. Shivering, and not only from the cold, she shuffled cautiously up to the railing and peered over.

The blue-white glow of the almost-full moon illuminated the bottom of Stephens Watch sufficiently for her to make out Walter's body. He was lying face down, head at an unnatural angle, arms and legs twisted out of shape like the soft boneless limbs of a rag doll. He wasn't alone, though. The bodies of a dozen women lay scattered around him, all in various states of decomposition, all slender, all wearing green dresses and nothing else, all possessing long black hair.

You have Laurie's eyes, Susan's figure, Karen's long black hair . . . and you're wearing my favorite outfit of Karen's. She wore that dress when we went to Mexico on our honeymoon. She had no bra or underwear on either. Said it made her feel sexy to go commando.

Laurie, Susan, Karen . . . Karen *Joy.*

She knew she wasn't looking at a dozen different women—women Walter had selected to kill because they fit a certain image out of his fantasies. She was looking at the *same* woman a dozen times over. Looking at herself.

Evidently Walter's special therapy hadn't worked the first time, or even the twelfth.

"At least you were persistent," she said. "I'll give you that."

As the women at the bottom of Stephens Watch began to fade into the moonlight, as Joy looked down and realized she could see the Chevy's headlights shining through her chest and stomach, she had the satisfaction of knowing that, if this play was finally over, at least one of her had been able to rewrite the ending.

Tim Waggoner is the author of the Nekropolis *series of urban fantasy novels and the* Ghost Trackers *series, co-written with Jason Hawes and Grant Wilson of the* Ghost Hunters *TV show. In total, he's published close to thirty novels, over a hundred stories, and his articles on writing have appeared in such publications as* Writers' Digest *and* Writers' Journal. *He teaches creative writing at Sinclair Community College and serves as a faculty mentor in Seton Hill University's MFA in Writing Popular Fiction program. Visit him on the web at www.timwaggoner.com.*

Raphael

Stephen Graham Jones

By the time we were twelve, the four of us were already ghosts, invisible in the back of our homerooms, in the cafeteria, and at the pep-rallies where the girls all wore spirit ribbons the boys were supposed to buy for them. There was Alex in his cousin's handed-down clothes—his cousin, who was in the sixth grade *with* us—Rodge, who insisted that *d* was actually in his name; Melanie, hiding behind the hair her mother wouldn't let her cut, and me, with my laminated list of allergies and the inhaler my mother had written my phone number on in black marker. Three boys who knew they didn't matter and one girl that each of us fell in love with every morning with first bell, watching her race across the wet grass to make the school doors by eight.

"We're the only ones who can see us," Rodge said to me once, watching Melanie run.

I nodded as Alex fell in beside us. When Melanie burst through the doors, each of us pretended not to have been watching her.

It was true, though, that we were the only ones who could see us, and there was power in it. It let us live in a space where no one could see what we did. The rules didn't apply to us. Maybe that freedom was supposed to balance out our invisibility somehow. The world trying to make up for what it had failed to give us. We used it like that, anyway, not as if it were a gift, but like it was something we deserved, something we were going to prove was ours by using it all up, by pushing it further and further, daring it to fail us.

Or maybe we pushed because we'd been let down so many times already, we had no choice but to distrust our invisibility and our friendship. Anything this good, after everything else, had to be the opening lines of some complicated joke. We were just waiting for the punch line. By pushing what we had each day, testing each other, we were maybe even trying to fast-forward to that punch line.

But, too, it felt so good to finally be part of something and then act casual, like it was nothing, even if it was the reject club—the ghost squad.

Maybe that was where it started, right? Maybe one day one of us would understand in some small but perfect way what it felt like at a pep rally, to give a girl a spirit ribbon then watch her pin it onto her shirt, smooth it down for too long because suddenly eye contact had become an awkward thing, or just get swept away for once in the band's music. Believe in the team, that if they can just win Friday night, then the world was going to be good and right.

More than anything, I guess, we wanted to be seen, to be given a chance. We didn't want to be on the outside anymore. That's what it came down to.

And the first step toward getting seen is, of course, being loud, doing what the other kids won't or are too scared to do.

The days, though, just kept turning into each other. Nobody was noticing us or what we were doing, even when we talked about it in the cafeteria or in the hall.

It would have taken so little too. A lift of the chin, a narrowing of the eyes, somebody asking where we were going after school . . . if we could have gotten that one nod of interest, maybe Alex would still be alive. Maybe Rodge wouldn't have killed himself as a fifteenth birthday present.

Maybe Melanie wouldn't have had to run away.

Even if whoever saw us didn't want to go with us, but just had a ribbon for Melanie, because she really was beautiful under all that hair. The rest of us—Alex, Rodge, and me—would have faded back into the steel-grey lockers that lined the halls and we wouldn't have gone any further . . . ever.

But we were invisible.

Invulnerable.

Nobody saw us walking away after final bell. We were going to the lake. It was where we always went.

* * *

In a plastic cake pan with a sealable lid, buried in the mat of leaves that Rodge said was just above where the waves of the ski boats crashed, was Alex's book. It was one of a series from a television commercial; his mom had bought it and forgotten about it. We didn't hide it because we thought it was a Satan's Bible or Anarchist's Cookbook or anything—because it was powerful—we hid it simply because we didn't want it to get wet. If my mother ever missed her cake pan, she never said anything.

"Where were we?" Melanie asked, not sitting down but lowering herself so the seat of her pants hovered over the damp leaves. She balanced by hugging her knees with her arms. She'd told us once that her father had made her take ballet and gymnastics until the third grade, when he left them, and the way she moved, I believed it. We were all invisible, but she was the only one with enough throw-away grace that you never heard her feet fall. Sitting back on her heels like that, her hair fell over her arms to the ground.

The rest of us didn't care about our clothes, only the book.

What we were doing was reading from the book and trying to scare ourselves with alien abductions, unexplained disappearances, ghost ships, werewolves, prophecies, spontaneous human combustion . . . the person reading would have to read in monotone. That was one of the rules. No eye contact either.

The first entry that day was about a man sitting in his own living room when the television suddenly goes static. He reaches for the mute button, can't find it, then the screen clears up all at once, only it's not his show anymore, but an aerial view of . . . he's not sure what at first, but then he sees it's his house, with ambulances pulling up. He opens his mouth in surprise and stands, his beer foaming onto the carpet, and then he doesn't go to work the next day, or the next, and finally he starts getting his checks from disability.

"That's it?" Alex asked when Rodge was through.

"What's the question?" Melanie asked.

In the book, the editors would ask questions in italic after each entry.

"Was he stealing his cable?" I offered, my voice spooky.

Alex laughed. He wasn't scared either.

"Was it a warning?" Rodge read, following the text with his index finger. "Was TJ Bentworth given a prophecy of his own death and the opportunity to avoid it? And, if so, who sent that warning?"

Melanie threaded a strand of hair behind her ear, shook her head, disgusted.

The test now—and we'd sworn honesty, not, at any cost, to lie about it—was whether or not that night, alone, we'd think twice with our hands on the remote control. Would any of us think, even for a microsecond, that the next station would show our house.

Melanie shrugged and looked away, across the water. "This is crap," she said. "We need a new book."

I agreed.

Alex took the book from Rodge and buried his nose in it, determined to prove to us that this book *was* scary.

I left him to it, prepared to go to Rodge's house and raid his pantry before his brother got home from practice, but then Alex said, "We should tell our own stories, think?"

Rodge looked down, as if focusing on the ground. "Like, make them up?" he asked.

Alex shrugged, smiled, and clapped the book shut.

He was three hours from the Buick that was coming to kill him.

* * *

The story I told was one I'd already tried hard enough to forget, that I never would. It was one of my dad's stories. I was in it. The first thing I told Alex and Rodge and Melanie was that this one was true.

Alex nodded and said to Rodge this was how they all started.

"It should be dark," Melanie said, swinging some of her hair around behind her. There were leaf fragments in the tip-ends. I

343

looked past her, to the wall of trees. It *was* night, in a way. Not dark, but still, with the sun behind the clouds, the only light we had was grey. It was enough. I nodded to myself and started.

"I was like ten months old," I said.

"You *remember?*" Alex interrupted.

Rodge told him to shut up.

"My dad," I went on, "he was like, I don't know, in the bedroom. I think I was on the floor in the living room or something." I shrugged my shoulder up to rub my right ear, stalling—not to be sure I had the story right, but to make sure my voice wasn't going to crack. The first time I'd heard my father tell this, I'd cried and not been able to stop. I couldn't even explain why, really. Just that, you look at enough pictures of yourself as a baby and you imagine that everything was normal, that it didn't matter, it was just part of what got you to where you are now.

But my dad took that away.

The story I told the three of them that last afternoon we were all together was that I was sleeping on the floor, my dad was in his refrigerator in the garage, getting another beer or something, and my mom was asleep in their room. The television was the only light in the room. Wrestling was on— the reason my mom had gone to bed early. Anyway, there's my dad, coming back from the garage, one beer open, another between his forearm and chest, when he feels more than sees that something's wrong in the living room. There's an extra shadow.

"What?" Melanie asked, her eyes locked right on me.

I looked away, down, and swallowed.

"He said that . . . that . . ." and then I started crying anyway. Twelve years old, with my friends, and crying like a baby.

Melanie took my hand in hers.

"You have to finish now," Alex said.

Rodge had his hand over his mouth, not saying anything. When I could, I told them how my dad was standing there in the doorway between the kitchen and the living room, looking

344

down into our living room, past the couch and the coffee table, to me, on my stomach on the floor.

There's a boy squatting down beside me, blond like nobody in our family, a fourth-grader maybe, his palm stroking my baby hair down to my scalp. My father doesn't drop his beer, doesn't call for my mom, can't do anything. The boy just keeps stroking my hair down, looks across the living room to my father, and says "I'm just patting him," then stands and walks out the other doorway in the living room—-the one that goes to the front door.

" . . . only it never opens," Alex finished, grinning.

I nodded as if caught, pressed my palms into my eyes, and stretched my chin as high as I could, so the lump in my throat wouldn't push through the skin.

"Good," Melanie said, "Nice."

And when I could control my face again, I smiled, pointed to Rodge, with his straw-yellow hair, and said it had been him patting me.

Rodge opened his mouth once, then twice, shaking his head, but when he couldn't get out whatever he had to say, Alex clapped three times slowly, then he opened his hand to Melanie and said, "Ladies first."

"Guess I'll have to wait then," she said, flaring her eyes, but then shrugged, wrapped a coil of hair around her index finger like she was always doing, and walked her hand up the strands, each coil taking in one more finger until she didn't have any more left.

That was one of the things Alex and Rodge and I never talked about then, but we each loved about her—how she was so unconscious of the small things she could do. How she took so much for granted, and because of that, because she didn't draw attention to the magic acrobatics of her fingers, to the strength of her hair, she got to keep that magic.

We didn't so much love her like a girl, or desire her, though that was starting, for sure. It was more like we saw in her a completeness missing in ourselves—a completeness coupled with a kind of disregard that was almost flagrant. Maybe that's

345

what desire is, really. In the end, it didn't matter; none of us would ever hold her hand at a pep rally or tell her anything real. It wasn't because of her story, either, but that's more or less where it starts.

* * *

"Four kids," she said, looking to each of us in turn. "Sixth graders, just like us."

Alex groaned, as if about to vomit, and held his stomach in mock-pain.

Rodge smiled, and I did too, on the inside.

A safe story. That was exactly what we needed.

"The girl's name was . . . *Melody*," Melanie said, arching her eyebrows for us to call her on it. When we didn't, she went on, and almost immediately the comfort level dropped. Alex flashed a look at me. What Melanie was telling us was the part *before* the story—the part we didn't want and would have never asked for. We already knew about the thing between her and her stepdad, what they did together, only to amp it up for us, maybe make it worse, Melanie added to the nightly visitations Melody's mother, standing in the doorway, watching and mad at Melody for stealing her husband.

Desperate not to hear this, I latched onto that doorway as hard as I could, remembering it from my own story, and nodded to myself. All Melanie was doing was reordering the stuff I'd already laid out there, using it again because it was already charged. We already *knew* bad things followed parents standing in doorways; or maybe it was a door I opened by telling a real story in the first place.

After the one rape that was supposed to stand in for the rest, Melanie nodded, said, "And then there was . . . *Hodge* . . . ," at which point Rodge started shaking his head no, no, please.

"We only have an hour," Alex chimed in, tapping the face of his watch.

Melanie turned to face him and raised her eyebrows, waiting for him to back off. Finally, he did. As punishment, his character didn't even get a name. Mine was *Raphael*—what Melanie considered to be a version of *Gabriel*, I guess, even

346

though I was just Gabe back then. I couldn't interrupt her, though, even when her story had the four of us walking away from school to play our little 'scare' game.

But this one was different.

In the Lakeview of Melanie's story, Lake*ridge*, there wasn't a book buried in a thirteen-by-nine Tupperware dish, but in an overgrown cemetery just past the football field.

Over the past week, she told us, her face straight, the dares had been of the order of lying face up on a grave for ninety seconds, or tracing each carved letter of the oldest headstone, or putting your hand in the water of the birdbath and saying your own name backward sixty-six times.

"They were running out of stuff, though," she added.

"I *get* it," Alex said, holding his mother's book closer to his chest.

Melanie smiled, pulled a black line of hair across her mouth, and spoke through it. "But then *Raphael* had an idea," she said, looking to me.

"What?" I asked, looking behind me for no real reason.

Melanie smiled, let the silence build—she had to have done this before, I thought, before she moved here, or seen it done—and told us that *Raphael's* great idea was to take some of the pecans from the tree over in the corner, the tree that (her voice spooking up) "had its roots down with the dead people, in their eye sockets and rib cages."

"Take them and what?" Rodge asked, worried.

"Look at you," Alex said to him.

"And what?" I asked in a whisper.

"Take them to one of your basements," she said. "Then put them in a bowl with water for six days, then turn the lights off and each of you eat one."

There was a lump in my throat. I thought it might be a pecan.

"That it?" Alex asked, overdoing a shrug.

"Six days . . ." Melanie said, ignoring him, drawing air in through her teeth, "and the four of them collect back in the basement, turn all the lights off except one candle . . . and then they blow the candle out too."

"At midnight," Alex added.

"At midnight," Melanie agreed, as if she'd been going to say that anyway, and then she drew out the cracking of the shells in the darkness, how they were soggy enough to feel like the skin of dead people.

She places the pecan meat first on the Alex stand-in's tongue and he throws up, then on the Hodge character, who swallows it and gets stomach cancer two days later, then it's Raphael's turn. All he can do, though, is chew and chew, the meat getting bigger in his mouth until he realizes that, in the darkness, he's peeled his own finger, eaten *that* meat.

I liked the story and laughed.

Then it's Melody's turn to eat. With her thin, beautiful fingers, Melanie acts it out for us in a way we can all see Melody through the darkness of the basement, not so much cracking her pecan as peeling it, then setting the tender meat on the back of her tongue, only to gag when it moves.

In the darkness she's created, we all hear the splat, then, unmistakably, something rising, trying to breathe but not able to.

The lights come on immediately, and running down Melody's chin is blood, only some is transparent, like yolk, like the pecan was an egg and—

"C'mon," Alex said. "You don't try to out gore the gore of Gabe here eating his own *finger*, Mel."

"I'd expect that from you," Melanie said, smiling through her hair, "It was you who was born from that dead pecan," at which point Alex hooked his head to one side, as if not believing she would say that, then he was pushing up out of the leaves, tackling her back into them, and we were smiling again, and I finally breathed.

* * *

When Rodge wouldn't take his turn, saying he didn't know anything scary, Alex went. Instead of telling a ghost story, though, he opened his mother's book again.

348

"Cheater, " I said. "They're supposed to be real."

"Wait," he said, "I was just looking at this one the other—" and then he was gone, hunched all the way over into the book.

I lifted my face to Melanie and said, "Where'd you hear that piece of crap?"

She pursed her lips into a smile, eyes flaring, and said, "You listened."

"I heard it with a walnut, not a pecan," Alex chimed in, turning pages, only half with us.

"A walnut?" Melanie said, crinkling her nose, "Nobody plants a walnut tree in a graveyard."

Looking back, I can hear it, how she'd used *cemetery* in the story and *graveyard* to Alex, but right then it didn't matter. What I was really doing was saying it *had* scared me.

"You heard it at Dunbar?" I said.

Dunbar was her old school.

She opened her mouth to answer but then stopped. She seemed to be fascinated by something out on the lake.

I followed where she was looking.

"What?" I asked.

"I don't know where I heard it," she said, still not looking at me, still looking over the lake. "Somewhere, I guess."

"No, what are you looking at?" I said, pointing with my chin out across the water, and she finally settled her eyes on me.

"Nothing."

We were twelve years old, going to live forever.

When Alex finally got the book open to the right place, it was about witch trials all through history: Salem, the Spanish Inquisition, tribesman in Africa—a whole subsection of a chapter, with pictures of the devices used to torture confessions from the accused, pointy Halloween hats, all of it.

"I'm shaking," I said to him, trying to make my teeth chatter.

"Can it," he said, following his finger to the next page, where there was a blue box framed with scrollwork—the stuff that was supposed to be footnotes but more important.

"How to test for a witch," he read triumphantly.

"This is scary?" I asked.

One of the blue boxes from two weeks ago had given us a list on how to become werewolves: Roll in the sand by water under a full moon; drink from the same water wolves have been drinking from; get bitten by a werewolf without dying. Our assignments that night had been to try to become werewolves.

Or get grounded trying.

"Weigh *her* against a *bible?*" Melanie read, incredulous.

"Her," Alex said in a whisper, an intensity in his voice I knew better than to argue with.

By this time, Rodge was rocking back and forth, looking up to the road each time a car passed. When the noise got steady enough, that would mean it was five o'clock and this would be over. On a day the sun was shining, the sound of cars would slowly be replaced by the sound of boat motors, but that day, if there even was a boat, then Melanie had been the only one to see it . . . if she'd seen anything.

"Weigh *her* against a *bible,*" Melanie repeated, not letting it pass.

Alex smiled and looked up at her. "How do we know?" he asked.

"That I'm a witch?" Melanie asked.

Alex nodded. Melanie shook her head without letting her eyes leave him. "What do you want to do, then?"

Alex looked down at the blue box and read aloud, "Devil's mark . . . kiss of—do you, if I cut you, or stick you with a needle, will you, y'know, bleed like a real person?"

Melanie just stared at him.

"C'mon," I said, standing, pulling her up behind me.

She didn't let go of my hand after she was standing. Alex looked from me to her. Even though I was just twelve, I understood in my dim way what he was doing here. He wanted to be the one holding her hand, and if not him, then at least for this afternoon, nobody.

"Do you?" he asked her again. "If I stick you with a pin, will you bleed?"

"Do you have a pin?" she asked.

Alex scanned the ground as if looking for one, or trying to remember a jack knife or hypodermic one of us might have in a pocket.

He shook his head no.

Melanie blew air out and then held the sleeve of her right arm up, cocking her elbow out to him. It was the wide scab she'd got three days ago, when, to scare ourselves after reading about the jogger who disappeared mid-stride, we'd each had to run one hundred yards down the road, blindfolded.

Alex grimaced. "What?" he asked.

"You asked," she said. "It's blood. Want me to peel it?"

"But that's not scary," he said, returning his attention to the book.

Melanie lowered her arm and let her sleeve fall back down. Ten seconds later, Alex raised his face from the book. He was smiling.

"How about this?" he asked.

I stepped around to read what he was talking about.

"We can't," I said. "It's too cold."

Alex shrugged and made his voice spooky. "Maybe we have to, for her sake."

"What?" Melanie asked, her arms crossed now.

"Tie your hands and feet," Rodge said from below, where he was still sitting. "Tie your hands and feet and throw you in the water. See if you float."

"Bingo," Alex said, shooting him with his finger gun then blowing away the imaginary smoke—something he'd gotten from the football players who'd been doing it during class lately.

"How do you know?" Melanie asked Rodge.

"He's been reading it after we leave," I said. "Right, Rodge?"

Rodge nodded. I'd caught him doing it early on. It wasn't because he wanted to know or to be more scared, but because if he'd already read it *once*, then hearing it again wouldn't scare him so much. He'd made me promise not to tell. In return, I'd walked to what had been my spot in the leaves that day, dug my inhaler out, and held it up to him like Scout's Honor.

351

"Well?" Alex prompted Melanie.

"It's cold," she said.

"More like you know you'll float," Alex said, daring her with his eyes.

Melanie shook her head and blew a clump of hair from her mouth.

"Just tie my feet then," she said, and already I had a vision of her like she would have been in 1640 or whenever: bound at the wrists and ankles, sinking into the grey water, not a witch but dying anyway.

Because we didn't have any rope like the blue box said we should, Alex sacrificed one of his shoe-laces. Melanie tied it around her ankles herself.

"It's only a couple of feet deep out there," Rodge assured her.

He was standing now, facing the water, defeated tone in his voice I would come to know over the next three years.

"Then I won't sink far, I guess," Melanie said to Alex.

"That means we can tie your hands too," he said.

Melanie took the challenge and offered Alex her wrists.

"Not too tight," I told him.

He told me not to worry.

"This gets me out of homework for two weeks," she said, having to sling her head hard now to get the hair out of her face.

"Three," I said back.

"A month," Rodge offered.

"You ready?" Alex asked Melanie.

She was, but Alex should have asked me, though, or Rodge.

He couldn't lift her all by himself. He asked Rodge and I for help.

"C'mon," he said to Melanie, stepping into the water up to the tops of his lace-less shoes. The water had sucked the second one away and kept it.

"Cold?" Melanie asked.

"Bathwater," he said back, grimacing, then, because her feet were tied together, offered her his hand.

"Thanks," she said.

"It's in the book," he replied, smiling.

He was on one side of her, me on the other, both of us trying to pull her along, not ready to dunk her yet. Rodge still on the bank.

"Not *too* deep," I said, but Melanie jumped ahead of us, splashing me more than I wanted.

"It has to be a little deep," she said. "I don't want to hit bottom either, right?"

Right. I thought it, but didn't say it, because I knew she'd hear it in my voice: This didn't feel like a game anymore. It wasn't like rolling in the sand under a full moon or running blindfolded down part of the road that had one of us standing at each end, watching for cars.

Something bad could really happen here.

It was too late to stop it, though. Or that's what I told myself.

We followed her out until the water was at our thighs, then Alex nodded and Melanie turned sideways between us, so one of us could take her feet and the other her shoulders. She leaned back into me and I held her as much as I could, but she was already wet, her hair heavy in the water.

"If she's—" I started, taking her weight, trying not to hurt her, and when Alex looked up to me, I started over. "She walked out here, I mean. Like us. Didn't float. Is that enough?"

Alex refocused his eyes on the water and the silt we'd disturbed.

"Doesn't matter," he said. "It wasn't a test then. It was her doing it herself, not getting thrown. 'Cast,' I mean. She needs to be cast into the water."

"But you know she's not—"

"On three . . ." he interrupted, starting the motion, setting his teeth with the effort. I shook my head no but had to follow, like swinging a jump rope, only one as thick and heavy as a young girl's body.

If I could go back now, I would count to three in my head and never look away from Melanie, I think. But I didn't know.

Instead of watching her the whole time, I kept looking up for boats, for somebody to catch us, to stop us. All I have left of swinging her is a mental snapshot of her face, all of it for once, her hair pulled back, wet, inky, her skin so pale in contrast it was almost translucent.

We let her go, arched her up maybe two feet if we were lucky, and four feet out. Not even high enough or far enough for her hair to pull all the way out of the water. It was enough.

Without thinking *not* to, I raised my right arm to shield my face from the splash, but then . . . then the world we had known was over, gone forever.

Instead of splashing into the water, Melanie rested for an instant on the surface in the fetal position, eyes shut, all her weight on the small of her back, her hair the only thing under, and then she felt it too—she wasn't sinking.

She opened her eyes too wide, arched her back away from it, her mouth in the shape of a scream, and flipped over as fast as a cat. Once, twice, three times, until she was out over the deep water, where the gradual bank dropped off into the cold water. She was still just on the surface, writhing, screaming, whatever part of her that had been twelve years old, dying. Finally, still twisting away, she lowered her mouth to the laces at her wrists, then her hands to the laces at her ankles. She tried to stand but fell forward, catching herself on the heels of her hands, her hair a black shroud around her.

She looked across the water at us, her eyes the only thing human on her anymore, pleading with me, it seemed, and then whipped around and started running over the surface on all fours, across the mile and a half wide lake, leaving us standing knee-deep in the rest of our lives.

* * *

Thirty-two years later the two hours after Melanie ran away are still lost. There's an image of Alex, falling back into the water on one arm, of Rodge just standing there, limp, and then it's trees, maybe, and roads. The red-brick buildings of town; an adult guiding my inhaler down to my mouth; Alex running up the side of the highway to meet a Buick.

At Alex's funeral, Rodge held my hand and I let him, but then I couldn't hold on tight enough, I guess. Three years later, on his birthday, he bungee-corded car batteries to his work boots and stepped off a stolen boat into the middle of the lake, leaving just me.

Geographically, I moved as far away from Lakeview as possible. There are no significant bodies of water for fifty miles, and my children, Reneé and Miller, they each got through their twelfth years unscathed—probably because I stood guard in their doorways while they slept and I only allowed history and political books into the house.

My kids were each popular in their classes, unaware of the kids standing at the back walls of all the rooms they were in, their faces a combination of damaged hope and hopeful fatalism, ready to break into a smile if somebody looked their way, *at* them instead of through them, but knowing that was never going to happen. I didn't tell them that kid was me.

The day Reneé came home with a spirit ribbon on her sweater—Skin the Bobcats—I almost cried. When she forgot about the ribbon, I took it from the dash of her car. It's in my sock-drawer now. One Saturday morning I woke to find my wife Sharon studying it. She put it back afterward, patting it in place as if putting it to bed. I pretended not to have been awake.

It's a good life. One I don't deserve, one I'm stealing, but still mine. Last Sunday I dropped Miller off at basketball camp two towns over and on the way home, bought Reneé some of the custom film she said she needed for the intro to photography course she was taking at the local community college.

Three nights after that, on a Wednesday, I took Reneé to the carnival. She's seventeen and I knew I wouldn't get many more chances. I even broke out the Bobcats ribbon; she remembered it and held it to her mouth. At the carnival she took picture after picture, washing the place in silver light—clowns, camels, the carousel—and at the end of the night she put her hand over mine on the shifter of my car and told me thanks, that she wouldn't forget.

Like I said, I don't deserve any of this.

When I was twelve years old, I helped kill a girl. Or, according to the doctors, helped her kill herself to punish herself for what her stepfather had been doing to her. I never told them about the dead pecans, though, or about how her hands had been tied, just that we'd been daring each other further and further out into the water, until her hair snagged a Christmas tree or something. At first, I'd tried the truth, but it wouldn't fit into words. And then I realized it didn't have to. With Rodge clammed up, catatonic, I could say whatever I wanted—that I'd tried to save her, even, or that I'd thought something like I'd seen just couldn't happen. It would have been what any twelve year old kid would insist he'd seen, rather than a drowning. Especially a twelve year old kid in a 'scare' club and a book buried in a cake pan under the leaves that nobody ever found.

I told it enough that way that sometimes I almost believed it.

Then I'd see her again, running on the surface of the water, and would have to sit up in bed and force the sheets into my mouth until I gagged.

When I finally told my wife about her—the girl I'd had a crush on who I'd seen drown when I was in the sixth grade—I even called her Melody, I think, like the story. The main thing I remembered was her hair. The sheets I stuffed into my mouth were supposed to be her hair, I think. An apology of sorts. Strong emotions, like the way your lip trembles when your best friend from elementary tells you he's moving away forever, or what you feel when your mother tells you they found him out on the highway, crammed up into the wheel well of a Buick.

The story I told myself for years was that her body was still down there, really tangled up in a Christmas tree or a trotline. That Rodge was down there now for all of us, trying to free her, but his hands were so waterlogged that the skin of his fingers kept peeling off. Above him, a mass of fish backlit by the wavering sun, feeding on the scraps of his flesh.

"Keep her there," I'd tell him out loud at odd moments.

"Excuse me?" Sharon would say, from her side of the bed, or table, or car.

Nothing.

The other story I told myself was that I could make up for it all. That I could be the exact opposite of whatever Melanie's father had been—could be kind enough to Reneé that it would cancel out all the bad that had happened to Melanie, and that Melanie would somehow *see* this and forgive me.

So I go behind Sharon's back and buy Reneé film, she's supposed to buy herself. I take her to the carnival and hold her hand. I sneak into her room the morning after and palm the film canister off her dresser so I can pay for the developing as well, then, when I can't wait twenty-four hours for it, I go back and pay for one hour. I leave the prints on her dresser without looking at them, although later, when she's gone, I can't resist looking.

I'm reading a book in secret, preparing myself, cataloging points to appreciate when she finally shows them to me, proud: the angle she got the man on stilts from; the flag on top of the main tent, caught mid-flap; the carousel, its lights smearing unevenly across the frame.

The . . . *tinted* or heat-sensitive lens or whatever she had on her camera to distort the carnival and the shutter speed—it's like she has it jammed up against how fast the film is so that they have to work against each other. Like she's *trying* to mess up the shots, or—this has to be it—as if it might be possible to twist the image enough it would become just another suburban neighborhood. Maybe it's part of the project, though. They're good, all of them. She's my daughter.

* * *

Saturday, deep in the afternoon, with Sharon gone to get Miller from camp, I walk into the living room and Reneé's there. On the glass coffee table she has all her prints out, the table lamp shadeless, lying on its side under the glass, making

357

the table into the kind of tray I associate with negatives or slides. I see why she's done it, though: it filters out some of the purple tint in the prints and makes everything sharper.

She's in sweats and a t-shirt, her hair pulled back to keep the oils off her face. No shoes, her feet curled under her on the couch.

"Date?" I ask.

She nods without looking up.

I'm standing on the other side of the coffee table from her. "These them?" I ask.

Again, she nods.

"They're . . . wrong," she says, shrugging about them, narrowing her eyes.

I lower myself to one knee, focus through my reading glasses, pretend to be seeing them for the first time.

"What do you mean?" I ask.

"Daddy . . ." she says, as if I'm the thicko here.

"They're . . . purple?" I say.

"Not that," she says, and points to one of the carousel shots that, with her lens/shutter speed trick, has come out looking time-lapsed.

I lift it delicately by the edge and hold it up to the light, my back old-man stiff.

"See?" she says.

I don't answer, don't remember this one from when I flipped through them the first time. It's one of the carousel shots, when she was figuring out how to move her camera with the horses. The object is to keep them in focus, more or less. Not the children—their movements are too unpredictable to compensate for—but the horses, anyway, and some of the parents standing by the horses, holding their children in place.

I shrug.

"*Look*," she says.

I shrug, try harder, and then see it from the corner of my eye, as I'm giving up: what's been waiting for me for thirty-two years. I relax for what feels like the first time, careful not to drop the picture.

"Right?" Reneé says.

I make myself look again. Tell myself it's just a trick of the light. The special *film*. It was a carnival, for Chrissake. I even manage a laugh.

What Reneé captured and the drugstore developed—maybe *that's* where the mistake was. An errant chemical swirling in the pan is two almost-paisley tendrils of iridescent purple breath curling up from one wooden horse's nostrils, the horse's eyes flared wide, as if in pain.

Somebody with a cigarette, I reason. A mom or dad standing *behind* the carousel, smoking. Or cotton candy under neon light. I follow the high, royal arch of the horse's neck to the crisp outline of a perfect little child sitting on its back, holding the pole with both hands.

Standing beside him, out of focus, is his mother, her hand patting the horse's neck. All I can see of her is her hair, spilling down the sides of her legs.

This time I do drop the picture.

* * *

After Reneé's gone on her date, I take the flashlight into the backyard. Buried under what Sharon insists will be a compost pile someday is a cake pan I bought at the discount store. In it, a book. Not the same series, not the same publisher, but the same genre: an encyclopedia of the unexplained. The carousel horse isn't going to be in there, I know because it was an accident.

But Melanie . . .

That's the only page I read.

Her entry is in the chapter of unexplained disappearances. The woman jogger who disappeared is on the opposite page from her, like an old friend. The title the jogger gets, because of a later sighting, is "Green Lady Gone."

The title of Melanie's entry is "Roger's Story." They forgot the *d* for the thousandth time, I smile about it, then close my eyes and lower my forehead to the book the way Alex used to in class. It was a joke. By then we both knew enough about Edgar

Cayce that we wanted to be able to lay our heads on a book and absorb it.

It doesn't work, though, and never has. Or maybe the book is already in my head. All closing my eyes to it does is bring Melanie back, not as she was on the water, but as she was running across the wet grass for the last bell, fighting to keep her hair out of her face.

Did she even leave tracks in the dew?

If she hadn't, and if we'd noticed, it would have been because of her ballet training, her gymnastics, or that she was made of something better, something that didn't interact with common stuff like grass and water.

The wooden horse with smoke curling from its nostrils.

Melanie, the mother I always knew she would be. This is the kind of gift she would give her child if she could. If it wasn't just a trick of the light.

Rodger's story is what he left as a birthday card to himself. Not word-for-word—it's been edited into the voice of the rest of the entries—but still, I can hear him through it. It starts just like Melanie's, with four social outcasts creating their own little society. One in which they matter. How none of the four of us knew what we were doing, really. How we're so, so sorry. We never meant for . . . for her—

Rodger places us by the lake. The reason I've never been able to stop reading his version is the same reason I was never able to forget my father's story about me as a baby, sleeping on the floor: because I'm in it, just from a different angle.

In the light-blue box framed with scrollwork, the way Rodge tells it, he was just watching us, not as if he knew what was going to happen, but as if, in retelling it, reliving it, he had become unable to pretend that the him who was watching hadn't been through it a hundred times already. The way he watches us, he knows about the Buick coming for Alex, about Melanie writhing on the surface of the lake. How a car battery changes the way a boat sits in the water. Maybe the gases that escape from the cells of the battery on the way down are iridescent—the last thing you see before the strings of moss become hair and smother you.

According to Rodger, Melanie *asked* us to tie her hands and feet and throw her in the lake. I shake my head. He's protecting Alex. Protecting me. After that, our stories synch up, more or less, the viewpoint off a bit. Instead of an image of Melanie's face as I let her go, I see her rising, slipping out of mine and Alex's hands the way a magician might let ten doves go at once.

And then she hisses, throws her hair from her face, and crawls across the lake, her hip joints no longer human.

Her body never recovered.

The question after the entry is *What was Melanie Parker?*

I close the book, set it on the island in the middle of the kitchen, then look down the hall when the noise starts, but don't go to it.

It's the bathtub. It's filling.

I raise my chin, stretching my throat tight, and rub my larynx, trying to keep whatever's in me down, then am clawing through Sharon's cabinets in the kitchen, spice jars and sifters raining down onto the counter.

Finally I find what I know she has; three tins of nuts from Christmas.

The first is walnuts and the second two are pecans, still in their paper shells. I raise the blackest one up against the light to see if I can see through it. When I can't, I feel my chest tightening the way it used to—the asthma I've outgrown—and know what I have to do. My head wobbles on my neck in denial, though.

But it's the only way.

I place the pecan on my tongue, shell and all, afraid of what might be inside, then work it over between the molars of my right side, close my eyes and jaw at once. I make myself swallow it all and fall coughing to the floor, digging out one of Miller's old inhalers, left from when he had asthma too.

The mist slams into my chest again and again, my eyes hot, burning.

At the end of Rodger's birthday card to himself, which the editors chose to encase in their version of the blue-box, are the words *She's still down there.*

I envy him that.

* * *

When I was twelve, I helped kill a girl I thought I loved, helped give birth to something else, something she didn't even know about. Something that saw me before crawling away. What makes it real and undeniable is the way she looked up that last time. She spit out the piece of Alex's shoe lace she had in her mouth and had to shake it away from her lips.

Her tongue was any color—maybe the same as it had always been.

Because I don't know what else to do, I squat behind my chair with my back against the wall, every light in the living room on, random muscles in my shoulder and right leg twitching, as if cycling through the sensory details of letting Melanie go that day. My lap warms with urine and I sway back and forth on the balls of my feet, hugging my knees to my chest, Miller's inhaler curled under my index finger like a gun.

An hour later, eleven, midnight, something, I try to tell the story to the end, naming the out-of-focus kid on the carousel Hodge. I give him a good life.

The front door swings in all at once and I know I'm dying, that this is what death is. I have to bite the knuckle of my middle finger to keep from screaming.

From behind the chair, all I can see is the top of the door. It closes and my vision blurs, a grin spreading from my eyes to my mouth. After so long, this will finally be over, but then a sound intrudes. Keys jangling into a brass bowl—the one on the stand by the coat rack.

Reneé.

She swishes past me in slow motion and never sees me. I stand in the doorway behind her, my slacks dark enough that she won't be able to see the stain.

Instead of putting stuff back into the cabinets, she's looking through the book I left out, opening it to the place I have marked with her spirit ribbon. Slowly, she cocks her head to one side, studying the ribbon, then holds it to her mouth again, breathing it in.

I cough to announce my presence as I move up behind her. She sucks air in, pulls the book hard to her chest, and turns to me, leading with her eyes. She looks at me for too long, it seems, then beyond me, into the living room.

"You okay?" she asks.

I nod and make myself smile.

"How'd it go?" I ask.

"You know," she says, opening the book again. "Sandy and his music."

I nod and remember: Sandy's the one with the custom stereo.

"What is this?" she asks about the book.

"Just—nothing," I say. "Old."

"Hmm," she says, leafing through, wowing her eyes up at the more sensational stuff, like aliens or maybe God.

"She did it to herself," I say suddenly.

Reneé holds her place in the book and looks up at me.

"She was . . . she was sad," I say. "She was a sad little girl. Her dad, he was . . . you've got to understand."

Reneé shrugs, humoring me, I think. I rub my mouth and look at all Sharon's cooking utensils spilling onto the floor.

Her eyes follow mine. "A surprise?"

"Surprise?" I say, trying to make sense of the word.

"Reorganizing for Mom?" she asks, holding her eyebrows up.

I nod, make myself grin, and feel something rising in my throat again. I have to raise my shoulders to keep it down.

I close my eyes. When I open them again, Reneé's sitting on the island, the book closed beside her, just watching me.

"I could have stayed home tonight," she says, but I wave the idea away.

"You need . . . to go out," I tell her. "It's good. It's what you should be doing.

The heels of her hands grip the edge of the countertop. I can't *not* notice this.

"Okay," she says, finally, "I guess . . ." but then, sliding the book back so she won't take it with her when she jumps down, her hand catches on the stiff upper part of the spirit ribbon and pulls it from the book. "Oops," she says, doing her mouth in the shape of mock-disaster, "Lost your place."

It's all right, I *know* where my place is, but she has the ribbon again, studying it, remembering too.

We were ghosts, I want to tell her, and then the rest. Instead, I watch as she pulls the stick pin from the head of the ribbon.

"Stacy showed me this," she says, holding her right arm out, belly-up, in a way that makes me see Melanie's again, waiting for Alex to tie his shoe-lace around it.

"No," I say, taking her hand in mine, but she steps back and says, "It's all right, Daddy."

What she's doing is placing the pin in the crook of her elbow, the part of her arm that folds in. I shake my head no, reach for her again, but it's too late, she's already making her hand into a fist, drawing it slowly up to her shoulder.

I feel my eyes get hot and my mouth open.

When she unfolds her arm, the pin slides out of her skin like magic. No blood.

"That's . . ." I begin, trying hard to make the words, "in a blue box, that's the . . . Devil's Mark."

She looks at me, not following.

I smile, touch her arm, and say, "You didn't bleed," and then I'm crying, trying to swallow it all back, but it's too late. The pecan is coming up.

I step back and throw up between us. It's not just a pecan, but bits of shell and meat and blood. Not red blood, like the movies, but darker. Real.

Renée steps back, raising one of her shoes, to keep it clean maybe, and I look up at her, wipe the blood from my lips with the back of my forearm.

"Daddy?" she says, and I nod, sad that it's come to this, but there's nothing I can do anymore. With trembling hands I pin the ribbon to the chest of her shirt, through her skin maybe, I don't know. It makes her pull back anyway, look up at me, her eyebrows drawing together in question.

"Skin the Bobcats," I whisper to her, then, when I pick her up in my arms like a little girl, I say it at last, that I'm not a good person, I've done bad things. She doesn't fight; she doesn't know to. She doesn't know we're going down the hall to the bathtub, which is already full.

Afterwards, my shirt wet like my pants, I stand again in the kitchen, hardly recognizing it. I have to go outside onto the balcony, my face flushing warm now my teeth chattering against each other.

Standing at the wood railing, I feel the tip ends of hair, silky long hair, lifted on the wind, trailing down from the roof.

I know she's up there, one knee to the shingles, her long fingers curled around the eave.

"Reneé?" I say weakly, unable to look around. It's not so much a question as a prayer. This isn't real. It's Reneé on the roof, maybe trying to scare me.

But then Melanie speaks back in the breathy, adult voice I knew she was going to have someday: *No, Raphael.*

I nod, seeing my shadow stretching out over the gravel drive, how it's split, doubling from two sources of light, and I know that this is all right, finally as it should be, as it's always been ever since that day.

Then Sharon pulls in under me, my son in the passenger seat, and I'm invisible again, a ghost, able to do anything.

Stephen Graham Jones is the author of nine novels and two collections. Most recent are Zombie Bake-Off *and* Growing Up Dead in Texas. *Stephen also has some hundred and forty stories published, from Asimov's to Weird Tales, and has been a Stoker finalist, a Shirley Jackson Award finalist, and has been an NEA fellow. More at http://demontheory.net.*

Taken

Felicia Merkler

My mind races in every direction; it won't slow down.
I try to grab a single thought; it slips through my fingertips.
My heart is beating loud, like a drum;
I try to scream, not a sound.

It is so cold, so dark.
Where am I?
I remember walking through the park.

I try to move; something holds me tight.
I'm peering through the darkest night.
I see it moving slow.
I must be dreaming . . .

I hear footsteps coming toward me.
They get closer and I see.
I begin to shake; my skin crawls.
Tears stream down my face.

My eyes are wet,
But still no sound.
Do I hear yet?

My body lies on the cold table;
I feel the warmth of his skin.
He seems so calm, so stable.

I feel something tear into me.
I try to move;
I try to break free.
I can't do anything.

Pain shoots through me;
No beginning or end.
Getting through? I begin to doubt.
There is no defense.

As he rips me apart,
I can't stand the pain.
Inside my heart.

The warmth of my blood
Washing over me,
Thick as mud.

My breathing slow;
My body weak.
My eyes close;
A final tear upon my cheek.

Felicia Merkler lives in North Carolina, where she writes poetry whenever she gets the opportunity. Her poetry is her voice in the world and an outlet for her thoughts and emotions. Her poems have been published online and in print. Visit her on Facebook.

Blood Bath

Wrath James White

Jan. 15, 1999

Dear Diary. Okay, that's corny. It makes me sound like a teenaged girl. I've never kept a diary before. Mother would have found it. That's not an issue anymore. I guess I still feel a little guilty about that. It wasn't my fault, though. She chose to go out like that. Anyway, I met a girl today. I was just walking down the street minding my own business when the most flawless woman I'd ever seen walked right by me. Bitch didn't even look at me. I said hi and she just walked right past without even acknowledging me. Pretty women are always mean. That's why momma was so mean sometimes. God made her too pretty. She was like a princess surrounded by maggots. It was hard not to want to squash them.

My mother used to be a model before she got pregnant with me and lost her figure. I think this girl was some kind of model. She had the same long, flowing, brown hair, the same pouty lips, high cheekbones, long legs, large breasts, and narrow waist. She had that same arrogant tilt to her head, that same superior stride. This woman wasn't my mother. I knew that. I'm not crazy. Still, she'd make a satisfactory surrogate. It's not that I hate Mom.

That's not it at all. I love her . . . uh . . . loved her.

I smiled as the woman walked into her apartment building and held the door for me. I rushed to catch it before it closed. I'd been following her ever since she'd passed me in the street and that was the first sign she'd shown that she was the least bit aware of my presence. I stopped by the mailboxes and fiddled with my keys, acting as if I was looking for my mail key. I watched as she pressed the elevator button for the fifth floor. When she stepped into the elevator I sprinted to the stairway and up the stairs. I made it just in time to see her step from the elevator into the hallway. Even though she didn't know anyone was looking, she still swayed her hips seductively as she walked. I stepped from the stairwell just as she reached her door. This time, as I rushed to catch the door before it closed, she had no intention of holding it for me. She had no choice.

She had a round bathtub with Jacuzzi jets. When we bathed, it was warm and bubbly and red . . . very, very red.

Feb. 2, 1999

Followed the checker home from the supermarket today. She looked nothing like mother; soft and fat, but still pretty . . . still pretty mean. I enjoyed my bath. I was in it up to my neck. This time I got my face wet too. I dunked my whole head under. I walked home with my hair still wet and slicked back. The paperboy even complimented me on it as he struggled up the street with a grocery cart filled with the evening edition. He said it made me look like a rock star. I couldn't help but feel flattered. I know vanity is a sin, but fuck it. I'm probably already going to hell.

Tomorrow I'm moving downtown. The neighbors are starting to complain about the smells coming from my house. Maybe it's time mother and I parted ways, cut the apron strings. I always wanted to live downtown, where all the action is. Perhaps it's time to move mother to some place more quiet and peaceful, some place where she can rest. I don't need her anymore. I'm a big boy. I can prepare my own baths now. I'll miss her, though.

March 11, 1999

"A serial-killer who police say forces his victims into the bathtub and slits their throat and wrists, apparently bathing in their blood, is stalking young ladies in the downtown area of Philadelphia. So far three young women have been found in bathtubs filled with blood. The police have no leads."

The bubbly blonde anchorwoman was smiling inappropriately, showing too much cleavage, and talking about me. I'm finding my new celebrity status oddly satisfying. I turned off the television and walked back into the bathroom. Everything was all fuzzy and pink. Fuzzy pink throw rug. Fuzzy pink toilet seat cover. Fuzzy pink towels.

The bank teller with the huge silicon enhanced breasts was still alive, but just barely. The faucet was wide open, squirting, spurting, gushing down into the fiberglass tub. Her eyes were fixed and dilated, but there was still a whistling and gargling sound coming from her lacerated throat as her lungs continued to inhale and exhale. The bath was almost full. I stripped down, neatly folding my clothes and setting them on the toilet seat. As I was taking off my new running shoes, I thought I saw her eyes turn to look at me. The hairs on the back of my neck stood up, but when I looked closer, her eyes were still staring off into space. It was all in my head. I guess I'm kind of starting to freak out.

Probably some latent guilt for taking the $130.00 for the fancy new shoes from my last "bath buddy." Maybe I just miss Momma.

I took off my socks and slid down into the warm, dark bath. The bank teller looked like she was smiling. But I doubted it.

March 20, 1999

The anchorwoman with the over exposed cleavage was talking about a task force being formed to catch me. They had a witness on TV who'd seen me walking from the grocery clerk's house with blood dripping from my hair. He couldn't remember much about me except the blood and my black, burning eyes. I laughed. My eyes were brown. Next the cleavage lady brought some criminal psychologist on via satellite, telling the world I was a bed-wetting, sexually abused, fire-starting mama's boy.

Note to myself: kill her.

March 23, 1999

I searched all over the Internet for the anchorwoman's address. I had to get her. Nobody spreads lies about me. Nobody! If I let her get away with it, pretty soon I'll wind up as just some crude locker room joke. The bitch has got to go. No luck on the Internet. I called the TV station three times.

First I claimed to be her brother. They wouldn't give me her address, but they promised to put me through to her office as soon as she got off the air. I called back pretending to be a police detective. They still wouldn't give me her address, but they did tell me what time she got off work. I only had thirty minutes to get down to the station. I caught her just as she was getting into her convertible BMW sports car. There was no way to follow her on my ten-speed, so I had to take her right there. I jumped into the front seat beside her and put the knife to her throat. The rent-a-cop that patrolled the parking lot was heading right toward us. I cut into her a little with the knife and told her how easily I could kill her, then I made her kiss me. Cigarettes and coffee. Yuck!

The rent-a-cop turned around and went the other way, obviously thinking he was about to interrupt two impassioned lovers. I made her drive back to her house, telling her that I would release her as soon as she promised to deliver a public apology and retract the statements that shrink had made about me. She said she would do me one better and bring in another expert to refute the first shrink's analysis. I made her think this satisfied me. She never asked why I was still going with her to her house. Not until we walked through the front door and I forced her into the bathroom. She knew what was coming and fought me when I grabbed her.

She kicked and punched and I had to stab her in the chest to get her to settle down. Then I shoved her into the tub before she could waste any more of my bath water on the bathroom floor. She was still struggling when I plunged the knife into the side of her neck and ripped it across her throat. So much blood was coming out of her chest and neck that I didn't even bother

371

to cut her wrists. The bath would be full in minutes. Her heart was still beating and it was pumping her dry. I had exerted myself so much this time that when I finally slipped down into the bath, I found it particularly relaxing.

March 25, 1999

They did an hour-long segment on the dead anchorwoman. They talked about her life, did interviews with her friends, family, and co-workers, and then the fat, lazy-looking detective who was heading the investigation came on and talked about her death . . . talked about me. Of course he made me sound like a monster. He didn't understand me.

Naturally he pretended he did. They had an FBI profiler come on and restate what the psychologist had already said about me, adding a few embellishments of her own. She was dressed far too casually for a Fed, in a tight skirt and white blouse with enough buttons undone to reveal an ample bosom. She looked like bait. Which of course was exactly what she was.

She said I was sloppy and reckless, out of control, and probably not too intelligent. I may be out of control, but I'm smart enough not to fall for her trap. If they're going to draw me out, they'll have to at least try to be less obvious. I don't feel like taking a bath tonight. Instead I think I'll order a pizza and watch a few old Saturday Night Live reruns.

April 1, 1999

April Fools day! Today I drank my bath water. It made me sick.

April 23, 1999

The new anchorwoman looks so much like the old one that I spent twenty minutes looking for the scar around her neck. She even wears those same tight, low-cut blouses and sweaters. Her breasts aren't as large as the other woman's, but they will no doubt increase along with her economic status. Breast augmentation seems to be a job requirement. She was talking about me again. This time she had the fat detective on with her. They were calling me the "Vampire Killer" now because they found some vomit at the last crime scene with blood in it, and I guess because vampires are in fashion. You know . . . the whole Anne Rice thing. The detective was trying his best to downplay the vampire angle. He wouldn't want me getting any sympathy from the gothic scene.

"Although it is true that we did find vomit that contained blood at the scene of the latest murder, I think the fact that he regurgitated it is proof enough that it didn't agree with him. We have no reason to believe he drank any of the other victims' blood." The detective droned on in a lazy, sonorous voice that sounded as if he was reading off the teleprompter. Somehow the idea of this ponderous, awkwardly built cop catching me makes me giggle.

"Detective, is it true that you found semen mixed in with the blood at several of the crime scenes?"

Sometimes I get a little excited.

"Well . . . uh . . . no. . . . I mean . . . I can't comment on any specifics of the investigation at this time. You mind if I ask you where you're getting your information?" The news lady smiled a superior, knowing smile and said: "No comment." I couldn't help but laugh. I liked her. She reminded me of my mother.

May 18, 1999

I had a bad dream tonight. I dreamt that mother was giving me a bath, just like she used to, and she started bleeding. There was blood everywhere.

It got all over me. When I started screaming she slapped me. She kept slapping me until I stopped screaming. I probably just need some cocoa. Hot cocoa always helps me sleep. Maybe I'll take a bath tonight.

June 2, 1999

The fat detective was back on TV this morning. He was at the police headquarters trying to explain to the press why he hadn't caught me yet. He looked even more tired than normal. I almost felt sorry for him. I stopped by his house this afternoon and met his daughter. She was home from college for a few days. She said she needed a break. I told her I was collecting donations for the homeless children. She gave me five dollars and her phone number. I can be quite charming when it suits me. I think I'll call her this evening.

June 19, 1999

I've been talking on the phone with Crissy almost every night. I think I like her. She's into Marilyn Manson and Rob Zombie. She also reads Anne Rice. Oh, and she thinks the Vampire Killer is cool. Tee hee. Her and her dad don't get along very well. She blames him for her mom's suicide. She overdosed on Valium two years ago and her dad's been drinking himself to sleep every night ever since. I haven't had a bath in over a month.

Mother wouldn't be happy.

June 30, 1999

I dreamt about Mom again tonight. It was about a time when we were in the bath together and she started bleeding the way women do. I touched her. I wasn't thinking, I guess. I just wanted to see where all the blood was coming from. She started slapping me and calling me a pervert. I woke up with an erection. The sheets were all sticky. Maybe I am a pervert.

Fuck it. I don't want to think about this right now. I'm calling Crissy. More later.

July 12, 1999

Happy birthday to me! Crissy invited me to her parent's house for dinner to celebrate my birthday. Her dad stared at me funny all through dinner. He hardly said a word. I thought I saw the detective slip my wineglass into a zip-lock bag. I volunteered to help wash the dishes. Sure enough we were one glass short. What gave me away? How does he know?

I wonder if bathing with a guy makes you a homosexual?

July 13, 1999

Crissy didn't seem freaked out at all when I told her I was the Vampire Killer. She showed me the scars where she had tried to cut her own wrists. She told me she belonged to a vampire club where the members drank each other's blood. I showed her her dad bleeding in the tub upstairs.

I'd had to stab him quite a few times to bring him down. He was stronger than he looked. I was afraid she'd be mad at me. You never know with women. They may say they hate their dads, but then when you kill them for them they freak out. Crissy was cool about it, though. She and I bathed together. I think I'm in love. She looked so beautiful covered in her father's blood I almost cried. Looks like I'm not alone anymore.

This time we cleaned up the bathroom and drove the body over to New Jersey. We buried the detective on our way to Wildwood. They had a new roller coaster on the boardwalk that did a triple loop and then went backwards upside down. I won Crissy a stuffed Tasmanian devil playing squirt the clown. We're in love.

July 20, 1999

The police keep coming around Crissy's house asking about the detective. Crissy is getting nervous. She looks depressed all the time.

Nothing I do seems to cheer her up. I don't think I like her anymore. Women always disappoint you eventually.

July 28, 1999

I got caught red-handed. Ha ha. Get it? The cops busted in just as I was settling down into my bath. They were looking for the detective again and this time they had a warrant. They jimmied the front door and heard us upstairs in the bathroom. Crissy was still whistling and gargling from her new ear to ear smile. At least, it looked like a smile to me. I thought I saw love in her eyes even as they went blank.

The cops were a little rough with me. I think I have a broken rib. I must remember to tell my lawyer about this. Someone is going to lose their badge! I still think about Crissy. She came to see me the other day. I didn't even know she was still alive. They don't tell me shit in here! She told me they'd found the detective. That was good. I felt bad about leaving him out in the woods all alone. Now he could be buried in the family plot. They found my mother as well. They had a ball with that one. They said I killed her. But that was a lie. She slit her own wrists in the bathtub. It was our last bath together. I promised Crissy I wouldn't tell anyone about her bathing with her father and me. She promised to bring me some butterscotch krimpets. It's funny the things you crave when you're in jail.

Sept. 1, 1999

The DA is pushing for the death penalty. I like him. He's silly. I managed to get a plastic spork from the cafeteria. There's a slow kid who works down there in the kitchen. He likes krimpets too.

They have me in solitary confinement for the safety of the other prisoners. They want me to stay dirty. Still, I've managed to prepare my last bath. It's damn hard trying to cut your wrists with a sharpened spork. I decided to stab myself in the femoral artery instead. The pages are getting all bloody now. I guess it's time to stop writing. Besides, I'm getting sleepy.

The faucet is almost dry.

WRATH JAMES WHITE is a former World Class Heavyweight Kickboxer, a professional Kickboxing and Mixed Martial Arts trainer, distance runner, performance artist, and former street brawler who is now known for creating some of the most disturbing works of fiction in print. Wrath's two most recent novels are The Resurrectionist *and* Yaccub's Curse. *He is also the author of* Succulent Prey, Everyone Dies Famous in a Small Town, The Book of a Thousand Sins, His Pain *and* Population Zero. *He is the co-author of* Teratologist *co-written with the king of extreme horror, Edward Lee,* Orgy of Souls, *co-written with Maurice Broaddus,* Hero, *co-written with J.F. Gonzalez, and* Poisoning Eros, *co-written with Monica J. O'Rourke. Wrath lives and works in Austin, Texas with his two daughters, Isis and Nala, his son Sultan, and his wife Christie.*

Big Fat Pig

Timothy Maxon

Vicky was sweating. She wiped her brow with the back of her hand and took a deep breath. She looked down and saw red streaked across her forearm and laughed.

"And you said I was lazy," she said, poking The Big Fat Pig's chest with the blunt edge of a cleaver. "What were your exact words?" Gazing up at the ceiling, still mindlessly jabbing with the cleaver, "Oh, I know. I remember now. You called me a 'no-good, lazy cunt.'" She laughed again and tilted her head to the side, smiling as she looked down at the man on the floor. "Isn't that right? A 'no-good, lazy cunt'?"

She raised the cleaver high above her head and yelled between each blow, "Well . . . this . . . is . . . very . . . hard . . . work." On the last swing the blade broke through the femur and stuck into the hardwood floor. "Whew." Her chest was heaving. "*Very* hard work," she said.

She stood up slowly. The pool of blood that surrounded her coated the floor and made it slippery beneath her bare feet. She carefully leaned over and grabbed The Big Fat Pig's severed leg, dragging it behind her as she padded down the hall and into the kitchen.

Bending down, she worked the leg into the cradle of her arms and heaved it up onto the Formica countertop. It was heavier than she anticipated and she had to take a moment to lean against the counter and collect herself.

She looked over her shoulder through her stringy, blood- and sweat-soaked hair, gazing at the footprints in the long red smear trailing across the oak floor. Resting her hip against the counter and crossing her arms, she looked at the mutilated body lying in the hallway.

"Would you look at the mess I'm making. I know, I know what you would say." She straightened up and tucked her chin into her chest so she could speak in a low, gruff voice. "'You better clean that up, bitch.' Or, oh, *this* was always my favorite, 'No good for fuckin', no good for cleanin', no good for cookin'.' Well, you aren't saying that no more, are you?"

She turned back to the leg on the counter, reached over to the knife rack, and pulled out a nine-inch filet knife. Grabbing hold of the ankle with her left hand, the knife in her right, she started slicing meat off the leg just above the knee. She moved the knife quickly back and forth. Her entire body wiggled as she worked at scalping off pieces of ragged flesh. Once she was down to the bone on the inside of the leg, she used the foot to turn the slab over so she could start on the outside of the thigh.

Her hair dangled in her face, swaying with the motion of her body. Sweat dripped from her nose and chin as she fell into a rhythm, getting a feeling for the cutting. The portions of meat became longer and cleaner cut. She smiled to herself, proud of the new skill she was learning.

With the leg stripped to the bone from the knee up, Vicky flipped her hair away from her face with her sticky hand and turned to the island in the middle of the kitchen. She opened a drawer and reached in to retrieve an aged cardboard box, which she put on the counter. Lifting off the lid, she removed the steel gears and hand crank and began assembling a meat grinder. Once complete, she rested it on the edge of the counter and tightened the wing-nut underneath until the apparatus was clamped securely to the island.

Bending down, she opened the base cabinet door and, pushing aside the Pyrex cookware, pulled out a large Tupperware bowl and placed it on the floor beneath the grinder. She looked back at The Big Fat Pig's body in the hallway.

"I think I need some music. What do you think?"

Vicky walked across the kitchen to the hallway, carefully tip-toed through the reservoir of blood so as not to slip, braced her hand on the side wall to step over The Big Fat Pig's head, and strode into the living room.

Standing in front of the CD rack, she paused, looking for the right disc, trying to gauge her mood. Something classic was in order. Classic but upbeat. She ran her bloody finger down the CD cases as she scanned titles, pausing briefly at the Beatles *Sgt. Pepper* album before quickly deciding against it. Although a classic, she was in the mood for something with a peppier rhythm, a more bubbly vibe. A few discs down, her eyes caught *Billy Joel's Greatest Hits*. Perfect. Billy hadn't played in this house for years.

She placed disc one of the double disc set into the carriage and pressed play. The disc retracted and after a moment the sprite, gentle notes of *Piano Man* flitted through the speakers. Vicky closed her eyes and began to sway her hips as the notes tickled her ears. She began humming along to the lyrics and felt a melancholy calm consume her body.

But she wasn't in the mood for melancholy calm. She reached out and hit the eject button, stopping the music immediately. The tray slid out. She switched disc one for disc two and pressed play again. As the CD whirred and queued in the player, Vicky turned her attention back to the body in the hallway.

"That's a great song," she said, "but a little depressing. This is fun stuff we're doing here."

The first song began to play and the rhythmic chops of *My Life* filled the house as she danced her way down the hall and squatted near The Big Fat Pig's head. She gently slapped his slack, lifeless cheek as if she were trying to get the dead man's attention. The head lolled a little but mostly just absorbed the impact like a slab of moist clay.

"Hey, come on now," Vicky said. "Don't be like this. You've been having your fun with Shelly for years. She couldn't take her turn, so she gave it to me."

She picked up the lyrics and started to sing along with "My Life." She smiled and picked the cleaver from the red, viscous puddle, wiping the handle on her oversized t-shirt. "And that's what this is now, *my* life."

She dropped to her knees and hacked away at The Big Fat Pig's left arm, severing it at the shoulder joint. She flipped her head back to toss her hair away from her face, then she settled her bottom down on her feet.

"You have to admit, this has been pretty wild," she said, grabbing his severed arm around the bicep and rising to her feet. She started laughing again, harder this time. "You should have seen your face. You came stumbling down the stairs, naked as you were when you passed out on Shelly, screaming your fool head off. 'Where the fuck are you?'" She yelled, again lowering her voice to mimic the dead man on the floor. "'I wasn't finished with you yet.'"

Vicky smiled and looked off to the side, remembering the match that lit this fuse. "Priceless," she muttered. "Absolutely priceless."

She stepped over the body and started into the kitchen, singing along to the second track. "Well, you had to be a big shot, didn't ya? You had to open up your mouth." She paused and turned back to The Big Fat Pig. "It's like these songs were written just for us."

Vicky plunked his arm on top of the counter and started slicing off the flesh with the filet knife. "Your face, though. You got to the bottom of the stairs screaming and hollering, almost tripping over that yappy little dog of hers. The poor thing, you booted it clear into the living room."

Vicky flipped the arm over and started carving the other side. "Then you saw Shelly in the kitchen and came bumbling down the hallway, bouncing off the walls on both sides, calling her every nasty name you could think of."

She put the knife down on the counter next to the pile of meat and turned, facing the hall. "That's when she came and got me," she said. "That moment, after all this time, she finally let me take over."

Vicky collected all the cuts and carried them—sopping, dripping, oozing—over to the kitchen island, where she plopped them on the counter with a wet thud. "Once I had the reigns," she went on, "I didn't even have to think about it. I had pictured going after you for so long, so when I finally got my chance, I grabbed the biggest knife I could find and just charged. And your face! Oh, so funny. I thought you were gonna shit yourself right there in the hallway. You were so surprised. Shelly would never defend herself, never mind bury a cleaver in your neck. But you see," she said, glancing over at The Big Fat Pig, "Shelly isn't here anymore."

Vicky started to stuff cutlets into the grinder and pack them down. "Shelly is gonna take a break for a while. She's not cut out for this." Vicky stopped what she was doing, "Cut out for this—that's kind of funny."

She began turning the crank. The gears rubbed together and churning teeth chewed through the meat, forcing it down through the grinder until it fell, splatting into the Tupperware bowl below.

"I've been waiting a long time for her to come around. A real long time. I've been here from the beginning. Did you know that?"

She kept cranking, feeding cuts into the grinder's opening and pressing them down with the tips of her fingers, careful not to get pinched by the rotating metal jaws.

"I've been here for every visit to the emergency room, every lie you forced her to tell the doctors. I was here biding my time. When you broke her hand, stomping on it while she was wiping up the beer you spilled on the floor, I felt that. The time you hit her in the head with the plate because she burnt the pork chops, I bled too. Or how about the time you were docked a day's pay because you were too hung over to get to work on time? You blamed her for not getting your drunk, fat ass out of bed, but you know what? Those bruises on her face were my bruises too. I had to wear them just as much as she did."

She looked over at the dismembered body in disgust. "I can't believe she made me wait so long. I mean, I get it, I guess. On some fucked up level I even understand the sickness behind it. You didn't know, but when she was a little girl, she used to climb into her toy box and hide when her father beat on her mother. She would cry for hours and I was there with her, in that box, the only one she could ever talk to, and do you know what she used to ask me? She used to ask me what Mommy did to make Daddy so angry." Vicky paused and shook her head. "I guess some of the things parents pass on to their children are the worst things they could ever give them."

She continued feeding the flesh into the grinder, letting the grinder chew it up until it passed through the gears and teeth and came out the other side, mangled and unrecognizable.

"And now you are stuck with me." She smiled and picked up on the lyrics coming from the other room. The song was "You May Be Right."

She continued churning the meat through the grinder. Her shoulder muscles started to burn from the continuous cranking, but she did not slow her pace. Blood pooled in the mouth of the grinder and flowed over its rim in a steady stream to the bowl below.

"You know where you went wrong, don't you?" she asked absently. "The dog. You should have never touched the dog."

The mound of cut flesh finally gone, she bent down and picked up the large bowl. Using her hand as a strainer to hold back the ground meat, she tilted the bowl down, allowing the excess juices to flow through her fingers and onto the kitchen floor.

"All the shit you put her through—and she would have suffered through so much more—but you had to go and hurt her dog."

She carried the bowl to the side of the refrigerator and placed it on a small pink mat shaped like a dog bone. The words 'Calm and Assertive' were printed on top of the mat.

"Stupid move," she said. "Shelly would have kept taking the beatings. She was raised to keep taking the beatings, but once you hurt the one innocent thing in her life, that was it. That she couldn't take." Vicky looked down at The Big Fat Pig, "I always knew you'd take things too far one day. It was simply a matter of time. And now, thanks to the dog, I'm free." She smiled. "I owe that dog a lot."

She looked past The Big Fat Pig's body and down the hallway. "Belle? Come here, sweetheart. Come here good girl. Mommy's got a treat for you."

Timothy Maxon is the author of The Fear Maker Chronicles. *His second novel,* The Hidden Place, *will be available on Amazon in summer 2012. When he is not people watching and taking notes, he is working on the second installment of* The Fear Maker Chronicles. *Tim Maxon can be contacted at tmaxon5@gmail.com, http://twitter.com/tmaxon5, http://twitter.com/thefearmaker, or join him on http://www.facebook.com/tmaxon5.*

Cognitive

Joseph Mulak

You want to know the worst way to die? Alcohol poisoning. Trust me on this. As if the dying process wasn't bad enough— all that vomiting, the worst nausea you have ever experienced, your shitty life flashing before your eyes, and having to listen to the paramedic bitching about his wife to his partner while they load you onto the stretcher—I woke up dead, with a massive hangover.

The only thing that could have made it worse was if Heaven existed and I would have had to walk toward that bright light people who've had near-death experiences keep talking about.

It was an odd sensation. At first, I thought I'd survived, which sucked. I mean, I drank all that booze because I was trying to escape from my shitty existence. However, a few things tipped me off to the fact I was dead. First off, I wasn't in a hospital but a coffin. Second, I no longer had the comfort of a pulse or breath. Also, I was pretty sure I was at my own funeral.

I know, right about now you are marveling at my impeccable powers of observation. I should have been a PI.

Lucky for me, no one noticed my eyes open, even though it was an open casket funeral. Once I realized where I was, I quickly shut them again. I decided to keep lying there, since my best friend Dan Robbins was giving the eulogy. I mean, come on, how often is it someone gets to hear all the nice things people say about them at their funeral?

" . . . I mean, the guy was such a loser . . ." Dan was saying.

Huh?

" . . . I was only friends with him for so long because his mom was paying me . . ."

Well now, this was an interesting piece of information. If it turns out I came back as a zombie, I'm eating that dipshit first.

" . . . the idiot didn't even know I've been banging his wife for the last ten years . . ."

I guess I'll be eating her second.

I waited for the priest to cut in any second, ending Dan's beautiful recounting of our friendship, but he never did. I quickly stole a glance in his direction. I'm pretty sure he wasn't even paying attention. I could be mistaken, but I thought I caught him checking out the altar boy.

The eulogy went on like that, describing all the mean things he did to me behind my back. He even gave Mike Loren half the money he was getting from my mom to pick on me in junior high because he thought it'd be funny.

Once Dan shut up, the priest called for anyone else who'd like to say a few words about me. Lots of people got up, but not one of them had anything nice to say. Not my wife, not my folks, not even my kids. I always suspected I was a loser, but this confirmed it.

If you were wondering before why I decided to kill myself, you should have your answer by now.

The idea that I might be a zombie occurred to me while I lay there listening to friends and loved ones bash me, but I dismissed it pretty quickly for a few reasons: a) I was pretty sure people became zombies quickly. Since I was at my funeral, my death had to have been several days ago; b) I was thinking clearly and, in movies, zombies were always brain dead idiots; c) I'm pretty sure a grown man believing in zombies is just pure stupidity.

This really depressed me since, if I was still alive, that meant I hadn't succeeded in killing myself. You have any idea what it's like going through life as a complete and utter failure, and then to choose suicide as your way out of the gigantic hole you've dug yourself into, then to fail at that? That is the epitome of loser right there.

One thing I couldn't explain, though, is how I possibly could have survived my autopsy. They give autopsies to everyone, don't they? I'm pretty sure they do. Of course, I'm getting my information from those stupid forensics shows my wife loved to watch on TV.

Once everyone was finished discussing every stupid thing I'd done during the course of my life—my mother even felt the need to discuss my decision to drop out of college and how that only led to the disaster of me marrying my first wife, which in turn led to the disaster of marrying my second wife—I decided it was about time I made it known I wasn't dead. I kind of liked the idea of scaring the shit out of these people after what they had said about me.

I sat up, and the idea I might be a zombie popped back into my head as several people pointed at me and yelled variations of, "Oh my god! A zombie!"

Despite this—or maybe because of it—my plan to scare them was successful; they all ran out of the church faster than I could get myself out of the coffin. My decreased motor skills were yet another clue I was, in fact, zombiefied (is that a real word? I should look it up sometime. I wonder if I can patent it. Can you patent a word? Maybe copyright is the correct term).

I looked around the church. Even though I hadn't set foot inside it since I was old enough to start refusing to attend mass, it hadn't changed in the slightest. They were even still using the same ragged hymnals.

I spent a few moments pondering what I should do next. I thought about trying to go to my house, but it was all the way across town, and I figured my widow and her lover would probably be there. Besides, I didn't have any change for the bus on me, though it would have been neat to see the look on the driver's face as I dragged my rotting carcass onto the bus. I tried to smile at the thought, but it seemed I no longer had the ability. I didn't even have the key to the house on me, so I probably wouldn't be able to get in if I was able to get there.

I was hungry. I literally hadn't eaten in days. However, getting food wasn't going to be an easy feat to accomplish. How do you get food when you're homeless and broke? I know most homeless people stood on the sidewalk holding cardboard signs with phrases like "Will work for food." What would my sign say? "Will resist eating your brains for food?" "Give me food or you will be food?" Neither of those sounded like much of an incentive to give me anything except a ride to the nearest sanitarium.

Since my body didn't work as well as it used to, it took me a hell of a long time to get out of that church. Once I did, I noticed a guy walking past me on the sidewalk. I tried to call out to him, "Hey buddy, I haven't eaten anything in a while. Do you think you could help me out?" Apparently there was something wrong with my nervous system because the message from my brain got skewed on its way to my mouth and what actually came out was, "Braaaaiiiiinnnnnns."

The guy ran away. Can't say I blame him.

I would have chased him but, being slower than a herd of turtles stuck in quicksand, there was no way I'd catch him. I had to figure something else out.

I sat down on the curb and tried to figure out what to do. Based on what I saw in movies, the only way to kill a zombie was trauma to the head. Since I didn't have a gun to shoot myself with, I wondered if bashing my head several times on the cement might do the trick. Only problem, I wasn't sure if I would feel pain or not. I wasn't really gung-ho about trying. I don't do well with pain.

Pain sucks.

"Hey, buddy," a voice called from behind me. "You all right?"

I turned to look at a guy standing right behind me, looking down at me with concern. What a nice guy! Just when you start to lose hope in humanity and think there's no goodness left in the world, someone like this comes along and proves you wrong.

I jumped on him faster than I thought I'd be capable of doing. He screamed as I tore his skull apart and started to eat his brains (they're kind of squishy, by the way. Thought I'd mention it in case you were wondering). The slurping sound they made as I dug them out of the poor guy's skull grossed me out a bit, but I found I couldn't help myself. I felt I was just as much a victim as him. In my head, I was apologizing profusely, trying to explain that I couldn't help myself, but in reality I could hear myself saying, "Braaaaiiinnns. Slurp slurp."

He didn't scream long. I was grateful for that, since I was still a bit hung over. I'd have complimented him on his consideration but, in all honesty, he only stopped because he died, otherwise I'm sure he would have kept on. I was grateful for the quick death, since I wasn't happy about making the poor guy suffer. I felt bad enough as it was.

There was a car parked at the curb and I caught my reflection in its window. I didn't exactly like what I saw. There I was, looking like death (get it?), holding this corpse in my hands, blood dripping down my chin like sweet and sour sauce, my skin already beginning to deteriorate. I also noticed my eyes had changed. I used to get a lot of compliments about my eyes. It seemed to be my only attractive feature. Now they were lifeless and hollow. They looked the way I imagined a serial killer's might. I guess the best way to describe them would be cold. Maybe even heartless. Either way, I didn't like what I saw, but there was no way to change what I had become.

When I was done eating, I stared down at the body on the ground, feeling ashamed of what I had done, but knowing I couldn't stop myself from doing it again. I had to find some way to prevent it from happening in the future.

I started to make my way down the street. I'm not sure why. I really had nowhere to go. What I should have been doing was trying to find a way to kill myself before I killed someone else. The other thing I felt I should be doing was killing Dan and my wife. I mean, really, who announces an affair at a funeral? Especially the funeral of the victim of said affair? How tactless can you get? Those two deserved to die more than anyone.

It was daytime when I left the church, but by the time I made it to my home—well, former home, I guess—it was well into night. The lights were on, and when I looked up to the bedroom window on the second floor, I could make out two shadows. They appeared to be kissing.

389

It was bad enough they were having an affair, but on the day of my funeral? That really pissed me off. I thought it especially weird they would do it after I had burst out of my coffin as a zombie (yes, I am well aware I didn't quite "burst out" of it, but it sounds so much better than "climbed out with great difficulty"). I guess they felt safe since they were inside the house and probably figured I was still on the other side of town.

They had locked the door, but I was determined to get in. The top half of the door was mostly glass. I'd seen in movies where people would punch through it and stick their hand in to unlock the door from the inside. I figured Kate and Dan were probably making enough noise upstairs they wouldn't hear me, so I gave it a shot.

In doing so, I learned two important lessons. The first was punching through glass makes a lot more noise than I thought it would. The second was zombies do, in fact, feel pain.

Ow!

I listened for a few moments, but didn't hear anything, so I figured it was safe. I unlocked the door, went inside, and began the long process of climbing the stairs to the upper floor.

At the top of the steps, I could hear them going at it on the other side of the door. The thought of the look on their faces when I walked in on them would have made me smile, if I'd been capable of smiling.

It would have been nice to be able to quietly open the door, sneak up to the bed, and tap whoever was on top on the shoulder. That would have really freaked them out. But again, one needs to be aware of his limitations. So instead, I burst through the door. I guess in my excitement I forgot about my limitations. I attempted to say, "How could you do this to me you fucking whore? And you're supposed to be my best friend! You deserve what's coming to you."

Instead, what came out was "Uuuuuuhhhhhhhhhhhhhh!" Not exactly witty, but it would have to do, I supposed.

Kate screamed as soon as she saw me. I'm not sure if it was out of terror or simply a scream of surprise at being interrupted while in the middle of riding her lover. Either way, the sound brought a feeling of satisfaction.

I went for her first. This was mainly because I knew both of them as well as they knew themselves. Maybe even better than they knew themselves. If either of them was going to attack me from behind while I was mauling the other, it would be Kate. I wouldn't describe Dan as the hero type. He was more of the crap-his-pants-while-he-cries-in-the-corner type.

Apparently, I knew him better than I thought. While I was on top of Kate, tearing apart her skull—relishing in the act of sinking my teeth into her brain matter—Dan was cowering in a corner, pissing himself. Weird how some odors don't bother you as much when you're dead.

Not having a camera was the first of two disappointing things about that event.

The second disappointment was the whole time I was ripping open Kate's skull and eating her brains, I kept thinking of jokes involving her giving me head. The wittiest comments I had ever come up with, and no one—not even my victims— would ever hear them. But listening to Kate scream and plead for her life more than made up for it.

My wife did struggle during the ordeal. She managed to tear off my ear—and I do mean literally. Apparently my body was in the decomposition stage. It hurt like hell and I screamed, but my anger ensured I didn't let go of her; I was still able to keep chomping down on her until she died . . . eventually. I made sure it was nice and slow. Despite my craving for human brains, I still wanted to enjoy the act itself.

The remorse I felt during my first kill was gone. I don't know if it was simply because in my zombie state I still felt emotions like anger and jealousy, or if it was because, as my body and mind became more zombified (I really need to find out if that term is taken yet), I was becoming more primal and developing a taste for killing.

Either way, it was a blast.

Once she was dead, I found Dan still in his corner. I advanced on him, surprised he didn't make a run for it while I was busy with Kate—probably because he was naked, though I'm not totally convinced that would have stopped the chicken shit from running out into the street like a maniac.

As I got closer, I stepped in the puddle where he had pissed. That pissed me off even more—no pun intended. Okay, it was intended.

The closer I got, the more Dan whimpered and pled for mercy. Man, I wish I'd been able to talk, just so I could make fun of him.

He was so easy to kill, it almost wasn't fun. That didn't stop me, though. The jerk was so paralyzed, he couldn't even fight, which took most of the satisfaction out of it. Most of it, not all. I was still glad he was dead.

But now I'm sitting here wondering what to do next. I got my revenge. Now what? Do I want to spend the rest of my life as a zombie? I doubt it. My life as a living person sucked. I can't see life as one of the living dead being any better. The whole point was to end it all and escape from life. That hasn't changed.

As far as I can tell, I'm the only zombie. Life would be lonely as the only one of my kind. Maybe more will come as more people die, but there's no way to know for sure, especially since I don't even know how this happened to me. I'm not sure I'm willing to take a chance like that.

No, I think it's time for me to go.

Maybe I can find a cop and attack him. If I'm lucky, he'll shoot for the head. If not, well, I guess I'll just have to cross that bridge when I come to it.

Joseph Mulak is the author of several short stories which have appeared in such anthologies as Masters of Horror: The Anthology, Dark Things II *and* Death Be Not Proud. *His collection of stories* Haunted Whispers *will be released shortly, followed a collection of two novellas entitled* Angel Dust. *He currently lives in North Bay, Ontario with his four children and can be contacted through his website http://josephmulak.com.*

Three Fingers, One Thumb

Stephen Volk

Frankly, I wasn't taken in by the castle. It looked fake. But of course, that was what it was all about. Fairytales. Make believe. *Fake.* Of course, it didn't matter. Our five year old, Elize, was completely spellbound, and that was what counted. This was her world. *Their* world. Children.

Stupid grown-ups, a thousand lollipop-lickers were thinking, rightly. *What do they know?*

It was the holiday we had promised ourselves for years, ever since Elize was born. The first year, Val seemed to be postnatally ill or morose most of the time and I was overworked or depressed—which was increasingly normal in my line of business. The second year, we were in the same stressful lethargy. By the time Elize was three, the idea of a holiday had evaporated—we'd got lazy with our lives. Then we both realised it was all part of the drawn-out grief which was sucking us down. Elize didn't save us from it, as we'd prayed, but buried us in it. Now was the time to get our lives in order, shake ourselves up. Or else.

I was head-hunted by a firm in Swindon, a goodish leap in salary. It meant Val could stop part-timing and study something afresh—which she needed to do badly. Something self-expressive, to let out that pernicious anger I could see burning inside her. Crass as ever, I decided that what we needed was a holiday before I started the new job. I booked four weeks in the States, with an Avis hire car we picked up in that microwave oven they call New Orleans (or rather, *Noo ORRlins*).

A year before Elize came on the scene, we had lost our first child. I had seen and heard him inside my wife's body, but he had only a fleeting glimpse of our world. After nine months in darkness, in a sea of vague, dimly-grasped sensations, Christopher died the first night he spent at home.

We'd worked so hard for him. As Val bulged and bloomed, our love for each other became almost uncontainable. Painting the nursery ready for the new arrival was an unbridled joy. We chose bright pom-pom circus colours and that wallpaper with the endlessly repeated cartoon animal—big ears and black olive-shaped nose, trail of stars striping from a white gloved hand. We heard our kiddie's laughter in our mind as we smelled the drying paint, but it was never to be. Not in real life.

It was a dark house afterward. The non-eye contact of friends begged with us to try again. We were in two bubbles of horror and emptiness. The little we talked, we bandied self-accusations and guilt. All we saw in each other was a mirror screaming back at us the memory of that tiny being, lost from the moment it breathed air. We never said it, but we wished we could kill each other and say, "There. All gone. All over." I think the only thing that stopped us was Elize.

Elize was born, perfect, beautiful. She arrived like Pinocchio. Like we'd made a wish. She saved us, God bless her.

Val and I felt a natural trepidation bringing her home to that room. It was unchanged, of course. We couldn't even bear to repaint the furniture pink instead of blue. I don't think we had even touched the door handle since the doctor came and knelt beside the cot that morning. I remember he joked about his cold stethoscope and I laughed. God above, how could I have laughed?

That night I dreamed of Christopher sleeping in the next bedroom, his inadequate breathing coming through the baby listening device.

When Elize awoke, crying, I went in and cuddled her to my chest. She stared wide-eyed around her at the cartoon animal—the animator-created buck teeth, bow tie, happy whiskered cheeks—duplicated on the wallpaper like some kind of saccharine but sinister modern-day hieroglyphics. I wondered what was going on behind my daughter's gleaming, bewildered, tear-filled eyes. I kissed her roasting cheeks.

The same cartoon animal stood there, in the flesh now, in sunlight, gloved hand raised and waving good-naturedly in big trousers. The fixed upturned snout, the clown shoes. He gave me the creeps, the way only images of enforced happiness always do: clowns, dolls.

Who was inside? Was anybody inside?

He held hands with the crowd. They loved him.

America the beautiful.

Land of make-believe, where you can be anything—even sane.

Noo ORRlins.

I bought a Diet Coke. I was dry as a rock.

Children chuckled and roared all round me. I took Elize on a ride and she clung to my body, terrified and screaming with pleasure. Fear and laughter beamed from her face and she was eager for more. But did she know real fear? Could she? She felt so fragile, like a trembling leaf.

Elf-like minions ran around ensuring the enchanted realm was litter-free. Fairies and frog princes paraded comically under the beating sun, half a world away from the Brothers Grimm. But for all its staggering banality, I found myself enjoying the place—the force-fed feel-good factor, the unembarrassed kitsch, the simple born-again faith in Goodness. It was forbidden here to be unhappy. Depression did not compute in Fairy Land. It didn't *exist.*

How could you fail to have a good time when dragons in dungarees were dancing and playing banjos?

Val came back from the Haunted Wood to find me sitting on a large concrete ladybird. Before she stopped striding she was saying, "Where is she?" I couldn't see her eyes behind the Ray-bans. The sun had reddened her nose. She said Elize had run ahead to meet me while she, Val, searched for the ladies. I looked round stupidly. Val's head darted like a chicken's. "She must be round somewhere; she can't be *far,* for God's *sake.*"

"She's not here," I said.

She looked at me.

The earth—this pit—opened up.

Trying not to panic, we retraced Val's steps. The crowd was thicker. There were hundreds of kids like Elize—God, why didn't we dress her in polka-dots or a hat with great orange plumes or something instead of bloody blue jeans and a white fucking T-shirt?

The heat and sudden activity started to slosh nausea—*NOR-sha*—round the pan of my skull like someone panhandling for sense. I shoved Val in the direction of one of the elves to get an announcement over the speakers. *Quickly!* Anything.

Oh, Jesus.

I ran after the parade, following the kazoo music. I trodded on heels, side-stepped pigtails. I fought against the rapids of people. My eyes lost focus.

Maybe it was a mirage in the heat haze. I saw a familiar shape in the crowd, towering higher than the little kids—the enormous ears, black in silhouette, the round nose, the whiskers. A girl at his side. The cartoon-red lips in a fixed grin. I thought of the wallpaper in the house we'd long sold—the wallpaper peeling, faded, rotten, decayed.

"Elize!" I screamed, clawing through the crowd in pursuit. I tore at the jungle of t-shirts and Nikons, sun tans and shades.

When I reached the merry-go-round, its bongo-drumming beating against my forehead, nobody was there.

Her name piped over the speakers. I ran to every ride we'd been on, every shop. I pulled little girls by the shoulder—never the right one. They were alarmed when they saw the tears running down my face.

I elbowed past Rumpelstiltskin. I smacked the head off a Dodo. I crossed rainbow bridge after rainbow bridge. The children's universe closed in on me with pirate parrots and Nutcracker toy soldiers and the Woman Who Lived in a Shoe.

Christopher, no! I was gibbering inside. *We loved you—we did love you! We will always love you!* I began calling for Elize again. The sound of her name seemed abstract now.

Dusk fell violently red. The crowd thinned. I wandered aimlessly. I lost all sense of time.

When it was dark, the elves swept the streets and *Make Three Wishes* played as some bulbous American cops arrived and my wife wept in my arms.

At 3 A.M. the cops wept too, when they found Elize curled up like a foetus in the trash behind a pink-and-white striped cotton candy stall. The smell of burnt sugar was sickly in the air.

Now Val and I are dead again. We're walking and breathing, but we're dead. Christopher knows that. He knows there'll never be another child now to take his jealously guarded place in our memories. And he knows when I identified my daughter's little broken body, though I'll never—*could* never—tell my wife, I saw the bruises on her poor, small neck.

Three fingers, one thumb.

Stephen Volk is the British creator/writer of the paranormal drama series Afterlife *and the notorious BBCTV Halloween Hoax* Ghostwatch. *His latest feature film is* The Awakening *starring Rebecca Hall and Dominic West. His many other screenplay credits include Ken Russell's* Gothic *and* The Guardian, *directed by William Friedkin. He has also written stand-alone scripts for Channel Four's* Shockers *and BBC1's* Ghosts, *and won a BAFTA for his short film* The Deadness of Dad. *His first collection of short stories,* Dark Corners, *appeared in 2006 and, more recently, his novella* Vardoger *earned him a nomination for both a Shirley Jackson Award and a British Fantasy Award. www.stephenvolk.net*

When Shadows Come Back

Nancy Kilpatrick

Fe's earliest memories were of her mother's gnarled, heavily veined hands twisting into unidentifiable shapes. Shapes that resembled nothing until the pale hands moved behind the light bulb. Then, suddenly, a form sprang to life and attached itself to the wall. Dark. Shifting. Fe remembered shrieking with delight at the familiar and benign animals—horse, dog, or rabbit.

But sometimes her mother created scary things. Vague, swarthy beings that throbbed and writhed through the wallpaper flowers. It was during those moments, when the blackness contorted, threatening to come alive, that Fe looked to the wall and then to her mother's tense fists. The wall. The fists. She could find no connection. "They come back," her mother whispered. "Whenever you need them." And finally Fe would search her mother's eyes, pleading. Always a mistake.

Fe stored her childhood memories the way she had finally packed up her dolls and sealed them in the toy chest in the basement. The fears vanished too, or so she believed.

"Huge house," Philip said.

"As big as I remember." Fe reached for his cigarettes on the dash and quickly lit one. After the first drag, he took it out of her hands.

"I'm not starting again," she protested, but he'd already stubbed it out.

The red brick row house where Fe had lived with only her mother until she was seventeen could hardly be distinguished from its neighbors. Four stylized whitened cement strips across the tops of the windows looked like eyebrows. They made the two windows on each of the first and second floors resemble eyes. Beneath the peaked roof the attic had only one eyebrow-less window. Its dark shade was drawn. A third eye, permanently shut.

Philip cupped her chin and turned her face. "Want to go in?" He was the best thing she'd run across. He cared about her dreams; protected her, sometimes from herself; kept the loneliness at bay—he was solid like no one else she'd known. If a man can be maternal, she'd often thought. His face in the sunlight: courage—squared jaw, licorice eyes, mouth permanently crinkled at the corners because his full lips turned up so easily.

"Let's do it!" she said. The empty street at noon felt the way she remembered it. Kids in school. Mothers and fathers away from home.

Fathers away.

At the top of the three wide marble steps she rummaged in her straw bag for the key. Weather had rusted the lock. She fumbled and her hand trembled, but she opened the door. They stepped into the short hallway and collided with moldy gloom.

"Whoa!" Philip yelled. "Didn't your mother ever clean?"

"Not often." She felt hurt and embarrassed. He knew her situation.

He turned and slipped an arm around her waist and kissed her forehead, running a hand through her hair, as if to say, I'm a jerk.

Philip empathized automatically; it was one of the things she loved about him. She returned his kiss.

The living and dining rooms were bare. It had been a long time since anyone had used most of the house. During the four years Fe had been away at school in another city, and while her mother lay dying, illness had forced her mom to retreat here, to the enclosed back porch, the kitchen, and a bathroom in the basement, where she'd wasted away. The windows were blocked with black oilcloth and Fe ripped it off. Soot–filtered sunlight revealed charred pots stacked by the sink that she had hastily scrubbed after the funeral.

She opened the refrigerator. Inside the door, a bottle of thick ruby liquid and a jar with emerald contents, each half full, fungus flourishing in both. The furniture in the back room was dusty—the daybed's damask pattern hardly visible, the walnut coffee table grimy. A dead pathos had collapsed over the edges of a hanging pot; sunlight cast the dry brown leaves into silhouette against the cupboard door. Fe glanced at the twisted shadow. It did not resemble the plant. It didn't look like anything identifiable. She turned away fast.

"Let's go up," Philip said.

They climbed the stairs to the second floor, their soles printing tracks in the dust. As she opened each door, the rooms lay empty, barren wallpapered wombs that could not support life. The sewing room. The bathroom. The guest bedroom, dark for lack of a window, where no guest had ever slept. Her room at the front. The windows, from inside, like huge cataract-covered eyes.

"You'll have to get somebody in to clean if you want to put it on the market," Philip said. "And we should strip the walls and floors. Get a better price." He flipped a light switch in the hallway and a dim bulb high in the ceiling sputtered to life. "Maybe we should live here ourselves."

Of course, he was joking. Still, terror snaked the length of her spine. She must have been holding her breath because he clutched her around the waist, looked seriously into her eyes, and said, "Breathe," then smiled.

Fe sucked in stale air. As she exhaled, they both heard a little wheeze.

"The dust," she told him.

"The cigarette."

"I'm okay," she said, and Philip nodded.

He started up the narrow stairs to the attic but stopped. "Any ghosts?" He inclined his head upward, his voice again mock-serious.

"Maybe you should go first. Not that I'm scared. No way. It's just that, well, you'd better introduce me. After all, it's your family."

Fe was only half listening. Behind Philip, against the wall, a reflection crouched. The wattage of the light bulb barely allowed her to make out the shape. Philip but not Philip. Smaller. Darker. Lurking close to the steps. Lying in wait.

He glanced to where she looked. "What?"

"Nothing. The dust is getting to me, that's all."

"We can come back."

She didn't want to come back. Ever. She pushed up the steps, past him, and he waved her ahead. Fe ascended to her mother's bedroom, the room she had not been permitted to enter without her mother. The room she had entered alone only once. Memories devoured the present.

The steps creaked. Every night. Phoebe followed her mother up for the bedtime ritual. When THEY came back. The steps had creaked on the night Phoebe entered Momma's room alone.

Fe stood at the top of the stairs before the small crimson door and shivered. It was too dark to actually see, but the color had imbedded in her memory from the many lonely nights she had come this far, only to retreat downstairs into light and quiet and safety. She did not turn the handle.

"We going in or what?" Philip wanted to know.

Her voice snapped through the dense air, "In a minute!"

He touched her shoulder and she jumped. "Take your time."

They're gone, she told herself. Mother took them with her. She promised she would.

Sweat slid down Fe's backbone. The knob, cut glass, pressed into her wet palm. She turned it and pushed. The door opened silently and blackness rushed to greet her. Dead air. The pressure of silence heavy against her eardrums. Fe's legs locked and she could not catch her breath.

"How about a little light," a voice behind prodded. A voice harsh with impatience. She felt along the wall. Paper rough and torn. She imagined the pattern, giant raven flowers with grey leaves and lead stems. 'Alice in Nightmareland,' her mother had laughed. Then she remembered: there was no overhead light.

Fe felt her way across the room to the night table. The switch clicked but the lamp refused to go on.

"Probably the bulb. I'll get one from downstairs." He paused. "Want to come?"

But the tone did not sound inviting and she heard herself say, "You'll hurry back?"

"What do you think?" Footsteps descending. Fainter. Silence.

Fe's heart pumped triple time. But all the adrenaline in the world could not translate into action. She felt trapped in the heart of darkness.

A darkness that absorbed everything.

"I've gotta go down to the kitchen. These ceilings are too high to reach," Philip called from below.

In desperation Fe pushed the switch again. White light exploded, blinding her. When her eyes adjusted, she cried, "It works," but Philip must have been out of earshot.

The little room was unnervingly the same. The peaked roof sliced it into an A. Inky swags guarded the shaded window, killing stray light. The ebony loveseat, matching parson's table, and vanity nestled against one low wall; mother's bed clung to the other. And everywhere sketches—figures like ink blots, easily twisted and bent to be anything Fe wanted to see.

She had an urge to run. "Philip?" But he did not answer.

The box on the table under the lamp caught her eye. She lifted the onyx lid and music bubbled out. Inside, the tiny white female and black male figures spun together to the melancholy tune. The tune she recognized as having become the melody of her life. Each note lulled her, blossoming into memories.

"Come here, Phoebe. I want to show you something."

Phoebe ran to her mother. The black box was playing that pretty music again. The couple inside swayed. Mother stretched out her arms. Phoebe crawled onto the bed and was enveloped.

"Watch carefully," mother said, "and remember."

Hands so delicate. Vulnerable. They joined, pale, nervous fingers interlocking, bending oddly. Phoebe watched the fragile blue wiggle beneath the skin.

"The wall," mother directed.

A slithering through the dark flowers. Phoebe shrieked, "Snake!" half in hope, half in fear. Mother shook her head. She struggled to catch a glimpse of what she could not see. As it skillfully darted for cover, the room shifted. Phoebe looked around. She was alone in the dark forest.

"Momma?"

An iron–gray leaf quivered at the sound of her voice. Something hid behind it. Watching her. The music grew loud, the foliage dense and moist. Phoebe screamed, "Momma, make them go away!"

A crash below brought Fe to her senses. She raced to the door and down to the second floor. "Are you alright?" A distant and muffled curse. Moments passed. He came to the first floor stairs as Fe looked over the banister.

"The chair leg broke when I was unscrewing the goddamn light bulb. I'll be up in a minute."

"Want me to come down?"

"Stay there!"

The music box was still playing and she intended to go up and close the lid then leave. But as she picked up the box, she noticed the female within, gracefully sculpted in virgin white marble, gazing adoringly upward. Her features were finely detailed, the face almost recognizable.

The dark male was disturbing. Rigid posture. Hair severe, tied back in a classical style. Brows arched. Haughty. The eyes hollows that swirled inward like obsidian pools. Pools with a threatening undertow. Why had she never noticed? Suddenly Fe remembered.

Mother was out. The knob on the door at the top of the stairs turned easily. Phoebe entered mother's room. The box that played music rested next to the bed. She would just listen a little, then hurry back downstairs before mother got home.

She opened the lid. Notes tinkled, a high one then a low one, the melody bitter–sweet and rhythmic. The man had the woman locked in his arms and they swirled in time. Phoebe leaned back against mother's pillows and closed her eyes. She dreamed she was dancing in the forest of shades with a darkly handsome prince. They dipped and swayed as the song lilted and plunged, lilted and plunged. The music wound in circles and they spiraled together.

Phoebe looked up at her partner. His hair was tied and black, dark as the drawings mother made with India ink. As severe as his skin and clothes. As his shadow eyes.

Even as those eyes hardened to black diamonds and pierced her, they melted to ebony pools which would float her to his land. The land where black flowers grow and never die.

"Like the dark?"

She dropped the lid shut at the sound of Philip's voice.

When had the light gone out?

He moved through the darkness until she sensed him near.

"The lamp." His demand jolted her to action and she guided his hand.

Light followed a click. His shadow appeared on the wall, at home among the midnight flowers.

"You came back," Fe whispered. Delighted. Terrified. She opened the box and the music flowed between them, connecting them. Suddenly she felt like dancing.

He walked to the door, closed then locked it. She watched his enormous silhouette stalk through the flowers until it reached the bed. The dark form towering above grabbed her in his arms. "Whenever you need me," he said.

His black-ice eyes melted into licorice pools, and Fe sank into the bittersweet darkness.

Award-winning author and editor Nancy Kilpatrick has published 18 novels, over 200 short stories, 1 non-fiction book, and has edited a number of anthologies including Evolve: Vampire Stories of the New Undead *(2010) and* Evolve Two: Vampire Stories of the Future Undead *(2011). Upcoming books include a graphic novel,* Nancy Kilpatrick's Vampyre Theater *(Brainstorm Comics); a new collection of her short fiction and novellas* Vampyric Variations; *and as editor, the anthology* Danse Macabre: Close Encounters With the Reaper *(both from Edge SF&F Publishing). She is currently editing her 13th anthology,*

Expiry Date. *Check her website for details (www.nancykilpatrick.com) and she invites you to join her on Facebook.*

The Sum of a Man

David B. Silva

1.

He returns . . . to the eleven year old, thin and gangly, moving across the cool winter shadows behind the carport. The boy steps over a puddle of water and stays low across the opening between the carport and the mobile home three spaces down. The aluminum siding is cold against the palms of his hands. He crosses the back of the home, beneath a bedroom window, then moves along the side, which borders a white rock garden. The side door, opening to the hallway, is unlocked. He opens it, slips inside, then listens to make sure no one is home. He has been here before. His best friend, Steven Marano, lives in this house. He moves down the hall, past Steven's room, to the master bedroom at the back. In the top drawer of the dresser, under a stack of blue work shirts, he uncovers a cigar box. In the cigar box there's a gold watch, two gold coins, forty dollars in cash, and a stack of credit cards bound together by a rubber band. He pockets the gold coins and the cash, then leaves the way he came in. His heart is pounding when he arrives back home. He feels exhilarated and terrified, all wrapped together in a tight knot in his throat. He is never caught, but for days he finds himself worrying that someone will come for him. The guilt reaches such extremes that he finally wraps the coins and cash in an old tee-shirt and tosses the shirt into the garbage can behind the snack bar at the park swimming pool.

* * *

He returns . . . to a summer night in 1962. It's hot and muggy, the hour well past midnight. He wakes up thirsty and calls to his mother. When she doesn't come, he climbs out of bed. Dragging his teddy bear behind him, he walks down the hall to his parents' room. There is yelling coming from the other side of the door. He looks through the crack and sees his father's hand come down across his mother's face. The sound it makes is thunderous. She whimpers. He closes his eyes. When he opens them again, his father is cradling his mother in his arms. They rock back and forth. "Shhh," his father says, comforting her. "I didn't mean to," she says. "I know." The boy hugs his teddy bear against his chest, then wanders back to his room and climbs back under the covers. He falls asleep with his mother's whimpers still fresh in his mind.

* * *

He returns . . . to Sarah Lancaster, age sixteen, dark mysterious eyes, a sad smile and wonderfully full breasts. She lies back against the sleeping bag. The night air is cool, the sky studded with stars that are as clear and as bright as her eyes. She giggles, and he can hear the uneasiness at the back of her throat. They have never found themselves in this position before, alone, under the stars, and it fills them both with an undercurrent of excitement and fear. He brushes the hair away from her face and kisses her. Her eyes close. She cradles the back of his head in her hands, pulls him tighter against her lips. *She's eager,* he thinks. His fingers grope blindly for the top button of her blouse, find it (and it's magic) as the button slides loose from its trappings. The next button follows close behind. And the next button after that. And his whole body is trembling. This is so different from anything he has ever imagined. It's . . . it's as if he has never been *real* before . . . as if until this very moment he has always been a ghost, and now at last he is finally. . . . *becoming.* Sarah Lancaster's blouse is tossed aside, then her bra, and he can't stop himself now, his body has taken over and all he can do is follow. She whimpers, then cries and says, "No." But it's a faraway, meaningless word that bounds past his ears without recognition. "No," she says again. When he doesn't respond, she tries to push him off. "I said no!" He's not listening. He doesn't *want* to listen. The world has been reduced to this singular act, at this singular moment, and the rush of the current sweeps him mindlessly down a river of no return. He shudders and in an instant it's over. He's a ghost again. Sarah Lancaster's whimpers pass through him, cold and stark. She slips back into her clothes, her dark mysterious eyes cast downward. Long after she's gone, he can hear her whimpers trapped beneath the starry night. They are the last sounds he ever hears from her.

* * *

He returns . . . to Margaret, his wife of seven years. She's sitting on the couch in the living room, her eyes red from crying. There's a box of tissues in her lap, the phone to her ear. She looks up at him as he stops in the doorway. "He's home," she says to whomever it is on the other end of the line. Probably her best friend Anne, though it might be her mother. "I'll call you tomorrow." She hangs up, sniffles, and waits for him to say something that will explain the reason he's coming home after midnight on a work night. He has gone over this moment in his mind a hundred times, only half-believing it would ever come to pass, but now it is here. "Well?" she finally says. His voice takes leave for a moment. His throat tightens. "I'm sorry," he says. "I should have called. I stopped off for a quick drink with Frank Pollard in marketing and the time just got away from me." The hurt on her face softens slightly. She wants to believe him. She wants to trust him. He wishes he were worthy of her trust, but that hasn't been the case lately.

* * *

He returns . . . to the fifth grade. The teacher is on a tear. The classroom of ten-year-olds has been rowdy all morning and she's had enough. One by one she calls the troublemakers to the front of the room. One by one she ridicules them in front of their peers. Bobby Taylor can't sit still if his life depends on it. He's a nervous tick, and he drives her crazy. Molly Merriweather smells like a sewer. Wouldn't it be nice if she took a damn bath once in a while? David Lloyd is an overweight bully who only feels good when he's making someone else feel bad. One by one she grinds them down with her anger. And then it's his turn. The last one. He doesn't know why she's lumped him in with these others. She stands behind him, her hands on his shoulders. "You try too hard," she says. "You're

408

always trying to please me. You're always raising your hand to answer the question. You're a little goodie-goodie and no one likes a goodie-goodie." The words sting, because he wants her to like him. He has always wanted her to like him. Now he just wants to shrivel up and disappear.

* * *

He returns . . . and finds himself in bed at the dorm. His vision is blurry, dark around the edges, out of focus. His head hurts. His mouth is dry and cottony. He sits up and wipes the drool from his chin. There's a stain on the pillow that distantly reminds him of pizza. He glances out the window at the lights over the parking lot. It's night. He struggles to latch onto a memory, any memory, but the headache is nearly blinding and he sinks back against the wall, nearly in tears. The dorm room opens. Brad Sawyer, his roommate, walks through, balancing a stack of books in one arm. He stops and leans back against the door. "Welcome back to the real world," he says. "You have any idea what day it is?" It's a question he cannot answer. "Sunday. It's Sunday. You've been wasted for nearly two days. And let me tell you, man, you're one angry drunk." Brad dumps the books on the nearest desk. He pulls out a chair, then sits down. "You got in a fight with Cochran and tossed him through the window. You remember that?" He doesn't remember anything and says so. "It was bad, man. You did some serious damage." He never sees Cochran again, the psych major drops out for the rest of the semester. Six weeks later, after another binge and another blackout, he's kicked out of the university. For a time, he blames it all on Cochran. Later he blames it on the university. Before he's done, he blames his roommate, the guy who threw the last party, the pressure of trying to maintain his grades, even the fact that he can't ever seem to catch a break. The blame never seems to find its way to his own doorstep.

* * *

He returns . . . to the long country road. It's mid-summer, high-nineties, humid and miserable. Next week he will be packing up the last of his belongings and moving into a studio apartment in the city, where he'll be starting a new job. Now,

409

though, he's in the process of reducing the excess baggage he's collected over the past few years. Shelby, a black cocker/collie mix, is lying on the floor of the passenger side of the car. The dog has always liked to travel. Miles pass by. Finally, there's a turnout that borders an open pasture. He pulls the car over, stops, then climbs out. Shelby jumps out behind him, excited about this new adventure. The dog follows him into the pasture, then takes off after a covey of quail, completely absorbed in the pursuit. The man watches a moment, then hurries back to the car, starts up the engine, and pulls out. In the rearview mirror he watches as Shelby realizes what's happening and changes direction. The dog stumbles out of the pasture, his legs pumping madly, then races up the road after the car. The man accelerates. Within a matter of seconds it's over. Shelby becomes a disappearing dot far behind him. He has a difficult time erasing this picture from his mind, and for a long time he feels the lingering shadow of guilt. He often wonders whatever happened to the dog.

* * *

He returns . . . to his wife, who is carrying an extra forty pounds after the birth of their second child. She's sitting in the recliner, breast feeding the newborn, who has been fussy all night, keeping them both awake. There was a time when a moment such as this would have reminded him what an incredible wonder it is to bring a baby into the world and how fortunate he is to be sharing his life with a woman he loves. But he's in a nasty mood and when he looks at her, he finds himself sickened by how overweight and unhealthy she has become. "You need to lose weight," he says in disgust. "I'm trying." "Not very hard." He shakes his head and walks out of the room. Later, he returns and apologizes, but the apology is never enough to erase the look of devastation on his wife's face. It will haunt him forever.

* * *

He returns . . . to his sister, Sadie. She's eight years old, playing in the sand not far from where he's hammering a nail into an old piece of wood. She says something he finds

410

disagreeable (he can no longer remember exactly what she said, only that it was something that angered him). He tosses the hammer at her. The clawed end strikes her in the forehead. For a moment he is stunned by what he's done. She appears stunned as well. Then she slowly climbs to her feet and wanders to another part of the yard without saying a word. He picks up the hammer and returns to his play. Several minutes pass before his sister finally lets out a piercing scream that brings him running. He finds her standing in the middle of the lawn, rivulets of blood streaming down her face and over her jumpsuit. He takes her by the hand and runs with her to the neighbor's house, where Mrs. Dunn, a retired nurse, bandages the wound and calls their mother at work. It takes seventeen stitches to close the cut, but it's years before his sister forgives him.

* * *

He returns . . . to dinner with his adult son, Nathan. The restaurant is The Hatch Cover, a modestly-priced, rather nice place that overlooks the Sacramento River. It's not often that they eat out together. They've never been close. He orders a crab salad. Nathan orders steak and lobster. The waitress collects the menus, then hurries away. He removes his glasses, which he's had to start wearing in order to read, then cups his hands and gazes across the table, not knowing quite where or how to start. It's so late in the game now. Time just passes so fast. "I know it's a little late," he says. "All these years after the fact, but I was wondering if it ever bothered you that I didn't spend more time with you as you were growing up." Nathan doesn't flinch in the slightest. He unfolds his napkin and places it in his lap. "Why now?" *A good question,* he thinks. Because he's older and wiser now. Because his perspective is different now. Because he knows he didn't do his best, and if he had, maybe his son would love him now, maybe he could look in the mirror in the morning when he climbed out of bed. "I guess it bothers me," he says. He recalls one incident in particular, not sure why this one bothers him now when there were so many others. "Do you remember when you were eight? You came into the garage where I was working and you wanted to play catch, but I was busy and I told you to stay out of the garage. That it wasn't a place for little boys?" Nathan doesn't remember this and he says so. "I've been thinking about that time lately, and all the others when I didn't give you the time you deserved." His son, who is thirty-three now, with a family of his own, shakes his head. "Amazing. Where's all this coming from all of a sudden?" He doesn't know, he says, but that's not true. It's coming from regret. "You were always working. You loved to work. On the car. On the house. In the garage. And you never had time for anything else. Not for me. Not for Sadie. I swear to this day, I don't have a clue why you ever had children." The words sting something awful, but they're true. Every single one of them.

* * *

He returns . . . to the Chevrolet in front of him on I-5. He checks the speedometer. 68 MPH. Traffic is light. The sun is still a force in the western sky, partially blocked by the visor, which he has lowered and moved so it covers the driver's side window. It's been a long drive up the state. He's tired. He looks up from the speedometer, surprised to see the Chevrolet start across the three lanes. The car takes a diagonal path, straight and steady, from the right lane to the far left lane, then onto the shoulder. A cloud of dust kicks up. He begins to slow down as the car sideswipes an overpass pillar then takes to the air. By the time the car completes the last of three rollovers and comes to a rest on its roof, he has come to an abrupt stop on the right shoulder. On the other side of I-5 an eighteen-wheeler grinds to a stop. In the rearview mirror, he can see a VW van pull onto the shoulder behind him. One by one, more cars pull over, stunned spectators too curious to drive by without stopping. The dust settles, almost eerily. An uneasy quiet falls over the scene. Then a tendril of smoke begins to snake its way out from beneath the wreckage. *Flames are going to break out,* he thinks. He opens the door, steps out, and watches. Gradually, others begin to emerge from their vehicles as well. For the longest time no one moves. Then the first yellowish flame becomes visible and everyone is moving at once. On the passenger side, a heavyset elderly woman is hanging upside down. He tries to pry the door open. The metal is already hot to the touch and twisted into an unrecognizable shape. It will not give. Across the seat, the driver is also hanging upside down by a belt. He appears to be unconscious. A lappet of the man's scalp dangles freely from his head, blood coursing down the hair and dripping onto the ceiling of the car. "Get me down from here," the woman says. He tries the door again, still unsuccessfully. The truck driver discharges a fire extinguisher that briefly dampens the flames before they flare up again. Two others from the crowd manage to pry open the driver's side door, cut the seat belt, and drag the man to safety. Then something explodes. Everyone backs away. Flames rise up and engulf the entire vehicle. The woman trapped inside begins to scream. She never makes it out of the car. For months he tries to find a way to rationalize her loss. He had tried. He had done his best. It had just been one of those things. Fate. But her screams hound him ceaselessly. If only he had acted without hesitation. If he'd been a little faster. If he had asked for help. If he had been willing to tolerate the heat. If he had been a braver man. The screams. They never stop.

* * *

He returns . . . to his first summer job, working for a local landscaper, mowing lawns, trimming bushes, raking leaves, watering. This particular afternoon the sun is beating down on them with sheer misery, and it's not long before the elderly woman whose yard they're grooming invites them inside for some lemonade. Her name is Mrs. Hathaway. She's well into her seventies, lives alone since her husband died in an automobile accident seven years before, and has the most precious smile he thinks he's ever seen. They drink the lemonade and she talks about what it was like growing up in a small town in the Midwest when she was a little girl and my how the times have changed since then. It's easy to see how much she craves the company. When she finally gets up to go look for an old photo album, his boss quickly rifles through the

413

nearby china cabinet drawers until he comes across a sterling-silver sugar cup. He removes the lid and discovers a wad of money inside, nearly $400 as they find out later when they count it. He tucks the money into his pocket. The old woman returns with the album and they look at photographs until they finally excuse themselves and finish the yard work. His boss offers him half the money. He turns it down. But that's all he does. He never tells another soul. And when the old woman dies in her sleep the next summer, he finds himself wondering how much of an extra burden the loss of that $400 had put on her. Did she have to borrow from friends to make the rent that month? Did she miss a granddaughter's birthday because she couldn't afford the trip or a present? Too late, he realizes. The time to do something about it passed long ago.

* * *

He returns . . . to the Christmas he drove into the mountains and eventually onto a winding back road paved with gravel. He pulls off and hikes down a short path, jumping a barbed wire fence with a sign that says: Private Property. Keep Out. On the other side, he finds the tree he flagged weeks earlier, cuts it down, and drags it back to the car. It's a fir tree, thick and perfectly balanced. It makes a beautiful Christmas tree, the best one yet. Only distantly does it occur to him that he has taken something which does not belong to him, in order to celebrate the birth of a man who would have abhorred such behavior. He tries not to dwell on the thought any longer than necessary.

* * *

He returns . . . to the lumber mill where he has worked as an apprentice for nearly a year before realizing it isn't for him. This is his last day. It's a job in which he has found not a moment of pleasure and he's looking forward to moving onto greener pastures. His boss, a man in his late forties with the temperament of a cornered bobcat, is riding him about changing the blade on the band saw before he goes home. He flips the old man off and gets shoved up against a nearby wall. The man's hands have his shirt tied into a knot, and he can feel

414

the crushing pressure against his throat. "You fucking little prick," his boss says. "You've been prancing around here like a spoiled brat since the moment you arrived. I'll be damned if you're leaving here before you change that blade. You got that?" He changes the blade, angry, hateful, then leaves under the derisive eyes of the other workers. But he returns later that same night, long after the mill has closed. With him, he brings a sledge hammer from home, and a flashlight. He uses a key he had copied the week before, in case he ever needed to use one of the saws, to enter through the back door. The building is a black tomb, but he has no trouble finding his way to the band saw. "This is for talking to me as if I were dirt," he says, slamming the sledge hammer into the side of the beast. "This is for laying your fucking hands on me." Another blow, this one across the blade. By the time he's done, the band saw is a jumble of twisted, worthless metal. "There you go, sir. Blade's all changed. Just liked you wanted."

* * *

He returns . . . to his father's death in 1974, at the age of seventy-six, after his third heart attack in as many years. He has come to the small apartment to look in on his father after being unable to reach him for nearly a week. The front door is unlocked. He enters, curious, assuming the old man has finally found some sort of social activity to keep himself busy. He calls non-stop sometimes, and it used to drive him crazy until he changed his phone number. Immediately, though, he becomes aware of the strong, unpleasant odor in the air. He calls out and makes his way past the living room, the kitchen, and down the hall. He discovers his father lying on the floor in the bathroom, naked, a towel clutched in one hand across his chest. Apparently, he had just stepped out of the shower when his heart had finally given out for the last time. How long he has been lying here on the cold floor is anyone's guess. The man is as thin as a toothpick, skin hanging loosely around neck and waist. He hadn't been eating. *Seventy-six,* he tells himself, as if it makes a difference. *He was seventy-six.* He stands in the bathroom doorway, staring down at the old man, and he knows

415

he should have done more. He should have called more. He should have brought food. He should have spent time. But he had done none of those things, and here is where it ended. His father died here . . . in this place . . . on this floor . . . alone. It's hard to imagine a more disturbing end to a life, to die alone on a bathroom floor.

* * *

He returns . . . to his Tuesday night bowling league. It's a mixed league. Bowling is not a passion, just a way for him and his wife to socialize a bit. One of his teammates, a jovial guy by the name of Tony, brings out a new ball. It's a plastic ball, red, with glitter. "Good for picking up those single-pin spares," Tony says. "Just bought it." There's a name engraved on the ball. It says: Roman. As the evening unfolds, someone asks Tony if he knows this Roman guy. "You haven't heard?" Tony says. Nope, no one has heard anything. So Tony tells them how Roman was a bowler, loved to bowl, *lived* to bowl, and because Roman was always happiest when he was bowling, after he died, his wife had him cremated, then sealed his ashes in the center of the ball. No one believes him, but they all get a kick out of the story. Tony swears it's true. He doesn't know how the ball ended up in the Pro Shop, which is where he bought it. Apparently, Roman's wife finally gave up bowling and decided her husband would prefer to spend eternity at the bowling alley instead of the top shelf of the hall closet, gathering dust. *An odd little story,* he thinks. *What kind of woman seals her husband's ashes in a bowling ball?* Then he looks at his wife, who has been with him for nearly thirty-five years, and he knows his marriage has hung on a thread for much of that time. All for the blessing of his wife, who put her whole into their union while he went through an affair, spent every spare moment working, and did his overall best to undermine it all. What kind of woman seals her husband's ashes in a bowling ball? Maybe a woman like his wife. A woman who has endured long enough.

* * *

2.

Henry Walstead opened his eyes and it didn't make a difference.

Another morning had come and *it* didn't make a difference either.

He rolled over in bed, replacing the sheets he had tossed off during the rough night's sleep. According to the clock on the nightstand, it was past nine. Might as well have been the middle of the night. The curtains were closed, and behind them, the horizontal blinds. It was getting harder to face the world each new day.

I don't want to sleep again.

I don't want to go back there.

He sat up and swung his legs over the edge of the bed. A cough came up from somewhere deep inside him, followed by a low grumble that had become his morning mantra. God, he hated mornings. He hated the taste in his mouth, the ache in his knees, the full bladder. All of it.

He forced his feet into a pair of slippers, tied the sash of his bathrobe around his waist, then shuffled into the bathroom. He relieved himself, then brushed his tongue to get rid of the taste left over from his dreams. They always left a bad taste in his mouth.

A man does stupid things in his life.

In the mirror above the sink, his father's reflection stared back at him. Thin as a toothpick. Four day's stubble. That turkey-gobbler neck of loose skin. Eyes that had lost their soul a long, long time ago. Maybe it wouldn't be on the bathroom floor, but he was going to die like his father had died—a lonely old man whose death goes unnoticed for days or weeks or maybe even months.

If I could do it over . . . change a few things . . .

Another cough came up. He wiped the spittle off on a towel, then splashed water on what was left of his hair and tried not to think about what his life had been like as a younger man. His grandmother had once told him, when he was still a young boy, that the mind had a way of blocking out all the bad things in life and leaving a person with only good memories. She had lied to him. He knew that now. The mind didn't remind you of the good things, it haunted you with the bad.

Henry didn't bother to change clothes. He never changed unless it was the end of the month and his Social Security check was expected. What was the point? He wasn't going anywhere. There was nowhere to go, no one to see, nothing to do. Life's little pleasures had dwindled to one.

He stared a moment longer at the reflection in the mirror, wondering where all the time had gone and how he had found himself here, alone, in these pathetic surroundings. Then he went back through the bedroom, out to the only other room in the tenement, with a kitchenette off to one side. He headed straight for the cabinet next to the refrigerator, brought out a fifth of vodka, and carried it with him to the chair next to the darkened window.

Time goes so fast.

He unscrewed the bottle cap and took the first long tug. A warmness washed through his body as sweet and loving as a mother's embrace.

The little things you do, he thought. *The spur of the moment things, without thinking . . . suddenly they're out in the open and you can't take them back. . . . those are the things that haunt you. Those are the things that play forever on your mind.*

Another drink.

Another wash of warmness.

So fast.

Time goes by so damn fast.

If only he could go back and do things right.

If only.

David B. Silva's first short story was published in 1981. His short fiction has since appeared in The Year's Best Horror, The Year's Best Fantasy & Horror, *and* The Best American Mystery Stories. *In 1991, he won a Bram Stoker Award for his short story,* The Calling. *His first collection,* Through Shattered Glass, *was published by Gaunlet Press in 2001. In 2009, Dark Regions published his collection of eleven new stories and one reprint, In* The Shadows of Kingston Mills.

Remembrance

Christopher Fulbright

Winter came. The nights grew longer and darker, the aspen branches like barren bones of the dead. The earth grew colder. Frost came. Then snow. Still she sat at the foot of her son's grave till late in the evening. Few saw her arrive early in the morning, a weary woman wrapped in wool and scarves. Her old black Buick Regal would roll in beneath the wrought iron arch that read: C E M E T E R Y.

Just another old cemetery on a hill. The quietest place in town. Full of loved ones grieved for and laid to rest, most of them years ago. The cemetery was barely even cared for anymore—just a small-town lot of land in the piney forest of evergreens and aspens. In the summer, weeds grew up through a crispy blanket of pine needles. Little grass grew here, and that which did grew sparsely and in patches. No one seemed to care.

Until she came.

She arrived every morning at the misty break of dawn, even on the coldest of days. Her path was well worn. She kept her son's plot clean, with fresh flowers once a week, always on Monday. She would sit on a small stool at the foot of his grave, head bowed, keeping silent vigil long through the winter. She piqued the curiosity of some kids who lived in the nearby apartments and had jumped the fence to have a snowball fight. They viewed her from a distance, but she never moved her head to look at them. It was as if she herself were a ghost in mourning.

But she was real enough. She drove her car to an empty old home in the evenings, struggling to keep a fire lit, scraping together scant funds to raise a meal. Once a week, a Social Security check came, and once a week she'd buy flowers and head up to the grave. Her son, her good son. He had loved her so much. More than any mother could hope for.

Some days she sat there and hoped for death, staring through teary eyes, a pit of loneliness filling with grief. Other days she just sat and remembered him. His smile, his laugh, how much she loved him, how it felt to hug him, everything he meant to her. Some days she stayed until gray shades of dusk fell over the rotting land.

And then she would drift away again.

Spring came. The trees began to bud. Leaves unfurled and opened to the welcome rays of sun. Untrimmed and uncared for, they grew wild and thick, a complete ceiling of foliage that filtered the light of day. A breeze fragrant with the scents of new life would carry across the plots, speckling the land with golden dapples of sun, whispering through the branches. The woman was there every morning, still wrapped in her coat as if nothing could warm her again, the breeze lifting wisps of gray hair that hid her sorrowful countenance. Flowers every week. Clearing the plot of overgrown weeds. Blades of grass pushed up through the mulch of pine, needles of new life from the earth. Her tears fell silently, shed for the death of love, for the only person who ever meant anything to her.

The seasons passed again. Summer flourished in warmth and shadow beneath the perpetual hollow. The kids came again, climbing under the fence to play among the graves, pausing at the sight of the woman, bowed in sorrow, bent with grief. Still there, always there. Always remembering. Some of the parents took notice, but hushed their children and turned them away. Just some crazy lady. But they never called the police.

Each day she lingered like a memory until twilight darkened the skies with violet hues. She was a symbol of dedication . . . of remembrance.

So neither did they call the police when the kids found the freshly overturned patch of grass atop that special grave and she never came back again.

The caretaker, such as he was, didn't bother to check the casket before properly re-covering the ground. He left as quickly as he had come.

421

The cemetery was lonely then, but a mother needs her son.

Christopher Fulbright is a recovering journalist turned technical writer. He received the Richard Laymon President's Award from the HWA in 2008, and is the author of numerous short stories and novellas, including the recent Fulbright & Hawkes collaboration Sorrow Creek. *For more information, please visit http://www.christopherfulbright.com.*

Hannah's Babysitting Blues

John Grover

The air smelled sweet as Hannah walked along Carlin Street. Swarms of rotting autumn leaves rushed toward her, reanimated by the cold wind picking up. It was getting close to Halloween, and close to Hannah's birthday.

Things were a little tight these days. Because of the recession all last year, Hannah barely got any calls for babysitting. People just weren't going out. They were staying in, cooking in, renting movies, and playing board games.

Thank God for the Harpers. They were new to the neighborhood and made fast friends with her parents. Judging from their Lexus and their taste in clothes, they seemed to have little in the way of money problems. Mrs. Harper was usually in glittering stones from head to toe and Mr. Harper was never caught wearing anything but a fine tailored suit.

Since moving to town, the Harpers were eager to get back to their nightlife. They invited Hannah's parents to show them around and enjoy a night of endless cocktails and a six course dinner, but they were worried about finding someone to watch their twin children, Charlie and Amy.

Hannah's mother was only too glad to sing her daughter's praises, babysitter extraordinaire. Hannah was simply the best, and children loved her, or so her mother had insisted. Mrs. Harper was sold, the night was set, and although Hanna feigned embarrassment, she was thrilled at the thought of making some of her own money again.

It was dusk when she reached the Harpers' front door, carrying a stack of schoolbooks in one arm, her backpack, Ipod, snacks, and cell phone in the other. She let the backpack drop to the steps beside her feet and knocked on the door.

The door swung open fast as Hannah's presence was known before she even knocked.

"Hannah," Mrs. Harper beamed. "We're so happy you were available to sit tonight. It's like a Godsend that we found you and your parents. We thought we'd be stuck with nothing to do in this boring town." She let out a throaty laugh before showing Hannah in and pouring herself a drink from the liquor cabinet in the corner of the parlor.

Mrs. Harper scooped some ice from the bucket on the cart beside the cabinet, then turned to Hannah with a big grin. "Cheers." She lifted the glass and took a gulp. "I'd offer you one dear, but I'm sure your parents would have my head. They seem like they'd frown on that sort of thing." She laughed again before fetching her husband.

Mr. Harper walked into the room, preoccupied with adjusting his tie. "Hi Hannah," he said cheerfully. "Nice to see you again. The twins are upstairs in their playroom. They'll be in there for hours. They won't give you any trouble. Just be sure they're in bed by ten. Help yourself to the fridge. There's a TV in the parlor with cable."

"Thank you, Mr. Harper," Hannah said as she placed her schoolbooks on the plush couch facing the 46-inch screen TV.

"Here you go dear," Mrs. Harper said. She handed Hannah a folded slip of paper. "It's my cell phone number in case you need us."

"Oh great, Mrs. Harper. I'm sure I won't need to call you."

"Well, it's okay if you do," replied Mrs. Harper as she drew her coat out of the living room closet. "Hurry dear, we don't want to be late."

"I'm right here," Mr. Harper called from the doorway, his coat already in hand.

"We'll try to have your parents home at a reasonable hour," Mrs. Harper laughed as she headed for the front door. "But who knows where the night will take us."

"Have a nice time," Hannah called as the Harpers left the house.

"Bye now, Hannah." Mr. Harper said, closing the door as they left the house, leaving Hannah in silence.

Hannah watched them drive off. Satisfied they were gone, she let out a sigh of relief and picked up the remote to the TV. She was about to turn the TV on when she heard a thump from upstairs.

"The twins," Hannah said to herself, smiling. She switched on the TV as another thump resounded. She looked up at the ceiling, then glanced at a rerun of a reality show on TV before settling back on the couch to check her phone for new text messages.

Another thump rattled the ceiling above.

"Okay," she said. "I think it's time to meet the twins." She thought she recalled that one of the Harpers had told her the kids were seven. Not a bad age. Still fun and full of curiosity, not yet full of sarcasm and rebellion. Everything would be a breeze as long as the two of them didn't have attention deficit, which would be a nightmare.

Hannah started up the stairs to the second floor. Another thud sounded. The hallway at the top was bathed in darkness, but the door ahead of her was dimly lit with amber light and slightly ajar.

Hannah eased the door open.

Inside the room, Charlie and Amy sat on the floor across from each other. Between them was a circle of marbles. Hannah's eyes widened when she entered the room. It wasn't the children that caught her attention, but all the clowns. There were dozens and dozens of clowns. The room was filled wall to wall with clown dolls, figurines, busts, and marionettes—every size, every shape, a rainbow of colors blared at her, a mix of pastel and bubble gum shades, a crashing array of textures and styles, polka dots and stripes, smiling red mouths and rubber noses.

The dolls circled the room on shelves, on the floor, suspended with twine, stuffed in a toy chest, and piled in the corners, but the one in the rocking chair stood out the most. Something about it unsettled Hannah. It was the only one in the room that was life-size, and it sat in the rocking chair and stared. Its eyes followed Hannah wherever she moved. Hannah tried to ignore it. It wasn't any of her business. She was there to watch the kids, not judge someone's overly indulged hobby. She mustered her nerve, turned her eyes away from the rocking chair, and approached the twins.

"Hi, guys, my name's Hannah."

"We know," Charlie said. "Mommy told us you'd be here tonight."

"We're playing marbles," Amy said. "Do you want to play with us?"

"That's okay," replied Hannah. "I'll just watch you guys. It sure looks like fun." She got down on the floor cross-legged and watched the siblings shoot and spin their marbles amidst a chorus of giggles.

She glanced up and noticed the clown in the chair.

It was grinning at her.

Just grinning.

The thing started giving her the creeps. Those glassy eyes watching from within a large stark white face. She tried not to show the kids her discomfort, although she felt the entire time as if she were being watched.

"Your mom and dad sure love clowns," she said. "Or is it you guys?"

"It's our parents," Charlie said. "They had these clowns even before we were born."

"That's what mom told us anyway," Amy said.

"Uh-huh," Hannah began. "It must be so much fun."

"It is," Amy said. "And they protect us too."

"Really? From what?"

"Anything," Charlie said. "Anything scary."

"That's wonderful." Hannah got up and rubbed her palms on her jeans. "I should go downstairs and finish my school work. Do you guys want a snack?"

"No," answered Charlie. "We're not hungry."

"Okay, well, I'm going to go downstairs and watch TV."

"Oh, we wanna watch TV too," Amy said.

"Yeah, we're tired of the marbles now," Charlie added.

He and his sister hopped up effortlessly and scurried downstairs.

When Hannah turned to leave the room, the big clown's eyes followed her again. A chill rippled through her and she shivered.

She looked into the hallway and spotted a closet across from the bathroom. She searched it briefly until she found a crisp white sheet, which she carried back into the bedroom and threw over the clown in the rocking chair.

"There. That's that." She wasn't about to pass by this room and see the clown staring from the rocker every time she checked the kids or needed to use the bathroom. No way. The sheet would do nicely, thank you.

* * *

After some TV and video games, the twins grew heavy-eyed and began to yawn relentlessly. Hannah ushered them from the living room and its massive TV to their rooms upstairs. Charlie was to the right of the hallway and Amy's room was on the left, nearest to the bathroom.

After tucking Amy in, Hannah left Amy's room. She passed the playroom with the clowns and stopped cold. The sheet she'd placed over the clown lay crumpled on the floor and, even in the shallow hall light, she saw the clown staring at her again.

"How did . . . the kids must have . . . no, they were downstairs with me. It must have slipped off." She started into the room, uneasy because the thing wouldn't stop staring at her. She tried paying it no mind as she reached down to pick up the sheet.

Something brushed her hair.

Quick, fleeting, gentle.

She jumped and stumbled backward. She flicked the light switch and illuminated the room. There was no one there but her and the clowns.

"Stupid." She shook her head and giggled, then she reached down, grabbed hold of the sheet, and threw it over the clown once again. She turned off the light and headed back downstairs.

This time she was able to get into her schoolwork. She cracked opened a book, opened a can of soda, and started on her math homework. Her phone vibrated off and on throughout the next hour—text messages from her best friend Melissa and her gay friend Tom kept her busier than her math work. She only managed to finish half of her assignment.

Another text from Melissa had her laughing out loud. She pushed the reply button and—

Thump, thump . . .

The noise came from the second floor. Hannah's smile instantly died. She put down her phone and looked up at the ceiling.

Could be one of the kids. Maybe they need help. Almost sounded like one of them fell out of bed. I should go check.

She got up from the couch and crossed the living room. As she rounded a corner, the carpeted stairway to the second floor came into view. The top of the stairs was shrouded in darkness. She flicked the light switch at the bottom of the staircase before she started up.

She reached the top of the stairs and saw the waiting playroom. The light at the top of the stairs leaked into the playroom, picking up pieces of the white sheet on the floor again. Hannah immediately went into the room and turned on the light. The sheet was on the floor; the clown in the chair grinned at her.

"That's it," she said.

She left the room and hurried downstairs. She snatched her cell phone off the couch and fished the Harper's phone number from her pocket.

"Hello, Mrs. Harper, I'm really sorry to bother you."

"Is everything okay, dear?"

"Oh yes . . . it's fine. I wanted to ask something. It's silly, really."

"What is it dear?"

"That's a really great clown collection you have in the playroom."

"Why, thank you. The hubby and I have collected them from all over the world. We just adore them and thought, what better place than a kids' playroom for such a fine collection."

"That's amazing," Hannah said. "I wanted to know if it would be all right if I moved the big one. You know, the life-sized one that sits in the rocking chair. I'd like to move him into the closet. He's starting to spook the kids and me." She thought the addition of the kids would add weight to her request. "I didn't want to move him until I asked you."

"I don't understand, dear," Mrs. Harper said. "We don't have a life-sized clown in the rocking chair."

Hannah's cell phone beeped as her call dropped. The battery had gone dead. Hannah's heart sank. Her eyes widened in panic as she glanced at the ceiling. Her throat went dry and her spine stiffened.

She looked down at her phone again, tapping numbers. Nothing happened. Frantically, she pushed them again and again. "No," she mumbled. She checked her pack for her charger, but she had forgotten to bring it.

Mrs. Harper's words echoed in her head. *We don't have a life-sized clown in the rocking chair.*

Hannah crossed back to the stairway. She could see the light was still on in the playroom. *The kids,* she thought. *I have to get them out of here.*

Her heart raced, pounding in her chest without mercy.

A creak resonated from somewhere upstairs and Hannah sprang into action. She took a deep breath as she ran to the top of the stairs, skipping steps until she reached the playroom. The rocking chair was empty and still rocking as she stepped into the room. *My God . . . Charlie . . . Amy . . .* She made her way to Charlie's room and threw open the door.

Charlie slept soundly, his blankets pulled over him snugly. Hannah listened to his breathing. She listened, unsure if she and Charlie were the only two in the room.

"Charlie, wake up," she said, pulling the covers away from the boy. "Please, honey, get up now, we need to get out of here."

"What's going on?" he yawned, rubbing his squinted eyes.

"We have to get your sister," she whispered. "I'll explain later. Let's go."

The two of them hurried down the hall, past the playroom and to Amy's room. Hannah pushed open the door and found Amy fast asleep.

"Amy, get up," Hannah whispered harshly. "We need to go."

"Huh," Amy said, shaking her head as she tried to wake up.

"Charlie and I are here. We all need to leave the house. *Right now.*"

Confusion left its mark on Amy's face, but she complied and got out of bed.

A door slammed from behind them as they hurried downstairs.

"What's going on," Charlie asked.

"Tell us," Amy demanded.

"There's someone in the house," Hannah said. "Don't be afraid . . . we just need to go next door to your neighbor's house."

"I'm not afraid," Charlie said. "Who's here . . . who's in the house . . . is it mom and dad?"

"No, honey, it isn't," Hannah said, ushering the kids to the front door.

She tried to open the door but it wouldn't budge.

"What the hell, it won't open." She tried with both hands, but the door still refused to give. "What's wrong with this? Why won't it open?"

"I want Mom," Amy whined.

"It's gonna be okay, Amy," Hannah said.

She spotted the home phone on an end table and scrambled to dial 911. She froze, her hand trembling as she placed the phone back on its cradle. "The line is dead," she murmured to herself.

"What are you saying?' Charlie asked.

A loud thud pounded through the entire upstairs. Hannah jumped. Amy began wailing, her tears staining her cheeks.

"Everything will be all right," Hannah said. She took the little girl into her arms and looked at the staircase, expecting someone to come downstairs at any moment. She could see the light in the playroom was no longer on.

Where is he? What is he doing up there?

She tried to recall if the kitchen had an outside door. Yes, it did, it had a door to the backyard. "C'mon," she said, rallying the twins. "We'll go out back."

Hannah led the twins across the living room, through the dining room, and into the kitchen, past the center island and to the back door.

When Hannah tried the door handle, she found that something blocked the door on the other side. She looked through the door's paneled window and saw a long metallic object preventing the door from opening.

"Let us out!" Hannah screamed, throwing herself against the door again and again.

The twins were both crying now, growing louder with every one of Hannah's crashes into the door.

"Okay . . . okay . . ." She turned to console the children and—

A tap at the door startled her. She turned and saw the clown's face hanging upside down in the door's window. The clown erupted in maddening laughter, cackling at her with gleeful menace.

Hannah screamed and pulled the children away. She took them back the way they'd come, ushering the kids forcefully, dragging them through each room.

She could hear the patter of feet throughout the entire second floor. A door upstairs clicked and creaked open.

We're not safe anywhere . . . not anywhere in this house. God help me, what do we do . . . I can't let him . . .

A shadow formed on the upstairs wall, stretching, growing longer.

"Do you have a basement?" she asked the twins in a hushed voice.

"Yes," Charlie said. "The door is in the kitchen."

"Quick," Hannah insisted, hurrying the children back to the kitchen. "We have to hide."

They climbed down the wobbly wooden stairs to the basement. The railing was loose, the steps creaked, and Hannah nearly lost her footing. She recovered quickly and descended with the kids into the basement.

She could hear footsteps in the living room now, right above them.

Please . . . please don't let him find us down here.

Her pulse raced and her body burned as if she had a fever. She was sweating. She guided the children as far back into the cellar as possible. She found a small window at the back of the basement. Moonlight streamed through the window like a beacon of hope, and a half smile played across Hannah's face.

"Come on guys, I think we can make it out." The window was a bit high for her, but there was a cot below it. Hannah jumped onto the cot and began working the window. It seemed to be jammed, but she had hope she could break it loose. "Almost there . . . almost . . . guys . . . hold on . . ."

The window had begun to slide up, squeaking and groaning as it did. A cloud of dust billowed around Hannah's face. She bowed her head, coughing back the dust, and for the first time saw the chains and handcuffs lying on the floor next to the cot.

Something shuffled behind her.

"Charlie? Amy?" She turned to see the twins standing with the clown. He was patting their heads, caressing their hair, and they looked up at him with adoration. The air rushed from Hannah's lungs. Her mind shattered.

"Get away from him," she urged the twins. "Run . . . for God's sake, run!"

"It's okay," Amy said with a giggle.

"This is our brother," Charlie added. "His name is Simon."

"He always dresses like a clown when we let him play with us upstairs," Amy said.

The clown grinned at Hannah as it left the twins and moved closer to her, staring at her endlessly. She stood frozen, unable to move or scream.

* * *

"Children! Downstairs right now."

When the Harpers arrived home at two A.M., Mrs. Harper poured herself a drink immediately. Mr. Harper stood with his hands on his hips. He searched for Hannah but found no sign of her.

Charlie and Amy trotted down the stairs.

"You promised not to let your brother upstairs anymore," Mrs. Harper sighed. "You promised. You've been very bad. I don't want us to have to move again. Your father and I are trying to keep our place in society."

"We're sorry," the twins said in unison.

"Sorry isn't good enough. You have to mind us. Now where's the body?"

"In the basement with Simon," they said, once again in unison.

"Honey," Mrs. Harper turned to her husband. "Simon's done it again. Come help me clean up, and don't forget the shovel."

An hour later the phone rang. Mrs. Harper rolled her eyes before answering. "Hello. . . . Oh, it's so good to hear from you. Excuse me? Why, no, I haven't seen Hannah since we sent her home at two. After we left you, we paid her and she left to go straight home. . . . You mean she's not home? Oh dear, that's horrible . . . yes, yes, that was a strange call from her. I don't know what the dear was going on about. . . . Of course. We'll help any way we can. I do hope you hear from her soon."

After returning the phone to its cradle, Mrs. Harper finished her drink in one gulp. It was going to be a long night.

John Grover is a fiction author residing in Massachusetts. He completed a creative writing course at Boston's Fisher College and is a member of the New England Horror Writers Association. Some of his more recent credits include Best New Werewolf Tales Vol 1 *by Books of the Dead Press,* The Epitaphs *anthology by The New England Horror Writers,* Monster Party *by Living Dead Press,* The Northern Haunts *anthology by Shroud Publishing, and* The Zombology *series by Library of the Living*

Dead Press. He is the author the new fantasy series Song of the Ancestors *and of several collections, including the recently released* Creatures and Crypts *for Amazon Kindle as well as various chapbooks, anthologies, and more. Please visit his website www.shadowtales.com for more information.*

Haunted House

Lisa Morton

"Take, for example, a haunted house . . . wherein some one room is the scene of a ghostly representation of some long past tragedy. On a psychometric hypothesis the original tragedy has been literally photographed on its material surroundings . . ."
—Sir Oliver Lodge, *Man and the Universe* (1908)

The Donegan house had stood on its hill in Angelino Heights since 1888. It had been added to, divided, remodeled, forgotten, and refurbished during its long life. It had withstood time, rain, sun, earthquakes, and smog; it had sheltered young couples, families, singles, grandparents, and boarders. In its time, it had seen one natural death (second owner Millie Chautauqua, who'd died in her bed at the age of 93), one suicide (a young boarder named Charles Pace, whose fiancée had jilted him, and so he'd hung himself from the extravagant overhead light fixture in his room), and two messy divorces. But it had also held laughter, whispers of love, exclamations of delight, congenial gatherings, squeals of playful children, purring cats, and the sound of canine tails thumping excitedly against its doors and walls.

The house was empty now and so it slept, until that time when it would once again partner in pursuit of a great dream.

* * *

An hour before sunset, two vans pulled up into the driveway of the Donegan house, just northwest of downtown Los Angeles. The vans bore the striking logo of a television show called *Ghostmasters*.

Men with cameras stepped out of the rear vehicle, then the doors on the front van flew back dramatically and the three "Ghostmasters" leapt out, lining up to pose between the cameras and the house. The trio wore jackets emblazoned with the series logo, and backpacks and utility belts full of

435

equipment. As they waited before the house in the late afternoon sunlight, tinged gold from the Los Angeles smog, the cameras captured the "For Sale" signs and panned across peeling paint and cracked paving stones. After a few seconds, a well-dressed middle-aged woman stepped out of the house and greeted them.

"Hi," she said, shaking hands, "I'm Eleanor Baker, the real estate agent handling the Donegan house."

The men introduced themselves: Martin Jones was a tall, dark-haired man with the sort of gaunt features that somehow translated as handsome to a television camera; David Pulaski was stocky, with thinning blonde hair and a short beard; Johnny Romano was barely twenty, with pierced ears and a perpetual baseball cap.

"So," Martin said, "we understand the house has been on the market for a while."

"About a year," answered Eleanor.

Martin knew the real reason was that the house was expensive and the world was in a recession, but the producers had spoken to Eleanor beforehand and briefed her on the answers they were looking for.

Eleanor complied. "There have been reports from previous owners and potential buyers of some disturbing activity, and that seems to be making the house a tough sell."

"It's a beautiful house," Johnny said, gazing up.

"Yes, it is. It was built in 1888 by Benjamin Donegan, who'd made a fortune in the insurance business back east and moved to Los Angeles for health reasons. Mr. Donegan and his wife ended up dying tragically in a train accident a few years later, and the house was taken over by an elderly aunt, Millie. Millie died here in 1910, and at that point the property passed through a number of owners."

David pointed to a room on the second floor. The window was curtain-less and the interior of the room, away from the sun, peered out like a dark eye. "There was a suicide here, in that room right up there . . ."

Eleanor nodded. "In 1938 the house was acquired by a couple who rented rooms to boarders. In 1940 a young man named Charles Pace was abandoned by his girlfriend and he hung himself in that room."

Martin, ever mindful that the show was in its fifth season and ratings had been slipping, asked, "And there have been reports ever since of creaking sounds from that room, right?"

"Yes, and one buyer was scared away when she claimed to see the figure of a man with a bent neck reflected in a mirror in that room."

"Full-body apparition," Johnny murmured. David nodded in agreement. Martin silently applauded.

"What else?" Martin asked.

"Well, we've had reports of a cold spot in the rear downstairs bedroom—"

David cut her off. "Where Millie was found dead?"

"Right."

"And wasn't there a rumor of a boarder who was a witch?"

Eleanor smiled. "There was once a tenant named Martha Joosten who dabbled in some odd things . . ."

"Okay. Let's go in." Martin held out an arm and Eleanor turned to lead the way, the cameras following.

* * *

The house stirred as it was entered, but this was no potential new owner hoping to fall in love, nor even a casual admirer. These men sought other rewards.

The house had felt Charles Pace's agonized final moments and knew that his grief had been so all-consuming it had left nothing of the young man behind. And it had watched as ancient little Millie Chautauqua had dreamed a last dream, smiling, before her heart stopped. It knew the lie of Martha Joosten, who had made herb teas for sick friends and nothing more.

The house, however, kept its silence and hoped the intruders would leave soon, allowing it to return to serenity.

* * *

After night fell, the Ghostmasters set up their cameras and their sound recorders and their thermometers throughout the house. At 10 P.M., they turned out the lights and entered the house, followed by their cameramen. They used small flashlights to find their way through the spacious three-story abode, starting on the ground floor, at the base of the large main staircase that rose to the upper levels.

Martin shone his light around, knowing that it would paint the house in broad swaths of high contrast black-and-white that would look appropriately stark and unsettling on high-definition televisions. "We're going to head into the rear bedroom first, since that's on the ground floor and there have been reports of a cold spot there."

The trio and the cameramen walked to the bedroom at the rear of the house. In the darkness, they passed a kitchen that loomed with shadows of cupboards and a center island, but they ignored it; they had no interest in a room that had harbored warmth and the pleasure of food. They reached the rear bedroom—a large, barren room—and David and Martin roamed the interior with handheld digital thermometers, while Johnny held out a small sound recorder.

"If anyone's here," Johnny called out, "we're friends who just want to visit. We're not here to alarm you or anger you, we'd just like to talk. If you're listening, just let us know; make a sound and we'll know."

Overhead, the ancient floorboards creaked.

"Did you hear that?" Martin called out in hushed, urgent tones, uttered with the ease of a natural actor.

"Yeah," both Johnny and David muttered. Johnny allowed a suspenseful few beats, then added, "do it again so we know it's definitely you."

The creak came again.

"We've got contact!" Johnny said, his eyes wide.

"Yeah," David answered, somewhat breathlessly.

"And guys, check this out . . ." Martin waved his thermometer in a circle near the ceiling. "Sixty-eight degrees . . . sixty-seven . . . sixty-five . . . sixty-four . . . we've definitely got some activity going on right here."

David nodded, then said, "Let's head upstairs to the suicide's room."

The others followed him out.

* * *

The house was angry.

Its boards were its bones; they were old and they often creaked. It knew of the cold place in the bedroom, where a space between a window and a wall, created by a small quake, had never been repaired properly. But now the house cursed its own infirmities and waited, biding, hoping for this intrusion to end quickly.

* * *

On the way up the stairs, Martin planned.

He knew he couldn't go too far—he couldn't claim to actually see the ghost of Charles Pace, for example, or viewers would feel cheated because they hadn't witnessed the sighting. He could claim that something had touched him; that was always guaranteed to incite a stab of music and a chill in viewers at home. He'd need to make it good, though, because otherwise *Ghostmasters* would be canceled at the end of the season, and Martin had no interest in returning to his previous life as a welder. He liked the money, the fame, the women.

They reached the second floor landing and David led the way down a long hall. He hadn't gone ten feet before he stopped, holding out his hands to halt the others.

"Did you hear that?"

Martin stopped, listening. He heard nothing but a car passing outside.

David continued. "Sounds like music."

Martin knew any music was likely to be emanating from the car, but he nonetheless nodded. "It *does* sound like music. Like . . . something old, from the '20s or even earlier . . ."

They listened for a few beats, allowing the cameramen to capture their raised faces and tense postures. David finally shrugged. "It's gone now."

They continued down the hall until they reached the last doorway on the left. The room was similar to the one they'd visited below—an empty room, with dingy paint and old wooden floorboards.

"This is it." David looked around the room. "This is where Charles Pace hung himself."

Martin gestured at the lighting fixture in the center of the room. It was obviously no more than twenty years old and couldn't possibly have supported the weight of a body, but that didn't matter when there were ratings to consider. "From that lighting fixture."

The two cameramen both swung their cameras around and zoomed in for a close-up. Martin stifled a grin.

Johnny stepped into the center of the room and looked up. "Charles Pace, if you're here, we'd just like to talk to you, that's all. We're friendly and we'd like to listen to you. We know what happened to you; you can tell us all about it."

Martin remembered the plan he'd made on the stairs, and he suddenly ran his hand over his face. "Is something on me? A bug or something?"

The cameras both swung his direction as David and Johnny examined him. "No, nothing," David said. "Did you feel something?"

"Yeah, I did . . . like . . . something light, brushing my face."

Johnny gestured at a digital camera set up in the corner of the room. "Let's see if we got anything else . . ." He pulled a walkie-talkie from his belt and thumbed the control, calling Marcus, the tech guy, out in the second van. "Marcus, you got anything in the upstairs bedroom?"

A voice crackled from the device's tinny speaker. "Not that I can see, but something might show up later on."

Martin stepped forward, letting the cameras linger on his sober expression as he said, "Guys, I think this house is very, very haunted."

He knew that would be a perfect commercial break.

* * *

The house was haunted. But it was haunted not by the dead spirits of those who had once dwelt there; rather, it was plagued by the living, who had exploited it and who now applied a label

440

that it hadn't earned and didn't want. It only desired to rest or provide a home, not be the object of desperate and deluded men.

The house was no longer patient.

* * *

"So," Martin said as he ran an EMF detector along the walls of the bedroom, "if the theory is that old houses act like recorders for everything that happens in them—and a suicide is a pretty big happening . . . then we should get something in this room."

"Oh, wait a minute . . ." That was David, scanning an opposite wall with his own gauge. "Yeah, I'm getting some spikes here." The cameramen descended on David, one punching in for a close-up on his EMF reading, the other pulling back for a wide shot.

Johnny joined him. "Wow, look at those readings! This is very serious evidence."

Martin half-smiled. "Hope Ms. Baker can find somebody who likes ghosts to buy this house."

* * *

No.

The house would no longer tolerate the presence of these caustic intruders. It wanted to feel the satisfaction of a job well done, to share in the contentedness of those living within it, and these men were jeopardizing its chances.

It fought back the only way it could.

* * *

Martin staggered and clutched at a wall for support. His mind had suddenly filled with images that had come unbidden, but which he knew to be true: Images of happier times, tableaux of bliss, pictures of comfort. He saw an old woman who he knew was Millie Chautauqua laugh as a grandchild rolled an old-fashioned ball to her. He saw Martha Joosten receive the gratitude of a friend who'd been helped by her teas. And he saw Charles Pace seated in a parlor room, his face alight with adoration as he gazed at a pretty young woman who batted her eyelashes at him.

Martin gasped as he realized these weren't his memories, but memories that could only belong to the house itself.

"Hey, Martin, are you okay?" That was one of the cameramen, who had turned his lens on Martin.

"No. Wait . . . turn the cameras off."

The cameramen looked at each other uncertainly. David stepped up and put a hand on Martin's shoulder, then spoke in low tones. "What's going on, bro? Are you in pain or—"

"Turn the goddamn cameras off!"

The two cameramen hesitated, then lowered their equipment.

Johnny joined his two companions. "What's going on?"

"This house . . . this fucking house . . ." The images had ceased unreeling in Martin's head, but the memories lingered— and they infuriated him. There'd been nothing there he could exploit. He couldn't sell a show on fucking pictures of grandmas playing ball or suckers like Charlie Pace drooling in love. For the first time ever, he'd experienced an actual paranormal happening, and it was useless to him.

"What about the house?" David asked, perplexed.

"There's nothing here. We're wasting our time. We're not going to get anything here."

David and Johnny looked from each other to Martin. "But . . . you said something touched you . . ." Johnny said.

Martin shouted his response. "I always say that, you stupid kid. You say it, David says it . . . so fucking what?! We're not being touched by anything but the occasional spider or fleck of dust, and we all fucking know it."

Before anyone could respond, Martin tore off his *Ghostmasters* jacket, then reached for the plain white t-shirt he wore underneath, yanking it over his head.

David watched warily. "What are you doing?"

Martin dangled the shirt, which nearly glowed in the dim light, and stepped just out of the room. "I'm going to step out of the room where you can't see me, and then throw this across the doorway while you guys all video it."

Johnny frowned. "You mean . . ."

"Fucking right, Johnny. By the time they play it back, it's gonna look like the best goddamn ghost we've ever seen."

"We can't do that, Martin," said David, jaws tightening, "That would be, well . . . fraudulent. That's not what we're about."

"Oh, bullshit. We're about giving the rubes a little thrill at the same time every week. They need to believe in this shit to give their lives meaning, so they tune into us. See? Look at it that way and we're doing a good thing." Martin stepped out of the room and called from the hall: "We gonna do this?"

One of the cameramen shrugged and raised his camera. "I'm good." His co-worker followed suit.

"Okay, here we go, on the count of three . . . one . . . two . . . three."

Martin tossed the shirt. It fluttered in the darkness and was gone.

"Got it," said one of the cameramen.

"You might want to punch it up a little in post, but it should work," said the other.

"I quit," Johnny said as he started out of the room past Martin.

Martin called after him, "Fine. Then there'll be a lot of people hearing about how much coke you do to get through these night shoots."

Johnny hesitated, his shoulders drooped, and Martin knew he'd won.

"Now let's get the fuck out of this stupid fucking house." Martin pulled his shirt and jacket back on, then led the way down the stairs and out the front door.

Eleanor Baker waited for them outside. "Well?"

"Oh, boy, Ms. Baker," Martin said with false enthusiasm, "you've got a severely fucked-up house on your hands here. Good luck with that sale." Then he turned and left the real estate woman gaping.

After the *Ghostmasters* vans had driven away, Eleanor turned and looked again at the house, which somehow always made her feel welcomed and warm, and she decided to see if the owners would accept her offer. She knew the house was worth more, but perhaps she could persuade them that it would be a tough sell once the *Ghostmasters* show aired.

She loved the house and wanted to take care of it.

* * *

The house had just experienced its worst memories ever. But it refused to let them imprint on its sensitive walls. It wouldn't force those scenes on anyone else, no matter how long it stood. It would leave those bad images for others to replay.

The house returned to slumber and its dreams were good.

Lisa Morton is a screenwriter, a novelist, a short story writer, and a world-renowned Halloween expert. Her fiction works include The Castle of Los Angeles *(winner of the Bram Stoker Award for First Novel),* The Lucid Dreaming, *and* Monsters of L.A. *2012 sees the release of two new non-fiction books:* Witch Hunts: A Graphic History of the Burning Times *(with Rocky Wood and Greg Chapman) and* Trick or Treat: A History of Halloween. *She lives in North Hollywood, California, and online at www.lisamorton.com.*

Triggering

John Shirley

It was one of those protect-plated Manhattan brownstones, rewired in the second decade of the 21st century, every square inch evenly coated with a thin, flexible preserving plastic. The old building was a jarring sight, snugged between the glassy high-rises. It was the distant past all neatly wrapped up and embalmed. It seemed appropriate, considering the job I'd been sent there to do.

I went up the slippery hall stairs, one hand on the plastic-coated wooden railing, wondering what unprotected wood felt like. They'd even preserved the 20th-century Keith Haring graffiti art spray-painted on the faded walls.

I pressed 2-D's doorbell. An eye goggled at the old-fashioned glass peephole. The place apparently had no inspection cameras.

The door opened—on real hinges—and I was looking down at a four-year-old boy. Behind him was the chair he'd been standing on. He pushed it aside.

He glanced at my cling suit, and at the department's suit-and-tie stenciled sharply on the front (the white hankie and the tie clip were beginning to fade), and chuckled grimly. He noticed my dark eyes, my short black hair, my duskiness, and his recognition of me as an Americanized East Indian showed in his face. Categorization. It was a very adult expression.

I stared. They hadn't told me what the Tangle was. I had a feeling it began here, with the boy. The boy had curly brown hair, big blue eyes, a pug nose, and pursed lips. He wore a neat little blue suit himself. It was an adult's suit in miniature. In his mouth was clamped a black cigarette holder containing a Sherman's Real Tobacco, burnt nearly to the butt. Smoke geysered at intervals from his nostrils.

A midget? But he wasn't. He was a four-year-old boy.

"You're staring at me," he said abruptly, his voice high-pitched but carefully articulated, accented almost aristocratically. "Is there some specific reason for this intrusive scrutiny, or are you simply a man who practices his penetrating glance on any unsuspecting citizen he encounters?'

"I'm Ramja," I said, nodding politely. "I'm from the Department of Transmigratology. And your name?" I covered my astonishment well.

He frowned at his cigarette, which had gone out. "Care for a smoke?"

"I don't smoke, thanks."

"Self-righteous, the way you say that. But you federal men are always self-righteous bastards. There was another here, fellow named Hextupper or something. You're the follow up. Very orderly. If you must know"—he gestured me inside and moved to close the door behind me—"my name's Conrad Frampton. How-do-you-do, salutations, et cetera."

"You're overcompensating a bit, aren't you?" I said.

He shrugged. "Could be. If you were a forty-one-year-old man trapped in a four-year-old body, you'd feel like overcompensating too. You'd feel like leaping out the window now and then. Believe me." He led me to a couch and I sat beside him.

"When did you die?" I asked, watching him. He made me nervous.

"I died in 1982," he said, not even blinking. "Care for a drink?"

"No, thanks. You go ahead."

"Damned right." There was a low yellow table beside the couch. He told it to make him a cocktail.

I looked around. The room wasn't antique; it seemed like a broken promise after the outside of the building. It was a standard décor-bubble, done in shades of pastel yellow, the curved walls blending cornerlessly into the concave ceiling; the floor was more or less flat but of the same spongy synthetic. The walls, floor, ceiling, and furniture were all of a piece, shaped by the inhabitants. The room spoke to me about those inhabitants.

"Who else lives here?" I asked. The department had told me nothing about the people involved in the Tangle, except the address. It's better that way.

Conrad took a silvery cigarette case from a table, his infant fingers struggling for smooth movements; he lit a thin Sherman sulkily with a thumbnail lighter.

"A couple of degenerates live here," he said, blowing smoke rings, "who call themselves my parents. Fawther is a musician. George Marvell, concert guitarist. Plays one of those hideous flesh guitars. They're both flesh machine fetishists. 'Mother' works at the genvats, helping make more genetic manipulation horrors. She's not so bad, really, though it nauseates me when she looks at me with those big brown eyes, hoping I'll turn into widdoo Ahmed again. Her name's Senya. They named me Ahmed, but I make them call me by my real name." He sipped his cocktail.

"I take it you don't approve of flesh machines." I sensed there was a flesh machine near at hand. A big one.

He wrinkled his nose. "Soulless things. Ugly. I don't know which is worse, the flesh guitar or that living pit they call a bedroom. They are soulless, aren't they? You're from the Department of Transmigratology. So you're allegedly an expert on souls. What's your stand on flesh machines, old boy?"

Who's the 'old boy' here? I thought. I didn't say it. "Depends on what you mean by soul. For us, a 'soul' is an IAMton field composed of tightly interwoven quantum particles, capable of recording its host's sensory input, and capable of traveling from body to body. From life, it evolves psychically so that species survival is more likely. It's not religion. It's a function of the first law of thermodynamics, but we use certain specialized techniques to work with it. Training for seeing life patterns, that sort of thing. Karma-buildup release. If we use words like karma and soul in our reports to the National Academy of Sciences, we'll lose our funding. It took us twelve years of regressing people, and tracing facts, to get them to admit it was a bona fide science."

"I don't know about science. But in my current circumstances . . ." The little boy grimaced. "I'm forced to believe in reincarnation." He looked at me. "Why the hell are you here? Level with me."

"We had a report of a Tangle here. The lines of spiritual evolution tangled. Sometimes a gross emotional trauma from one life surfaces in the next. The people involved in the trauma are reborn in close circumstances in the next life, and the next, until the thing's cleared up."

I considered telling him more. I might have said I came because a Tangle needs a Triggering. And they sent me, Ramja, specifically, because I'm part of the Tangle. Not sure how yet. But I'm one of the few department staffers who can't remember his last life. Part of it's repressed irretrievably.

But I didn't say that. "As for flesh machines," I said, "I don't know how much so-called soul they have. Or even how much awareness. The department believes that they're part of the evolution of the lower orders. Animal minds, animal souls." I shrugged. I was trying to keep the tone casual. "Conrad, what do you remember of your death?"

He hesitated, shakily relighting his cigarette. "I . . . I drowned. Scuba . . . uh, scuba diving. Sickening circumstances. Trapped underwater. My air ran out. Big pain in my chest. Gigantic buzzing in my ears. And a white rush. Next thing I remember is hearing this sad guitar song. Only it was a flesh guitar, so it sounded like they do—like a guitar crossed with a human voice. I looked around, and there was Senya looming over me, her arms outstretched, and I was staggering toward her. It must have looked like toddling. And then the guitar . . . it screamed. That's what brought me to myself. I remembered who I was. . . . My real parents are Laura and Marvin Frampton. Were. They died together in a nursing home fire, so I'm told."

He crossed his small legs and propped an elbow on one knee, his cigarette holder poised between thumb and forefinger. "George would like to have me adopted. He doesn't like me, and neither does his room. But then, the room is rude to George too. It shakes when he strokes it. Unpleasantly. I'll show you the damned thing."

We got up. I followed him to a doorway on the right and into the bedroom.

The room was in pain.

The cave-like walls were all rosy membranes, touched with blue, pulsing. Across the room and near the living floor was a blue-black bruise, swollen and pustular, a half-meter across. Conrad carefully didn't look at it.

"You're brim full of hostility, Conrad," I said softly. "You've been kicking the wall there. Or hitting it with something."

He turned to me with a very adult look of outrage. "If I have, it's in self-defense goddammit! I sleep in the next room, but I can feel this thing radiating at me. It won't let me sleep! It wants something from me. I'm half-crazy living in this kid's body anyway, and this thing makes it worse. I can feel it nagging at me."

"And you kicked it to make it stop. In the same spot. Repeatedly."

"What do you know about it?" Conrad muttered, turning away.

I felt uncomfortable in the room too. It wasn't hostility that I felt from the walls. It was the shock of recognition.

The moist ceiling was not far over my head, curving, soft and damp. It wasn't much like a womb. It was more like a boneless head turned inside out. The wall at the narrower end, to my left, contained the outlines of a huge unfinished face. The nose was there but flattened, broad as my chest. The eyes were forever closed, milky oblongs locked behind translucent lids.

The room was a genvat creation, a recombinant-DNA organism expanded to fill an ordinary bedroom. The old bedroom's windows were behind the eyes; the light from the windows shining through them as if through lampshades, defining the outside capillaries in the lids. The face's lips were on the floor, puckered toward the ceiling. The lips were the room's bed, disproportionately wide. They were soft looking, about the size of a single-bed; they would open out for two. There would be no opening beneath them, no teeth.

"It was grown from Senya's cells, you know," Conrad said. He dropped his cigarette, deliberately ground out his still-smoldering butt on the room's floor. The fleshy walls quivered.

I controlled the impulse to box Conrad's ears as he continued. "There's a tank of nutrifluid outside the window. Personally, I think the creature is disgusting. I can hear it breathe. I can smell it. You should see the lips move when Senya stretches out on them. Ugh!"

The room breathed through its nose with a gentle sigh.

Returning to the main room, Conrad said, "Sure you won't have a drink?"

"This time I will have one, thanks." The womb-room had shaken me.

I stood on a secret brink. My heart was beating quickly and irregularly. Waves of fear swept through me. I focused on them, brought them to a peak, shuddered, and let the fear vaporize in the light of internal self-awareness.

I sipped my plastic cup of martini, for the moment relaxing. Sitting beside Conrad, I said, "You said something about George's guitar being sick."

Conrad smirked. "George is hoping his guitar will be better today. But it won't sing for him. I know it won't. It's got an attitude now. Lately it starts screaming the instant he plays it. It sounds vicious—the most awful screams you can imagine. He may have to go back to playing electric guitar."

"It's screaming of its own volition? Maybe it's allergic to him."

"Possibly. It doesn't scream when Senya plays it." I felt my communion deepening. The outlines of the furniture seemed to hallucinogenically expand, emitting soft strobes. I glimpsed ghostly human figures on flickering paths; the apartment's inhabitants had left their life patterns on the room's electric field. In those subtly glowing lines I could see the Triggering foreshadowed.

450

"Conrad," I said carefully, trying not to show my excitement, "tell me about your life just before transition. Give me details of the death itself." I waited, breathless.

Conrad was pleased. He lit another cigarette and watched the smoke curl up as he spoke. "I was a copy editor for a book publisher. I was a good one, but I was bored with the work. I'd accumulated a lot of vacation time, so I accepted Billy Lilac's invitation to go on a cruise with him and his friends. All around Jamaica. I felt sort of funny about it—I was having an affair with his wife, you see. But she insisted that it would be good because we would remain casual for the duration of the trip—four days—and that would cool Billy's suspicions about us. Billy was rolling in the green. He owned a chain of the most appalling fast-food restaurants. Horrible food, which sold by the ton.

"His yacht had what he called a mousetrap aquarium built into it. The boat had a deep draft, and by pressing a button, he opened this little chamber in the hull. Water would be sucked into it, along with little fish and sometimes squid or a small shark. Then the gates at the bottom would close, temporarily trapping the creatures in there, and we would watch them through the glass deck.

"There were five of us on the cruise. Meredith Lilac, Billy's young wife, thirty years younger than Billy; his secretary, Lucille Dole; Lucille's son Patrick—"

"Who? Who did you say? The last two?"

Conrad looked at me with an odd fixity. "Lucille and Patrick Dole," he said. "Anyway, Billy asked a bunch of us to go down and scare some octopi into the aquarium. We were over a certain reef where they were quite common. So we went down in scuba gear. There was me and Meredith and—"

"And Lucille. You three went down?" I interrupted, feeling a whirlpool spinning in my head. Calm, I told myself. Perceive objectively. Perceive in the perspective of time. Evolutionary patterns. "You three went down," I went on, as he stared at me. "And when you approached the gate where the hull opened, good old Billy pressed the button that opens the gate and makes the current that pulls things in, and all three of you were sucked into the mousetrap aquarium. He closed the gate behind you, and then he stood in the hold, over your heads, watching. And you ran out of air."

"And—how did you know that, exactly?"

For a full minute I couldn't talk. I felt as if I were choking, though it hadn't been me who'd drowned—not then.

I was peripherally aware of Conrad gaping at me. I was seeing myself as fifteen-year-old Patrick, hands cuffed behind me, lying face down on the glass floor, watching as my mother drowned. My gasping and my tears misted the glass, but the blur emphasized their frantic movements as they tried to pry the gate . . . their frenzied hand signals . . . their fingers clawing at the glass while Billy Lilac stood with his hands in his pocket beside me, like a man mildly amused by a zoo, chuckling occasionally and sweetly chatting to me politely, explaining that he'd killed Conrad because Conrad had been having an affair with Meredith.

And he'd killed my mother because she helped them keep the secret and had permitted Meredith and Conrad to use her apartment.

I'd expected him to kill me. But he simply uncuffed me and put me ashore. He knew that my history of emotional disturbance destroyed my credibility. No one would believe me when there were three others testifying differently. He'd bribed his crew handsomely. Both the Lorimers claimed a mechanical failure had caused the gate to open prematurely, and Billy had been on deck and hadn't seen it. They'd been with him the whole time. Craig and Judy Lorimer, husband and wife, were his crew. Only, after a while, Judy began to have nightmares about the people drowning in the hold. She threatened to go to the police. I knew this because Billy came to me in the asylum a bit later and whispered it to me in the visitor room.

He enjoyed talking about it. Billy was the quintessential psychopath—with a twist of sadist. "I drowned Judy in the aquarium in my house, Patrick," he'd said, his voice mild and pleasant. Like a taxidermist talking shop.

"You want to explain yourself, friend, hmm?" Conrad said, in the present.

I was thinking about my own death. I'd been in and out of institutions for the four years after my mother drowned. Treated, quite persistently, for paranoia and drug abuse—the heroin use was real—'til I wondered whether I had hallucinated Billy's quiet enjoyment as he stood on the glass, watching the bubbles forced from exhausted lungs—watching the bubbles shatter on the pane.

I died of an overdose in 1987. Drowned when I choked on the fluids that fill the lungs of an overdose.

"No coincidences, Conrad," I said suddenly. "I'm here because I knew you in your last life. I was Patrick Dole. I watched you die. You and Meredith Lilac—and my Mother. Strangling under glass." I paused to deepen my trance. "Really, Conrad," I went on distantly, gazing down the corridors of time. " . . . you ought to slow down on the drinking."

But he gulped another cocktail, swearing softly.

I turned my eyes toward the doors—first the front door and then the door to the bedroom. The orifice in the womb-room had contracted a little, twitching, so that its blue-pink flesh showed at the open door's corners.

I felt its excitement subliminally, and I shared its half-slumbering yearning. Conrad felt it too, and glanced at it, irritated.

But only the womb-room and I were aware that George and Senya Marvell were climbing the plastic-coated steps to the apartment. Now I felt them stopping on the landing to rest, and to quarrel. I felt the Trigger near. I hadn't quite located it.

"Conrad," I began, "Senya is . . ." I hesitated. How to say it?

The door opened. Senya came in, toting something behind her. She and the man I took to be George were carrying a large transparent plasglass case between them. Within the case's thick liquids, something wallowed like a pink sea animal. A flesh guitar. An expensive one.

I could hardly take my eyes from Senya. She was lovely. I had a disquietingly powerful sense of déjà vu, taking in her

453

strong, willowy shape; a campy Old Glory flag pattern worked into the thick spill of flaxen hair flipped onto her right shoulder. The amused curiosity in her face fascinated me; it seemed to go with her black, clinging Addams Family Revival gown and her transparent spike heels.

"Who the hell is he?" George puffed, looking me over as they carried the flesh guitar into the bedroom.

"He'd be the man from the Department of Transmigratology, George," she replied offhandedly. "I had them send someone over about, umm, about Conrad."

The déjà vu resurged when I listened to her voice. The tone of it wasn't familiar. The familiarity was in the way she used it.

George and Senya returned from the bedroom. In contrast to Senya, George was stocky and pallid, his hair permaset into a solid yellow block over his head. His smoky-blue eyes swept over me, then flicked angrily at Conrad. "The kid's drunk again."

As George bent to punch for a drink, his motions set off reverberations containing within them, coded, all the actions of his lifetime. And implications of earlier lifetimes.

"Actually, I'm not here to clear anything from Conrad in particular," I said, crossing my legs and leaning back against the couch. Watching Senya, I went on, "In this lifetime my name's Ramja; in the last it was Patrick." Her eyes met mine. She was puzzled. I hadn't hit the Trigger yet. I smiled at her, felt a flush of pleasure run through me when she smiled back.

"No, George, I'm here," I continued, trying to keep eagerness from my voice, "to deal with a rather complex transmigrational entanglement. It results from a past-life trauma shared by everyone here. A memory that brought us back together. For Triggering. And the funny thing is, George, I don't really have to do much of anything. My being here completes the karmic equation. I'm not sure how it's going to Trigger . . ." I sipped my drink and asked, "How did your guitar perform today, George?"

George just shook his head at me. He was close to throwing me out.

Senya answered for him. "It screamed. As usual! Every time George touched it."

"I kind of counted on that," I said. "I assume there's a growing alienation between you and George lately, Senya. Since the day the guitar started screaming—and Conrad appeared in your son. ."

"What the hell do you know about it?" George blurted. He was tense with fear. He could feel the Triggering coming on some level.

"The man's right, George," Conrad put in, grinding his cigarette out on the table, his little-boy fingers trembling. "The guitar's screaming and my, ah, my coming out came together. And then the tension between you and Senya got nasty. But it's not like it's my fault. The damn guitar may not have more than the brains of a squirrel, but it knows a creep when it senses one. George was playing it, and this scream came out of it. It finally got fed up with the creep."

George said suddenly, "If you think there's some link between him"—he jabbed a thumb at Conrad without looking at him—"and what's wrong with my guitar, then maybe you can, I dunno, uh, clear it away so the guitar works again, like, I suppose I send the kid here away to, I dunno, a relative or . . ."

"Maybe," I said, smiling. "Let's go into the bedroom. And just see."

He glanced at the bedroom, shook his head. "Department of Transmigratology." He sighed. "What horseshit. Probably a boondoggle. But if there's a chance you can get us back to normal . . ."

A moment later we were standing around the plasglass case, beside the bed-sized, up-thrust lips at one end of the womb-room. Senya opened the case and lifted the guitar free as the floor's lips quivered and the room's walls twitched. The guitar cried almost immediately. It was the approximate shape of an acoustic guitar, but composed of human flesh, covered in pink-white skin, showing blue veins. The neck of the guitar was actually fashioned after a human arm with its elbow fused so that it was always outstretched. The tendon-like strings were stretched from the truncated fingers, which served as string pegs. The guitar's small brain kept the strings always in tune. Its lines were soft, feminine, its lower end suggesting a woman's hips. Where the sound hole would be on an acoustic guitar was a woman's mouth, permanently wide open, its lips thin and pearly-pink; toothless, but with a small tongue and throat. There were no eyes, no other physical suggestions of humanity.

Senya held it in her arms, leaning its lower end on her lifted knee, her right foot propped on the brim of the open guitar case. She played an E chord, her fingers lightly brushing the tendon-like strings. The strings vibrated and the guitar's mouth sang the note. The tone was hauntingly human, melancholy, sympathetic. An odd look came over Senya's face. She glanced up at me, and then at Conrad, who reeled drunkenly to one side, then she looked back at me.

"Well?" George asked.

"You play the guitar, George," I said. "Go on. I think all the integers of the equation are here, in place. You play it."

"No, thanks," he said, looking at the pink, infant-like guitar in his wife's arms.

I could feel the lines of karmic influence tightening the room. Unconsciously we'd moved into the symmetrical formation around the glass case: myself, Conrad, Senya, George, and the guitar, which Senya held over the case, her arms trembling with its weight. We were the five points of a pentacle, encircled by the waiting, brooding presence of the womb-room.

"Go on, George," said Conrad, slurring his words. "Don't be a simpering coward. Play the guitar." Like a defiant midget, he sneered up at George.

George snorted and took the guitar from Senya. Its strings contracted with a faint whine when he touched it. He strummed a chord and relaxed as the notes came out normally. He strummed again, shrugged, and glanced nervously at the living blue-pink ceiling and the bruise low on the ceiling walls.

The guitar's scream shattered the glass of the window hidden behind the flesh wall and made me clap my hands over my ears. The walls rippled and from somewhere gave a long sigh. Blood ran from the lower edge of the closed eyelids, like crimson tears. An ugly, ripping sound made me look up; the ceiling had ruptured. Blood rained on us in fine droplets.

Conrad began to laugh hysterically, his voice piping manically. His eyes rolled back into his head.

George flung the guitar down furiously. I had to look away as the flesh guitar struck the edge of its case. It howled again as something vital within it snapped. It rolled onto the floor, face down, moaning. The room moaned with it. Panic flaring in his eyes, George looked at each of us. He looked as if we'd suddenly become strange to him. He was seeing us differently now, all his self-assurance gone.

I said loudly, staring hard at George, "Yours was the sort of crime that required a major effort at karmic justice, Billy."

"You call him Billy . . ." Conrad said, staring at George.

"Billy Lilac," I said, smiling at Senya. "By now you should be remembering. And wondering, maybe, why a man should be punished for things he did in another life. Was Billy the same man as George, really? He is the same man, at the root. Remember what he did? That sort of crime, Billy . . . oh yeah! The womb-room remembers, on some level. The guitar remembers. Their brains are small, but their memories are long. You drowned three people and you took pleasure in it. You destroyed my life. Me? I was Patrick Dole." I waited for the full impact of my words to hit the others.

The red mist sifted down on us. The floor's lips snapped open and shut soundlessly. Senya and Conrad listened raptly, their eyes strange. "You killed my mother, Billy. But she's here with us. Everyone you killed is here. It's going to be a big shock to the genvat industry when I tell them we've got evidence that human soul can incarnate into flesh machines. It will shake up my department—I think I'll enjoy that, really . . ."

George licked his lips. "You said . . . we're all here?"

I nodded. "My mother incarnated into the room that surrounds us, Billy. And Meredith is here in Senya. The guitar woke up in your arms one day and remembered what you had

457

done. So it screamed. The guitar is Judy Lormer. Remember Judy? The crew woman you drowned when she threatened to talk?"

George, aka Billy Lilac, wasn't listening. He was backing into a corner, making funny little subhuman sounds and swiping at his eyes, overwhelmed by the sudden remembrance I'd triggered. And by the realization of who he was and what he'd done and how it had always been a shaping influence on his life. The room's walls were closing in around us. The room itself was undergoing contractions, squeezing us. We felt waves of air pressuring us, slapping us toward the door. We staggered, heading for the way out.

Howling, his voice almost lost in the room's keening and the discord of the dying guitar, Conrad struggled on all fours after us. He looked like a frightened child.

Senya and I stumbled out into the main room, both of us fighting panic, shuddering with identity disorientation.

Choking, I turned and looked through the shrinking entranceway. The aperture was closing. I glimpsed George standing over the guitar case. The bleeding flesh guitar yowled at his feet. George swayed toward us as the room got smaller around him, his arms outstretched plaintively, face white, his expression alternating terror and confusion, mouth open in a scream lost in the room's clamor. Behind him, the fused lower edges of the lids over the room's eyes tore free; the lids snapped abruptly open. The eyes glared, pupils brimmed with blood. The room contracted again, and George tripped. He fell against the open plasglass guitar case, face down over churning liquids. The aperture closed.

"Ahmed," Senya shouted, recovering herself. "Ahmed's trapped!" She was calling Conrad by the name she'd given him. The doorway was blocked by a convex wall of tense, damp human tissue; it was puckered into something like a closed cervix at the middle. But slowly the "cervix" dilated. The top of a head poked through. Conrad's head. His eyes were closed, his face blank. Gradually the room pressed him out. He was unconscious but breathing. Senya held him in her arms. His clothing was badly torn and slick-wet with blood.

When the child opened his eyes a minute later, he said nothing, but gazed up at her, all trace of Conrad gone. Conrad had withdrawn to whatever closet of the human brain it is that erstwhile personalities are kept in.

The womb-room had shrunk to a bruised, agonized ball of flesh less than two meters across, clamped rigidly around the plasglass case. It died, mangled by the corners of the big glass case, and inwardly burst from its own convulsions.

George—once Billy Lilac—died within it. He'd been forced by the shrinking enclosure into the glass case and its glutinous, transparent fluids.

He died under glass.

He died by drowning.

John Shirley is the author of numerous novels, story collections, screenplays ("THE CROW"), teleplays and articles. A futurologist and social critic, John was a featured speaker at TED-x in Brussels in 2011. His novels include Everything is Broken, *the* A Song Called Youth *cyberpunk trilogy (omnibus released in 2012),* Bleak History, Demons, City Come A-Walkin' *and* The Other End. *His short story collection* Black Butterflies *won the Bram Stoker Award and was chosen by Publisher's Weekly as one of the best books of the year. His new story collection is* In Extremis: The Most Extreme Short Stories of John Shirley.

The Evolutionary

Tim Lebbon

The man should never have been there.

Daniel knew the woods well. He was familiar with the sounds and sights that prevailed when he was here on his own, and they were ever-present today. There was no one else to disturb his wandering and wondering, no one to spy on him or hide away, slinking between trees like a shadow looking for a home. He was alone. The man should never have been there. And yet, there he was.

He stood beside the old tree that Daniel had named Sparrow Oak. It was where Daniel had seen his first dead bird. That had been the previous year, when Daniel was ten and his parents had at last allowed him to leave their garden and venture into the woods beyond. The sparrow's corpse had come as a shock. Though his parents' garden was alive with birds, Daniel had never seen one of them dead. He had never even thought about it until the sparrow, and then the reasons he'd never seen one dead began to plague him: they rarely died, they lived to a hundred, they were *immortal*.

Or perhaps they came here to pass away in secret.

The man was a flicker at first, a haze in the woods that Daniel had to second-glance to see properly. And then when he did see him, Daniel knew he had not been there before, not like this, not *solid*, the definite shape of a man standing in the shadow of a tree. A second before, he had been only maybe, perhaps possibly, an echo still considering being.

In his hands the man held a dead bird.

"Hello, Daniel," he said.

Daniel was not afraid. Surprised and startled, but not afraid. His parents had always warned him to stay away from strangers, and one rainy night when they were out, his older sister Josie had told him what strangers *did* to small boys, smiling as she stoked his terror. But this man was not a stranger. Daniel had never seen him before now, but there was no doubt in the boy's mind he was a friend.

"Hello," Daniel said.

He left the path worn through the woods and approached the tree, pressing between a spray of ferns to the left and a wood ants' nest of pine needles to the right. The nest came up to his waist, and its surface was a constant blur of motion. At any other time he would have looked for a caterpillar or beetle to throw in, watch the ants swarm across it and pull it down into the darkness. But not now. The man had said hello, and in his voice there was a calling.

"Is that a sparrow?" Daniel asked.

The man smiled sadly, and though he *was* sad, the smile lit his face with something approaching joy. It was a strange blurring of expressions, and Daniel was confused.

"Alas, the common sparrow has its problems," the man said. "Its food sources destroyed by deforestation, its habitat ever-changing. But today isn't the sparrow's day. No, this is a siskin. See?" He lowered his hand to show Daniel.

The bird was splayed across the man's grimy palm, its wings spread, yellow streak on its head level with the man's thumb, its claws raised and clasping at the air. One side of its head had been flattened by an impact.

"What happened to it?"

"It flew into the tree," the man said. "Its eyesight isn't what it should be. Its nest is on the far side of these woods, in an old sycamore tree that grows right at the edge of the farmer's fields. That sycamore is dead. Its pores have sucked up so many pesticides and chemicals from the field that it gave up on life a decade ago. Yet little fellows like this still choose to nest there, giving the dead tree a semblance of life. And sometimes, those chemicals bleed through. This bird isn't quite blind, but will be in a few more months. Unless I fix it."

Daniel felt sadness at the bird's death, and confusion at the man's comments, talking as though the bird were still alive. Its head was flattened, skull crushed, brain turned to mush.

461

One of its wings twitched.

Daniel stepped back. "I thought it was dead!"

"Well, yes," the man said. "But this is a very special bird. An exceptional siskin. It has a future, and it should never have died. I'm here to see what I can do."

There was something not quite right about the man and his words, not quite *here,* as if he were acting in a film instead of standing in the woods with Daniel. "Can I watch?" Daniel asked.

The man smiled. "I was hoping you would. Now, sit down here at the base of the tree—"

"Sparrow Oak."

"Is that what you call it? I suppose you would. All birds die, Daniel. That was just the first dead one you saw."

Daniel wondered how the man knew his name. But only briefly. The bird and the man had grasped his interest, and such matters seemed unimportant.

They both sat at the foot of the tree—Daniel conscious that wood ants could be swarming over him in seconds, the man calm and quiet, holding the dead siskin before him—and the woods seemed to pause. Birds and animals and the breeze in the canopy waited to see what would happen next.

"A few days ago, this little siskin uncovered seed buried under the carpet of dead leaves on the forest floor. It used its claws. Small birds like this usually use their beaks to do something like that. This one found the seed whilst keeping its head up to watch for any dangers."

Daniel frowned. The dead bird twitched again. Perhaps it was the man moving his hand.

"It will teach its young how to do that," the man said.

He fell silent, and seconds later he started to touch the bird with the fingers of his free hand. Its claws first, then its small feathered body, and then its head, crushed and bent out of shape from where it had flown into the oak's trunk. His fingertips smoothed across the bird's body, pausing here and there and pressing down, shifting its feathers, changing the way light fell upon them and subtly altering their colour. Daniel knelt up so he could see better, leaned in until his head cast a shadow over the bird. The man did not seem to mind.

"But it's dead," Daniel said, as if in anticipation of what he was about to see.

The man did not reply. Instead, his fingers slipped inside the dead bird's skull. Daniel felt the world tilt around him, dizziness threatening to spill him to the forest floor where the wood ants would overwhelm him. It felt as though reality had stumbled. But the man glanced up, and one look from him restored Daniel's balance.

"Watch," the man said. His fingers delved and twisted. He worked quickly and confidently, remoulding the brain, going deeper, fixing links and connections that had been torn away, mending thoughts and restoring instincts destroyed by death. Somehow Daniel knew exactly what he was doing, as if the man's efforts were charted in a book or on a TV programme. The brain reconfigured, the skull knitted together by a delicate touch, skin and feathers folded back into place, the bird rolled and sat on its clawed feet, stroked, whispered to in a language and tone Daniel could never understand.

The siskin blinked.

A breeze gasped through the trees overhead, astounded.

"That bird was dead," Daniel said.

"That's why I'm here," the man said. "I have to look after the future."

The siskin sat on the man's hand and looked around, its head jerking this way and that, amazed at everything it saw. *And it should be,* Daniel thought. *It should be amazed. It's seen death, and now there's life in front of it again. What can that be like?*

"I don't understand," said Daniel.

The man sighed and stared off between trees. "None of you do." He threw the bird into the air and, having little choice, it flew away into the tree canopy, singing its surprise.

"Time for you to go home," the man said, smiling at the young boy.

"But I came here to play," Daniel said, thinking of everything he had wanted to do today: dam the stream, explore the basement of the demolished house in the woods, climb trees.

"You've come here to learn."

"What's your name?"

The man's smile slipped from his face. He averted his eyes, searching as though he would find a name pinned to a tree. "I had one once," he said, "but now it's long gone."

"But what do I call you?"

"You don't need to call me anything." And the nameless man stood and walked away without saying another word.

Daniel thought to follow, but suddenly his sister's gleeful description of what strangers did to little boys kicked home. So he sat there and watched the man pass away between the trees, listened as he pushed through the undergrowth, and finally he was seeing and hearing nothing but the woods. Birds sang, and maybe the siskin was one of them. *Its head was crushed*, Daniel thought. *It was* dead!

Suddenly the forest sights and sounds felt less friendly.

Daniel ran home, and every step brought the woods pressing in around him. The bird song sounded louder, trees felt closer together, leaves and mud stuck to his trainers to slow him down, and when a startled bird took flight past his ear he lashed out, striking himself instead of the bird, his ear burning red as if the man in the woods was talking about him somewhere else.

He leapt the stream, vaulted a fence, and then he was running across a field toward the village, his house already in sight.

His parents were in the garden, trimming bushes and cutting the grass.

"There was a bird in the woods!" Daniel gushed as his dad halted the lawnmower, "and it was dead and its head was crushed and it was a siskin, but it flapped its wings and then took off again 'cause it used its claws to find food, not its beak, and it'll teach that to its young!" He gasped for breath, and his smiling father ruffled his hair.

"Calm down, Dan. Catch your breath. Have you been looking for dead birds again?"

"No, Dad, I wasn't. I was just walking and then I saw the man and—"

"Man?" his mother asked sharply. She held her secateurs open, ready to take the next snip. "What man?"

"There was a man in the woods, and he couldn't tell me his name. And he picked up the bird—"

"I've told you to never talk to strangers!" she scolded. "Daniel, what did he say to you?"

"Nothing, Mum. Just that the bird was dead but it was special, so he brought it back to life."

His parents glanced at each other, and his father sat on the stone steps. "Listen Dan, what was the man like? Did he ask you to go anywhere with him? Did you know him?"

"Dad!" Daniel said. "You know I wouldn't have gone anywhere. I'd have kicked him in the bollocks like you told me."

Daniel's mother uttered a short bark; a laugh or a gasp, Daniel could not tell. "Did your father really tell you that?"

His father smiled sheepishly. "Well, yeah. But that was supposed to be man's talk, wasn't it?" He reached out and grabbed his son.

Daniel laughed, trying to tear away from his father. The familiar smell of him was a comfort; the tang of aftershave, the staleness of coffee on his breath. Daniel was home and he was glad.

"I don't want you going in those woods again for a while," his mother said.

"Aww, Mum!"

"I mean it! Unless you recognised this man from the village, we don't know where he's come from."

"I don't think he does either," Daniel said, realising the truth as he spoke it. *He's lost,* he thought. But he decided that would not sound good in front of Mum and Dad.

"So you and he had a good chat?"

"Well, I watched him fix the bird, then it flew away, then he left."

"And he didn't ask you anything? Didn't invite you anywhere?"

"No, Mum. I know all about pervs and stuff."

"Okay, Dan. Go in and wash, we're going to the pub for dinner."

"Yay!" Daniel ran inside, cleaned up, changed, read a comic book, watched some TV while his parents got ready, and as they walked to the local pub, the memory of the man and the siskin was as clear in his mind as ever.

* * *

Daniel's summer break from school was filled with new things and he welcomed them all. He and his mother went bowling, his father took him to an archery range, and the four of them spent a weekend in Cornwall hunting through rock-pools for crabs, eating fudge, and trying to prevent sea gulls from stealing their chips on the sea front. Dan recalled the man in the woods less and less, though there were a few occasions when he came to mind. Once, they found a dead crab washed up on the beach—a huge specimen almost as big as his head. Its shell had been holed and some of its insides eaten, and Dan thought, *I wonder if he could fix that?* The man's memory followed him across the beach for a few moments but was gradually eroded by the waves. Another time, when they were driving through the narrow Cornish lanes, Daniel heard a crunch beneath the car. His parents exchanged a brief glance and Josie said, "Gross!" *That was a rabbit,* Daniel thought, *squashed by the wheel. Beyond hope. Beyond even him.* They arrived at the outdoor water park, and with every slip down a slide, the man's shadow was diluted more and more.

By the time Daniel returned to school, the man was gone from his day, haunting only the occasional dream. And these were dreams where there was much more going on. "I wonder about diseases," he said to his mother one day, "and why we just can't take them out bit by bit."

"I'm sure the doctors have thought of that," his mother said, still reading her book in the back garden.

"But they try to stop it or kill it with drugs instead of just taking it out and throwing it away."

She put down her book and sighed. "Well, sometimes they do. If you have a disease growing in you, they cut it out and burn it."

"Yuch," Daniel said, thinking, *well maybe they should teach people to take out* every *disease like that, whether its growing in you or not.* But he said no more, because his mother was reading again.

That night he dreamed of pulling a disease from his head and drowning it in the garden water butt. The disease was black and greasy and it screamed.

* * *

It only took a few weeks for Daniel's mother to forget about his forest ban. He guessed his talk of a stranger had receded in her list of Important Things—adults seemed to be preoccupied all the time with new things that seemed to matter so much— and he chose the right moment to ask.

"Be back at five for dinner," she said without even looking up from her newspaper.

Daniel ran before she could change her mind.

Approaching the edge of the forest was strange. It had grown up. He was not really afraid, but as memories of that time with the stranger and the dead siskin resurfaced, the trees and undergrowth seemed to take on a whole new sheen. A fir tree waved, beckoning him in. Brambles at the edge of the wood rustled secretively, though there was little breeze. The darkness in there stared right back at him. It could have contained a million eyes.

He was not scared. But he *was* aware.

Passing between the trees seemed to draw the memories out and lighten them. The bird had not really been dead. The man without a name had meant no harm, he had simply been playing a joke on Daniel. But every bird Daniel saw could have been the resurrected siskin, and he scanned the forest floor for shapes uncovering seed with their claws.

He explored far that day, arriving home half an hour late, though his parents seemed not to mind. They ate dinner together, chatted, but nothing he said seemed to make sense to them. He and his sister bickered as usual, and his mum and dad had their own grown-up thoughts to contend with. After dinner, he returned to the woods.

He found a sick squirrel close to the stream. It was lying on its side, breathing fast, its eyes wild and terrified. He picked up a long stick and prodded at the rodent. It hissed but barely moved. Its front paws clawed at the air.

"What's wrong with you, then?" Daniel asked, looking around for the man. But he did not appear. Perhaps this was not a special squirrel.

Over the space of a few minutes Daniel crawled closer and closer to the creature, nudging it with the stick, frustrated by its lack of movement. It seemed to be dying before his eyes and he wondered about illness, what was killing it, and why now. Finally he flipped the squirrel over. There was no sign of any injury. It still panted, foaming slightly at the mouth now, its back legs shoving at the ground and kicking up a pile of dead leaves.

Why can't I just take it out? Daniel thought. *Open it up— just like that man—and take out its illness and make it better? Why should it die just because it's here on its own? It's not fair.* He thought about sickness and things going awry. He thought about death and why it could not be prevented. It seemed so wrong that someone could catch a disease and die, so pointless, and buried deep within those concerns were forbidden images of his parents fading away in a hospital bed. His darkest nightmares, surfacing now because of this squirrel.

"That's not right!" he said. Nature should be perfect. Why allow its imperfections?

He took out his pocket knife, opened the largest blade, held the squirrel with his left hand, and cut it open to see what had gone wrong.

Daniel gasped as the creature's blood pulsed over his skin. His idea of delving inside for the sickness suddenly seemed mad—a young child's bloody fascination—and he fell back onto his rump, crying. He wiped his hand on his shirt. The dying animal's blood was sticky and warm.

It hissed as it faded away.

And then he saw the man standing on the other side of the stream.

"Have you come to save the squirrel?" Daniel asked tearfully.

The man shook his head. "Why? It's just a dead squirrel. Death is essential for moving on."

"But the bird . . . you saved the bird!" Daniel was shaking now, shocked at what he had done. It had been dying anyway, but he had quickened its death.

"The bird was special and should not have died. I told you that."

"This squirrel isn't?"

"Not in the same way. It wasn't fit, so it didn't survive."

"That's not fair!" Daniel shouted.

"Fair is something for people," the man said, "and they're the least fair of all."

Daniel cried some more, taking some strange comfort in the tears. Perhaps because they prevented him from seeing the small grey corpse.

"I *travel*," the man said, and his voice was so filled with a child-like wonder that Daniel stopped crying instantly and looked up. The man held out his hand and smiled. "Will you travel with me?"

Don't go with strangers, his parents said.

They *touch* you, Josie said.

"Travel where?"

"Everywhere!"

Daniel held the man's hand; in his grip there was only goodness.

* * *

They walked together, strange man and confused boy, and slowly they faded away from the forest. Daniel saw the familiar path changing, the geography of his memory struggling to keep up, and the man took them left into an area of evergreens, finding a path that had never been there before. They were remote from the forest. It existed around them, but there was little interaction; no spider webs breaking across Daniel's face, no smell of freshly fallen pine needles, no spongy give underfoot. As they moved, time seemed to shift. It lapped against the shores of his consciousness, making itself felt and yet showing little. He had a staggering sense of time passing in huge waves—ten, a hundred, a thousand years with each breath. The trees remained the same, but with every step other aspects seemed to alter. He felt the forest flexing around him, just out of sight, shrugging time from its shoulders. The man's hand clasped his own, as if afraid to let him go. Daniel wondered what would happen if he did. He wriggled his fingers and the man squeezed even harder, glanced at him in alarm, shook his head.

"You'd be lost," he whispered, and it seemed so loud.

The forest settled down, and the man and boy became real again. Daniel's feet sank into the carpet of pine needles, the sun slanted through the tree canopy and speckled his skin, and birds chattered in a startled symphony at their sudden presence.

"Where are we?" Daniel asked. He knew every inch of the forest behind his house. He did not know this place.

"The forest," the man said. "Just not when you think."

"Then when?" Daniel asked.

Something was coming at them through the trees. A grey shadow, slinking from trunk to trunk, feigning covertness and yet destroying its effort with a long, low whine.

"A long time ago," the man said, "I came here to fix something. I'll do it again now, and you can see what it is I do. It's important you see this. Watch, Daniel. Take note."

"Do you want me to do it?" Daniel asked. *Is that what he wants?* he thought. *Is he teaching me? Is he—*

470

And then he saw the wolf. It emerged from behind a fallen tree, glanced at them, and tried to slink away. But it was injured. Something had cut it from behind its head, around its shoulder and down across its front left leg. The wound was open and raw. Blood soaked its pelt, black and dry, red and wet. Its eyes held a dozy sheen, like pain-induced cataracts.

"This one shouldn't die," the man said. "A human slashed at it with a sharpened stick, caught it with a lucky blow, and now it's looking for its own death in these woods. It will die, rot into the ground, add its essence to the trees and bushes and ferns, and it will be forgotten. Its cubs will be abandoned by its pack and they will be picked off by eagles and bears. One of them will find out how to catch fish. Not soon, but later in its life. If this wolf dies now, that will never happen."

"But you can't change time," Daniel said. Every film he had ever seen, every science fiction book he had read, assured him of that fact. *You can't change time, because . . .*

The man looked down and touched Daniel on the back of the head. "Daniel, it's already been changed. I've just come back again to show you."

He knelt and held out his hand to the wolf. The injured animal lay down on its stomach, whining as the movement opened its wound some more. Daniel saw the cut went deep; the white of bones, the dark purple of something inside that should never be seen. It growled as the man approached, but it seemed to have no energy to wrinkle its lips. By the time the man held his hand beneath its nose, the wolf was almost dead.

"It smells me," he said. "It knows I'm not here to harm it."

Daniel saw the beast's nose twitch slightly. *Dry nose,* he thought, *must be really bad.*

"Come and watch."

Daniel moved closer and knelt beside the man.

The man touched the wolf's head first, stroking the fur to calm the animal. It had started shaking, as if cold. Its eyes shimmered. The man's hand went in deeper than the cut. The tendons in his wrist flexed, muscles danced, and as he drew his hand out, the slash melded together, skin fused, fur closed over the wound. He put his hand in again, further down its neck toward its shoulder, and pulled down as if zipping up the injured animal. The blood was still there on the wolf's fur, incongruous now that the wound was gone. When the man's hand plunged into the wolf's wounded shoulder, the wolf opened its eyes and howled.

Daniel fell back, terrified and exhilarated at the same time. *There's a wolf howling in the woods behind my house!* he thought. When he got home he would listen for its echo every night.

The man worked quickly, using his other hand to press the wolf's body on the outside. His fingers massaged the grey pelt in ways that could not have been random. He frowned in concentration. Sweat ran into his eyes and he shook his head to clear them, his hands and fingers never halting for an instant. His mouth twisted into a grimace and he cursed, a word Daniel had never heard, a language that seemed impossible from the man's mouth. It was as if he were talking animal.

The wolf growled and grumbled deep in its throat, then stood and pulled away. The man's hand left its body, fingers clawed like a dead spider, and its pelt fell closed. The animal staggered sideways a few steps. It leaned against a tree and looked around, as if amazed it was still here. The blood on its pelt was almost all dry now, and the wolf sat like a dog and began to clean itself.

Daniel realised the animal was beautiful. In his astonishment at seeing a wolf, he had failed to appreciate its grace, its grandeur. And now, fixed and better, it stared at him with eyes yellowed by sunlight refracting through the tree canopy.

"That's it," the man said, sighing and sinking back onto his haunches. He seemed to be lessened somehow, and Daniel reached out to touch his arm.

"What's wrong?" he said, and he thought, *how will I get home if anything happens to him? Where is home? Where am I, really?*

"Tired," the man said, "I'm just tired. I'll sleep for a while, and then we need to travel again." He lay down on his side, asleep before his head touched the ground.

Daniel sat alone and watched the wolf disappear between the trees.

* * *

They travelled.

They remained in the forest but faded in and out of existence, passing through the years and settling here and there, places where the man had performed his work in the past. He had been here already, he told Daniel, but it was important for Daniel to see what he had done and to understand.

Why? Daniel asked.

It will all become clear, the man replied.

Near a rocky outcropping Daniel had never seen, where the stream burst from the ground as if forced by some pressure from below, they found a dying frog.

"Someone stepped on it," the man said, and when Daniel asked *who?* he shook his head and smiled. "We're a long time ago, and you'd barely recognise the people who live here right now. But even in its earliest days, humankind was interfering with nature."

Daniel was confused, but as he watched the man go to work again, fascination smothered his bewilderment. Fingers moved across the frog, searching for the injuries, finding them inside even though its skin was unbroken, forming no hole yet *going inside* the frog to touch its organs, meld its flesh, restart its heart, and set it down again. With a slight nudge from the man, the frog launched itself into the stream and disappeared.

They travelled again, and this time Daniel saw signs of humanity. At first he thought there were fallen trees, but as he and the man hid behind a screen of ferns he realised he was looking at an ancient settlement in the woods. Trees had been felled to form the backbones of several shelters, constructed from heavy branches covered with moss, mud, and sheets of bracken. They blended so perfectly into the forest they were all but invisible, but the people wandering around gave them away.

Daniel could hardly believe what he saw. These people wore animal furs, had long black hair, dark skin, stumpy limbs, and only one or two of them stood any taller than him. A woman sat with a baby suckling at each breast while she gutted a rabbit; a man squatted by the fire and worked at other animal corpses, spearing and resting them high above the flames on timber spits; two children tumbled and rolled across the carpet of pine needles, naked yet hardy, one of them growling as if pretending to be a bear.

"This is like prehistoric times!" Daniel said.

The man smiled. "Not as long ago as you think, Daniel. No dinosaurs here. But yes, pre-history, in a time when humanity was thought to be at one with nature. But there has always been that destructive spark." Daniel looked up at the man and saw a glimmer of anger in his eyes, reflected from the fire.

"What are you?" Daniel asked. The questions surprised him, and seemed to jolt the man as well.

"That's a big question for a little boy," he said. "Come on. We have work to do over here." He pulled Daniel away and retreated into the forest, still hunkered down low to keep out of sight.

We *have work,* he had said. Daniel followed, and that question echoed through his mind: *What are you?*

Though the man seemed to have no harm in him, its potential answers were terrifying.

Half an hour later they found the black bear. It was not as huge as Daniel had always imagined a bear to be, but it was twice as vicious. Its leg seemed to be buried in the ground and it lashed out as they approached, lethal-looking claws whistling at the air. It growled, dribbling bloody spittle, its whole fleshy body shaking with each lunge.

"Trapped," the man said.

"Where's its leg?"

"There, in the ground. They dig a small hole, set sharpened sticks in its base, and catch anything from a rabbit to a bear. A rabbit would fall in and impale itself, the bear just gets its foot trapped."

"Will they eat the bear?"

"That's their intent. And its pelt will be highly prized. But not this one, not this time. This bear is special."

Daniel had already been expecting this. *Special,* he thought, looking at the bear. "So what can it do?"

"Nothing unusual," the man said, "but it's fit and healthy, larger than normal, and now is not its time to die. Its bloodline is needed in the future. It's young and has yet to mate."

"But there are no bears in England now," Daniel said.

The man nodded and knelt next to Daniel so they could talk face to face. "Knowing the future doesn't change the many presents," he said. "If I disregarded this bear's predicament just because of what I know of its species' future, everything could change."

"What do you mean?"

The man shook his head. "Sometimes even I don't understand."

They travelled further, back and forth through the forest and through time. At one point during that walk Daniel thought, *this is it, this is where my house is at, some time later than now.* There seemed to be no pattern to their journey. One time they arrived during a terrible storm, another time it was daylight and parts of the forest were aflame from a clumsy human's fire. Of all the animals dying from fire and smoke inhalation, the man chose a small butterfly to pick up from the ground, mend its scorched wings, slip into its minute head to reassemble shattered connections, carry it away from the fire, and set it free. The butterfly fluttered into the sky and merged with the clouds of ash drifting through the trees.

"A butterfly flaps its wings . . ." the man said, and he smiled down at Daniel. "Every second of this journey you've seen me making the future into what it should be."

Later, back in the forest Daniel knew, he wondered what influence he himself had made on this time he called his own.

* * *

Though he had travelled far, Daniel arrived home just an hour after leaving. His mother was dishing up dinner, chatting with his sister as she laid the table, and his father arrived home from work just as Daniel ran downstairs after getting changed.

The excitement of where he had been and what he had seen carried Daniel through the usual argumentative meal, and afterward he ran upstairs to his bedroom. Sitting at the window, staring out over the fields to the forest, he wondered where the man was now, and what he was saving from death. Special, he had called all the creatures he saved. *Who's to say?* Daniel thought. *Might there be special people too?*

A butterfly fluttered past his window, hanging in the air outside for a few seconds like a memory demanding recollection. Daniel stared, amazed. It was different from the butterfly the man had rescued—larger, its wings a deeper orange—and yet the boy saw it as a sign. Of what he was not yet sure, but he was plenty old enough to see the relevance in such coincidences.

He opened his window and reached out to touch the butterfly. It danced further away, dipping and rising like ash on the breeze, and Daniel stretched some more. His arm burned with the effort of holding the windowsill, his feet lifted from the floor, and for a few seconds he was balanced on his stomach and hand, swaying there fifteen feet above the ground. His heart jumped and stuttered, and he was certain the only factor affecting his fate—tumble back into his bedroom or fall to the hard patio below—was whether or not the butterfly landed on his outstretched hand. It fluttered closer to him, flew beneath his hand, and he tilted back into the room. He slammed the window closed and gasped.

Was he here then? he thought. *Did I actually fall into another time dimension and he came and changed it and now I'm back here again?*

Daniel was a boy who fought with problems until he had a solution, real or not. He was tenacious. He went to bed that night dwelling on what had happened. And when he woke up he knew how he could find out how special he really was.

On his way to school next morning Daniel saw a snail squashed into the pavement. He paused and let his friend walk on, kneeling beside the glistening remains, leaning in close enough to smell it.

"Dan?" his friend said. "What you doing?"

"Dead snail," Dan said. He had almost forgotten Billy was there. Someone must have stepped on the snail recently because its insides were still oozing out under their own pressure, catching the sun in bubbles of goo. He reached out and touched the remains. They were cool, wet, and he closed his eyes, waiting for the rush of whatever power he may feel at that moment, wishing it in and yet fearing it as well. *What will it be like?* he thought. *Will I know what I'm doing. Does* he *really know?*

"Gross!" Billy said. He stepped back from Dan, uttering various expressions of disgust. "Dan, what the fuck you doing?" Fuck was a word the boys knew and used on occasion, and usually its shock brought them out of whatever they were up to. But Dan did not move. He barely even heard Billy.

"Come on," he whispered, prodding, poking, working his finger in beneath the crushed mass and trying to find the centre of things. "Come on snail, maybe you shouldn't die yet, maybe you'll go on to grow wings or something." But the snail remained crushed, his finger dripping with its innards. After a few more seconds he sat back, looked at his finger, and gagged.

"Your head's messed up!" Billy said. "You going to taste it now?" He sounded appalled and fascinated.

Dan looked at his friend and shook his head. "Just thought I saw something," he said.

"What?"

Dan shrugged. "Pearl. Or something."

"That's oysters, you turd!"

"Well they have shells as well. Maybe . . ." Dan trailed off. He could not talk to Billy about what he had been trying to do. All the way to school his friend quizzed and mocked him, and eventually grew angry. But Dan remained silent on the subject.

By the time their first break arrived, Billy had forgotten the incident.

Not Dan, though. As he ran around, he was wondering what he should try next. *That snail just wasn't special,* he thought. *Something will be. Eventually.*

* * *

But nothing ever was.

Over the next few weeks Dan realised how many dead things were lying around, if only you went looking for them. One Friday evening he found a mouse in his back garden behind a flower pot. It was still breathing, even though it had been holed by something; perhaps thrown there by his father when he had cut the grass. Its little grey sides shifted with its rapid breathing, its eyes were shiny and black, and when Dan picked it up by its tail, a slick of something grey and wet exited the wound in its body.

He held it in one palm and stroked it with a finger, slipping his fingertip across the wound, trying to press inside, all the while thinking, *get better, get better.* But the mouse did not get better. As he forced at the wound, the mouse stiffened and then died. It suddenly seemed heavier.

The mouse was not special.

A week later Billy told him about a cat that had been run over on the other side of the village. It lay in a ditch, stiff and dead. Dan slipped away later that day and found the cat. He probed its cold, hard body, scraping aside blood-dried fur, but he found no way in. The cat remained dead, not special.

A blackbird, shot with an air rifle, already crawling with maggots. A woodlouse, poisoned by his mother's rose spray and curled into a ball. A spider, light and dry in a saucepan beneath the sink. He even found a rabbit hauling itself into a field, back legs crushed by a car.

None of them were special.

Daniel tried, but all he received for his efforts were fingers both bloody and cold. He would nurse the dead or dying things and project his thoughts, *get well, get well.* He would search for the power he thought he must have, the same power as the man in the woods, and even though he found nothing, he was convinced there was something about *him,* something special that set *him* aside from his sister and Billy and his other friends. He believed this so deeply that eventually he began to feel it as well. It was deep down inside him, past dark places he had never seen, and sometimes it itched. He began scratching at his stomach and back, and he closed his eyes and imagined the man's fingers and hands slipping inside the siskin, the wolf, the bear.

Daniel spent that Christmas holiday hearing about Jesus and how special He was, and he cried himself to sleep one night, wondering whether the man had watched Jesus' crucifixion with a tingle in his fingers that could never be answered.

* * *

I could try to kill myself. The man will come. He'll save me. He'll have to, and he'll let me know what I can do. He'll let me know what the itch is inside me and help me scratch it. I know there's something there, I can feel it, I can taste *it when I sit still long enough and don't eat or drink anything else. Mum and Dad don't even notice. Billy hasn't called me for days; he says I'm going weird. He says I should have a wank, but I'm afraid that'll lose the itch. I don't want to lose it. I never want to lose it. All I want is for it to grow bigger and clearer.*

I could try to kill myself.

He'll come . . .

I could try . . .

Daniel had seen films and read books where people killed themselves. Shotguns to the face, pills, jumping in front of cars, leaping from cliff tops, lying across train tracks, slitting wrists in the bath . . . each image haunted and disturbed him, leaving a deep-felt sense of wrongness he could not shake. He felt as if he had witnessed something not only sinful, but not of nature. The suicides shifted themselves out of reality. It was not only death, but the manner of death that mattered. The more he thought about it, the more Daniel believed that nothing the man could do—no touch, no muttered invocations—could ever save a suicide.

Still, the thought lingered for a while. *I could try, just try, not actually do it. I could pretend. And then he'll come and tell me what I am and why I'm here.*

I could try . . .

But as time ran and fate frolicked, choice was taken from him.

* * *

The following spring, Daniel and his family spent a weekend in a caravan on the Cornish coast. Daniel had shaken loose any ideas of trying to do himself harm, moving on and leaving that troubled boy behind. He was glad. Christmas had seemed to act as a point of change, and successive weeks and months had blurred the memory of the man, diluted the impact of those strange journeys. By the time buds appeared on trees and flowers pushed their way up out of cold soil, the man had become a dream. Sometimes Daniel could remember him, sometimes not. He thought of a wolf and a frog and a butterfly, but he could not see them in his mind, could not picture whatever wounds should have killed them. Sometimes a dream will edge into reality, but more often the opposite will happen. Part of Daniel's life became a dream, and he was happy to sleep the sleep of the innocent and let it play itself out.

On their trip to Cornwall the family did a lot of walking, tracking the coastal path as far east as the little village of Polperro. It was lunchtime when they arrived and the cafes and pubs were filled with tourists eager to stake their claim on table-space. Daniel and his family bought fish and chips and sat in the harbour, relishing the strong afternoon sun on their flushed cheeks. Seagulls buzzed them, darting in to snap up any scraps that fell to the stone breakwater. His sister smiled at him. His mother and father held hands and sat close together. It was the sort of day that goes by in a pleasant haze but lives in your memory as one of the best. And Daniel knew that. He was more than aware of growing up, and he knew times like this would not happen for very much longer. He would soon be a

480

teenager, and much as he looked forward to discovering his own place in the world, he was still young enough to mourn what would be lost. His mother kissed his forehead. His father took him down onto the beach and followed him into the narrow cave, and they both jumped back in shocked fright when they found a dead seagull with flies buzzing its open stomach. Daniel even held his sister's hand as they walked up through the town, heading for the bus stop to catch a bus back to their caravan site.

The bus did not stop. It ploughed straight into Daniel and his family, throwing his father and sister across the road into the front of a building, and his mother into the stream. Daniel was caught beneath the front wheels and scoured across the road, flesh and bone tearing and splintering, living long enough to feel the bus grind to a halt against a stone wall.

* * *

Why do you think you met me?

The voice came from far away, so quiet it may have been a memory.

You always knew I'd be here if you needed me.

Pain, in rhythm with the voice, as if controlled by its shifting cadences.

And here I am, and here you are, and there's not long left until you know.

Daniel tried to open his eyes, but he was not sure they were his anymore. None of his body felt like his. He could feel something happening—agony here, there, erupting at random points, flaring and then subsiding again—but feeling it did not mean he belonged.

He had come back from a place where he had known nothing, been nothing, and now he was trying to accept something again. He did not know what that something was, but it felt important. It felt like life. Behind him the gravity of emptiness struggled to haul him back. He felt its endless weight, always there and always known, and it seemed to snatch away his thoughts as soon as they happened. He could recall nothing, and nothing fresh arrived. Back there, in the heavy void, lay everything he sought.

But there was a problem.

You can't go back, the voice said. Daniel felt pain blossoming and he heard a sound. His soul was touched and slapped, as if to wake it up. That sound again, a croak, and he recognised it. His voice, crying out in pain.

"Lie still," the other voice said, and Daniel heard rather than sensed it. "Time doesn't matter to you right now."

When Daniel opened his eyes, the pull of the emptiness suddenly faded and let him go.

A shape knelt by his side. The man from his dreams. He looked no different, although his face was washed of humour by the splashes of blood speckling his skin. His eyes shifted and met Daniel's and he smiled.

"Trust me," the man said. "There's lots to do." He leaned forward and Daniel felt something happening in his chest. At last, his itch was being scratched.

Other voices rose up, filled with shock and concern and something that could have been disgust. *What are you doing? Look at that. Is that his hand? Lucky to be alive, all of them . . . except the poor boy . . . no way he'll live . . . That man, is he a doctor? Ambulance on its way.*

Daniel opened his mouth, emptied himself of the scream that had been building, and then said, "Am I going to be left behind?"

"You'll never be on your own," the man said.

"My mum, dad, Josie?"

"Alive, but you're the special one."

Daniel tried turning his head, but the man held it there somehow, pressing down inside so it could not be moved; Daniel felt another galaxy of pain fade away.

They're all special, he thought. *I can't live without them.*

"I've been waiting for this," the man said. "You're the special one now." That phrase again, as if it was a reason, an excuse, an answer, all rolled into one.

482

Daniel tried to shake his head to deny the truth, but he could not move. Perhaps the man had yet to reach his spine. "Why?" he asked instead, verbalising the endless question. So many people ask it, so few ever hear a reply. He suddenly realised that perhaps he would be one of the few.

"If I told you that," the man said, "it could never be."

And suddenly he was gone.

Faces appeared above Daniel, professional concern failing to hide the shock, and then his mother with blood in her eye and cuts on her cheek. Her tears speckled his face and he was glad to feel them.

A mask shut him off from the world, but only for a while. Daniel knew he would be given back very soon, and then he would grow into a future that would be, in every way, extraordinary.

Tim Lebbon is a New York Times-bestselling writer from South Wales. He's had over twenty novels published to date, as well as dozens of novellas and hundreds of short stories. Recent books include The Secret Journeys of Jack London *series (co-authored with Christopher Golden),* Echo City, The Island, The Map of Moments *(with Christopher Golden), and* Bar None. *Future novels include* The Heretic Land *from Orbit UK,* Coldbrook *from* Hammer, *and the* Toxic City *trilogy, and a Young Adult trilogy from Pyr in the USA. He has won four British Fantasy Awards, a Bram Stoker Award, and a Scribe Award, and has been a finalist for International Horror Guild, Shirley Jackson, and World Fantasy Awards. Fox 2000 recently acquired film rights to* The Secret Journeys of Jack London, *and several more of his novels and novellas are currently in development. He is also working on new screenplays, solo and in collaboration. Find out more about Tim at his website www.timlebbon.net*

That Last Day, Those Final Moments

Gary McMahon

I'm sure you remember this better than I do. Your powers of recall were always so much stronger and clearer than mine.

We certainly put on a great show that final evening in the campsite bar, making jokes, having conversations, pretending that we were still in love. I drank some kind of dark ale—a local brew—and you sipped bottles of apple and blackcurrant J2o. The flames of the fire were too hot and I took off my sweater to cool down; you made a quip about man-boobs and the couple sitting next to us on the long pine bench exchanged a glance and smiled.

Later that night, as we walked from the pub to our tent, we giggled in the dark and I switched off the torch to scare you. You held onto my arm. I tried to fool myself just for a moment that everything would be okay. I pretended that we were still a proper couple and we'd be back here in Ullswater next year. When we got back to the tent you undressed with your back turned toward me. I slipped off my jeans and climbed into the sleeping bag, wishing I could touch you just one last time.

You turned off the light and crawled into the tent bedroom, trying not to touch me. I could feel the warmth of your body, smell the scent of your skin, and when my erection became uncomfortable, I turned over onto my side so I could no longer see your outline in the darkness.

I'm not sure if you slept well—you never said—but I struggled to sleep at all. I kept listening to the sound of your breathing and wondering what would happen if I reached out to hold your hand.

We didn't need an alarm that next morning; your body clock, as usual, had us awake before 6 A.M. I remember lacing up my boots slowly, as if I were trying to extend the moment. You waited patiently beside the car, leaning against the bonnet.

Your jeans were skin-tight and you had on that black bobble hat with the hanging ears—the one that made you look like a child.

Barely anyone else was up and about as we left the camp site and walked in the direction of Great Mell Fell. You stumbled when we crossed that first wooden stile, and I made some lame joke. You walked several paces in front of me as we made our way across the farmer's field. The craggy Fell loomed ahead of you like the ragged skull of some great dead giant whose body was buried beneath the land.

Did I pause, then, and have second thoughts? I'm not sure; the strength of hindsight is warping the memory into something it might not have been.

But I do remember the cold. It was freezing that morning; a crisp blanket of frost lay across the long grass and your boots cracked it open as you walked. Our breaths misted white in the air. The landscape was empty of figures other than our own.

We didn't talk much on that first part of the hike, and I walked behind you most of the way, admiring your backside in those tight jeans. You'd lost a little weight and it suited you. You'd always carried a few extra pounds when we'd been together.

The woodland we passed through was gloomy, and the cold underneath the canopy of trees was more intense where the daylight failed to penetrate and add any warmth. You hung back and walked at my side, your arm brushing against the arm of my thermal jacket. I could've held your hand, but was afraid to try.

We hit the high ground a couple of miles before Great Mell Fell and it seemed like a tougher climb than before. The last time we'd done this we had still been an item, and some kind of intuitive teamwork—a sense of togetherness—had aided us as we ascended the rocky path.

We reached the place just before 8 A.M. The small mound of stones—the tiny cairn—was still there. The lookout point looked solid, as if man-made rather than a natural occurrence. We walked to the edge and looked out over the boulder-strewn landscape. We must only have stood there for a minute, two at most, but it felt like an hour. Our breath misted, came together, blended in a pale white cloud before us, and I wished not for the first time that everything could be different.

Something moved in the bushes below. You glanced down, raised a hand to point. It was a rabbit or some other small mammal, and I missed seeing the animal before it dashed into the sparse undergrowth, but at least it made you smile. We both stared down and across the glistening lake, where it was too early for many boats to be out but late enough for people to be readying their craft. The lake had always seemed immense—a symbol of something larger and greater than us and the things we had shared—but this time it felt eternal. When we were dead and gone, that body of water would remain. The lake would outlast us all.

The weak sun gave off a surge of light, drawing my attention. I took a step backward, away from the edge, and stood directly behind you. A bird circled above us, white and with long wings. It looked like a seagull . . . I recall thinking, *What's a gull doing this far inland,* and then I reached out my hand and pushed you hard in the small of the back.

You hardly made a sound as you fell—just a sharp little cry and the scrabbling of stones as your boots slipped on the loose earth. When I looked over the edge you were already dead. It was a short fall, but all those rocks made it lethal. The hat had fallen from your head and there was blood on your face. The stuff that had leaked out of the fracture in your skull was thick and dark, but I didn't linger long enough to form a more detailed mental picture.

I turned and walked away, out of the shadow of the hill, knowing that I'd come back here again. The bird trailed me for a while as I descended the hill, and then finally it wheeled away.

I've missed you every day since, but nothing I can do or say will ever bring you back or stop the moment from playing out again and again in my dreams. Even my yearly pilgrimage to this spot can never erase the pain of separation. Your many drunken betrayals and infidelities remain like scars on my soul; the thought of your naked, eager body as it was passed around town stings like poison in my blood. I am haunted by all those different men, each of them an assassin killing off a small part of my happiness. I despise the abuse of my trust. I cannot forget the smell of sex on your underwear.

These are the things that continue to tear me apart.

But we will always have that last day, those final moments. I will always have these images to carry with me: a surge of sunlight, the rocks, the looming gorse-covered fell; that lone bird, and of course, the sad glistening of the great and deathless lake in the distance.

Gary McMahon's short fiction has been reprinted in both The Mammoth Book Of Best New Horror *and* The Year's Best Fantasy & Horror. *He is the acclaimed author of the novels* Hungry Hearts *from Abaddon Books,* Pretty Little Dead Things *and* Dead Bad Things *from Angry Robot/Osprey and* The Concrete Grove *trilogy from Solaris. He does not own a cat but he does have a wife and son who somehow manage to live with his madness. Website: www.garymcmahon.com*

Trapdoor

Tim Curran

They gathered together by the fence in that wind-blown September field like mourners at an open grave. They were expressionless, gathered in silence, waiting, waiting, shoe-button eyes whispering of black abyssal depths, lips pulled tight in gray lines, hands lying limp at hips.

"Is that him?" Lisa Weiser asked. "Is that him coming?"

Her voice rose up and faded away, broken apart by the wind, scattered like the leaves that tumbled through the field.

A single hunched-over figure came over the hill above, holding onto the rickety, weathered fence for support as it ran down the slope. It pulled itself forward like a little old man pressed down and compacted by too many years, too much despair. The wind blew waves through the yellow grasses and the figure clutched its cap tightly so it would not seek higher environs in the clouds, lodge in some craggy elm, or in the mast of some telephone pole scratching the sky.

"Yeah," Charlie Heidigger said, "that's him, all right."

Donny Provo looked up at Charlie, then at the figure dragging itself in their direction. "Does he even see us? Does he know we're here?"

"He knows, all right," Lisa Weiser said, vines of blonde hair whipping over her face.

"Sure he does," Charlie said. "He knows we're here without even looking."

There were seven of them gathered—Donny, Lisa, little Helen Weiser, Chuck Vandermissen, Violet Lanager, Stubby Desmond, and, of course, Charlie Heidigger. The oldest, he towered over them in years, experience, and knowledge.

Charlie was every boy who'd ever climbed the tallest tree, held an exploding firecracker in his fingertips, entered a haunted house on a dare, and played chicken with a knife. He'd soaped windows and smashed pumpkins and snowballed cars and skipped school, even slipped out his bedroom window long after curfew to spend midnight in the graveyard just to prove he could. Charlie was fearless. And in those green drowning pools of his eyes, there was wisdom and achievement and ambition the others could only dream of. There was nothing he hadn't done or was afraid to do.

So under Charlie's huge, encroaching wing, they waited as the figure came into view—the figure that belonged to Lester Tryan. When he got near, he just stood there, leaning against the fence. His left eye was black and his lower lip was swollen. A livid bruise like a misshapen handprint spanned out over his cheek and touched his jawline with hurting fingers.

"Oh, Les, oh no," Helen said, her big heart throbbing on her sleeve. She began to cry and Lisa put an arm around her.

"What happened?" Stubby asked, even though they all knew, and knew very well.

Lester just stood there, lips trembling, eyes fighting back oceans. His face pinched-up, unfolded, seem to lay loose on the bone like a sheet on a line, found its contours again, and held them carefully. "He already knew when I got home," he began. "The school called . . . told him . . . he was waiting for me in the doorway . . . he was drunk . . . he's always drunk."

"But you can't do math!" Helen said. "It's not your fault you failed!"

"So he hit you," Violet said, her eyes narrow slits.

"And he kept hitting you?" Chuck said—a question, but he ended all sentences with a question.

Lester wanted so badly to tell them they were wrong, that his father wasn't like that, that they didn't know him, didn't know him at all . . . but he couldn't. It had been going on for years and Lester had long since grown weary of the lies—the fishing trips, the camp-outs, the hikes, the ball games, all those things a father did with his boy but Lester's father never did with him. He no longer had the energy to weave those fabrications from whole cloth and spread them like blankets over his lap, to protect the man who abused his own son.

489

"I can't stay," Lester said, fighting the rising tides in his eyes again. "I . . . I have to clean the garage and rake the yard and . . . and . . . darn it, I gotta go, that's all."

He loped away, back in the direction he had come. They watched him until he made the top of the hill and was swallowed by the bleary, blowing September afternoon. A tempest of autumn leaves marked his passing.

"He shouldn't do that to Les," Helen said, her eyes gone red and puffy. "His own father."

"No, he shouldn't," Lisa said to her sister, who had yet to see eight.

"Hitting your own kid," Stubby said.

"Just because he failed a class?" Chuck said.

"There's something wrong with that," Violet added.

Charlie just stood there, leaning against the fence. He was stuffed with September's grim bluster and had late afternoon sunlight for eyes. He licked his lips. "Do you remember Mr. Carnaby?"

Lisa did. "Yeah, I remember."

If the others didn't, they did not admit to it. They nodded, murmured, murmured, nodded.

Charlie said, "Remember how he kicked me off the football team because he didn't like me? Remember that?" Charlie was grinning now. "Then, remember a few weeks later . . . how he just didn't show up for school that day?"

"Yeah," Lisa said. "That was funny, huh? He must've run away."

"But why does a guy run away and leave all his stuff in his house?" Chuck wanted to know, though it seemed he knew the answer. "Why does he leave his car? And a nice car too. Remember that car?"

"People are funny," Violet said. "Sometimes things happen to 'em. Sometimes they make things happen to 'em. And sometimes things . . . just . . . happen . . ."

They waited by the fence in that big empty field on that windy September afternoon and knew it was all too true. Sometimes things just happened if you weren't careful . . .

490

Lisa worked her pot roast and potatoes carefully with her fork, corralling them to different sections of her plate, careful that they should not linger with the green beans or mingle with the applesauce. Across the table, Helen mixed everything together into an unpleasant mush and ate it with a spoon.

Mom and dad were talking politics with cousin Frank just in from Milwaukee and getting his opinion on everything from death to taxes. They filled their mouths and talked and gestured with knives and forks.

"You know what's strange, what's really strange?" Mr. Weiser was saying, a spot of gravy glistening on his tie. "This business with Tryan. Roger Tryan. Just up and disappearing like that. That's damn strange."

Mrs. Weiser merely shrugged. "You ask me it's a blessing—a blessing."

Cousin Frank just nodded amicably; he did not know the Tryans.

"Yeah, that family—that whole damn family—is better off without old Rog around, that's for sure. Drunk all the time, couldn't hold a job, beating those kids, but it's still strange," Mr. Weiser said.

"He was trash," his wife pointed out. "Plain and simple. He probably ran off with someone. Good riddance, I say."

Mr. Weiser nodded, speared a bit of roast, gesticulated with it. "But if you ask me, it's still odd. Can't imagine him running off. Can't imagine him drumming up the ambition."

"Well, somehow he did."

"But to think . . . on the heels of that coach from the school. What was his name?"

"Carnaby?"

"Yeah, that's him. Those two dropping out of sight only a month apart."

Helen had stopped eating. She winced when they mentioned Tryan and winced again at Carnaby's name. She looked gray and small and stiff. Her fork clattered against her plate.

"Something wrong, baby?" Mr. Weiser asked.

Helen opened her mouth but saw Lisa looking at her. Knew better. So she merely shook her head and held Lisa's eyes until they both began to grin.

Cousin Frank seemed to notice now that the girls were present. He smiled and dabbed his neat gray mustache with a napkin. "So, how are you kids, anyway? You still running around and causing trouble?" He laughed. "When me and your dad were kids, we always were into something whenever I visited. Did you know I used to spend the summers with your dad? No? Oh, we had a ball. The lake, the woods, the park, the ball diamond . . . we had a blast. And that old mill! Ha, now that was a creepy place! You kids don't play up there, do you?"

Lisa shook her head. "Nobody plays up at the old mill. Not anymore . . ."

* * *

Charlie Heidigger was bouncing a basketball against the wall of the garage, his back to the alley and the trash cans beyond, when Stubby and Chuck showed. They stood in the leave-strewn grass, captured in an arc of autumn sunlight like insects in amber. It washed them down, made them glow.

Stubby looked to Chuck, knew Chuck wouldn't start talking until somebody else did, so he went first "There's some kind of trouble, Charlie."

Charlie kept bouncing the ball. "Big trouble or little trouble?"

"Big trouble," Chuck said. "I think it's big trouble."

Charlie stopped bouncing the ball, looked over at them. "Give."

Stubby shrugged. "I talked to Lisa. She said some weirdo was bothering Helen."

"What do you mean 'bothering' her?"

"You know, bothering her. He tried to get her in his car."

Charlie's mouth tightened. "Does she know him?"

"No. Never seen him before."

Chuck said, "What is that guy, Charlie? A pervert or something?"

"He drove by their house today. Twice," Stubby said.

Charlie tossed the ball into the yard and watched it roll to a stop at the back porch. He could hear his mother doing dishes and singing in the house while his father swept leaves from the walk out front.

"Okay," he said. "Okay. If he bothers her again. You tell her this is how it works . . ."

* * *

Helen stood there by the side of the road in the tall grass, looking lost in her sister's hooded blanket coat. She felt small and alone and helpless, but she knew she wasn't, because somewhere—maybe in the woods or the bushes or up a tree— she was being watched and it was really okay, as long as she did what she was told. Charlie wouldn't let anything happen to her.

The man was leaning out the window of his sedan. He had bad skin and a big belly, but arms that looked thick and strong like stout roots pulled from the earth. His eyes were very dark. "It's okay, Helen," he said. "Just hop in and I'll give you a ride home. I know your dad real good. It's okay."

Helen's brown curls fell over her eyes in the breeze. "I'm not supposed to talk to strangers."

"But we're not strangers, Helen. I already told you my name is Joe, and I know your name is Helen. We're friends, right? And you want to be friends, don't you?"

"I guess. I don't know."

Joe laughed, and such a merry laugh it was. A clown should have such a laugh. "Sure you do."

Helen felt her blood hot beneath her skin. She couldn't be afraid; she had to remember how to do this. "If you're my friend, how come . . . how come you don't get out of that car?"

Joe laughed again. "You want me to do that? I can do that." Joe stepped out of the car. He was short man, heavy and hard, but short. His hair glistened with tonic. "There? See?" he said, twirling around in a circle. "I'm out and about!"

Helen could see the town nestled in the hollow below where they were standing: rooftops and streets, the steeple of the

493

church, the park, the band shell, the lake lying out there huge and dark and frigid. She wasn't far, not really.

"I'll be your friend," she said, "but you have to catch me first!"

Before Joe could intercede, she galloped away, slipping beneath a fence and finding a trail that twisted through a thicket, her feet pounding through a down of leaves and pine needles. Joe—calling out, hollering, laughing—gave chase. Helen kept going, casting glances over her shoulder to see that he wasn't too close or too far. She didn't want him losing sight of her. Lisa had told her Joe was a monster. Maybe he looked nice and acted nice, but underneath, he was all claws and teeth and death—just the most awful things you could imagine.

And Helen was imagining plenty.

Soon the forest gave way to meadow, which gave way to a stream and rocks you could hop across, then there was an overgrown drive, and finally, parting the trees like a withered hand, came the mill. Helen didn't know much about the mill except what Lisa and Charlie told her. She knew it had been empty for a hundred years and maybe more. A weird, rambling structure, it was both standing and falling like a Medieval keep, dark and gloomy and downright scary. At night—if you dared come there at night—the wind blew through it and made a high, howling sound that wasn't good to hear.

Helen ran into its towering, leaning, yawning shadow and felt its cold breath blown from dark cellars and musty spaces; saw its empty windows leering at her. She thought it looked like something from a storybook—a place an ogre or a giant might live, except what lived there was none of those.

She slipped beneath the fence with the NO TRESPASSING signs hanging from it, gray and worn like dingy laundry, then she was inside and she could hear Joe coming, getting closer. She knew, as spooky as the old mill was, it was not half as spooky as Joe was.

She moved down dusty corridors, around heaped jackstraw piles of lumber black with fungus and green with mold, and up rickety steps. Her nose was filled with the smell of the place—

an old smell, an ancient smell, a smell of tombs and mummies and basements shut up for too long. And something else. Something malignant and vast and threatening.

She paused in a rough-timbered room with a high, high ceiling. There were great holes in it. She could see the blue of the sky and the reaching limbs of the bog willow around back. Rays of sunlight captured specks of dust, held them, made them churn and worry.

"Helen . . . Helen . . ." It was Joe's voice as he lumbered up that tight stairwell and then fell into the room, covered in grime and cobwebs and a snowfall of dust. He was panting, breathing hard. "Is this . . . is this where you play?"

Helen nodded. "Over here, over here."

Joe came toward her, his appetite raw and glaring now, raging inside him with an unspeakable lust. You could smell it coming from his pores in a sour miasma. There was a trapdoor across the room; it was splintered and warped and unsafe-looking.

Then came motion as the others seemed to bleed from the walls like moisture—Lisa and Stubby and Violet and Chuck and Lester (dear, good Lester) and Donny and then Charlie, who looked dire and angry and somehow excited at it all.

Helen looked upon him and trembled. Charlie was fun and full of laughter and sunshine and good, warm things. He was always smiling and throwing her up in the air and carrying her piggyback and watching over her, telling her silly stories and teasing Lisa. But when someone or something threatened them, their little group, he got like this. He got dangerous.

He was the one who first found out about the mill.

"Well, well, well," Charlie said; the words were cold, mechanical, spoken by a machine.

Joe's Adam's apple bobbed up and down like there was a golf ball lodged in there tight. "Hey," he said. "Hey, what's this?"

But no one answered him. Lisa pulled Helen to her, tucked her in tight with the others who became first a line, then a half-circle, then a noose that encircled Joe. He took a step backward,

495

then another and another as they moved slowly forward, all the childhood leeched from them now, replaced by something stark, something savage, something hungry.

Joe's foot brushed the trapdoor; there came an arcane rustling from below.

"Hey, hey, hey, you kids! Hey!" Joe said, looking small and powerless now, a Christian in the clutches of lions and tigers and bears. "What do you think you're doing? What do you—"

His words were blotted out by an explosion, a crashing, a rending. The trapdoor set in the floor behind him—big enough, yes, big enough to swallow a car maybe—dropped away and black abyssal depths yawned below. The children fell back and away like dominoes tumbling. Joe balanced precariously on the edge of that black pit on one heel, but only for a second before there was a rap and a blurring phantom of motion—an oozing darkness, a creeping black storm of legs, and a fury of too many eyes.

Something took Joe. Something grabbed him and skewered him with fangs. Something that should've lived under a rock or hung beneath an eave or scurried in a sewer, but instead was here now, blown up to the size of a Holstein cow, moving in a flurry of crushing jaws and bicycling legs.

Then Joe was simply gone.

Gone in a blizzard of spidery motion, drawn like thread into the eye of a needle, drawn down surely into the secret, sticky, webby darkness of the bowels of the mill to be cocooned and leeched dry, and hung with the others. For five or six seconds after the trapdoor swung shut, Joe's screams could be heard, and then something wet like a kiss silenced him, followed by the drawn-out, horrible noise of hollow, hungry sucking.

The children stood there, touching each other, feeling each other, breathing in the smells of each other—fear and wonder and joy and terror and shock—until the mill seemed to rustle with great sighing vibration and everything was quiet.

* * *

Charlie led them back into town, dispersed them, collected them, made them dance and even laugh and, soon enough, they forgot to brood, forgot there was anyone or anything named Joe, and that was a good thing. Charlie led on, making them walk curbs and dive into leaf piles and collect rotten apples from beneath trees and play tag in the vacant lots and march with sticks in their hands.

It was just like any other day in that small town blown orange and yellow and brown by September; the children were scattered by the winds, constantly straying and re-grouping and enjoying one another and the bond they shared. They were happy and they sang and played and fell and tumbled until it began to grow dark and the voices of mothers and fathers and older brothers and sisters echoed through the neighborhood, calling them home, one and all, to supper.

Life in a small town. It was good.

Tim Curran is the author of the novels Skin Medicine, Hive, Dead Sea, Resurrection, Skull Moon, The Devil Next Door, Biohazard, *and* Hive 2. *His most recent books have been* Graveworm, *the short story collections* Bone Marrow Stew *and* Zombie Pulp, *and the novellas* The Corpse King, Fear Me, *and* The Underdwelling. *His short stories have appeared in such magazines as* City Slab, Flesh&Blood, Book of Dark Wisdom, *and* Inhuman, *as well as anthologies such as* Flesh Feast, Shivers IV, High Seas Cthulhu, *and,* Vile Things. *Find him on the web at: www.corpseking.com*

The Long Wait

Christopher Shearer

Though it was the last place he wanted to be, Greg Blatt had visited the hospital for two days, watching the muted Channel 8 news until the nurse told him to leave. He'd held his wife's hand while silent stories of carjackings and murders played out on the screen, then came the daily profile of an orphaned child on a segment called *Heather's Kids*. The segment had been hard to watch. Harder than he could have imagined. When the segment came on the first day, Greg had started shaking so badly that he feared pulling out his wife's IV if he didn't let go of her hand. On the second day, as it profiled a four-year-old blonde with brown eyes and a missing front tooth, unwanted tears began to slither into his beard.

That's what she would have looked like, he thought as he watched the TV segment on the little girl.

Later that night, he thought of the little girl again. He needed a couple of Xanex and a six-pack before he was able to stop thinking about her. It worked for a short time, but when his buzz was gone, thoughts of the little girl returned.

He was sitting on the couch in his underwear when it happened. A rerun of the *Big Bang Theory* was playing on TV. As much as he wanted his escape to be permanent, he knew that wasn't going to happen. He'd learned throughout his life that the memories he didn't want were the ones that kept coming back—the ones that continued to haunt him.

His stomach turned. His eyes stung and his lids were stuck to them. A film had formed on his glasses, clouding everything he saw. That must have been how his grandmother had seen the world before she'd had her cataracts removed.

She'd died the year after her cataract surgery; he missed her too. He remembered the stories she had read to him when he was younger—stories he might have passed on to his child, but now . . .

The lights flickered and came back. He wasn't sure if it had happened or if it was his imagination. All he wanted in the world was to sleep, but when he tried, the things he saw forced him to turn on the lights and reach for the nearest pill or bottle. Last night he thought that if he drank enough and took enough pills he'd pass out, but that hadn't been the case. He'd only felt the shadows that much more, and they were closing in.

A sticky string of dried sweat clung to his forehead and greased the palms of his hands. His brown hair was plastered to his head in dueling cowlicks. His mouth tasted like rancid cotton balls and curdled milk. His back and face itched. There was a large zit on the crease between his right cheek and his nose.

He flipped through the channels. *Jersey Shore,* a *Twilight Zone* marathon, news, football—he turned the TV off and sat in the soft glow of his wife's reading lamp, watching the blank screen. Most of the room was in shadow. The chair, his grandmother's piano, the pictures on top of it, the bookcase, all swallowed by darkness. He hugged himself and pulled his legs to his chest, avoiding the shadows that lingered beneath the couch.

And he held the bottle in his lap. It was empty, but he moved his thumb and fingers across the logo, back and forth. He rocked slightly and closed his eyes, but when he did, he saw her. He saw the bloody mess his daughter had been—the deformed bundle his wife had birthed. Her arm had been in the middle of her chest. He'd never forget that. The doctors had advised him to wait outside. They knew what it was going to be like. Maybe his wife knew too, but no one had prepared him. He stood back, away from his wife and the doctor and nurses and orderlies, next to a sink and in front of a stool set out for him (once they realized he wasn't going to leave).

He still tasted the blood in the air.

The lights flickered again. This time he knew it wasn't his imagination. He listened for the sound of rain, but there wasn't any. All he heard was the subtle roar of passing cars and the quiet beeping of a distant garbage truck. He touched his head, ran his fingers through his knotted and greasy hair. He smelled awful and he knew it. It didn't matter anymore. Nothing mattered anymore.

He looked at the clock. It was almost time. He headed toward the bedroom he shared with his wife. To get there he had to pass what would have been the nursery. The door was cracked. Through it, submerged in shadow, was the empty crib. The blanket he'd bought last week—the one with a pony emblazoned on it—was behind the bars. For an instant he thought he saw movement in there, but then he realized it was only the lights of a passing car.

The room still smelled of fresh paint. Its newness sickened him. He pulled the door shut. He never wanted to look in there again. He never wanted to go in there again.

* * *

In his bedroom, he popped a Vicodin and chased it with a full bottle of warm Budweiser. It was only eleven A.M. and he'd already polished off five beers and only God knew how many pills.

He sat on the bed, wishing for sleep, although now, sleep was out of the question. Despite his inability to go to sleep, he had to pick up his wife. She was being released at noon; it was at least a half-hour drive to the hospital.

He looked at the shower and even thought about getting in, but he decided against it. Instead he changed his shirt and pants, though not his undershirt or underwear, and he swiped a bar of deodorant under his arms. As for his hair, he put on his old black hat with his high school's logo on the front. He sat on the cold comforter covering the bed and ran his fingers over the sheets, still smelling his wife's perfume.

He sat and waited for the clock to inch closer to 11:20. When it was time, he waited five minutes more.

When he finally left, the Toyota sputtered to a start. It was cold, and though he hadn't heard it earlier, it was raining—a sad sort of drizzle that required him to flip his wipers every minute or so. The Village of Maplewood passed slowly. There was a traffic backup on the South Bridge and people were cutting through town to bypass it. Greg took the Market Street Bridge across the Oneega into Harrisburg. He hated bridges; this morning he considered jerking the wheel and plowing through the concrete barrier, barreling into the dark water twenty feet below. It was a child in a passing car who waved at him that changed his mind.

And he didn't want to leave his wife sitting in the hospital.

When he pulled into the lot outside Harrisburg Hospital, he finished off the bottle he'd brought with him, then he simply stared ahead, hands pressed to the steering wheel, listening to the tick of the engine.

The hospital slumped squarely across the street. It was pale brick with red trim. The ambulance port stretched from its side like a deformed arm. There were barred windows on all the floors. Scraggly bushes brushed its sides and a stray, naked tree scratched the second and third floors with its unruly branches.

A gaggle of nurses dressed in green and pink smocks left from the ambulance port. The large doors slid out of their way and closed behind them. Two were blonde. They talked and never looked his way.

Greg wiped his mouth.

Inside the hospital smelled of Lysol and death. Greg passed through a waiting area where an elderly woman read a back issue of *Cosmopolitan*. She wore tiny, gold-trimmed glasses and sipped a Sprite. He tried not to look at her as he passed, but she raised her head and smiled. Her smile faded quickly, though. Greg knew it was because he looked horrible, but he didn't care anymore.

CNN was playing silently on the TV in the corner. No one was watching.

Greg went to the reception desk and asked if his wife was ready to go. He recognized the receptionist from past visits. She didn't ask his name, so he assumed she recognized him too.

"They should be bringing her out shortly. You're welcome to head up to her room if you'd like," she told him.

She was on the second floor. Greg looked over his shoulder at the elevator. "How long do you think it'll be?"

"Just a few minutes. It looks like they're discharging her now."

"I'll wait here, then. There isn't much I can do up there anyway."

The receptionist smiled. She had dark hair, pale skin, and wore a pink blouse. Her eyes were dark and she had one crooked tooth. "As you wish, Mr. Blatt. We have coffee on the table. I doubt it's fresh anymore, but there are sodas and snacks just around the corner."

"Thanks."

Greg sat down as far from both the receptionist and the old woman as he could. He grabbed an issue of *Sports Illustrated* from a nearby table and flipped through the pages, watching the elevators and the TV instead of looking at the magazine. Though it wasn't hot in the hospital, he began to sweat; he swiped his forehead with his sleeve. The sweat was beading on his chest and back. His heart sped up and his breath came in short, quick bursts.

His eyes began to close. He did what he could to keep them open, including pinching himself several times and drinking a cup of the reception area's rancid coffee, but three days without sleep had caught up to him. His head tilted forward and the world began to swim.

A little blonde girl appeared from around a corner. She was maybe six, her hair in pig tails, wearing a pink dress. She skipped toward him with a smile on her face that showed her missing front teeth were beginning to come in. She was carrying a basket marked donations. The little girl passed the old woman without even a look and came straight to him. "Would you like to donate, sir?"

Greg felt his pockets for loose change, but there wasn't any. "Hold on," he said. He stood up and took out his wallet. All he had was a $20 bill. He handed it to her.

"Wow, mister! Are you sure? No one ever gives this much."

Greg smiled at her and patted her head. "I'm sure. Take it."

"Thank you," the little girl said. She turned to walk away, but then turned back. "You okay, mister. You don't look good."

"I'm fine," Greg said. "Don't you worry."

She started away again and stopped. "My daddy misses me," she said. "He says he thinks about me all the time. I never met him."

A chill began at the small of Greg's back and spread throughout his body.

"I wish I could have met him. And mommy," the little girl said. When she turned to face him again, her face had changed, sunk. Her rosy skin had become gray, even green in places. Most of her teeth were missing, and an open fissure appeared where her nose should have been. One of her eyes looked off to the side; the one staring at him was yellow.

The little girl dropped her basket. "I wish I'd met them," she said again, then her hands shriveled to bone.

Greg tried to look away but couldn't.

The little girl wasted away before him. Her blonde hair first grew out, then fell to the floor. Strands of it clung to her pink dress, which now hung loosely from her cadaverous body. Her eyes fell back into her head one at a time. The dress faded to brown, then black. Her skin seemed to recede until all that remained was a yellow skeleton in a soiled dress. She tried to take a step toward Greg, but her leg gave way and she fell to the ground.

Greg started to go to her but held himself back. He didn't want to touch her or go near her.

The little girl managed to get up and tried to take another step; her body imploded. Bones twisted in strange ways and fell inward. Her skull stared at him. "A child shouldn't be without parents," she said. "I wish I could have met them." She tried to move again, but her bones just shifted inside her dress.

Then she was gone.

Greg rubbed his forehead. He looked around.

The TV played silently. The old woman read *Cosmo*, and the receptionist talked on the phone.

Greg looked at the empty foam cup next to him, stained brown with coffee. He set down his magazine.

"They're coming down now," the receptionist said.

Greg looked at her.

"Your wife. They're bringing her down now."

Greg nodded and stood up.

"Are you alright?" the receptionist asked. "You don't look good," she said.

"It's been a tough few days, but I'm fine."

"Are you sure? Do you want me to call a doctor for you?"

"No doctor. I'm fine, thank you."

The receptionist gave him a look somewhere lost between pity and disgust. She must have known why his wife was in, what had happened, but of course she wouldn't say anything specific. Her eyes lingered on him longer than he would have liked, and Greg started to feel uncomfortable. He turned toward the TV in the corner and fingered his cup.

When the elevator opened, a tall man in a grey suit and bright red tie stepped out industriously. He had a briefcase dangling from one hand and a newspaper curled beneath the other. He wore his hair close to his scalp, the way businessmen tend to. Behind him came Greg's wife. She was in a wheelchair, with a nurse pushing her. Her purse was on her lap; her hair hung limp and greasy. She smiled at Greg, but he knew her real smile and this wasn't it.

Greg tossed his cup in a small can beside the coffee table. He waved at the receptionist, who still watched him, and she waved back pertly, like a pageant queen in a fall parade. She smiled when she did it.

The nurse pushing his wife had square shoulders and a drooping jaw that fell nearly to the top of her smock and jiggled with each step. Her heavy breasts were flattened beneath that smock. She had grey hair done up and held in place with blue clips. He'd seen her before.

She pushed Lucy toward him. The closer they came, the sicker his wife looked. Her skin was pallid, as if everything she'd once been had been sucked out of her. New wrinkles curled at the folds of her eyes and lips. She was thinner. For a woman who'd once been both prom and homecoming queen and liked to keep up appearances, this was totally wrong.

Greg knelt down and kissed her forehead. Her skin felt like dull sandpaper.

"Ready to go home?" he asked.

Lucy smiled at him, but again, there was nothing behind that smile. Her blue eyes were tinged with yellow, but worse than that, they just weren't the same. He didn't know what had changed in them, but something was missing. He almost didn't recognize her eyes, just as he almost didn't recognize his wife.

He supposed he looked different too. What had happened to them was enough to change anybody, sometimes irrevocably.

Greg pushed a limp strand of black hair from his wife's face.

She kept her head bowed, studying her purse.

"We took care of the discharge upstairs," the nurse began. "She has a prescription for pain, and something to help regulate her mood, waiting at the CVS off Bridge Street. She said that would be most convenient for you."

"Yes."

"She's going to be sore for a few more days, maybe a week. If she wants to lay in bed all day, I'd say let her for the time being, but try to get her out, get her back to doing the things she likes, when she's ready. And give her plenty of fluids. Juices, water, that kind of stuff. No soda or caffeinated beverages if you can avoid it. And gentle foods, nothing spicy or acidic. We've scheduled a follow-up appointment with her in a week." She handed Greg a slip. "The time and place is there. We've suggested she visit our psychologist that day. The appointments are back to back, so it should be convenient. He may wish to see her more than once, but that isn't uncommon. Neither are mood swings or feelings of depression. If you can be at the appointment with her, that'll help."

Greg slid the slip of paper into his pocket. "I will be. Thanks for everything."

"If you have any questions or concerns, please call. This isn't an easy thing for her, or for you, I imagine."

Greg took the wheelchair from the nurse. "It's not easy, but we'll get through it." He started to push his wife toward the door. "I'll bring the chair back once I get her in the car."

The nurse watched him leave.

* * *

It was still spitting rain when he pulled into the CVS's side lot. The sky was clouded in grey, like God had tossed an old moth-eaten blanket over Maplewood. It was getting colder as the day wore on.

"I'll only be a minute," Greg told his wife. "You wait here."

Lucy only stared at him.

He kissed her cheek.

When he got to the CVS's sliding doors, he looked back at the car. Lucy's head was a silhouette in shadow, unmoving. All she'd done so far was stare out the window. She hadn't said anything, hadn't moved. He stood where he was for a few seconds, watching her shadow, before going into the store.

"Should be something here for Blatt," he told the young blonde woman at the pharmacy counter.

She turned around and riffled through the wire basket of ready orders marked "B." Greg couldn't help notice her shape beneath her short white coat when she bent over.

"That'll be $180.92," she said after she'd rung the sale.

"Jesus!"

"They ain't cheap," Tom Freeman said, approaching the counter. Tom was the regular pharmacist—a big man, both in height and weight. "How you doing?" Tom sidled up next to the girl.

"We're getting by," Greg replied.

"I heard what happened. I'm so sorry, Greg. How's Lucy handling it?"

"I'm just bringing her home now. It's been tough on her, but you know Loos. She'll be back to normal in no time. Busting my balls."

506

Tom smiled. "She certainly does that. Hey, you know, I was thinking. We haven't gotten together in a while. You two should come over sometime soon. Just got a new TV. Movie night or football or something?"

"Sounds good. I really should be getting back . . ."

"And you know, if you need—"

Greg grabbed his bag and started toward the door. "I'll be in touch. I'm sure Loos will want to do something soon. Thanks."

Tom gave a little wave. His chin shook like a turkey's caruncle. Greg had always liked Tom, but Tom had been in the mood to talk—something Tom would do for hours and hours if given the chance. The man didn't have an off button, which was normally part of his charm. Now, however, wasn't the time for talk. Greg only wanted to get his wife home.

On the way out, Greg saw Lucy sliding up the makeup aisle. Her limp hair clung to her jacket and the sides of her face. She was hunched, as if she carried a massive weight, and paler than she'd looked in the car.

"What are you doing in here?" he asked, taking her hand.

She looked at him like a stray and hungry puppy. Tears had gathered around the folds of her eyes and her lips quivered.

"Okay," Greg said. "It's okay. Let's get home." He put his hand on the small of her back. Her spine poked through her clothes in odd mounds. Greg had a sudden sense he was touching a corpse—a living corpse. Lucy smelled of sweat and hospital rooms, but something else as well—something rotten and old, something stale.

He pulled his hand away from her.

"C'mon, Loos. Let's get you home. Don't you want to go home?"

She looked at him again, her eyes vacant and her lips still quivering.

She doesn't want to go home, he thought.

Where else would they go?

He touched her spine again. The feel of it made him nauseous.

"Let's go home," he insisted, leading her out to the car.

She went to bed right away. Greg spent the afternoon watching television. At six o'clock, he brought Lucy a bowl of chicken soup and some fruit. He set it by the bed and kissed her forehead.

Two hours later she still hadn't eaten it, so he took the food away.

The room that would have been their daughter's room— they hadn't picked a name (though they had gone back and forth over a few and even bought a book with a bald newborn on the front at the Barnes and Noble in Camp Hill)—was open. As Greg passed by the room, he tried not to look inside, but he did anyway. He couldn't help it.

Shadows rested in the empty crib, along with the gifts from Lucy's shower, still unopened. He would have to return those.

Greg stepped into the dark room just enough to grab the door knob. A cold finger touched the base of his spine. The finger turned into a hand, and then two, and they worked their way chillingly upward.

Just as he was about to pull the door closed (maybe forever) the clock in the room chimed. It was an old cuckoo, but there was no bird, just an annoying bong from its antiquated black bell. Lucy's mother had given it to her. It had once been in her grandparents' house. The clock was old fashioned, made of wood, and it lost time. You had to adjust the hands because it ran about a minute and a half slow each hour. Long chains dangled from it, and on their ends were metallic ears of corn. Greg's heart pulsed thickly in his ears. It wasn't anywhere near the hour and the clock should not have been sounding off.

Greg left the room behind. He fell asleep on the couch sometime between eight and eleven, but he slept restlessly. He dreamed of a thousand things, all mingling together . . .

He and Lucy were at the Daytona 500 (her parents had given them tickets a few years back). He'd just brought her a hot dog and Coke. She'd taken both eagerly, and smiled at him the way she had back then. She touched his leg, just enough to let him know. She was about to take her first bite of the hot dog when a car jumped the track, flying in their direction. Greg grabbed Lucy and swept her out of the car's way.

The car, tattooed with ads, crashed where they'd been sitting. Pieces of it flew in every direction. One of the pieces cut Greg's cheek.

Heat radiated from the accident before there was an explosion. Greg put himself between the wreck and his wife. The force of the explosion knocked the two of them over. People screamed. A roaring fire broke out.

Lucy was limp in his arms; he shook her and she came to. The car was engulfed in a ball of orange flame. The people nearby writhed in pain from the heat. Screams and crying. When he was sure Lucy was safe, he went to lend assistance.

People wandered, some cut and bleeding, others burned, their skin rising and falling in blisters; others were simply dazed. A few of them were helping those who needed help. Sirens moaned in the distance.

"Daddy," she said.

It was the little blonde girl from the hospital, only a little older, and she looked scared. She sat next to the flames. Her hair was messed and her jacket was torn and bloody. Thick tears smudged the black stains on her face. "Daddy, where are you?"

Greg tried to reach her, but the heat was too much. Too intense. It was like putting your head inside a Thanksgiving oven, sans turkey. He called for her and she turned toward him. Half her face was gone—her skin charred to the bone, a black, crisp mess. One eye had burst and liquid from it boiled on the bone. "Daddy?" she said again, while stumps of her hair singed and steamed. "Daddy, where are you?"

Greg started awake. His heart was like a hammer in his chest and in his temples. He was dripping sweat.

The clock had chimed.

Greg pried himself from the couch and went to the kitchen, where he tugged a cold one from the back of the fridge. He downed it with a Xanex and two Tylenol, then went upstairs to check on his wife.

His tee shirt was soaked through with sweat and clinging to his body and bunched up high on his stomach like a belly shirt. He didn't think he smelled very good, but then, that didn't matter. He didn't care and seriously doubted Lucy would care either.

His thoughts were jumbled, blocked by pills, booze, and lack of sleep. He almost didn't feel the pain anymore. He'd numbed himself too much for that, but he knew it was still there somewhere, waiting. It followed him like a shadow, and like a shadow, it would never be gone. You couldn't see your shadow at noon, but that didn't mean it wasn't there. Ten minutes either way, and there it was, same as before, looking at you with a sardonic smile that said, "You'll never get rid of me, bucko. Oh no. No way."

Greg wiped his forehead. It was clammy and warm, feverish. He wished the fever was the cause of his dreams, but he knew better. His subconscious was playing games with him. All of the pain he'd worked so hard to numb. All the loss, the blame, the anger. All of it was there, waiting. It was his shadow now.

And the fear. He didn't want to admit that one, but it was there too. Fear for Lucy. Fear for himself.

Fear for her . . .

As he turned the corner at the top of the stairs, he noticed his daughter's room was open again. God, he didn't need this right now. He stumbled toward the door, using the wall for support.

(Who says you need eight hours of sleep a night?)

When he reached it, he grabbed the knob and started to close the door. A shadow moved inside the room. At first Greg thought it was the girl from his dream—the hospital girl. He jumped back, startled.

The shadow crossed from the crib to the door. Lucy looked at him with dead eyes. She held their daughter's blanket in her hands. She was paler than a full moon. Even her lips were white.

"Loos. You scared me. What are you doing in here?"

Lucy stroked the pony's fuzzy head.

"You should be in bed." She walked with a strange gait, and he could see in her face how much each step hurt her. "It's late."

"I heard the clock," she said. "It was off."

"Yeah. I haven't set it. Been . . ." He let the sentence end that way. He didn't feel like saying anything else.

"The weights were almost touching the floor," she said. It was an old clock, run by weights. Every so often you had to pull the chains behind the weights to make them rise and keep the clock working. "It's not good for the clock when they fall that far."

Greg touched her hand. "Between us, I don't think it matters what happens to that thing. It can't keep time anyway."

"You just have to watch it," she said, and she moved her thumb against his hand while she looked at the drooping ears of pewter corn.

"Let's go to bed, honey."

She fingered the blanket.

"Leave that here." Greg took it from her gently. She didn't fight.

He got her a cup of water in the bathroom, then led her to the bedroom and climbed into bed with her. She kept to her side, and when he moved closer to her, she moved further away.

Greg finally drifted to sleep, and with it came the dreams.

"Mister! Hey Mister!" the blonde girl called to him from her car.

He was raking the fall's first drop of leaves. Brown, black, yellow, red, orange. They skittered on the wind, covering what he'd already done. Mounds of them stood sentry at the curb.

"Yeah?"

"Do you know where the library is? I've got a project due on Monday, and I can't find it. Just moved here."

Greg dropped his rake and waded through the part of the yard he hadn't gotten to yet. At the curb he said, "Easy. You continue down this road. Now this is Poplar. When you reach Third, you take a right."

The girl was tall and thin. The bite in the wind had reddened her cheeks. Sandy hair leaked from beneath her hat.

"When you reach Bridge Street—that's the main road—the Lutheran Church will be on your right. Take a left there, then go up to the Middle School. That's Brandt Avenue. Take another left and you're there. Can't miss it."

Greg patted the top of her blue Kia.

"So I go out here? This way?" She pointed.

"You got it."

"Thanks, mister. I've been driving around forever."

"Happy to help." Greg waved to her and started back toward his yard.

"Hey! One more thing, if you have the time."

"Sure."

"Have you been to Rolling Green?"

Strange question. "Not recently. Do you need directions?"

"No. I know my way there. I think you should go."

The hairs on Greg's neck began to rise. He suddenly felt ill. Sweat beaded on his shoulders and streaked the length of his spine in icy runnels.

"Why should I go to the cemetery?"

"Because she misses you," the girl said. She smiled, and her smile was strangely familiar. It was part Loos, part his mother. It was part the little girl he'd seen earlier, and yet it wasn't. Her smile twisted into a maul.

Greg took a stumbling step backward.

The girl in the car leaned toward him. "Have you seen my father?" she asked. Her voice had changed, become thinner It was the voice of a child half her age. "Have you seen my father? Have you seen my father?"

Greg tumbled to the ground and scrambled away from her.

The girl's face blackened and shriveled. Yellow orbs where her pretty eyes had been watched him. "Have you seen my father?" Her voice rose and rose until it was a scream. "HAVE YOU SEEN MY FATHER?"

Greg felt a pain in his chest. His world swam wildly before him.

He awoke from the dream. His heart thundered in his ears. He was soaked once again in sweat. He touched his head, then turned toward Lucy's side of the bed. She was no longer there.

He reached for the light on the nightstand and almost knocked it to the floor. The light swayed, sending dancing shadows around the room.

"Lucy?" he said, barely able to catch his breath.

He got out of bed. "Lucy?" He started toward the stairs. The clock in the room that would have been their daughter's room rang out. The door to the room was open. Greg entered the dark room. "Lucy?"

She was sitting in the rocking chair her mother had given her a month after Lucy had told her the good news. She was clutching the blanket, rocking slowly. "Shh," she said to him as he came further into the room.

Flecks of electricity raced up his spine. "Lucy? What are you doing in here?" He touched her shoulder.

"The clock's off again," she said. Her voice was soft and hollow, as if her words had been tossed carelessly from the pit of a deep cave.

"You shouldn't be in here." He took her by the arm.

"I think you damaged it by not pulling the weights sooner," she told him. "It's worse than it was before."

Greg couldn't believe what he was hearing.

"I don't want you in here." His voice had risen. He tried pulling her from the chair.

"Stop it!" she shouted. "You're hurting me!"

He let go of her.

"This isn't healthy. It isn't right."

Lucy stroked the blanket and rocked. Her eyes were glazed over.

What was she seeing? Where was she?

"Come to bed," he insisted.

She began to hum a nursery song he remembered from his childhood.

"Lucy?"

He moved his hand in front of her, but she didn't seem to notice.

"Lucy?!" he shouted.

She only rocked and hummed and petted the blanket's equine face.

Greg left her there.

* * *

When morning elbowed its way between the blinds in the bedroom, casting striped shadows across sections of it, Greg rolled over. He'd managed to fall asleep again, but that sleep had been fitful—though he hadn't dreamt. Thank God for that. Lucy hadn't come back to the room.

He rolled again, twisting the blankets into a long sleeve that surrounded his body. One of the sun bars touched his face warmly. His breath was sour and his gums ached a little. He wanted a beer and something else to numb the pain. Besides everything in his life going to hell, he hurt physically. Dull aches stretched the length of his back, his stomach, and his left arm. He had a killer headache (Tylenol for that) and every joint in his body was stiff and swollen.

He moaned. A few tears slipped free. He'd done his best these past few days to hold it together. He wiped the tears away with the bed sheet and composed himself, fearing that if he let the waterworks begin, they wouldn't stop. His hands began to shake. Then the rest of him. He would make it through this. He had to make it through this.

He went to the bathroom and then made his way toward the room that would have been their daughter's room, where he knew Lucy would still be. As he approached the room, he could hear Lucy's voice, high and excited like a child at play. There was a smile in her voice and she seemed to be talking to someone.

He wondered what he should do. Should he call the doctor? Play along? He only wanted what was best for Lucy. He knew what this was like for him. How hard all of this had been. He knew how it felt to build up those expectations, and then have them dashed so suddenly. He knew what those great nobodies who came up with all the world's slogans meant when they said, "A parent should never outlive their child," even if the parent had never met the child, had never had the opportunity to hold her.

He passed by the room without looking in. He went to the kitchen and cracked his first beer of the morning, then popped a Xanex and a Vicodin for good measure, along with a fistful of Tylenol. He called his boss and told him he wouldn't be in again. He was the Acquisitions Editor of Count Zero Publishing, a small press out of Hershey. Normally Rich, his boss, was a hard ass, but Rich had told him again and again to take all the time he needed, and to take care of Lucy. Rich was a good man, even if he did drive Greg like a slave and pay well below the salary range Greg had seen listed online for his job.

After hanging up, Greg sucked the last of the beer, tossed the bottle in the recyclables, and started to dial the hospital's number. The nurse had told him to call, hadn't she? The way Lucy was acting wasn't right. She needed help. (more than I can handle. too much. too much. this is too much) He stopped before he finished dialing the number and set the phone down.

She was struggling, yes, but who wouldn't be? She'd get past it. Maybe not today, maybe not tomorrow, but it would happen. He just had to be patient. Be there for her. He finished another beer. The tears threatened again, but he held them back.

(too much. too much. too much. too much. too much)

("Have you seen my father? Have you seen my father? Have you seen my father?")

Greg went back to the room. Lucy was on the floor. She looked up at him questioningly. There had been a smile plastered on her face, a big toothy grin, but that faded.

"What are you doing, Lucy?"

She leaned back. There was some blood on the hem of her nightdress. She must have pulled a stitch. "Nothing," she said.

"I heard you talking earlier. Who were you talking to?"

"No one."

The clock read 9:15, but Greg knew it wasn't yet 7:00.

"Will you come to breakfast?"

515

"No. I think I'd prefer to stay in here."

"I think you should. I can make something or we can go out." Greg started to shake again. "Whatever you'd like."

"I'm not hungry." Her eyes went glassy and she said something under her breath that he didn't catch. The smile returned.

"You're a good girl," she whispered.

Greg didn't know what to do. He went back to the phone and started to dial the hospital again, but then he stopped. What would they do? Take her away? Take her to a psych ward somewhere? Put her back in the hospital? How would he pay for that? What if they didn't let her out? Would he forgive himself? Would she forgive him?

(too much. too much. too much. too much)

Would he forgive himself?

("Have you seen my father?" "Have you seen my father?")

She'd be fine by lunch. He knew she would. She had to be— he wiped tears and sweat from his face with one arm and took a deep breath—She had to be.

* * *

She was still in the room at noon. The clock had sped up considerably. It chimed every half hour now. He'd stopped in a few times to try and talk to her, but most of the time she didn't hear him. She had pulled some of the baby clothes and stuffed animals they'd been given from their packages and scattered them across the floor. She played with them and she laughed. Her whispering voice, her smile, her glazed eyes were bad enough, but when she laughed it tore his heart from his chest.

(too much)

Greg knelt beside her. He rubbed her back. More blood had stained her nightdress. "Come on, Loos, you need to eat something. Let's get you some food and get you cleaned up."

"I like the bear too. He has big eyes. He's so soft, isn't he?"

"Loos, please. I can't take this."

"Someday, when you're older, we'll go to the zoo and see a real bear. But not now. You're not big enough yet."

"Loos?" Greg began to shake and the shaking brought on the tears.

"Oh, you are a big girl. I know, but not big enough. Maybe next summer. How's that sound?"

"Loos . . ." Her name came out garbled. His face and neck grew hot and red.

(too much. too much. too much. too much. too much. too much. too much. too much. too much. too much. too much. too much)

"Please! Help me!"

She turned to him. "Earlier she asked me where her father was. Isn't that a strange question? I told her you were in the other room, but she said you weren't. She said you couldn't see her."

"Loos, *please.*"

("Have you seen my father?")

(too much)

"She's so big now. So fast. It all went by so fast, Greg. I can't believe how quick it happened."

"Please!" Greg tried to back away from her, but he was shaking so badly he could barely move. Tears streamed off his face, a torrent of emotion.

(too much. too much. too much. too much)

He chewed his lip.

What can I do? What should I do? She needs help. I need help.

This is too much.

(too much. too much. too much. too much. too much. too much. too much)

They'll take her away. They'll take me away. How will I pay for it? Will she ever forgive me? Will she ever forgive me? Will she ever forgive me?

He ran from the room.

He popped another Xanex and downed another beer in the kitchen. He could hear Lucy cooing all the way upstairs. The clock chimed again—a chime every fifteen minutes now.

He grabbed the phone and dialed. It rang once, then again. He hung up. She would never forgive him. He couldn't do it.

"Greg!" Lucy shouted. "Greg! Come in here!"

He was on the floor, his head pressed to his palms.

Salt and something coppery touched his lips.

("Have you seen my father? Mister, have you seen my father?")

"Greg! I need you!"

Greg went back to the room. The clock chimed again as he entered. Its hands spun quickly. The minute hand made its way from XII to XII in about 45 seconds. It chimed again. The corn hung limply at the bottom.

The clock shouldn't have worked.

"What?" he asked. His voice was tired, not harsh, but the words were broken by a raw throat and rawer emotion.

"Look," Lucy said. "Look at this."

The clock chimed.

Greg didn't move. Blood stained the floor beneath Lucy in a heavy, dark ring. Her nightdress weighted heavily in it. "Oh, Loos. I'm calling the hospital. You're going to be okay. Don't worry."

Lucy wore a big smile. "Isn't she bright? Isn't our little girl bright?"

Greg left her there and called the hospital. This time he stayed on the line. By the time he got through the automated service and to a real person, he'd rehearsed what he was going to say nearly fifty times, but the words came out in a jumble, so fast the operator couldn't understand.

"Ineedanambulanceat64WestgateDriveinMaplewoodMywife isdelusionalandbleedingseverely.OhGod,please,please,help!"

(it'stoomuchtoomuchtoomuchtoomuch)

"Slow down, sir. I can't understand you."

Greg tried to slow his breathing, but it came fast and deep. His head swam. "I need an ambulance. My wife is bleeding. Oh, God! Please hurry! Please!"

"Where are you, sir?"

Greg gave his address again.

The operator asked if he was able to take the phone to where his wife was; he told her no. They used to have a cordless, but Lucy liked the look of the old fashioned phones better. He'd found this one at a yard sale and gotten it as a birthday present for Lucy.

His cell was dead on the nightstand by their bed. He hadn't charged it since taking Lucy to the hospital three days ago. He hadn't felt like it.

"She had surgery a few days ago. Our daughter—"

The woman on the phone cut him off. "I see that in our records. The ambulance should be there shortly. I want you to go check on her and then come back. Will you do that for me, Greg?"

Greg dropped the phone and headed for the room. The hallway began to spin, and he put his hand against the wall to keep his balance.

The clock chimed incessantly.

Dong. Dong. Dong.

Again and again, getting faster

(too   much.   too   much.   too   much. toomuch.toomuchtoomuchtoomuch)

until it sounded like a fire alarm, shrill and quick.

("Have you seen my father?")

Then a muffled clang and the clock stopped.

Greg charged through the door.

Lucy was slumped over, her head resting against her chest. There was blood everywhere—a black, sticky circle. It stained her hands, their dead daughter's toys, the blanket . . .

He fell beside her. Warm blood soused his jeans.

"Lucy! Lucy! Wake up, Lucy! Wake up!"

He slapped her cheek gently, then harder. He raised her head. She stared, unseeing, at the far wall where he'd painted a blue unicorn beneath a rainbow, and at the end of the rainbow a kettle brimming with gold coins.

"Lucy, please! Honey, please! Wake up, Lucy! Wake up!"

Greg shook her and she toppled over.

The room smelled coppery. A drop of sweat fell into his eye. He tried blinking it away. "No! No! No! No!No!NoNONONO!"

(toomuch.toomuch.toomuchtoomuchtoomuchtoomuchtoo much)

("My father? Have you seen my—?")

Greg lifted her from the carpet and held her against him. His tears finally came full force and he knew they wouldn't stop. Not today. Not tomorrow. Not in a week.

Not ever.

He was warm and wet with his wife's blood. His daughter had died. Everything was gone. Everything he'd ever loved, all gone.

A sound fought its way through his clenched throat.

A sound like he'd never heard before.

He pressed Lucy's head closer to his chest.

(breathe, baby. please breathe!)

He stroked his wife's hair and pushed it from her face.

She was smiling.

She was happy.

When the police and ambulance drivers knocked on the door, Greg didn't move. He continued to hold his wife the same way he'd held her so many times before: as he had for the first time on their second date at Chocolate World, as he had when her father succumbed to the big C two years back and she'd broken down, as he had the night she'd told him she was pregnant.

And as he held her, he remembered it all: every fight; every kiss; every touch; every word and every silence.

And he knew it was gone—all of it.

She was gone forever, never to return.

He held her much tighter.

And their daughter's room faded away . . .

Until it was only them.

Christopher Shearer's writing has appeared in Cemetery Dance, Horror World, Big Pulp, From the Fallout Shelter, *and many more. Over the last five years he has received three Penn*

State University best short story awards, a Demon Minds best short story award, and two Pushcart Prize nominations. He is a freelance editor with Cemetery Dance Publications and a featured book reviewer on fearnet.com. In 2012, he was jury co-chair of the HWA's Bram Stoker award in long fiction. In addition, Chris is an MFA candidate in Seton Hill University's prestigious Writing Popular Fiction program, mentored by bestselling horror authors Tim Waggoner and Lawrence C. Connolly. You can visit him online at www.apulpsolemnity.blogspot.com or email him at shearer44@msn.com.

Family Tradition

Sebaston Milam

It happened one cold, dark, windy Halloween night. It was late and most of the house porch lights were off. The street was empty and silent except for the chilly moan of October winds. My friend and I were swapping trick-or-treat candy when something snarled in the bushes near Mrs. Cook's house.

I pulled the plastic Sherlock Holmes pipe from my mouth and whispered, "What was that?"

Tony shrugged, jiggling the candy in his trick-or-treat bag. "Let's cross the street," he said through the slit of his Star-Ranger mask.

We looked both ways, but as we stepped off the curb, a pair of bony hands grabbed us. Our mouths hanging open, we turned to look. There, looming over us with a skeletal grin was the Grim Reaper!

Tony and I dropped our candy bags and ran. We were halfway down the street when I recognized the howls of laughter. I spun around and saw my brother Dennis take off the Reaper mask. At his feet our candy bags floated in a greasy mud puddle.

"Dennis!" I shouted. "You need to stop scaring people!"

"Can't help it, little brother," Dennis said as he ran off down the street. "It's a family tradition!"

My brother is right. My dad loves to tell scary stories and scare people too. One time he told me there were spiders in our basement and sometimes they lay eggs in kids' ears when they're asleep.

After that, Mom had to get out my old nightlight.

If you think that's bad, Dennis is ten times worse. He *always* takes scaring me too far. Last summer, he told me the cabin where we were staying at was haunted by an evil lumberjack. Dennis was jumping around teasing me. I just wanted to get away. While he was chasing me, I slipped and fell down the porch stairs, hurting my ankle. I had to get an x-ray and we left the cabin three days early. Mom grounded Dennis from video games for the rest of the summer, but it didn't make me feel any better.

Looking down at my ruined snickers and jawbreakers bobbing in the puddle, I decided it was time to teach Dennis a lesson.

After saying goodbye to Tony, I cut through the empty lot near my house. I knew Dennis would eventually have to come that way to get home. I found a dark hiding spot between two green dumpsters and waited. Even though Sherlock Holmes isn't that scary, I figured I could still scare Dennis as he walked past. Besides, I should be good at it; scaring people is our family tradition.

I watched the moon float in the sky and listened to the crickets sing in the nearby woods. I waited a really long time and just when I was going to give up, I saw someone coming near. I waited as the footsteps got closer. Just as the figure came into range, I jumped out and let out my loudest, scariest scream.

When I saw what it was, I screamed again.

It was a werewolf!

I raced toward home. Behind me, I could hear the werewolf chasing after me, growling and snapping its jaws. I tried cutting through yards and jumping fences, but the werewolf kept coming.

Finally I reached home. Nearly out of breath, I ran inside and locked the door.

Dad called from the living room, "Hey, you're home!"

I yelled, "There's a werewolf after me!"

Outside, I could hear the werewolf snarling and scratching at the door.

"A what?" Mom asked.

I pushed against the door, holding back the werewolf as my parents walked into the hallway . . . but they didn't look like my parents. They were covered in thick brown fur and their faces were wolf-like with huge fangs.

"You're all werewolves!" I screamed.

Pushing past me, dad opened the front door and let Dennis inside.

"Sorry if we frightened you, son, but we've wanted to tell you for the longest time. I guess just like being a werewolf, scaring people is our family tradition."

Sebaston Milam was born with craniosynostosis, a serious genetic condition that can lead to blindness, deformity, and impaired mental development. Luckily, the Ronald McDonald House in Charlottesville, Virginia allowed him a place to stay during his surgery. Today, Sebaston is a healthy and happy thirteen year old. He enjoys basketball, video games, and telling stories. He lives with his family in Putnam County, West Virginia. This is his very first publication.

www.ingramcontent.com/pod-product-compliance
Lightning Source LLC
Chambersburg PA
CBHW051933020726
47501CB00001B/102